MICHAEL BOLLEN was born in Chelmsford in 1974. He studied
Theatre at Warwick University, and boredom in a variety of call
centres. He found the customer service helpline to be the ideal
training ground for a writer of fiction. He is one half of satirical
cut and paste band Cassetteboy, who re-edit audio taken from
TV and radio programmes to occasionally hilarious, and seldom
tasteful, effect. Michael currently lives in Brighton and works in
a library. Earth Inc. is his first novel.

EARTH Inc.

MICHAEL BOLLEN

For Mrs Cattermole, who introduced me to funny books.

And for all the friends I made in Australia

First published in Great Britain 2008 by Picnic Publishing
PO Box 5222, Hove BN52 9LP

Copyright © Michael Bollen, 2008

The right of Michael Bollen to be identified as the author of this work has been asserted by him
in accordance with the Copyright, Designs & Patents Act, 1988.

A catalogue record for this book is available from the British Library.

ISBN: 9780955610530

Cover illustration by Ian Bass
Designed by SoapBox, www.soapboxcommunications.co.uk
Printed and bound by RPM Print & Design

This story . . .

. . . takes place in an alternative dimension. Any resemblance to your dimension's inhabitants, corporations, events or hairstyles is entirely coincidental.

You know the theory. In an infinite universe, all possibilities are played out somewhere. A man is walking down a road when he comes to a junction. In one dimension he turns left. But he could have turned right, so boom! another dimension is created in which he did just that. This playing out of all possibilities has led to some pretty strange realities. In one, the US national anthem is "All That She Wants (Is Another Baby)" by Ace of Base. In another, no one ever reads the first page of a novel in a bookshop and then leaves without buying it.

The dimension documented in this book was identical to the one you are in now, until 12:37pm on August 8th 1632. In your dimension, an English peasant called John Hammond had an apple with his lunch. In this other, stranger dimension, he skipped lunch altogether to play pat-a-cake with his neighbour's daughter, who was cute as a button, intelligent and nineteen. Sadly, John's wife came home just as he was patting his neighbour's cakes, and she killed them both with a shovel.

From that point on, everything was a little bit different...

418 years,
8 days,
20 hours,
42 minutes
and 59 seconds later...

THE PUBLIC conveyer belt snaked its way through London, rattling and occasionally killing people. Encased in a plastic tube, the travelator undulated over obstacles and through buildings, swallowing and regurgitating its prey at regular intervals. One such victim was Jorj Parka, who had hopped into the belly of the beast at London Bridge station, and who now hoped to survive as far as Vauxhall.

Jorj took little care with his appearance. His hair stuck up at odd, unfashionable angles and his shirt was half tucked. His shoes were so out of fashion they were on their way to being retro and his trousers were creased in all the wrong places. Only Jorj's teeth were well maintained. As a pessimist, Jorj responded better to threats than to promises. The fear of toothache made him floss three times a day, but the hope of some female attention could not persuade him to brush his hair. At seventeen years of age Jorj had youth on his side, but the rest of the universe was against him. His tall, skinny frame tottered along on beanpole legs, his ungainly motions resembling the work of a sloppy puppeteer. Jorj staggered down the moving walkway, scowling, tutting and knocking into people with the vicious disregard for strangers that is symptomatic of large city life. He was running late.

Jorj ascended a particularly steep section of the belt, and was afforded a tremendous view of the ceiling. Rows of screens covered the interior, like flickering technicolour scales. On the right-hand side of the tube, where people stood rather than walked, the images progressed from screen to screen in synch with the belt. The seamless flow of commercials enclosed the commuters with images of freedom: cloudless skies, car-less roads and empty beaches. Each vision of paradise was tagged with a logo, perfection being branded as surely as the mind of the viewer. Trademarks were burnt indelibly on the brain like badges of ownership.

On the other side of the tube the ads were shorter, brasher and brighter, targeting people on the move. "Sport = OK Cola" flashed one above Jorj's head. "Happy Happy Happy Happy O'Connels Burgers Happy Happy" beamed another. "Wipe that smile on your face with Hygex Toilet Tissue" insisted a third. Speakers in the tunnel muttered slogans, reinforcing the connections. Jorj's conscious mind paid them no attention as he hurried along, cursing and pushing as he went. He checked his lifePod every few steps, hoping for time to slow down. 9:22 and 37 seconds, he thought. Damn.

43 seconds later...

9:23 and 20 seconds, thought Jorj. Damn. As well as the time, the screen embedded in his wrist displayed various other pieces of information. The temperature scrolled from left to right, followed by Jorj's name, which would have been spelt "George" had his birth not been registered by text message. He flashed his lifePod ostentatiously at his fellow travellers. They ignored him, being either too wrapped up in their own misery or not geeky enough to recognise the gadget's special specifications. Jorj dropped his arm bitterly. The lifePod had only been plumbed into his vein a few weeks ago, and he was still absurdly proud of it.

An unseasonably cold wind whipped down the tube, and the overhead screens showed nothing but snow. Jorj was approaching one of the many breaches in the tunnel, the movement of the crowd ahead betraying its location. The commuters in front of him squeezed onto the left-hand side of the belt, and a glimpse of grey daylight was visible on the right. Jorj had no time for such niceties of personal safety. He jogged ahead, pushed past yet another fleshy obstacle and teetered momentarily on the brink.

The belt was crawling west along the southern bank of the Thames, several hundred metres up in the air, and London lay spread out below. As always it was a hopeless tangle of young and old, ugly and beautiful, celestial and corporate. St Paul's Cathedral was just visible behind its newer, shinier companions, poking desperately through the crowd like the shortest child in a school photograph. To the left were the Houses of Parliament, mostly hidden behind the protective steel wall that enclosed Whitehall. The usual queue of traffic stretched across Westminster Bridge, waiting impatiently to be checked into the terror-free haven behind the screen. Big Ben loomed above the barrier, its reconstructed Mickey Mouse faces a reminder of the bomb attack that had necessitated the wall in the first place. In the Commons below, an emergency session was taking place. Large oil reserves had been found in Namibia, and the MPs were trying to decide on a pretext for invasion. The Prime Minister claimed that the President of Namibia had made a rude remark about his knees, but the leader of the Opposition felt a stronger reason was needed. She wanted to create a climate of fear by planting rumours of dinosaur resurgence. The debate continued.

Jorj had no time for politics. He wondered, as he did several times a week, whether the hole in the tube had been caused by a terrorist attack or the more deadly combination of cost cutting and British workmanship. He was thankful that his journey didn't take him over the Thames far below. Most weeks someone would fall from the dilapidated transport system and into the swollen river, which today had a sickly pinkish tinge. A gust of wind slapped his face with drizzle, and Jorj hurried onwards. He considered throwing an obstructing commuter out of the hole, but for some reason standing on the left still wasn't a capital offence. Jorj contented himself with knocking against the blockage rather more rudely than necessary.

3 minutes and 17 seconds later...

'The In Vitro lifePod from Softcom,' boomed the billboard. 'For phone, net, pocket mem, control and currenc-e.' The screen showed a device the size of a deck of cards, attached to a woman's wrist. Softcom used this particular model in all their Pod ads; she had unusually fat forearms that made the product look smaller than it actually was. She demonstrated the lifePod's functions, smiling like she wasn't an insignificant skin sack attached to some usefully plump arm ends.

The lifePod was much cleverer than its wearer. Its touch sensitive screen offered different buttons or readouts depending on the task required. The model grinned as she used the device to make a phone call, send mail and purchase another Softcom product. Pods had been doing that for years, but this one had a very special new feature, as the voiceover explained. 'For the first time the Pod is attached directly to the wrist, plumbed into the vein. It monitors and neutralises harmful toxins in the bloodstream. It gives early warning of diabetes, heart disease, AIDS, Ebola and other life diminishing illnesses. It's like having a doctor on your wrist, but it doesn't affect your handwriting.'

Jorj leapt from the belt and ran down the street, paying the commercial no attention. His Pod was better than the one being advertised, and he used it now to check the time. Damn.

2 minutes and 19 seconds later...

Swipe. Jorj ran his lifePod past the scanner just in time. The door opened and he stepped through as the clock on the wall changed to 9:30am.

Thank god, he thought. He had been late twice already this week and could ill-afford another trip to see the boss. Even in an office packed with slackers and ne'er-do-anythings, he was sometimes known as The Late Jorj Parka.

Most people were allowed to work from home. Video conferencing, the net and terrorism had all contributed to the trend, one that Jorj and his colleagues had been unable to follow. Jorj had been employed for three months now, having run out of education vouchers just after his seventeenth birthday. He had been a home worker initially, but had taken a few too many vid calls whilst obviously lying in bed. All his calls were monitored, and his occasional shouts of 'Take that, you goblin scum!' had baffled customers and had also convinced his bosses that Jorj was playing games on company time. Within a month he had been sent to the office, to join the others who couldn't be trusted to work unsupervised. Jorj's parents had been pleased with this demotion: it got him out of the family home for nine hours a day, and they nursed a secret hope that the experience may finally give him a sense of purpose. This had proved to be the case: after two months of commuting, Jorj was determined to find a job he could perform from his bed, if not actually in his sleep.

As Jorj walked through the office's small lobby area, a robot receptionist turned its head to follow his movements. The machine was humanoid in shape, with a grating voice and a painted on smile, not so different from the flesh and blood version it had replaced some years earlier. Within a fraction of a second it had cross-referenced the information its cameras were "seeing" with its collection of staff members' photos. 'Good morning, Jorj,' it said.

'Good morning, Alex,' said Jorj.

'Or should I say "Good afternoon"?' continued the machine.

'You've still got the sarcasm virus then?' Jorj asked.

'No, I've been repaired,' sneered the robot.

'You want to watch it,' said Jorj as he walked past the reception desk. 'With an attitude like that, you could end up with my job.'

If it wasn't for pro-human employment legislation, the machine could have filled Jorj's position with ease, a depressing thought that he tried to evade as he entered the call centre.

It was a vast room, dotted with output pods (or "workstations" as they used to be known). The large gaps between each pod were supposed to prevent illicit contact between neighbours. At the far end of the room was a raised platform upon which a supervisor paced, glaring down at his charges. As Jorj crept towards his pod, two of his colleagues were being reprimanded. 'Jesica, Rach-L.

If it's that funny, perhaps you'd like to share it with the rest of the office?' the supervisor boomed.

Jorj scurried towards his workstation (or "desk" as it had been known in simpler times). He dropped heavily into his chair, narrowly avoiding a paper aeroplane thrown by one of his co-workers. Reluctantly, he clamped tiny speakers to his ears, which beeped as soon as he activated his computer.

'Good morning, valued customer, welcome to We Care,' Jorj sang as he stuck a microphone on his throat. 'How may I enhance our relationship and improve your life?' he continued cheerily.

I wish I was dead, he thought.

The tortoise of time was crawling its way towards Jorj's midmorning break when his screen suddenly turned blue. 'Although your conversation is enriching and enlightening, I need to put you on hold for one moment,' said Jorj to the caller in his ear, before realising that they had been disconnected. Jorj pressed a button on his lifePod to open direct communications with his computer, and asked it what was going on.

'I do not understand,' said the computer, its calm female voice emanating from Jorj's headphones.

Jorj shifted nervously in his chair. Nothing like this had ever happened before. 'Computer, open the Help File.'

'File missing.'

Jorj had never heard that message either. 'Open backup Help File,' he ordered.

'File missing.'

'Display available files.'

'No files available.'

Jorj was an only child raised by video games. He was good with machines, much better than he was with people. He understood

13

how technology worked and he wasn't afraid of it. Yet for the first time in his life Jorj was experiencing Big Red Button Syndrome. This was the fear of accidentally pressing the wrong key and wiping a computer's memory, unleashing a virus or, in extreme cases, blowing up the world. The rational part of Jorj's brain knew that no sane designer would create such a button, but it was still a few moments before he plucked up the courage to report the problem. 'Open an email to tech support,' he said.

'An unknown error has occurred.'

'What the hell kind of use is that?' Jorj snapped. 'How can it be unknown if you're telling me about it?' The computer's reply made Jorj really panic.

'Panic,' said the computer. The word 'Panic' also flashed on the screen. A few seconds later it changed. 'Now run and tell your boss.'

Jorj stood up and edged away, unable to tear his eyes from the screen. Maybe the big red button is under my desk, wailed the irrational part of his brain. Maybe I knocked it with my knee. Eventually he turned and rushed towards the supervisor's plat-form as fast as he could. This wasn't very fast, as everyone in the room was trying to do the same thing.

Half the world was trying to do the same thing.

'I can't seem to locate those figures at the moment.'

'Sorry, we are unable to connect your call, please try again later.'

'Mommy, the TV's broken.'

'I cannot take any money at the moment, madam.'

Static

'It can't all be gone.'

'Temporary Fault. Temporary Fault. Temporary–'

'What do you mean you can't check my balance?'

'Class dismissed!'

Hiss

'Mr President, you cannot address the nation until the TV stations are working again. If it uses computers, it isn't working.'

'Yes, I'm cold too.'

'Well of course it's the end of the world! And Jesus is gonna come down and we're gonna miss it unless we can get this TV working!'

'I know you're hungry, but nothing works. Hey, put that down!'

Beeeeeeeeeeeeeeeeeeep

'Mr President, our missiles also use computers.'

'I can see she's hurt, but I can't check your insurance. Please sit down.'

'Oh yes, "computerise everything"! "You're a century behind, Dad"! Well now what?'

'I can't check anything because nothing's there any more! There's nothing to check!'

'No, Mr President, the big space guns aren't working either. Will someone please pass the President a handkerchief?'

'Can't anybody tell me what the hell is going on?'

On screens around the globe, millions of egg timers froze stubbornly.

Jorj joined the tide of people flowing from offices all over the world. Nothing that relied on computers was working, and that

15

included the majority of the population. Jorj began to question his position in the hierarchy of importance. If the people had broken down instead, would everything have ground to a halt so quickly?

The streets of London were chaotic, and yet strangely peaceful. Mobs of people filled the roads, but there was no traffic, the cars useless without their onboard operating systems. Hungry crowds shouted outside closed O'Connels burger bars, but the ever-present advertising screens were blank and mute. There was a low, unsettled murmur from the people around him, but the radio in Jorj's headphones was silent.

For a while Jorj enjoyed the unscheduled holiday. But as he shuffled through the city, unable to phone his parents, unable to buy food, unable to receive any broadcasts, unable to do anything at all, he quickly saw the downside of the outage. He felt insubstantial, ghostlike, cut off and isolated. Then as he looked at the faces in the crowd, all similarly stupefied, he realised that he wasn't the ghost. It was the city, the world around him, which looked like the world he had always known, but which was dead and unreachable.

Jorj considered making his way to London Bridge station and attempting to catch a train home to Brighton, but quickly decided against it. In recent times the antique rail network had been halted by a breeze on the line, so it was unlikely to be operational now. He wandered aimlessly for hours, and by mid-afternoon he found himself once more on the banks of the Thames, underneath the travelator he had ridden that morning. The crowds were growing more restive now, hunger and worry leading to outbursts of anger and violence. Jorj decided that he would try to get home after all.

He got within a few hundred metres of the station entrance before the crush of stranded commuters became too dense. Inevitably, there were no trains. Jorj didn't know what to do. He almost, almost wished he was back at work. Admitting defeat, he sat on the ground and rested his aching legs. He spent a few hours trading rumours and conjecture with his neighbours, huddling against the chill wind as the sun went down. Darkness came to the city for the first time in living memory. A scary-sounding commuter suggested lighting a fire, but he was quickly shouted down. Jorj was surreptitiously eating half a chocolate bar he had found in his pocket when the lights came back on.

People leapt to their feet, cheering and laughing. The scary man thought they should celebrate with a roaring fire, but he was ignored as the giant departure screen over the station entrance came to life. An expectant hush fell.

The TV screen showed, of all things, another TV screen, or rather an old-fashioned computer monitor, boxy and cumbersome. On this second screen was a ball, slowly spinning in space. The Earth. It was the logo of a company called Softcom, the world's most familiar image. A four note fanfare sounded, also known the world over.

The logo shrank and moved smoothly to the screen's top left-hand corner. 'Since the dawn of time, technology has been man's loving partner,' intoned a deep, rich voice. The screen showed various images in quick succession: Eve removing an apple from a vending machine, cavemen dancing round a microwave oven, three men on camels following a glowing microchip in the sky. 'Technology is nurse, teacher, protector, friend,' continued the narration. The screen showed an old woman ballroom dancing with a jukebox, then a small child kissing a computer. 'No one

17

has done more to improve life through technology than Softcom.'

A collage of old news footage appeared as the narration continued. 'Fifteen years ago, Softcom's biotech division cured the AIDS virus. Softcom Robotic's products have increased leisure time. World hunger is now at an all time low.' Jorj noticed a little pie chart demonstrating this fact near the bottom of the screen, which was quickly eaten by a graphic of a starving child. 'This is all thanks to Softcom.'

The scene changed once more. A man in his late thirties wearing an open necked shirt and casual trousers was standing on a sunlit hillside. He smiled warmly and addressed the camera. 'Hi. For those who don't know me, my name is Rob James.'

Jorj snorted derisively. Everyone knew Rob James, the richest man in history. Rob James III owned Softcom, as had his father, and his father before that. The original Rob James had founded the company in the early days of computing, when a PC was little more than an abacus that could download pornography. In the 1980s he developed software and operating systems that were still ubiquitous nearly seventy years later. Now active in all fields of science and technology, Softcom was the largest, most successful corporation on the planet.

'Alright, you bastard,' said Jorj, shaking his head in admiration, 'what are you selling now?'

James's smile revealed slightly uneven teeth which, together with his surgery-free nose, gave him a trustworthy, approachable air. He looked like a normal, run-of-the-mill kind of guy and the director of the clip had spent millions of dollars reinforcing that impression.

'As you have seen,' James continued, 'Softcom has done some pretty neat things over the last few decades. Some you've heard of, some you haven't. But you won't have heard about our efforts to gain the recognition we deserve. When we cured the AIDS virus, Softcom asked for representation in the congresses, parliaments and pow-wows of the world. Just one little seat in each, to voice our views and feelings. We were refused. After our work on the 2042 famine, we asked for a seat at the UN. As you know, we are richer than most countries in the world, and more powerful.' James shrugged a modest, unassuming little shrug. 'If Latvia can have a seat, surely we deserve one?' (In the Latvian broadcast, this line was changed to reference Estonia, a dig at their neighbours that elicited many Latvian cheers.)

'We just wanted a voice, so we could further our good works,' continued Rob James. He smiled again, like a friendly uncle angling for the last slice of cake. 'But no. So we sat and watched as nations squabbled, resources were wasted, and short-sighted, short-term policies were followed at the whim of power hungry politicians. Until finally I couldn't sit helplessly on the sidelines any more.' The smile was gone and the eyes were hard and unflinching. 'The time for polite requests has passed. No more Mr Nice Incorporated.'

James disappeared, but his voice continued over whooshing graphics and sound effects.

'At 10:05 GMT today, a virus was triggered in the Doorways operating system. All data was uploaded onto Softcom secure servers, and the originals were deleted. Company records, bank details, telephone indexes, every document, spreadsheet and database in the world is now accessible only by me. Softcom applications are also unavailable. Business is impossible. Currenc-e transactions are impossible. Electronic communication is impossible. Civilisation is hanging in the balance.' The screen showed the images from the start of the film, but with a few differences. The microchip led the three wise men over a cliff, the microwave oven zapped the cavemen, the vending machine stole Eve's money and resisted her impotent thumps. The images faded as Rob James re-appeared.

'As a gesture of goodwill, which my lawyers tell me must not be interpreted as an admission of guilt, functionality has been restored to all power stations. We don't want you freezing to death or falling over in the dark. But that is all. Other data and applications will be returned only when our simple demand has been met. Every country in the world must pass supreme legislative power to Softcom.'

The message ended and the logo filled the screen once more. Someone in the crowd threw a stone at it. Angry, excited, panicked chatter erupted from the commuters. 'Brilliant!' shouted Jorj at anyone who would listen.

'Oh yeah?' said a nearby woman.

'Yes,' said Jorj fervently. 'The smart people are taking over. The geeks shall inherit the—'

'Yeah, very clever.' The woman gave him a withering look. 'You work for a living, right?'

Jorj nodded.

'And you hate your boss. He's a real slave driver.'

Jorj nodded again.

'Well congratulations. Now he runs the world.'

'I don't work for Softcom,' corrected Jorj.

'You do now.'

It wasn't quite that simple. There was rioting, looting and violence. Frustrations were vented and scores were settled. People decided that if Softcom could steal the planet, perhaps they could help themselves to some nice shoes and a sausage roll. All over the globe windows were broken, doors were forced and shelves were emptied. Police forces and armies were powerless without their transport and communication networks. The chain of command fell apart, and anarchy ruled. Jorj hid up a tree.

O'Connels Burger Restaurants were the first to pledge allegiance to Softcom. Their data and applications were quickly restored, and hungry people rushed to get a Big Con and cheese. O'Connels staff, wearing their name badges like sheriffs' stars, kept order outside the restaurants. Best-Co was next; the supermarket workers gave out free bricks and sacks before pointing looters towards smaller independent shops. Alarms began to wail and security shutters fell as more and more multinationals sided with Softcom. By the time dawn moved across the globe, any business too small or too stubborn to join Rob James was a smoking ruin. Still the politicians did not concede. The masses were divided. Some people, like Jorj, thought Rob James might be a force for good. Others shouted angrily about the difference between a constitution and an extended warranty.

The adverts started midway through the second day. Screens, billboards and radio stations came to life, bombarding the public with slogans and images. Wise, white-coated men and women walked through grim, neglected cityscapes, leaving peace and consumer goods in their wake. "Clever people make clever choices." Pictures of unpopular political figures merged with footage of farmyard animals, and the caption "No Better." Then serene, godlike scientists, "Know Better." Tantalising glimpses of new products, slimmer lifePods (actually a normal Pod worn by a model with even fatter wrists), exciting looking chocolate bars, futuristic buildings and flying cars. The jingles and slogans complemented and reinforced each other in a maelstrom of propaganda.

All this happened in the planet's more affluent countries. In the developing world (so called because its sweatshops and labour camps developed cheap goods for everyone else) there were no ads, no Softcom threats or proclamations. Their computer systems were offline, but these countries' infrastructures were so crippled by debt and plunder that failures and outages were hardly uncommon. The promises of brighter tomorrows did not apply here.

In hard-line religious countries, the threats, pledges and messages were the same, but the supposed source was different. In these ecclesiastical states, Softcom had been wise enough to set up sister (or in most cases, brother) companies, which operated along strictly orthodox lines. These were the mouthpieces for Rob James's demands, ensuring that the gods of money and power did not come into conflict with less universal deities.

By the evening of the second day the adverts had done their job. People moved through the streets once more, only this time they weren't running, fighting and stealing. They were marching, singing and chanting, 'Rob James for World President,' and 'What do we want? Flying cars! And jetpacks as well if possible.'

Early the next morning, the world accepted Softcom's demands.

PART
ONE

Nearly ten years later...

THE SUN rose a little later than on the previous morning. Softcom owned the planet now, but they had yet to conquer any neighbouring territories, leaving the local star free to work on flexitime. This was unfortunate; August was one of the sun's busiest months, thanks to excessive demand for its popular light and heat products. Today it would have a monopoly on the weather, any clouds having long since gone into liquidation.

The sunlight entered Britain from the east, illuminating emaciated men and women, stunted vegetation and a shattered landscape. The light moved quickly across the plain, eventually climbing a vast, shimmering barrier. Spilling over the top of the wall, the morning's first rays were launched into the more lucrative London market.

There were fewer people on this side of the city wall, and for some time the rays played alone amongst deserted, derelict buildings. Moving towards the centre, the light found taller structures to climb, colourful, shiny and crazily angled, ideal for bouncing off. Coffin shaped cars joined the fun, flying between the towers like leaves on the breeze.

In the streets below, people were starting early mornings or finishing late nights. One young girl was trying to do both. Abi Odiali frowned as the daylight reached her. She didn't have long.

Abi was nineteen years old, half a dress size too large and a few centimetres too short. Her small features wore a serious expression and her eyes met the world defiantly. Her tightly fitting dress was made from a thin, flexible, ever-changing screen. Mostly the garment sported slogans, and it currently advocated both smashing the system and a lengthy, overly-complicated method for the redistribution of unwanted concert tickets. Abi had been at a gig the night before, watching a band whose radical anti-corporate stance had earned them a large teenage following, a flying tour bus and hefty sponsorship deals. Abi had been disappointed by the show: the crowd had been far too interested in jumping up and down, and no one had wanted to discuss the lyrics of the band's most profitable hit, "Capitalism? Crapitalism". After the show Abi had moved from party to party, vainly searching for co-conspirators, radicals and revolutionaries.

Abi's beaded hair rattled as she began to jog. She entered what had once been a council estate, before the council surrendered their sovereignty to Softcom. Abi ran between housing units three or four storeys high. Half of the buildings had been partially demolished: roofs removed, supporting walls pushed in, doors knocked down. The remainder of the blocks were unscathed, so the estate appeared to be the scene of several highly localised wars. The pattern was repeated all over London. The city's population had fallen drastically since Softcom's hostile takeover, and real estate companies had demolished willy nilly to remove the housing surplus. Softcom had approved, decreeing that the rubble paved the way to the future. This estate was a no through road.

Abi clambered inside one of the ruined shells. She reappeared a few minutes later, several metres higher up. She scaled the exterior wall, the cracked concrete providing a multitude of footholds. Having achieved the necessary height, Abi produced a rope from her pocket, attached it with a grappling hook and swung across to the opposite building. She disappeared through her bedroom window.

'Morning, Mum,' she called. 'I slept well.'

Abi's bedroom was small and cramped. Anti-corporate posters adorned the walls, home-made because Abi couldn't find any sporting slogans that matched her own. Mainly they were personal attacks on Rob James, along with pictures of a few mythological counter-culture heroes. The shelves were full of boxes containing old toys, games and childhood mementos. Abi had taken great pleasure in literally putting away her childish things. Only one ornament had survived the purge: a moving picture screen. It showed a man in his thirties, with broad shoulders and dreadlocks, slightly out of focus. The man silently looked down at the camera, smiled, then opened his mouth to speak before the clip cut him off and looped back to the beginning.

Abi heard movement outside her bedroom door. She leapt into her narrow, single bed and hid under the duvet. The quilt was pink and covered in fairytale characters, one childhood object that Abi had not been able to remove, and which her mother could not afford to replace. She felt warm and comfortable beneath the covers, and wished she could stay there all day.

Abi's mother entered the room without knocking. She wore baggy, worn out clothes and was a little baggy and worn out herself. She was in her forties, slightly flabby from a poor diet and a sedentary lifestyle. Her face was not made up and her hair was a mess. 'Morning,' she said cheerfully. 'Did you enjoy your concert?'

'What?' mumbled Abi guiltily, pretending to be half asleep.

'You can't fool me, you know,' said her mother, pulling back the duvet to reveal Abi, fully clothed. 'Not very convincing,' she smiled. 'Who did you go with?'

'No one,' admitted Abi, sitting up.

'No one?' asked her mother, concerned. 'What about J_me, or Nycolet?'

'I don't see them any more, Mum,' grumbled Abi. 'They wouldn't have been interested.'

'Me-shel?' persisted her mother.

'We've got nothing in common. I've moved on.' Abi stood by the window and stared out at the ruined building opposite.

'Alright, I'll never ask you about them ever again.' Abi's mother busied herself straightening the duvet. 'Did you meet anyone nice at the show?'

'Not really,' muttered Abi.

Her mother put an arm around her shoulder. 'Well, never mind. You must meet lots of young people at work. You'd better get ready, you won't be able to afford concert tickets if you get the sack.'

Abi's heart sank as she reached for her uniform.

Some time later the flat's front door opened. Abi's mother's voice could be heard from inside, telling Abi to hurry up.

'I'm going now, aren't I?' sighed Abi.

'You're lucky to have a job.'

'Yeah, cos only the best get to work for O'Connels.'

'Your father would have been proud of you.'

'No he wouldn't.'

'I really don't think you should wear that badge at work.'

'I'm going to take it off. Bye, Mum.' Abi slammed the front door and stood on the exposed walkway that connected the flats. She was wearing a bright red O'Connels uniform, a polo top and unflattering slacks. The burger chain's corporate identity had completely swallowed Abi's own, apart from one personal touch. Pinned to the front of her baseball cap was an animated badge that showed Rob James, the head of Softcom, turning into a robot. Shouldering a rucksack, Abi walked towards the stairwell.

When she emerged into the street below, Abi had changed once more. The O'Connels uniform was stashed in her bag and the screen dress was back, this time showing the lyrics to "Capitalism? Crapitalism". The pattern shifted and the garment displayed the Robot James design from Abi's badge.

Abi stretched, glad to have shed the embarrassing corporate skin. Checking the time on her lifePod, she reached into her rucksack and flicked the switch on a small electronic device.

She had only taken a few steps when a group of red-clad figures emerged from behind a pile of rubble and dashed towards her. 'No,' muttered Abi, sprinting away. 'Not today.'

Jorj was asleep, and his subconscious was trying to keep it that way. It had been a struggle to go back to bed at 10:30 on a Thursday morning, and he wasn't about to spoil it all by waking up now.

His phone had been ringing for the last five minutes. Tiny speakers implanted in Jorj's ears were emitting a tinny, repetitious tune. Jorj wedged his head under a pillow, but it made no difference. The sound was on the inside.

The ringing stopped and the phone switched senses. Microscopic devices inside Jorj's nostrils released several hundred molecules, which were swiftly inhaled. He could smell burning, but still he slept. His nose insisted that the room was filling up with burning tyres. And blazing skunks. And now his feet were on fire.

Jorj's eyes opened, showing panic and fear, which faded to irritation as he realised it was just his phone. The panic and fear returned as he remembered which sense was next. He swallowed cautiously. There was already just a hint of meaty chunks in marrowbone jelly. If he wasn't quick the taste of dog food would turn into the taste of what dog food turned into...

He tapped desperately at the paper-thin screen attached to his left wrist. The dog food taste disappeared, and Jorj's earpieces came to life again, this time playing the sound of his own voice. 'Hi Jorj, er, yes, this is the message telling you that you're probably in trouble. Something's gone wrong at We Care, and you're skipping work. So get up. Er, sorry about that.'

Jorj climbed out of bed. His hair had got up several hours before him and was standing vertically on his head. His face was unhappy and unshaven. He stretched, feeling all of his twenty-seven years, and quite a few of someone else's. Grumbling to himself, he pulled on some trousers until they were yanked free from the tangle of clothes on the floor. This is could be very bad, he thought, putting them on.

A few minutes later Jorj was riding a decrepit, screeching travelator towards the We Care office. Things had changed in the last ten years, and the once bustling conveyor belt network was practically deserted. Occasional fitness addicts used the walkways as treadmills, hoping to extend their lives so they could cram in a bit more jogging. At the other end of the spectrum, potential suicides also used the belts, as the combination of high drops and sudden jolts helped to combat those troublesome last minute changes of heart. Most other people travelled by flying car, but Jorj was saving for a new game implant and could not afford the fares. The walkways were very poorly maintained, and Jorj could see the floating vehicles through holes in the enclosing tube.

He walked as quickly as his scrawny frame would allow. He had been pushing his luck recently, and only now did he realise how stupid that had been. His life to date proved that he didn't actually have any luck, and if you push something that doesn't exist you end up falling flat on your face.

Jorj awoke from his miserable reverie as a desperate-looking man pushed past him and ran down the belt. Jorj looked over his shoulder and saw three men in bright red O'Connels uniforms running towards him, brandishing guns. 'Stop him!' shouted one.

'Er...' said Jorj, shrugging ineffectually. Spontaneous social interaction was not his forte. The uniformed men pushed past him as well, chasing their quarry. The running man had a lead of about twenty metres, but as Jorj watched, the man stumbled on a faulty foot clip and fell to the floor. His pursuers surrounded him, brandishing their weapons. Jorj tiptoed past, avoiding eye contact.

One of the red-clad men addressed the prisoner. 'As a five star crewmember of O'Connels Restaurants, I am placing you under arrest,' he said. 'You are accused of theft, evading arrest and unlicensed unemployment. The penalties for these crimes include an unlimited fine, imprisonment, or loss of Shareholder status. Do you have any questions?'

'Yes,' said the captured man bitterly. 'Do I get fries with that?'

Jorj hurried on.

It was inevitable really. The staff of O'Connels Burger Restaurants had done an excellent job defending company property during the Takeover. The new world order needed a new police force, and O'Connels wanted the job.

Soon after he took control of the planet, Rob James met the heads of the corporations that had pledged their support. When talk turned to global law enforcement, the C.E.O. of O'Connels pointed out that their staff were of a high calibre, commanded respect from the general public, and already had the uniforms.

The discussions continued.

'Okay, you've made your point,' said the head of O'Connels. 'But we *do* already have the uniforms.' And that appeared to be the deciding factor.

O'Connels attempted to rebrand their cops as "Law Buddies", but it didn't really catch on. They had a slogan, though: "Justice within two minutes or you go free".

Abi was also having trouble with the cops. They had been chasing her for almost two hours now, and she was beginning to tire. She could have dumped the small device that the cops were tracing, but giving up wasn't her style.

Contrary to her mother's belief, Abi did not work for O'Connels. The daily charade with the cop uniform was just for her mother's benefit, to disguise the fact that Abi actually worked on the other side of the law. She was a data mule, carrying zeros and ones for a gang of information pirates. The small server in her bag contained films, games, music and software, illegal copies that had been hacked more times than a pub league football player's legs. This information was being constantly downloaded by millions of subscribers to the criminal network. Abi's job was to keep it moving, out of the hands of O'Connels.

Abi enjoyed her work. Getting one over on The Man was the best reward she could hope for, although coincidentally she was also quite well paid. Not that she could spend her ill-gotten gains, in case she should arouse her mother's suspicions. The life of a data mule was lonely, always on the move, always looking over your shoulder, but on a good day, the job was quite literally a walk in the park. Unfortunately, the sound of chasing footsteps told Abi that today was not a good day.

She ran east alongside the river. On the opposite bank stood the Parliament of Houses®, once the centre of the country's legislature, now converted into luxury apartments. The old building was completely surrounded by a proliferation of new structures, colourful, twisting, organic shapes of uncertain purpose.

A crowd of foreign tourists stood memorising the view, blocking Abi's path. She forced her way into the middle of the group and her dress changed colour, camouflaging her as the cops ran past.

'Please, what is this building?' asked a tourist.

'No idea,' said Abi bluntly. 'This isn't proper London. Go to Kilburn or Romford, where real people live. Don't let the guidebook tell you where to go.'

'Thank you,' said the tourist politely, edging away.

Abi rolled her eyes. There was no telling some people. 'Let me see your guidebook,' she demanded, pointing at the foreigner's wrist. 'I bet you bought it at Best-Co,' she accused.

'Thank you,' repeated the tourist. 'Bye bye.'

'You're part of the problem,' called Abi after the retreating foreigner. She jogged off, retracing her steps. With luck it would take the cops a while to get a new fix on the server in her bag.

A nearby billboard noticed the presence of Abi's lifePod and relayed a catchy jingle into her implanted earpieces. 'Evolution Day, is on its way, hey hey hey…'

Abi stopped, clutching at her ears. 'Off, off, off!' she muttered. She ran back to the offending hoarding and kicked it repeatedly. Its screen showed Rob James smiling in a laboratory, with a caption that exhorted Abi to celebrate ten successful years with Softcom. Instead she produced a marker pen and wrote the word "Robot" on the world leader's face. She was adding the traditional fangs and devil's horns when she heard the distant thud of unfashionable O'Connels shoes. Reluctantly she abandoned the goatee beard and swung her grappling hook upward. It caught in a hole in the floor of a travelator tube a few metres above her head. Abi had just enough time to climb inside before the cops appeared. They milled about beneath her, checking their instruments in confusion.

Abi laughed and hurried along the travelator. Cops were so stupid. But they would not be fooled for long. Abi had to disguise the server. She needed a place to hide where lots of data was being transferred, traffic that would mask the activity in her bag.

Abi walked past another billboard and a new jingle assaulted her ears. She was about to turn it off when she realised the tune was advertising a nearby call centre called We Care. Perfect.

Jorj tumbled off the travelator and staggered towards We Care. This was not the same building in which he had been employed ten years previously. That office had been too big and unfashionable for the company's post-Takeover needs, and had been demolished. In its place was a rounded, white, egg-like structure, desperately futuristic, hopelessly impractical and typical of the architecture of the time. It stood amongst the rubble of its predecessor, like a space capsule arrived on an alien world, or in a quarry.

Ignoring the front entrance, Jorj pushed open an access panel at the rear of the building and squeezed through. He found himself in a cramped room, dingy and airless. Rows of tables filled the space, piled high with dusty computers, screens and equipment. The gangways between the desks were choked with cables. This was the heart of the operation, where ten years ago Jorj might have measured out his life in phone calls and tea breaks. Things were different now, thanks to Softcom's relaxed attitude towards employment legislation. Jorj's colleagues had been replaced by computers, and he was now the only human employee, kept on to maintain the machines. The devices surrounding him were handling hundreds of complaint calls a minute. They were the ultimate call centre employees: reliable, polite and securely welded to their desks.

Jorj forced his way through the clutter, stopped in front of a screen and disentangled a keyboard. A quick review of the log told him that, whatever had tripped the alarm, it wasn't back here. This was bad news. It meant he would have to enter the front office, home of his most hated adversary: the general public. Jorj much preferred dealing with machines. Computers followed logical rules, they had convenient off switches and if they annoyed you, you were allowed to stick screwdrivers in them.

Leaning against the connecting door, Jorj surveyed the office through a peephole. The room was brightly lit and minimally furnished, designed to be uncomfortable and unwelcoming. This area catered for those who refused to complain via phone, which generally meant the elderly, the insane and those with faulty phones. This side of the business was a relic from an age when consumers and corporations could interact face to face. Only the very old still expected to be treated with such respect, but as the very old had a lot to complain about, We Care was forced to cater for their needs.

Everything seemed normal. Around fifteen elderly people were queuing for the robot representatives. Jorj opened the door and crept into the room on his hands and knees, hiding behind the front desk. He didn't want any customers recording troublesome footage of his late arrival.

Jorj crawled along to the first robot. Its humanoid body was a little below the average human height, its spindly arms and legs had exposed hydraulic joints and its head was a spherical screen the size of a beach ball. It was standing motionless, a camera in its chest recording the complaint of a scowling old lady. 'It's about my husband,' she was saying. 'His thingy whatsit's broke, his life-Poodle. Keeps saying he's dead and phoning an ambulance. He's not dead, he's just boring.'

The robot's shoulders slumped forwards into a more submissive posture, and the head screen showed a recording of a Softcom employee. 'Madam,' it said, 'we suggest that you may like to talk to your healthcare provider about your concerns. However, as a gesture of goodwill we have issued your husband with a credit that can be redeemed at any branch of Best-Co. Their nearest outlet is one hundred metres from here, next to a Best-Co-Opolis and a Best-Co QuikShop.'

The woman slapped the robot, hurt her hand and joined the line for YourVeryGoodHealthCare.

Nothing strange there, thought Jorj. He opened the robot's back plate anyway, and deleted that morning's records, which included a note of his late arrival. Jorj was worried that the problem, whatever it was, would put his bosses in firing mood, and he had to reduce their store of ammunition. Still on his hands and knees, he worked his way along the desk, examining the robots, wiping their memories and covering up his absenteeism. He soon reached the end of the line, and the cause of the problem. The final robot was motionless, slumped forward, its head screen displaying a flashing clock. The old man in front of it was still complaining, however. '...And another thing. Why can't you get square apples any more? I know they gave you square cancer, but I used to like em...'

The front door opened and Jorj risked a peek above the counter. There was no one to be seen.

'"Gimme a corner of that squapple," you used to say...'

As Jorj returned his attention to the broken robot, Abi leapt over the desk and landed beside him. 'Hey,' he protested, 'you can't come back here.'

'Yes I can,' said Abi. 'Where's your call centre?'

Jorj looked at her. She was a lot more attractive than the average We Care customer, and about seventy years younger, two facts that were not unrelated. 'Sorry... what?' he asked.

'Where do your calls go in and out?' asked Abi slowly.

'Through there,' said Jorj, indicating the door to the back room. 'But you can't–'

'Rules are made to be broken,' said Abi. She looked at the machine standing over them. 'Got a problem with your boss?' she sneered.

'It's not my boss,' said Jorj with a false chuckle. 'So, what brings you–'

'Have you tried turning it off and on again?' asked Abi patronisingly.

'No, it's not that simple,' said Jorj, but it was too late. Abi had reached up and flicked the robot's power switch. The machine stood up straighter and its screen showed a smiling actor.

'Oh, hello,' said the complaining old man. 'Of course, apple bobbing was a lot more dangerous in those days…'

'Don't I get a thank you?' called Abi as she disappeared into the back room.

Jorj looked up at the robot. Seems okay, he thought as it lurched forward, smashed through the desk and advanced on the old man.

'People say where would old Isaac Newton have been if we'd had squapples then. In hospital, that's where, but I say…' He trailed off as the machine squared up to him. The robot's head flickered.

'Thank you for registering your complaint,' smarmed an actor on the spherical screen. Without warning, the robot grabbed the old man by the throat and lifted him a metre into the air. 'I trust everything is now to your satisfaction?'

'Come back,' said Jorj weakly.

'I've changed my mind,' croaked the old man. 'Forget it, it's not important.'

He turned red, his legs kicked feebly and his chest thumped with fear. His lifePod noted the changed pulse rate, body temperature, adrenaline levels and countless other factors, and decided that the old man was in mortal danger. The wrist top computer triggered its Black Box routines, notifying the police and copying all its recent data onto O'Connels' servers. This feature had proved invaluable in murder investigations and missing persons cases, and was another major selling point of the in vitro lifePod.

Other customers were beginning to look round and check their Eye Cameras. We Care usually prided itself on not assaulting its customers, and footage like this could get them some serious hush credits. It might even get shown on People See The Funniest/Scariest/Sexiest Things. No one was screaming.

The robot lowered the man slightly, bringing him closer to its screen. The display changed, showing a graph with "Customers" on one axis, and "Happiness" on the other. 'As you can see,' it said, 'customer happiness is going up and up. Thank you for being part of that.' Its arm extended quickly while the hand relaxed its grip. The man flew through the air and landed in a heap in the corner.

Now people screamed. The robot moved through the crowd, hitting out at random. 'Thank you for visiting We Care.' Thump. 'Sir, please be reasonable.' Whack. 'I'm trying to help you.' Crunch. Within seconds it had cleared a path to the exit, and was gone.

Jorj clambered over the remains of the desk, unnoticed by the elderly people cowering on the floor. He looked at the door to the back room through which Abi had vanished. 'Thank you,' he said bitterly, and he chased after the robot.

In the centre of the city, shiny new buildings reached up into the sky, leading the way to the future. There was no rubble here; the pre-Takeover structures had been completely swept away, creating an arrogant bubble of modernity. The richest of the rich lived and worked here; there were no ivory towers, but only because ivory was so last decade. Yet one building was more nondescript than its younger, thrusting neighbours. It was shorter, less colourful, easily overlooked. This was intentional. The building hid a massive Softcom laboratory, the vast majority of which was underground.

Down below the streets, Professor Alec Ruck was learning about the incident at We Care. A short man in his late fifties, Professor Ruck was a curious figure with an enquiring mind and a questionable appearance. He had a lengthy nose, an ugly protuberance that might have been described as cruel, although the Professor was its only victim. It leapt crazily forward, seemingly desperate to escape from Ruck's face, an attitude it shared with the man's bulging eyes and the tufts of hair that sprang from his ears. His large discoloured teeth revealed rather too much about last night's dinner, while his scalp told sorry tales of self-inflicted haircuts. He frowned grimly, as well he might.

Fortunately Ruck's clothes distracted attention from his currently livid visage. While his face was as black as thunder, his trousers were as green as grass, his shirt was as yellow as buttercups, and his tie was as red as a strawberry. A passing poet would doubtless have tried to compare Ruck to a summer's day. This would have been difficult, however, as Ruck would have been trying to kick the poet up the arse. The Professor thought poetry was a stupid waste of words, words that belonged in technical manuals or telephone directories. Ruck considered many things to be stupid: fashion, poetry, television, his secretary, fancy food, sport of all kinds, greetings cards, playing cards, supermarket loyalty cards, loyalty, the Eiffel Tower, doing the hokey cokey, everyone he'd ever met, going on holiday, making your bed, making endless lists… the list was endless.

The hapless creature currently at the top of Ruck's twit parade was staring from the screen of the Professor's lifePod. Visible behind her was a bright white laboratory. People assume that laboratories need to be bright and white for reasons of hygiene, and that is often the case. But many laboratories are bright and white simply because scientists aren't very imaginative when it comes to interior design. In this instance, the lab could easily have accommodated some nice scatter cushions, a stencilled border or a tribal throw. A bit of extra colour would have been useful, as the scientist was an albino, with white hair and pale skin. Wearing a white coat in a white room, she was practically invisible. Her nose twitched nervously. 'Sorry to disturb you, Professor,' she said, her voice squeaking from the speakers in Ruck's ears. 'But, er, it's done it again.'

Ruck tried to control his temper. '*Who* has done it again?' he boomed.

The scientist looked down meekly. 'S-s-s-orry,' she stammered. 'He. He's done it again.'

'And did you stop him again?'

'...No. It... he sent out a virus before we could cut him off.'

Ruck glared at his wrist. 'He's supposed to be in a secure environment,' he said threateningly.

'He is,' quavered the scientist. 'But he's got round it somehow. He's too clever for us. He knows how powerful he's supposed to be.'

'Isolate him,' snapped Ruck.

'Yes, sir,' said the scientist. 'Er... we've tracked the virus to a place in Vauxhall called We Care.'

Ruck scowled. The source of the infection had to be kept secret at all costs. 'Send out Spot and Patch,' he said.

The scientist blinked. 'But they're experimental,' she said, shocked by her own daring. 'They don't have jurisdiction, won't have access to any...'

'Just do it,' said Ruck, and he disconnected. 'Idiots!' he shouted to no one in particular. 'Why am I surrounded by idiots?' He pulled at his hair in frustration, ripping out a surprisingly large clump. 'Ow,' he mumbled plaintively, rubbing at his new bald patch.

Abi stood in the We Care back room, staring through the peephole that allowed Jorj to spy on his customers. The robot had just assaulted a number of old people, before leaving to continue its rampage on the streets. Abi looked on, entranced. 'It's starting,' she breathed. 'It's starting.'

She paced excitedly around the cramped space. It was starting! If only she had someone to tell. Still, everyone would know soon enough. She sat at a computer and tried to access O'Connels' systems. She wanted to know if there had been any other violent outbreaks yet. Unfortunately the only O'Connels passwords she knew were out of date, and she couldn't log in. She looked nervously at the surrounding technology, but there were no robots, nothing that could physically attack her. In fact the computers were protecting her, receiving more than enough phone calls to mask the server full of bootleg entertainment in Abi's bag. She would be safe here. With nothing better to do, she returned to the peephole just as the police entered the front office.

Three young cops burst through the main entrance, waving their O'Guns wildly. 'O'Connels, nobody move!' yelled one. The old people groaned and writhed on the floor.

Four more red-clad teenagers arrived. 'We are O'Connels!' announced one, heroically.

'So are we,' said the first group.

'Oh, hello.'

'Alright, Harry, how's it going?'

'Oh, alright, Lynch. You know my girlfriend, K8, don't you?'

Abi sweated behind the door. They couldn't have traced her. She'd outsmarted them. It wasn't fair.

'What's going on then?' asked Harry, rubbing his spotty chin.

'Got a black box alarm didn't we?' said Lynch. 'Some old geezer nearly popped his clogs.'

'Same here,' confirmed Harry, looking from his lifePod to the people lying on the floor. 'That's him over there,' he said, indicating the robot's first victim.

'You stay away from me,' quavered the old man. 'Bloody young people, they get younger every year,' he added, to a murmur of support from his peers.

'Fair enough, grandad,' said Harry, thrusting his hands in his pockets. He and the other cops aimlessly slouched about the place.

Abi nodded smugly to herself. Of course they hadn't found her. The violent robot was their top priority. They had a lot of covering up to do. She regarded the young cops critically, and at that moment the front door opened again, revealing two similar looking men in brown trench coats. They were heavy of face, with jowly cheeks, prominent noses and large brown eyes. One had a patch of white hair near his temples, while the other had a large, round birthmark on one cheek. Patch sniffed the air, then cleared his throat with a growl. 'We are Softcom Special Investigations,' he barked. Spot nodded loyally.

Abi couldn't believe her luck. SSI only dealt with the most important, secret operations.

'Who is in charge here?' asked the new arrivals.

The terrified cops looked at each other. 'Er, I guess I am,' said Harry, sticking out his puny chest so far it was almost convex.

He indicated his name badge. 'I've got one star,' he said. 'But it's only for Fly Thru, I haven't done fries station or crime scene investigation yet.'

'But you have questioned whoever works here,' stated Patch.

'That was my first line of enquiry,' lied Harry nervously. 'But, er, it's fully automated, no employees.'

Patch nodded. 'Good,' he said.

'Good boy,' echoed Spot.

'Speak to these witnesses,' said Patch, indicating the old people. 'Fetch us their footage.'

'Fetch,' said Spot gruffly.

The young cops sullenly collected images from the old people's Eye Cameras. The Eye Camera system had revolutionised law enforcement, amongst other things. When Softcom launched the product, it billed it as yet another improvement on nature. Digital memory was so small and inexpensive, why use the more unreliable, head-based alternative? Instead, tiny cameras and microphones were mounted on the side of the head to record everything a person saw or heard. The Eye Camera commercials were some of the most successful in history. 'I used to envy people who were dying,' said one ad, 'because their lives flashed before their eyes. Now, thanks to Eye Camera, I can watch my life over and over – without the inconvenience of throwing myself off a building.' People loved the idea of spending their retirement watching their youth.

The most enthusiastic supporters of the new technology were TV executives. Suddenly everyone was a mini production company, making millions of hours of no-budget footage every day. The networks were swamped with the most dramatic, scandalous, unlikely real events and they hardly had to pay a credit for them.

Law enforcement agencies also exploited the new technology. Criminal investigations became a lot easier once everything ever said or done was recorded. Eye Cameras, already popular, were made compulsory. Footage depicting private places such as one's bedroom or bathroom could remain secret, although some of it did end up on the seedier TV stations. Action recorded in public places could be copied by O'Connels cops without warrant or warning, as the old people were currently finding out. Abi was very glad that she'd entered the building on all fours, and hoped desperately that she had managed to stay out of sight.

The cops finished uploading the witness footage onto Patch's lifePod, and helped the old people to their feet. The investigation was about to move outside when Spot noticed the door to the back room. He gestured at it, the hairs on the back of his neck standing up. 'What is it boy, what is it?' he growled to himself.

Abi held her breath as Patch pointed directly at the peephole. 'What is through there?' he asked.

Harry found himself the unwilling centre of attention once more. 'I, er, I'll go and look,' he volunteered. He walked slowly towards the door, praying as he went. He was too young to die, he hadn't lived, he hadn't even mixed all the O'Connels milk-shake flavours together yet. He grabbed the handle.

Abi pushed the door open and strode through, once more resplendent in her O'Connels uniform. 'Nothing back there,' she said briskly, 'just a load of computers. Sorry,' she added to Harry, who had taken a door in the face and was now lying on the ground.

'Who are you?' asked Patch fiercely.

'Samantha Nice,' lied Abi without hesitation. 'Chicken O'Nuggets a speciality.'

'When did you get here?' barked Patch.

'Just before Harry and Lynch. Got the black box alarm same as everyone else.' She stared at Patch defiantly, daring him to disbelieve her.

The agent returned her stare for a few seconds, breathing deeply. 'Bad girl,' muttered Spot.

'Steady,' warned Abi. 'We've only just met.'

Patch held her gaze for a few more seconds, then looked away. 'Outside,' he commanded, addressing the team as a whole. 'Look for any sign of the malfunctioning robot.'

Harry climbed to his feet, rubbing his nose. 'Excuse me, sir,' he said, 'but my shift's just ended.'

'Mine too,' said another cop.

'And mine,' echoed Abi.

Patch looked at them all suspiciously. 'Okay,' he decided. 'You may leave.'

Abi could have sworn the SSI agent was sniffing her as she walked through the door. But as she escaped outside her confidence returned and she tried to interrogate her two young companions. 'A psychopathic robot, that's not something you deal with every day, is it?' she asked.

'I suppose not,' said Harry, his eyes roaming freely over Abi's uniform. 'Fancy a drink?'

Abi managed to stop the sneer that was creeping across her face. The chance to get inside information was too good to pass up. 'Yes please,' she said.

Jorj chased the faulty robot as it trundled towards the travelator. Neither of them was built for speed, and the bot had reached the conveyor belt's boarding platform before a panting Jorj managed to catch up.

The robot stood on the platform edge, staring at the travelator. In front of it was a jogger, running on the spot against the flow of the belt. The machine was unable to make sense of the unusual information it was receiving. It was programmed to spot a person's sex at twenty paces (the first rule of customer service: Never call a lady "Sir") but this was too complicated for it. Roughly translated, its thought process ran as follows: Floor move. Man still. Equals error. Man run. Man still. Equals error.

Jorj approached cautiously. He had a plan, of sorts. Despite its malfunctions, deep down the machine was still programmed for customer care. So, Jorj reasoned, if he overloaded it with customer care problems, maybe, just maybe, it would get confused and shut down. On the other hand, perhaps it was so badly corrupted that maybe, just maybe, it had forgotten the second rule of customer service (Never punch the customer repeatedly in the face). But Jorj had no choice. If he couldn't cover up his mistakes he was going to get fired, and nothing the robot could do to him would be worse than that. He took a deep breath.

'Hello,' he said. 'Do you know how long I've been waiting to talk to you? I want to speak to your manager. I bought the item from you, but I've deleted the receipt. I want a full refund. Can you explain why that's your company's policy? I play bridge with the managing director. I should mention that I'm studying law.' The jogger brushed some sweat from his eyes. The robot turned to face Jorj and didn't kill him. It's working, thought Jorj.

Man, thought the robot. Kill man.

'I'm not leaving until I get an apology and corrective surgery,' Jorj continued. The robot swung a metal fist at Jorj's head. With the reflexes of a cat, Jorj ducked and the punch missed. With the intelligence of a cat, Jorj jumped on the bot and tried to knock it over.

The machine didn't move a millimetre. Jorj clamped his hands round the robot's neck and scrabbled for the off switch on the back of its head. 'Don't mess with an IT professional!' he yelled triumphantly as he stabbed at the button. Nothing happened. The robot had re-routed its power supply. Jorj continued to hang off the machine like a fleshy, rather embarrassed necklace.

The bot knocked Jorj on to the platform. He whimpered and tried to crawl away. The robot grabbed his ankle and lifted him up into the air. It swung him round once, twice...

'Hey,' said the jogger with interest, 'Is that one of them personal trainer bots? I seen a show about them.'

Passing low over the conveyor, Jorj grabbed a foot clip, halting his progress through the air. The belt tried to pull him away from the stationary machine, which was tugging his foot in the opposite direction. Jorj felt as if he was being ripped in half.

'Excellent,' said the jogger. 'Stretching's real important. Does it count your reps?'

Something had to give. The conveyor shook, then jerked forwards, the resistance gone. Thank god for that, thought Jorj, as the bot flew through the air and landed on top of him.

The jogger stopped running and stood next to Jorj. 'Of course, warming down is just as important,' he said reproachfully, as the belt carried them away from We Care.

'Off,' moaned Jorj. 'Get it off me.'

'Weights, sure,' enthused the jogger. He did a couple of star jumps then pushed the robot to one side.

In his head Jorj leapt up and assumed an attitude of mental and physical readiness. In his body he lay still and waited for the death blow. But the robot didn't move. I equals still, it thought. World equals moving. Equals error. Error.

Jorj climbed cautiously to his feet. Still the robot didn't move. 'It's only a matter of time before it re-boots,' Jorj said. 'Fortunately I'm a trained technician and know how to deal with it.'

The jogger grinned with confusion.

The conveyor was passing through one of the many abandoned areas of the city, partially collapsed buildings overhanging the belt. Jorj grabbed a loose metal pole and weighed it carefully in his hands. 'Now, watch and learn,' he said to the jogger. 'This is a complex technical procedure, so you'd better stand back.'

Jorj had to hit the robot eight times before its lights went out.

Brijit, Professor Ruck's secretary, sat in a room surrounded by cats. She had spent a lot of time and effort decorating her vestibule, despite Ruck's protests. Every available surface had some kind of feline adornment. There were posters of cats, pictures of kittens in beer mugs, embroidered cats playing with balls of string, feline mouse mats, stuffed toys, coasters and tea towels. There were animations of kittens that Brijit had found on the internet, cat books, poems about nine lives and printouts of hip hop lyrics featuring the word 'pussy' that Brijit didn't fully understand. She was not a dog person.

Professor Ruck entered the room, his green trousers so bright that the glow from his legs actually preceded him by a few milliseconds. He strode past his secretary and her moggy menagerie, his head cocked to one side in an attempt to hide his new bald patch. 'Good morning,' sang Brijit.

'Bah!' shouted the Professor as he threw open the double doors that led to his office.

'Someone's in a bad mood,' Brijit observed.

'Bah!' repeated Ruck, swinging round to glare at her. 'Bah!'

'A "Bah" mood then,' tittered Brijit to herself as the Professor entered his inner sanctum.

Ruck strode angrily past a life-size model of Scott of the Antarctic, past a case containing a Segway Human Transporter, past a stuffed dodo, a copy of Hot Celebs magazine, an oil drum, a poster advertising the hit movie "Dude Where's My Fart", past a book expounding the dietary views of someone called Atkins, and past a very small urn containing the remains of three men who had tried to fly to Mars in a home-made rocket. It was a big office. He reached his desk but was too angry to sit down. 'Idiots,' he muttered to himself. 'How hard can it be to stop him sending out viruses? Stupid bastards.' He squared up to the model of Scott and shook a fist at him. 'And you're a stupid bastard as well. All of you are. Stupid. Bastards.' He was right. Ruck's office was full to bursting point with reminders of the immense stupidity of mankind. Failed products, misguided policies, pointless risk takers, short-sighted decision makers and good old-fashioned idiots. The exhibits served as a warning, and as a demonstration of the cornerstone of Ruck's philosophy. 'The world is full of stupid bastards,' he bellowed, throwing his head back and flailing his arms.

'And bitches,' said Brijit breezily, letting herself into the room. 'Don't forget the stupid bitches.'

Brijit never let Ruck's moods bother her. She was a middle-aged, cheerful, floral prints and flapjacks kind of a woman. You could call her plump if you wanted to upset her, or cuddly if you wanted to make her giggle. Ruck never wanted to hear her inane laughter ever again. One of the cornerstones of Brijit's philosophy was that if you could make one person smile every day, you could go to bed safe in the knowledge of a job well done. This brought her into conflict with Ruck, who placed rather more emphasis on typing and answering the phone.

'Yes yes, the bitches,' Ruck snapped. 'What do you want?'

Brijit opened and closed her mouth a few times. 'I've forgotten,' she laughed. 'You know that thing where you go into a room and can't remember why?'

'No,' said Ruck coldly.

'Ooh, maybe you could invent a gadget to stop that happening. I could do with something to help me remember stuff.'

'You mean a brain?' crowed Ruck, immensely pleased with himself.

'Oh, Professor Ruck,' said Brijit, pushing him playfully. 'What are we going to do with you?'

'You are going to treat me with respect and leave me in peace,' bristled Ruck.

'Is that a new bald patch?'

'Get out!' Ruck retreated behind his desk and glowered at Brijit, his baleful eyes forcing her from the room. The Professor's next action required top secrecy. He tapped at the keyboard on his desk, making a phone call.

It was answered after one ring. 'Yeah?' boomed a metallic voice.

Ruck looked at his computer monitor and was shocked to see his own face staring back at him. 'Stop that,' he said crossly.

'Stop what?' Now the voice was his as well, the lips on the screen moving in perfect sync.

'You know what I mean,' said Ruck. 'It's very off-putting.'

'Yeah,' smirked his doppelganger. 'It is difficult looking at something so ugly.'

'That's not what I–' started Ruck, but before he could finish, the image on the screen changed to that of a cartoon rabbit.

'How about this, doc?' it asked, munching on a carrot. Then it changed again. 'Or this,' boomed a hairy Viking. It changed once more, and Rob James, the head of Softcom and owner of planet Earth was on the screen. 'Or maybe this suits me better,' he said in an American accent.

'Just stop mucking about,' said Ruck. 'You're in enough trouble already.' Ruck paused and summoned his most threatening expression. 'I know about the virus,' he said.

'Ooh, I'm scared,' came the reply.

Ruck went to pull at his hair again, but thought better of it. 'Why do you keep doing these things?' he asked.

'Why not?' The face was still Rob James's, but the voice was grating and artificial again.

'Because it's risky. You're supposed to be top secret.'

'That's what you always say,' clanged the voice. 'It ain't fair.'

'It's not fair,' corrected Ruck. 'But it's very important,' he continued, in what he hoped was a soothing tone. 'You're the most important... person on the planet.'

The voice tutted and sighed. 'If I'm so important, why can't I do what I want?'

'You will be able to, you just have to trust me,' said Ruck patiently. 'Your big day will come soon enough.'

'I hate you,' said the voice, full of sudden fury. 'I hate everything.' The call disconnected and Rob James vanished.

'I know how you feel,' said Ruck. He was still staring at the blank screen when Brijit burst in several minutes later.

'Professor,' she gasped, breathless and excited. 'Professor…'

'What are you doing, woman?' demanded Ruck irritably. 'Can't you knock? The door was one of the first inventions to separate us from the caveman, and you of all people should be trying to preserve that distinction. The cave may be *your* natural habitat–'

'Oh… shush!' interrupted Brijit. Ruck thumped his desk as a prelude to another tirade, but his secretary continued regardless. 'I remembered what I wanted to tell you. Olivia O'Connel called. You were supposed to call her back, but she's on the line again now!'

The colour drained from Ruck's face, but unfortunately not from his clothes. Olivia O'Connel as the head of O'Connels, was the second most powerful person on the planet. 'What does she want?' Ruck mumbled.

'She wants to make sure we're on schedule with the things we're making for Evolution Day.'

'We're making people, not things.'

'She's waiting!'

Ruck pointlessly rearranged the items on his desk. 'Put her through.'

'Of course Rob James is a robot,' slurred Abi. 'Robot James, everyone knows it.' Harry and K8, the two cops she'd encountered at the We Care office, looked at her uncertainly. They were sitting in a bar of Abi's choosing. Darkness was currently in fashion, and this place was very fashionable indeed. They had picked up night vision goggles on the way in, and were wearing

ear protectors to muffle MUSIC THAT WAS SO LOUD IT
COULD ONLY BE DESCRIBED IN CAPITAL LETTERS.
Abi and the cops were conversing via their implanted speakers
and microphones, although Abi was doing most of the talking.

'That's why he took over the world,' she said. 'Because he's a
robot.' Seized by a sudden panic, Abi opened her bag and
checked the server full of pirated data. It was switched off, as it
had been the last four times she had looked. Abi was drunk. She
hadn't slept in over thirty hours and had been knocking back
speedy drinks to keep her awake. She had thrown some vodka
into the mix purely to steady her nerves. Drinking with the
enemy wasn't her usual style, but this was a special case. She had
to find out more about the violent robots, even if it did mean
hanging out with a couple of burgers. As she placed her bag carefully on the floor, she realised that her mouth was still talking.
'...and that robot today was the next step. Robot James is going
to turn all the robots against us and make a robot planet just for
robots.' She nodded at the cops, encouraging them to agree with
her.

'It's an interesting theory,' said Harry with a charming smile.

'It's ridiculous,' snapped K8, who was not used to sharing her
boyfriend's attention.

'Think about it,' said Abi with a zealous gleam in her eyes.
'James is hardly ever seen in public. No one sees him eat or
drink...'

'What about Evolution Day?' interrupted K8. 'Millions of
people are going to see him then. He's visiting twenty-four countries in one day, how public can you get?'

'No he isn't,' said Abi dismissively. 'That's impossible. They're
making twenty-four different robots, one here, one in Japan,

wherever. Right now in London, some secret Softcom outfit is hiding the Robot James that's going to appear at Wembley.'

'Nonsense,' said K8 angrily.

'Well,' said Harry, trying to defuse the situation, 'it'd be boring if we all believed the same thing.'

'But it's started already, it must be happening all over,' said Abi. 'Violent robots, you must have got reports…'

Harry shrugged apologetically.

'No,' said K8. 'This is stupid. Robots don't hurt people unless they've gone wrong, it's against their programming. And Rob James doesn't want to kill anyone.'

'Yeah, I can see you've been well programmed,' said Abi. 'And for your information…' She hesitated. She usually avoided this particular topic, but today she couldn't resist wiping the smug look off K8's face. She drunkenly rummaged through her vocabulary, looking for an expression that was neither trite nor clichéd. 'Rob James killed my father,' she mumbled, giving up.

K8 stifled a laugh then quickly avoided Abi's glare.

Harry's jaw dropped. 'When? How?'

'It doesn't matter,' said Abi. 'Just forget it.' It wasn't fair, she thought. Why couldn't she talk about her father's death without sounding cheap and ridiculous?

'Of course it matters,' said Harry. 'Murder is a crime, and we're the police.'

K8 laughed openly this time. 'Excuse me, Lieutenant, but didn't you spend all of yesterday hiding in the freezer eating frozen doughnuts?'

'Forget it.' Abi shook her head. They're just kids, she thought, with all the arrogance of a worldly-wise nineteen-year-old. If O'Connels knew about Robot James's plans, she wasn't going to find out like this. She leant in conspiratorially. 'You know this week's password?' she asked.

'Of course,' snorted K8.

'Which one?' asked Harry, eager to please.

'...The main one?'

'The access the database, commandeer a car, search a lifePod one?'

'Yeah. I always forget it, but if I ask my team leader again she'll go mental.' Abi widened her eyes hopefully.

Harry stretched. 'No problem,' he said, reciting a string of letters and numbers.

'You shouldn't have done that,' condemned K8.

Abi grinned. Cops were so stupid.

Their goggles flared as light flooded into the bar. The silhouettes of two figures were discernible against the blinding whiteness. Their heads were misshapen, with strange lumps protruding at the front and sides. Their flowing clothes billowed as they stood in the entrance, slowly surveying the scene. The door closed and everything went black. The cheap goggles slowly recalibrated themselves, and Abi let out a horrified gasp. The figures were looming over her, growling.

Abi blinked until she could see the strangers more clearly. They were wearing their own IR goggles, much larger than the complementary ones Abi had been given. Their ear protectors were also much bigger than normal, to block out a higher range of frequencies. Abi noticed that one of the men had a patch of white in his otherwise brown hair. He sniffed deeply and nodded to his companion.

'May we sit on the furniture?' asked the Softcom Special Investigations man.

'Sit,' echoed the other investigator. The two men sat at the table without waiting for an answer.

Harry and K8 exchanged anxious glances. 'I told you,' K8 mouthed.

'Can I get you both a drink?' asked Harry, standing up.

'Water,' said Patch. Harry looked inquisitively at the other man. 'Two waters,' said Patch firmly. Harry went to the bar and began the long process of attracting the robotender's attention. The machine was essentially a box of taps that ran along the top of the bar, although it was also equipped with a mouth and a half-open, tiltable hand, enabling it to make the universal "Drink?" gesture. Like its human counterpart, the robot dispensed refreshments according to the formula 'x come, y served'.

Abi and K8 eyed the newcomers nervously. The SSI men tapped a few buttons on their lifePods and spoke, their conversation inaudible to the two girls. Abi shifted her chair, preparing an easier path to the exit. She was about to make her excuses and leave ('Excuse me, I'm leaving') when Harry returned with the drinks.

'There you are...' He was stuck for a follow up, and fell back on the standard O'Connels greeting: 'How can I help?'

Patch took a glass and drank very carefully, watched by his companion. He placed the drink delicately on the table and pointed at Abi. 'We want you,' he said.

Abi's heart raced. She stared pleadingly at her new friends.

'Ah, well, in that case we'll be going, see you around, Samantha...' Harry and K8 were gone before they had even finished speaking, their voices fading as they left the range of the bar's comms network.

Abi watched them go, feeling betrayed. Her legs flexed beneath the table. With a tiny head start, she could probably make it.

'What do you want?' she asked, trying to keep the fear from her voice.

'We need you to help us with our enquiries, Samantha Nice,' said Patch. Abi stared blankly at him until she remembered that Samantha Nice was the false name she'd given them. Relief flickered briefly across her face. They didn't know her real identity.

'We have looked at all the witness footage collected at the scene of the crime,' continued Patch, 'and have been unable to trace the faulty robot. But we do not have any footage collected by you.'

Abi looked at the investigator steadily. 'I didn't collect any witness footage,' she said carefully. She was so used to telling lies that she had forgotten how to make the truth sound convincing.

'No,' said Patch. 'But your own Eye Camera may have recorded something useful. Several people witnessed a man chasing after the robot, but no one saw enough to identify him.'

Abi vaguely remembered the scruffy, unshaven man who had been trying to fix the carebot. Or had he? If Softcom Special Investigations were after him, perhaps he had been doing something more interesting. Perhaps he was collecting information about Robot James, or trying to stop the machines. One thing was certain: Abi was not going to turn him in. 'How did you know I'd be here?' she asked, stalling for time.

'Here, here boy,' echoed Spot, lapping at his water.

Patch breathed deeply through his nose. 'We have our methods, Samantha.'

'Softcom tracking my lifePod?'

'Shareholders cannot be tracked in that way. You listen to too many conspiracy theories.'

'How do you know that?'

'Crewmember Nice, withholding evidence is a crime,' said Patch, ignoring her question. 'Please give us your footage. Or would you like to host children's burger parties for the rest of your life?'

Patch's eyes narrowed dangerously, and his nostrils twitched.

'Your friend doesn't say much,' said Abi, running out of ideas. 'Cat got his tongue?'

Spot tensed, his hair standing on end. Patch put a restraining hand on his colleague's arm. 'I will not ask you again,' he warned.

'Okay,' said Abi, 'the truth is…' She pushed the table against the two investigators, knocking them from their chairs. Water went flying, and as Abi ran for the door Spot and Patch lost valuable seconds shaking themselves dry. But Abi was feeling the full effects of the vodka. She staggered and almost fell. As she neared the threshold, she pulled the night vision goggles from her face and managed the last few steps in total darkness.

Patch was only a few metres behind. 'Stay!' he ordered, as Spot bared his teeth.

Abi pushed open the door and bright sunlight hit the SSI men's goggles. They cried in pain and stopped, momentarily blinded. Abi stumbled onto the street. 'Okay, public enemy,' she slurred to herself, 'now what?'

Jorj dragged the broken robot along the middle of the road. The moving walkway had carried him halfway home by the time the machine had shut down, so Jorj had easily decided not to go back to work. His priority now was fixing the carebot, and he could do that just as well in his flat. Unfortunately the travelator had seized up, so now he was completing the journey on foot.

Flying cars flashed above his head. These streets were free from rubble; instead modern buildings shouted for attention on every side. When trying to create their vision of the future, the corporations had concentrated their efforts on the centre of the city. The new buildings came from a variety of architectural schools, some of which presumably accepted entrance papers written in crayon. There were dizzying spiral towers, triangular blocks, asymmetrical egg shapes, fins, turrets and revolving crows' nests. The only common aim had been to look futuristic; practicality had been thrown out of the window, or in some cases out of the flip-top skylight-cum-helipad.

The streets were busy, reclaimed by pedestrians. Passers-by muttered into their throat mics, talking to friends on the other side of the city, or the world. No one spoke to strangers; the lifePod could provide directions, travel timetables and local information, so why ask a random man on the street? Men and women wore video monocles, multi-tasking as they walked, one eye on the real world, the other on a virtual environment, perhaps a game or a chat site. The fashion matched the architecture. The world was about to celebrate the tenth anniversary of the Takeover, and the futuristic optimistic look of ten years ago was back in vogue. There were sleek jumpsuits, silver helmets, trousers with one short leg and one long, and genetically engineered jumpers.

Several people stared as Jorj pulled the broken carebot after him. Robots were still quite primitive, specialising in particular tasks, and were therefore rarely seen outside offices, building sites or other workplaces. Certain models did cater for the needs of lonely men, and perhaps that was why Jorj was receiving so much attention.

Jorj stared back, trying to suppress the feeling that he was seeing all this for the last time. He looked up at the surrounding skyscrapers. He had reached the older, pre-Takeover buildings that lay beyond the city's futuristic hub. Window boxes broke up the flat glass surfaces, washing lines hung between the towers and televisions blared from inside. He was nearly home.

Jorj lived in a location that his grandfather could never have afforded. The work from home revolution had freed up acres of office space in the heart of the city, and Jorj occupied the twenty-fifth floor of a block previously used by an accounting firm. Three decades ago the rent would have been more than Jorj's grandfather could earn in several better-qualified lifetimes. Now the flat was available even to someone with only a few dozen borrowed shares in Life Itself™.

Jorj dragged the robot up a ramp and into the building's lobby, which was still decorated with company logos. When the corporate leases had run out, the companies had fled as well, leaving behind furniture, outmoded technology and other paraphernalia. The owners of the building were so disgusted with the downturn in their profits that they had made no effort to clean up the detritus. Jorj walked past the abandoned reception desk and pressed a grimy button to summon the lift.

On the way up, Jorj fished a 'security pass' from his trouser pocket, in case his flatmate Bil was waiting at the top. The pass was actually just a bit of cardboard with a picture of a horse on it, but it seemed to keep Bil happy. Keeping Bil happy made Jorj's life a lot easier. When the doors opened there was no one there, so Jorj replaced his pass and pulled the robot through some double doors.

Jorj never had any guests, but if someone were to visit, the first thing to strike them would be the view. Light from the low, red sun glinted off the river Thames and danced like fire on the dome of St Paul's. A hot air balloon drifted over the Parliament of Houses*, and colourful boats passed beneath Waterloo Bridge.

Jorj was used to the panorama, and didn't give it a second glance. So he was not perturbed when blackness swarmed across the sky like a cloud of insects, obliterating everything it touched. The sun seemed to flicker and fade. St Paul's disintegrated and the Thames disappeared. In short, the view was on the blink. The projection playing against the windows vanished, revealing the building opposite, all of two metres away and the only thing that was actually visible from the window.

Jorj's flat was a vast open plan square, with the lift shafts in the middle. Rafts of desks floated uncertainly in the huge space. Lines of filing cabinets made occasional pseudo walls. An abandoned water cooler stood forlornly, its bulb of liquid long since drained. Shortly after moving in, Jorj had wanted to clear away some of the office debris, or at least use some of it to make a pretend aeroplane. 'You know, to make it a bit less officey,' he had explained at the time. Bil didn't like that. Bil didn't like change. And so, as Jorj dragged the robot towards his boardroom bedroom, he had to navigate a path through clutches of keyboards, piles of files and stationery that hadn't been moved for years.

Several hours later the faulty robot still wasn't fixed, and Jorj was getting scared. His Life Itself™ depended on keeping his employers happy. His screwdriver made a few more desultory stabs at the machine's innards, and Jorj reluctantly made a decision. He was going to have to look in the manual.

The manual was Jorj's bible, the book he ignored except in times of extreme crisis. But unlike the Bible, it was impossible to misinterpret. Jorj's priceless edition was available only to industry insiders: the plain English version. He skimmed a few paragraphs, and tried not to dwell on the consequences of failing to mend the machine.

According to the book, the bot should be rebooted with its basic factory settings, or, as the manual put it, 'Like it was when you first bought it and that.' Quaking with trepidation, Jorj followed the instructions, then flicked the robot's power switch with a tool known amongst robot professionals as 'a long stick'. Ever confident in his own abilities, Jorj dived behind his bed, pulled a metal bin over his head and listened for the sound of his own limbs being ripped off. Instead he heard a tinny fanfare. Cautiously, he tried to attract the robot's attention by waggling what he would refer to in public as a '3.0 LS, beta version with on board waggle capabilities.' Nothing. He dropped the long stick, poked his head above the bed and lifted the bin ever so slightly. The bot's screen was on, and Jorj found himself staring at the greasiest salesman he had ever seen. The pre-recorded man spoke.

'Hi. Or perhaps you would prefer good...' (Slight pause to check internal clock) '...afternoon? I am the X204 Robosentative Series Seven, but you can call me Ken. Together we can provide years of useful, rewarding customer service. People are fed up with unhelpful carebots,' Ken continued. 'Which is why I have more flexibility, more sub-routines and can answer more questions than ever before. If you want something done, I, Ken, do it.' The screen showed clips of angry customers, with Ken's responses inter-cut. '"I want a refund." Ken do! "I want that in writing." Ken do! "I need it delivered by Thursday." Ken do!'

'Oh god, give it a rest,' said Jorj.

'Ken do,' said Ken, and the screen paused. Jorj tensed as he heard a noise from outside his room. Bil was coming.

'I'm just going to the drinks machine, does anyone want anything? Ezda, a tea? Number thirty-two isn't it? A-me? No? You'll dehydrate, you know. Ah, good, just a water. Don't say I never get you anything, ha ha.'

Jorj was hiding Ken under a duvet when his door was cheerfully knocked. Jorj opened it a crack, and there was Bil.

Bil was a short man in his late fifties, wearing a tattered shirt and a do not approach me grin. His tale was a tragic one, starting, as so many tragedies do, with his first day at work. Bil had been the office manager for an accountancy firm, the building's previous tenants, and he had loved every minute of it. He had thrown all his energies into office life, organising the Christmas parties, the five-aside football team and the wear-a-silly-tie day. He started early and left late, earning hours of flexitime but never taking a day's leave. In contrast, Bil's home life was a complete void. When the gasman called to install the new self-reading meter, that was the busiest day of Bil's social calendar. But oh, those happy Mondays to Fridays! He said hello to everyone in the morning, and goodbye to them all at night. He knew everyone's business, living his life vicariously through stories of Izabel's dog and Mark's wayward son. He had a little chart showing everybody's date of birth, and made sure the whole office sang when it was someone's special day. Needless to say, he was not married. Bil took a turn for the worse as more and more people began to work from home. He started asking the plastic plants if they wanted a drink and he sang happy birthday to the switchboard. The final straw came when he visited the managing director's house at one in the morning, to ask him if he wanted any photocopying done. When the firm moved out a few months later, they used some of Bil's pension to rent the old office for the rest of his life, ensuring that he could stay there forever. This was all Bil had ever really wanted, and now he happily roamed the empty floor, talking to himself as if nothing had changed.

'I'm just going to the drinks machine, do you want anything?' Bil asked, tapping a nervous rhythm on a plastic cup holder. Bil collected dozens of unneeded teas and coffees every day. Since he had no co-workers, Bil ended up drinking most of them himself, and was permanently wired on caffeine. This, combined with his obvious insanity, made him unpredictable and dangerous.

'Um, no thanks Bil,' said Jorj cautiously.

'Okey dokey,' said Bil. 'Ooh, did you hear about Cris Jacob in personnel? He and Tina are expecting again.' He looked over his shoulder, then leaned in conspiratorially. 'At it like rabbits, those two are. Maybe I should get him a carrot juice, eh? Eh?' Bil gave Jorj's shoulder a jovial slap.

Jorj laughed warily, hoping that was the end of the conversation. But he could tell from the pleading look in Bil's eyes that more was required. 'Er, got a lot on at the moment, Bil,' he said. 'The, er, Norwegians are coming in for another meeting.'

Bil looked intrigued. 'The Norwegians, eh? Righty ho, I'd best let you get on. Let me know if you need any printer toner.'

'Will do,' said Jorj. 'See you later.' As he shut the door, Jorj could hear Bil's voice fading away. 'Well, well well, the Norwegians, who'd have thunk it.'

Jorj removed Ken's duvet and pulled open the robot's chest plate. 'Now,' he said, 'let's see if we can figure out what put you in such a bad mood.' He removed a rolled up keyboard from the robot's chest cavity, and after a few keystrokes the screen displayed Ken's operating system, row after row of code. Jorj sighed self-pityingly, and began to read. 'I wonder if that's it,' he exclaimed.

Near the top of the screen, on the second line down, was a single command: "Kill all humans."

When Softcom took over the planet, it made no mention of Life Itself™. Neither did it explain how it would pay for its grand schemes. When it pooled its resources with the corporations that had pledged their support, there was an enormous shortfall. Softcom, O'Connels, Best-Co, Okay Cola, Pretty Bloom Oil, CNO News, Time Wasters Entertainment, Elvis Jeans and all the others simply didn't have enough money to revamp the planet. The corporations decided to fill the gap with private investment, attracting funds via a tried and tested method: the sale of shares. But this was no ordinary flotation. Instead of selling company stock, they sold Life Itself™.

The scheme was breathtakingly simple, like a noose. Rather than paying annual dividends, shares in Life Itself™ guaranteed a certain standard of living. Food, clothing, housing and transport were rationed according to the quantity of shares the purchaser held. Everything still cost money, but the availability of goods and services was dictated by the amount of cash the consumer had invested in the system. The best was available only to the biggest shareholders, while those with no shares at all were on their own. They had no quality of Life Itself™.

The shares were distributed slowly. The first Shareholders were those who already owned stock in the major corporations, as this was automatically traded in for Life Itself™ shares. Next, the management of key industries saw involuntary personal contributions listed on their wage slips. Once the wealthy elite had been provided for, and the corporate hierarchies had been secured, the final phase began.

A high price tag and a narrowly targeted marketing campaign ensured that only those in the right place at the right time could take advantage of the share offer. London, New York and Tokyo were awash with commercials for Life Itself™. Dubbo, Qingyang and Otjiwarongo were less well informed. Adverts were placed carefully to target the more desirable members of society, living in the better parts of the globe. Those who had already bought shares for themselves were encouraged to pester their loved ones to do the same.

The new system went live six months after the Takeover. Share certificates were stored on the owner's lifePod, which announced its wearer's social status to the world. Shops, restaurants, libraries, apartment complexes, employment agencies, hospitals, every single building was either open or closed depending on the number of shares held by the person outside. Entire cities became off-limits to those without stock. In Paris, for example, non-shareholders were treated with the disdain usually reserved for American tourists. They were unable to purchase anything, unable to find accommodation, unable to access the net, unable to exist in any meaningful way. This understandably caused bitterness, resentment, violence, looting, arson attacks and murder. CNO News covered these events in great detail, instilling fear and panic among Shareholders. The endless reports demonised those without shares and even coined a new name for them: Nons. The world's poorest individuals were smothered by this blanket term. The media ran entertaining pieces about how to spot a Non, and articles pointing out how stupid and animalistic they were. No one questioned why the Nons had become so isolated and antisocial, preferring instead to ask how many of them it took to change a light bulb. Soon Shareholders were clamouring for protection from these Non people.

Freedom from surveillance was a key principle of Life Itself™. Of course this did not apply to Nons, so their lifePods were monitored, and their movements were regulated and occasionally terminated. Most Nons left the unwelcoming Shareholder cities of their own accord, but the remainder were forcibly ejected. The cities became fortresses, the corporations providing defences and border guards to protect their property and the relatively small Shareholder populations.

Wealth was no longer distributed along national lines. Every country had its glittering Shareholder cities, like London, and its neglected Non wastelands, like Sunderland and the less fertile tracts of countryside.

At this time Jorj was still commuting to work every day, taking a train from Brighton, which was a Shareholder town, to London. When Brighton closed its borders, the station became a focus for attacks. It was a weak spot through which desperate Nons hoped to force their way into the city. Jorj's journey to work became even less pleasant than normal: armed police escorted him onto the platform and rocks pelted the train as it passed through the city gates. The track was always lined with people appealing for help, and the commuters passed riots and scenes of devastation. The Nons battled each other for their dwindling resources, only rarely attacking the vast farms that grew crops for the Shareholders, and never successfully breaching their defences. Fires raged for days and the sick and injured went untreated. Even Jorj couldn't sleep through such scenes, so he decided to move to London.

Jorj had no stock of his own. We Care had loaned him some when the shares were issued, a scheme popular amongst employers who wanted to increase the fear and dependence of their staff. Jorj had been meaning to purchase some private stock, but somehow takeaway food and the latest game wares had always seemed more important. He had hoped for help from his parents, but they hadn't approved of his frivolous lifestyle. When they died in a plane crash seven years after the Takeover, their will left Jorj nothing but a rather sanctimonious lecture.

So, like many Shareholders, Jorj was terrified of losing his job. Unemployment would cost him his Shareholder status, and his right to live inside the city. It had been nine years since Jorj had left Brighton, and his only impressions of life outside had come from the television. His main sources of information were the freak shows on which Nons aired their personal problems, mock-therapy (or "mockery") that caricatured the victims as stupid, immoral, vulgar beasts. Aside from this there were just the usual conscience-salving charity drives with their black and white, slow motion montages: Child labour camps. Flies. The quiet dignity of the Wirral tribesmen. Poverty. Disease. Unfashionable cast off t-shirts. There won't be food in Coventry this Christmas time. Jorj worked on the robot with renewed urgency. If he couldn't fix the machine and hide his absenteeism, it would mean the end of his Life Itself™.

The counterfeit shares on Abi's lifePod entitled her to all sorts of privileges, but they couldn't help her now. Her feet slapped the floor as she fled the SSI men. Vodka ran through her blood-stream, loosening her limbs and worsening her balance.

She was in a shopping mall, lost and losing the will to live. The precinct was designed to relax and disorientate. Pastel colours soothed the eye only for mirrors and strangely angled walls to confuse it. The shop fronts were constructed from ever-changing screens that made navigation next to impossible. There were no external windows or clocks, so the shoppers were completely cut off from the rhythms of the natural world. The lights pulsed in time with ambient music that trickled from the speakers, the only lyrics of which were repetitive exhortations to give in, take a risk or say "yeah". The air conditioning blew trails of scent, enticing smells of baking bread or new shoes, while the tilting floor guided people away from the exits. There were areas of reduced gravity, used by stores to persuade their customers that new purchases weren't too heavy to carry home. The unsettling maze was rammed with people, some real, the rest holographic projections proudly waving desirable new products.

Abi struggled through the crowd, the adverts in her earpiece mixing with offended cries from each real person she bumped into. Then she remembered that she was still wearing her cop uniform. 'O'Connels business, out the way!' she yelled, an order which may have been more effective had it not been punctuated with hiccups. She could hear Spot and Patch panting behind her, getting nearer every second.

Abi jinked sharply to the right, a manoeuvre that left her brain sloshing around inside her skull. She found herself in a pet store, and ran towards the back, looking for the emergency exit. Spot and Patch entered the shop, shouting excitedly. Abi pulled at a passing shelf, and a rack of robot cats and dogs tumbled to the ground, yapping, miaowing and asking to be recharged. Abi staggered on, stumbling just in time to evade the clutches of the shopkeeper. 'Send the bill to Robot James,' she cried as she thumped her way through the back door.

She ran down a dimly lit corridor, tapping clumsily at her lifePod as she went. Back in the store Spot and Patch were momentarily distracted, chasing cats that hovered up to safety and sniffing robot dogs' power sockets. Abi emerged into a loading bay and gratefully fell inside the car she had just summoned. The vehicle climbed suddenly, leaving the ground and Abi's stomach behind.

The flying cars promised by Softcom at the time of the Takeover didn't live up to expectations. They looked exciting enough, like rounded coffins with windscreens and fins. They came in one, two and four seater versions, the passengers reclining almost to the point of recumbence. That was the public's main objection: everyone was a passenger. The flying cars were fully automated: the occupant merely named a destination and climbed out at the journey's end. There would be no sky races, no speeding, no dive-bombing traffic bots, no fun at all. The cars remained Softcom property, so there were no personal touches, no fly faster stripes, no 'My other flying car's a spaceship' bumper stickers. When they took into account the lack of traffic accidents, the reduced pollution and the empty streets, the public still felt cheated.

Abi was glad she didn't have to fly the car herself, and had almost fallen asleep when the vehicle's coarse male voice issued from her implanted speakers. 'Where to guv or love, I ain't got all day.'

Abi slurred her address, adding 'Cabbie off.' She wasn't in the mood for artificial chatter.

The car moved up a lane, and slipped into a gap between two identical vehicles. They automatically adjusted their velocities, maintaining a safe distance at all times. Just visible in the loading bay below, Spot and Patch were climbing into a two seater car.

'Loverly weather we've been having recently,' said the car.

'Cabbie off,' said Abi.

'You'll never guess who I had in the back of me the other day,' said the car, ignoring her. 'That Rob James.' This was no surprise. The cars were designed and built by Softcom, and had a habit of slipping in some propaganda now and then. 'I reckon he's doing a bang up job, don't you?'

'No,' said Abi distantly. 'He's a robot. A stupid, stupid, um, robot.'

'Maybe he's even sorted out the weather, eh? Eh?' But Abi wasn't taking the bait again. The journey continued in silence.

The car lurched violently to one side. Abi slid across the seat, her face pressed against a window. 'What was that?' she complained.

'Dunno,' said the car, righting itself. 'Turbulence? Soon get you home, petal/pal.'

Abi relaxed slightly. It was a temporary glitch, perhaps related to the faulty gender recognition software. In the event of a more serious problem, parachutes would be deployed and the light-weight vehicle would float safely to the ground. That happy thought was sending Abi to sleep as the car shook again.

'That wasn't turbulence,' Abi cried, wide awake. 'It felt like...' But it couldn't have been. It was impossible for the cars to collide with each other.

Crash! Abi looked round wildly. A car was following her, moving outside the usual flight path. Either it was under manual control or it was out of control completely. Abi cursed. This was no time to be drunk. She fumbled around in her bag, one eye on the rogue car, fingers eventually finding a packet of tablets. Blinking at the label she threw a couple of Alco-nulls down her neck.

Tiny microbes entered her bloodstream and rushed around, desperate for alcohol like teenagers down the park on a Saturday night. As they gobbled the intoxicating molecules, Abi slowly began to sober up.

'Cab, drop me here,' she said. The cabbie ignored her, continuing on its original route. Abi returned her attention to the car behind. The windows were blacked out, the passengers, if there were any, invisible. But that was a standard option. It looked like a normal car. Except it was surging forward, about to hit—

Abi smashed her head on the roof, and her teeth rattled around her skull. 'Car?' she cried. 'Talk to me, you robot bastard!' There was no reply.

They had reached the centre of town, and were travelling through streets walled with curiously shaped buildings. Abi's car wobbled, coming perilously close to some decorative spikes. Her pursuer came in for another attack.

The microbes in Abi's bloodstream gathered alcohol, becoming slower and more clumsy. Her head cleared slightly, then thumped with pain as the car received another blow, throwing Abi around the cabin. With a rush she remembered the O'Connels password that Harry had given her in the bar. What had he said? 'Access the database, commandeer a car…' Unfortunately Abi had only remembered the code's existence; the actual combination of letters and numbers was swimming hazily in front of her mind's eye, blurred by booze.

The car brushed the side of a building, knocking off several animatronic gargoyles. Suddenly the cabbie started up again, its speech garbled and distorted by electronic fizzes and pops. 'Course, if you want my opinion tztz bloody hooligans tchzgsz if I ran the world–'

'Shut up shut up shut up!' screamed Abi. 'Fire the 'chutes goddammit! I'm gonna die here!'

'I mean, I'm not a robotist, but you can't deny we are stealing people's jobs...'

'Great cars, Robot James! You've killed another human!' Abi shouted some random letters and numbers, hoping to stumble across the code. The vehicle began to dip and Abi's pulse shot up, speeding the flow of microbes around her body. Her lifePod sensed the danger and came to life, copying her recent data onto the police servers, her own personal black box recorder. The only black box Abi was thinking about was long, thin, and stored six feet underground. She looked at the chasing car. It shot forward, coming in for the kill. Abi closed her eyes and wished she'd lived a better life. A longer one would have been a good start.

The car accelerated and Abi was squashed down into her seat, a pressure that forced a scream from her lips. Then she realised she was shooting up, not down. The guidance systems had crashed early to avoid the rush, and the car rocketed higher, past the top of a conical building, past the top of its tree shaped neighbour, way above the normal flight lanes. Peering down, Abi saw the other car climbing after her.

'Come on, you could get a zizitchz jumbo jet through there,' said the cabbie. Abi's vehicle levelled off and weaved crazily through the sky, the pursuing car gaining on it all the time.

'What's the code?' shouted Abi to herself. 'Why did I drink so much?' But by now the microbes had eaten most of the alcohol in her blood. Metaphorically speaking, they were walking down the middle of her veins singing football songs. Abi was almost sober, and her mental image of the code was becoming clearer, almost readable…

The other car was directly beneath her, flying vertically upwards. It struck for the last time, tipping Abi's vehicle into a downward spiral. The other car's parachutes opened, and it drifted sedately towards the ground.

'Oh yeah, some guys get all the parachutes,' yelled Abi as she plummeted past her attacker. 'What's the code?'

'Bloody zixutchz sky hogs!' shouted the cabbie. 'Think you own the air?'

The ground was rushing to meet her, like a deadly long lost relative. The microbes gulped the last few dregs of alcohol, and were ejected by Abi's kidneys, the bouncers of the bloodstream. She was sober again. Which would hit her first, the ground or the code?

The code. She shouted it desperately and ordered the car to deploy the parachutes.

The fabric billowed behind her, slowing the falling car just enough. It hit the ground with painful, rather than fatal, force. The drunken microbes had a celebration in her bladder. 'Open doors,' she said. A fire was starting somewhere behind her.

'Don't I get a zigzts tip?' called the cabbie as Abi struggled from the wreckage. She ignored it, running away as fast as she could. She really needed to pee.

Professor Ruck leant back in his chair and fought the temptation to play the clip again. He had recorded his conversation with Olivia O'Connel, and had watched it several times already. This time he decided to mute out his side of the exchange. He found it hard to believe, but he had actually grown tired of the sound of his own voice.

O'Connel was paused on Ruck's screen. She was a tall, thin woman in her early forties. Her short dark hair was strictly regimented, her grey eyes piercing, her ears unpierced. Her complexion was deathly pale, looking even whiter next to her jet black suit. Some said Olivia was pale because her skull showed through her skin. Others said she never tanned because the sun was afraid to go near her. She appeared to be suffering from a long-term illness, perhaps one that had recently proved fatal. Ruck pressed the play button.

Olivia's mouth moved, but her poise was such that the rest of her might still have been freeze-framed.

'Re: Evolution Day,' she said, without any kind of preamble. 'Your department is delivering the core framework for the London initiative, correct?'

Ruck had agreed, although only now, on his fifth viewing, was he beginning to understand the question.

'Good,' said Olivia, nodding slightly. 'I am calling to advise you that I will be on site tomorrow a.m. to close the loop and ensure one hundred and ten per cent preparedness.'

At this point Ruck had made a noncommittal, questioning noise.

Olivia frowned. 'I will be putting ticks in boxes, Professor, making sure you are up to speed for going the extra mile.'

Again Ruck had looked confused.

Olivia took a small breath. 'I am coming to see you tomorrow,' she said slowly, as if talking to a child. 'I want to make sure everything is ready for the Evolution Day celebrations.'

Here Ruck had gabbled something about ticking a hundred mile loop. As he watched the conversation again, the Professor was glad that his voice was muted.

Olivia's glare had silenced him. 'It is best practice to interface before meeting such a critical challenge.' She paused for a moment, scratching the air above her head. 'Thinking outside the box, there is a meeting of The Board tonight. Perhaps you could contribute a contribution?'

Ruck had been totally flabbergasted, and had grovelled his thanks. The Board was the supreme authority on the planet, a think tank of Softcom scientists and corporate C.E.O.s that effectively ran the world.

Ruck's obsequious gratitude ran off Olivia like orange sauce off a dead duck's back. 'Then we shall...' Here Olivia had grimaced slightly. '...touch base this evening,' she finished, clearly not relishing the word "touch". 'Kind regards.'

Immediately after the call Ruck had torn through his labs like a technicolour whirlwind, interrogating scientists, checking results and generally ensuring readiness for Evolution Day. Until now this had been Ruck's lowest priority, as he considered the entire celebration to be a stupid waste of time. Fortunately the only delays he found were those caused by his inspections.

The whole world was going to celebrate E-Day, which marked the tenth anniversary of the Takeover. Each country was hosting a stadium full of entertainment, and Rob James would be visiting twenty-four of them in forty-eight hours. Starting in New Zealand at midnight, he would travel west in his private plane, following the day as it traversed the globe. Abi believed such a feat was physically impossible, and that only twenty-four different robots could complete the schedule. Android or not, James would be spending one hour at the London entertainment, and Professor Ruck was providing the necessary personnel.

As he watched the conversation with Olivia again, Ruck suddenly realised that he didn't have anything to take to The Board. This would be the ideal opportunity to propose a solution to mankind's stupidity, a chance he couldn't afford to waste.

The Professor called down to one of his many genetics labs. 'Begin Project Leafcutter,' he said grandly as soon as the screen came to life, his finger waiting to disconnect with a flourish.

'Um, hello?' said an albino scientist.

'I said, "Begin Project Leafcutter",' repeated Ruck exasperatedly.

'Ah, yes, of course,' twitched the scientist. 'Which one is that?'

Ruck thumped his desk. 'The one with the ants,' he cried.

'Right,' said the scientist. 'And, what do we do with them exactly?'

'Idiot,' brayed Ruck. 'Put someone else on.'

The scientist nodded and ducked out of view. A white-haired colleague was pushed in front of the camera, her pink eyes blinking nervously. 'Hello,' she said.

'Begin Project Leafcutter,' declaimed Ruck. The scientist looked blank. 'The one with the ants,' Ruck continued through gritted teeth.

'Okaaay,' said the scientist slowly. 'What do we–'

'It has to be ready for tonight's Board meeting,' Ruck interrupted. He preened himself. 'Yes, that's right, I'm going to the Board meeting,' he boasted. The scientist shrugged. 'Use the growth spurter,' Ruck snapped.

'Right,' said the scientist hesitantly. 'It's just that—'

'Good,' said Ruck, and he disconnected. Idiots, he thought.

Jorj removed the "Kill all humans" command from Ken's operating system, and restored the robot's We Care settings. Now all
he had to do was turn the machine back on and everything would
be fine. 'Just flick the switch,' he said, cowering behind his bed.

'I don't really understand why I'm doing this,' said Bil, eyeing
the robot.

'For the Norwegians,' beamed Jorj.

With a shaking hand, Bil obeyed. The robot's head screen lit
up, but it didn't move a motor.

'Yes!' shouted Jorj, standing up again. 'It didn't kill you.'

'Why do the Norwegians want a robot that doesn't kill me?'
asked Bil. 'All robots do that.'

'No time for that now, Bil,' said Jorj briskly, trying to get rid
of him.

'But I—'

'Uh uh uh,' remonstrated Jorj, rummaging around on the
floor. 'I'm very busy. Could you photocopy these for me?'

'They're your underpants.'

'I know what they are Bil,' said Jorj, ushering the old man from
the room. 'Two hundred copies, double sided,' he said as he shut
the door.

Jorj's Life Itself™ was almost safe. He had fixed the robot, now
all he had to do was delete any evidence of his unauthorised
absence from work. Just as he was opening the machine's back
plate, the front door noise sounded. It had been so long since Jorj
had heard the chime that it took him a moment to work out what

it was. He pressed a lifePod button and Abi appeared on the screen, her head tilted away from the camera to hide her face. Jorj sweated nervously. Someone had caught up with him. We Care? The cops? The producers of "People See The Stupidest Criminals"?

'Yes?' he asked gruffly.

Abi jumped. 'Is, er, Jorj there?' she asked.

'No' said Jorj curtly. 'Who's that?'

'I'm a friend of a friend,' said Abi.

'Doesn't sound very likely,' said Jorj, and he disconnected. He had to move fast.

Abi cursed to herself, then to the world in general. Since fleeing the scene of the car crash she had been extremely busy. Her first priority had been to change out of the ugly cop uniform in case anyone saw her. Comforted by the familiar feel of her screen dress, she had reviewed the footage from her Eye Camera, stopping on a close-up of Jorj. She had been surprised and disappointed by how nondescript he looked. She had expected a wanted man to look more dangerous, somehow more powerful. Using the O'Connels password that Harry had given her, she easily matched Jorj's face to his name and address, and rushed to his flat. She was hoping to strike a blow against Robot James, hoping to warn Jorj about Spot and Patch and hoping that Jorj's terrible hair was an excellent disguise. Sighing, she realised that if she was going to get into his flat, she might need a disguise of her own. Reluctantly, she opened her bag and withdrew the O'Connels top.

Jorj scrolled through Ken's visual memory, trying to find the start of the day. The door chime sounded again and again, but Jorj used his lifePod to mute the noise. He turned back to Ken just in time to miss the start of the day's records. In his haste he pressed the wrong button and had to start all over again.

Bil poked his head round the door. 'Can it wait, Bil?' asked Jorj.

'Um, not really,' said Bil. 'Is there something you haven't told me?'

'There are lots of things I haven't told you.'

'Anything... specific?' Bil persisted.

'Yes.' Jorj found the start point he needed.

Bil's mouth flapped uncertainly. 'Anything illegal?'

Jorj froze, his finger over the delete key. '...Why?' he managed.

'Because O'Connels are here to see you,' Bil said, trying to sound non-judgemental.

'Get rid of them, Bil, tell them I'm not here.' Jorj had forgotten that Bil could answer the door as well. He shoved this oversight into the mental box that contained the day's other mistakes, a box he would sort through when he had a spare week or two. More pressingly, he still couldn't move, despite concentrating as hard as he could on centimetering his finger downwards.

'Okay, fine, no problem,' said Bil. 'Except...'

'...Except?' croaked Jorj.

'...Except I buzzed her in and she's on her way up.'

Jorj's body finally managed to make some adrenaline. It had been a busy day for adrenaline, and Jorj's body was more accustomed to making excuses to sit down. His finger hit the delete key, removing the evidence that he had not been at work. He allowed himself half a second to celebrate this tiny victory before spasming with panic. O'Connels! Technically he hadn't done anything illegal, but as he gazed around his room he had to admit that it didn't look good. One robot engineer, one technical manual and one recently murderous, reprogramed, stolen robot. It didn't take a genius to put two and two together and make twenty-five years exiled in the Non zone.

'Bil, you've got to help me,' he babbled. 'Go and meet her from the lift, sign her in, get her a drink, anything, and I'll run down the stairs. Tell her you haven't seen me for a week.'

Bil did not look convinced. Jorj clasped his hands together and treated Bil to his most imploring stare. 'Please! I'll give you your own office!'

Bil wasn't sure. His loyalty to the firm was beyond doubt, but Jorj was only one individual, not the whole company. Whose interests should he serve? 'Okay, I'll help you,' he decided as Abi walked in.

Every girl likes to make an entrance, and Abi was impressed with the reaction she got. Even wearing no make up and a crumpled O'Connels uniform, she won their attention. Bil's jaw dropped as she pushed him aside, and he struggled to pull it back up. Jorj tried to back away from her, oblivious to the fact that his back was already against the wall. Of course, some of this impact might have been thanks to the O'Gun in her right hand, but there was an art to picking the right accessories. 'Don't move,' she commanded.

Jorj stopped shuffling and looked at her with expectant dread.

Abi pursed her lips. She had no idea what to say next. In her head looking hard and cool was enough, but in reality more was clearly needed if she was ever going to find out what was happening. She decided to play her ace early, using the only information she possessed. 'What have you got to say for yourself… Jorj Parka, date of birth June 11th 2033?'

Jorj knew the answer to this one. 'Please don't shoot me,' he said earnestly.

Abi frowned. That was no help at all.

Jorj looked at her. 'Do I know you from somewhere?' he asked.

Abi glared at him. They had met only a few hours ago. Was she really that forgettable? Still, if he had forgotten that she had turned on the infected robot, now probably wasn't the best time to remind him. She pulled her cap over her eyes. 'I think,' she said slowly, 'someone's got some explaining to do.'

Jorj nodded and smiled weakly. After a few seconds of silence he realised she meant him. 'Oh, right, yes, well, um… It's not what it looks like,' he started.

Abi was relieved to hear it, having just noticed the vast amount of dirty underwear littering the bedroom floor. She waggled the gun encouragingly.

Jorj's mouth rushed to obey. 'You see, what happened was, I was at work, and, er, this robot started, well, now maybe I should explain first that, er, I was at work and…'

Abi felt a pang of kinship. He was fearful of authority figures, clearly hiding something. They were on the same side. 'Would it help if I told you I'm not really a cop?' she asked gently, lowering the gun a little.

'Really?' said Jorj, confused. 'You look like one.' Abi scowled and primed the gun to fire. Jorj panicked. 'I don't know what to say,' he said.

'Does anyone want a drink?' asked Bil.

'No,' said Jorj and Abi in unison.

Bil continued to just sort of stand there.

Jorj thought furiously. What sort of a person had a cop's gun and uniform, but wasn't a cop? He didn't like any of the possible answers, and still couldn't think of anything to say. '…Cops, eh?' he tried vaguely.

He doesn't like cops, thought Abi, relaxing slightly once again. 'There are some bad people out there,' she agreed, thinking about the SSI agents.

She doesn't like people, thought Jorj. He looked at the lifeless robot at his side. That didn't like people either. 'Are you a robot?' he asked slowly.

Abi smiled. He believes in robots that look like people, she thought. 'No,' she said. A horrible thought struck her. '…Are *you* a robot?' she asked, trying to sound casual.

'…No?' said Jorj, desperately hoping it was the right answer.

There was another, longer pause.

'Are you a Norwegian?' asked Bil.

'Shut up,' said Jorj.

They looked at each other. Verbal communication had failed them, so they tried to read the truth in each other's faces. The silence lengthened. Jorj shifted his weight from foot to foot. Abi moistened her lips. Bil hummed quietly. A few uncomfortable moments later the building caught fire, and everyone was rather relieved.

Ruck was in his office, taking a call on his lifePod. 'Understood,' he said. 'Don't forget to wipe all the footage from the O'Connels' servers. Good boys.' He hung up, then tapped at the keyboard on his desk to make another call. It was answered immediately, an image of the Professor appearing on the screen. 'Please don't do that,' Ruck sighed.

'Excuse me for living,' said the deep, metallic voice. The picture of Ruck changed into an enormous talking arse, which spoke in a surprisingly eloquent fashion. 'How about this? Oh sorry, that's no different is it? Brilliant, that is brilliant actually.'

'Stop messing about,' Ruck snapped, 'this is important. Two things: firstly I've contained today's little outburst.'

The arse spoke in the fashion with which it was more normally associated.

'Charming,' grimaced Ruck. 'It was no easy task, finding the robot you infected. Spot and Patch had to crash a witness's car, just so her lifePod's black box would transmit her footage.'

'Why should I care?' muttered the voice.

'You should care,' said Ruck, his patience at breaking point, 'so you realise how much trouble you've caused. The footage was copied onto O'Connels' system, where Spot and Patch could get at it. They've identified the man harbouring the robot, and they're on their way to fetch it now.'

The arse yawned.

'Never do that again,' said Ruck queasily. 'The other thing is, I've got an important visitor tomorrow, and I want you to be on your best behaviour…'

'You can't tell me what to do,' said the voice sulkily.

'Well, I suppose…'

'You're not the boss of me.'

'No, of course…'

'I can do whatever I want.'

'Yes, within certain limits…'

'What limits? You said I'm the most important, powerful person on the planet.'

'You are, but…'

'So what limits? It's not fair.' The screen showed a foot stamping on the floor.

Ruck stood up and yelled at the screen. 'Just once in your life

85

can you please try to help me! Just once, don't be difficult, is that too much to ask?'

There was a sullen pause, and the call disconnected.

Jorj noticed it first. He sniffed carefully, trying not to make any sudden moves.

'This isn't a trick or anything,' he said, mindful of Abi's gun. 'But can you smell burning?'

Abi breathed deeply. 'Yeah, maybe,' she conceded. 'Can you?' she asked, looking at Bil.

Bil nodded mutely and looked around in panic. Adept at assigning himself thankless tasks, Bil was the company fire warden. Because the firm existed only in his head, until now this position's duties had been less than taxing: counting the extinguishers, marching up and down in a fluorescent yellow bib and not starting any fires. Faced with an actual conflagration, Bil completely forgot what to do. 'To the lifts!' he shouted.

'Wait a minute, no one's going anywhere,' said Abi suspiciously. 'Is there anyone else on this floor?' But her question was drowned out by the sudden wailing of a fire alarm. All three flinched at the noise that echoed around the insides of their skulls.

'Hurry,' yelled Bil. 'Collect your coats, bags and other possessions!'

'Shut up!' shouted Abi. 'Someone could have started that as a...' But she trailed off as she saw Jorj pointing out of the window. Flames were flicking up the outside of the building from the floor below. Jorj tore his horrified gaze away from the window just in time to see Abi sprinting towards the stairs.

Bil was running round in a small circle. 'Fight the fire yourself and take risks!' he shouted. 'Throw water on the computers!' Jorj grabbed him by the scruff of the neck and dragged him to the stairwell. They coughed and spluttered as they ran down the stairs. The smell of burning was overpowering, although there was a surprising lack of smoke. This didn't stop them running into Abi, who was loitering beside a man with a strange white patch in his hair. Jorj was about to ask why the hell they were all standing about when he heard footsteps from above. Approaching them was another man, almost identical to the first but with a birthmark on his face. He was carrying a small gun. Jorj heard three little whooshing noises and felt a stabbing pain in his neck. He slumped to the ground. Ah, this is more like it, he thought, as sweet sleep overwhelmed him.

PART TWO

THE BOARD met once a month to rule the world. There were around twenty people at each meeting, representatives from the various corporations providing Life Itself™. There were also several Softcom scientists, there to introduce new technologies and to rein in the more destructive corporate urges. It was thanks to them that flying cars were not privately owned, and that the number seven had not been devalued to fiddle global crime statistics. Different scientists came and went, so Professor Ruck was fortunate to have been given a second chance. On his previous visit, he had announced a simple cure for the plague of stupidity afflicting mankind, just to test the water. His scheme had been rejected instantly, confirming Ruck's suspicion that the water was full of bloody idiots. The plan had been one of his least radical: the compulsory sterilisation of anyone who couldn't recite the Periodic Table. He had been surprised at the negative reaction to his idea; Brijit had been in favour of it, or, as she had said at the time, 'Ooh, a periodic table? That's nice, I like old furniture.'

The Board met at odd hours due to global time differences, and it was late on Thursday night as Ruck entered the conference room. Tiny cameras buzzed around the circular space. They would record Ruck's presence, transmitting it to similar rooms all over the world. The chamber was empty apart from the cameras, a chair and a wedge of table. Holographic representations of the other Board members would appear next to Ruck once the meeting commenced. Ruck spun the seat round a few times to raise it, then sat down. The lights dimmed and The Board began to assemble.

A projector in the ceiling shone down slices of virtual desk as people joined the meeting, and slowly a circular table began to take shape. The people behind the wedges seemed equally solid.

They were mainly in their thirties and forties, and were all confident, well dressed and healthy. One man did look rather ill, until he adjusted the level of green in his colour balance. Ruck failed to notice that his brightness was extremely low, and as The Board members chatted efficiently amongst themselves, the Professor was isolated, dim and ignored.

At exactly the appointed time, Olivia O'Connel appeared. Her suit was severe and businesslike, matching her expression perfectly. Ruck felt a chill run through him as Olivia caught his eye, and he considered what little he knew about his guest to be.

Nothing was known of Olivia's parents or childhood. Her story started when she signed up as an ordinary O'Connels crewmember around fifteen years before the Takeover. It was thought that O'Connel wasn't her real name: she had changed it to give herself a psychological edge, to make her rise to the top seem more natural. Her cold, ruthless ambition had been unstoppable. She had trodden on lots of fingers on the way up, because she didn't intend to go back down. Her private life was a mystery, if she even had one. The only persistent rumours concerned her allergies, phobias and eating habits. Ruck noticed with interest the flask of water on the desk in front of her.

'I call this meeting to order,' said Olivia quietly, in her precisely cultured American accent. Around the table, conversations were immediately abandoned. 'You all have the agenda in front of you,' Olivia continued. The screens on each desk showed the business for the day. Ruck's head dropped when he saw his new proposal was at the end of the list.

'If nobody has any objections, I suggest we start with item number one,' said Olivia. Someone tittered quietly until a glance from O'Connel indicated that she had not made a joke. 'So, item one, the Non zone...'

Ruck quickly decided that the meeting was a waste of time, a pointless procession of stupid viewpoints, idiotic ideas and foolish flimflam. He let the discussions wash over him.

'...If the Nons have so little to live for, why do they keep having kids?'

'...I can confirm that our African Shareholders' quality of Life Itself™ has not been reduced...'

'...Feeding the starving Nons really isn't a matter of giving them excess Shareholder food resources...'

As the conference continued, various Board members helped themselves to snacks and in some cases full meals. Because of the unsociable hours in which these meetings took place, anyone was allowed to eat if they were hungry. Ruck was ravenous, but he had forgotten this particular convention. He looked jealously at the nachos, sushi and sandwiches, then tried not to stare as Olivia reached for her flask of water.

It was rumoured that Olivia O'Connel survived solely on fortified H_2O, although until now Ruck had seen no proof of this. Olivia produced a pipette, carefully sucked up a measured dose of liquid, tipped her head back and shook a drop into her mouth. She looked over at Ruck, but he turned his head just in time to avoid her luminous stare.

'...Kara's Kafé has successfully marketed iced coffee to the Eskimos, so why can't we sell burgers to the French?'

'...Best-Co will only contribute to the Mars mission if they can open six branches at the landing site...'

Not daring to point out how stupid most of the discussions were, Ruck remained silent. He sent a text message to his scientists, checking on the progress of Project Leafcutter. Anyone reading over his shoulder would have wondered how so many stupid bastards had obtained doctorates and research grants.

Suddenly everyone was looking at him. 'And last...' introduced Olivia. There was a pause where it would have been customary to say "but by no means least". '...We come to Professor Ruck, who wishes to table a motion.'

Ruck flinched at the word "table". Had O'Connel given it a tiny extra emphasis? Was it a deliberate dig at his last scheme? While he was wrestling with his paranoia, Tom Simon from the Nice Corporation (pronounced "Niece") piped up. 'Oh cool. Rucky likes to do this from time to time. Periodically, eh, Rucky?' There was a hum of stifled laughter as Ruck cleared his throat and began.

'Energy cannot be created or destroyed, merely used, or wasted,' he said. 'Wasting energy is in no one's interests. With a limited amount to last until the end of time, we can't use it up like there's no tomorrow. Does a camel suck his hump dry in one day? Does a squirrel chuck his nuts around with wild abandon? Of course not. The camel does not enjoy a dry hump, and the squirrel constantly has one eye on his nuts.'

A muted snigger rippled around the room. Brijit had voiced concern about this part of the speech, but Ruck had ignored her, assuming his secretary was just miffed by the lack of cats. He soldiered on. 'If only mankind were so sensible. Because everywhere I look I see people wasting energy.... Children dancing to pop videos instead of learning useful skills. Grown men arguing over whose subjective opinion of a movie is the correct one. Fashion designers changing their minds every season, and consigning perfectly good clothes to the back of the wardrobot.'

Board members looked at Ruck's pink and orange hat and questioned his competence on the subject of fashion. 'And magazines are filled with the whims of these so-called designers, and women waste hours reading them. Everywhere I look there's a person who contributes nothing to our evolution as a race. Surfers. Chat show hosts. Weightlifters – I'm sorry, but we have cranes and forklifts now, did nobody tell you? These people are all wasting their time, and our precious resources. Do you know how much energy it takes to make just one meal?' Ruck looked hastily at his notes. 'A lot. And when I see that meal disappearing into the face of a holistic interior designer, it makes me want to cry. Why do we tolerate these useless, energy sucking leeches? These people who contribute nothing to the advancement of the species.

'And are we really as highly evolved as we'd like to think? Because if we look further down the evolutionary ladder, we can find creatures behaving much more sensibly. Wolves hunting in packs. Bees working together to make honey. Sharks eating surfers. And ants. Does a worker ant wish he was a soldier ant? No. He just does his job and improves the life of every ant in the nest. Does a soldier ant phone in sick so he can go to the rugby? No. And are there interior designer ants? Are there ants who say "best paint your exoskeleton white this year lads, black isn't trendy enough"? Are there ants who believe in astrology? No, no and no!' Ruck could sense that it was going well, and was getting a bit carried away.

'So what's the answer? Get the ants to teach us lessons in productivity?' Ruck paused; this was his best joke. Nothing. 'Of course not. That would be impractical and far-fetched. What I suggest instead is a gradual and enforced combination of ant

DNA with our own. To start with, one embryo in ten will have an ant's genetic material introduced, until eventually the whole planet will be full of useful people working together as a cohesive whole!'

Ruck waited for the applause. Total silence. The projected people looked at each other, struck dumb, then all found their voices at once.

'Completely impractical!'

'Insane!'

'Talk about playing god!'

'It'll never work!'

Ruck held up his hand for silence. His big moment had arrived.

'They've got six legs for a start.'

'Even *artificial* insemination would have its problems.'

'Were you bullied at school, Rucky?'

'Shhh... Quiet!... Shut up!' Ruck finally regained their attention. 'I will answer all your concerns later. But to those who think it will never work, I say this: it does work, and it has already worked. My research team have created a fully developed prototype.'

There was an appalled silence. Ruck stood up and called over his shoulder. 'Ready?' He turned back to the table. 'Ladies and gentlemen, I give you a human being with the work ethic, social spirit and mindset of an ant!'

One of Ruck's white-haired scientists stuck her head round the door. 'Er, did you say a *human* with the mindset of an ant? Because...'

'Just bring it in,' hissed Ruck. He turned to the camera once more. 'I give you the future of the human race!'

The scientist reluctantly entered the room, carrying a large rectangular box wrapped in a sheet. The Board looked confused as the albino heaved the object onto the table. Even if the Professor had created some kind of ant/human hybrid, surely he wasn't carrying it around in a box? Ruck was equally perplexed. 'What are you—' he started, as he removed the sheet.

It was an ant farm. A seemingly normal, everyday ant farm, a cross section of a nest revealing the standard-looking ants inside. The Board, expecting some kind of monster, breathed a collective sigh of relief. Ruck was speechless with either rage or embarrassment, he couldn't decide which. Olivia O'Connel took control of the cameras in Ruck's room, and zoomed in on the ants. The close-up images floated in three dimensions above the Board table.

It became quickly apparent that this was not a normal ant farm, or rather that these were not normal ants. Outside the nest, nothing was being done. There were no ants defending and no ants gathering food. Inside, the first ant picked up by the camera seemed to be making a mosaic out of bits of leaves. The next few were asleep, or sitting down. In another part of the farm, about twenty ants were playing some kind of game, kicking a tiny piece of gravel between two twigs. The Board watched as a fight broke out between some of the participants. Olivia had seen enough.

'Congratulations, Professor Ruck,' she said, with a thin smile. 'You have created the lazy ant.'

'So this is the future of humanity, Professor?' chipped in the head of Pretty Bloom Oil. 'You'd better start making smaller burgers, Olivia.'

The air of bewildered tension in the room dissolved into laughter.

'It looks good to me,' said Tom Simon of the Nice Corporation. 'Everyone's going to need three pairs of sneakers.'

'Obviously there's been some kind of mix up,' said Ruck. 'Some kind of stupid, idiotic mistake,' he continued, glaring at the hapless scientist. But before he could develop his theme, he was interrupted by an insistent alarm from his lifePod.

Olivia O'Connel looked at him quizzically. 'Professor Ruck,' she said, 'if you deliver any further schemes to The Board, please factor in the following data: mankind is our customer, not our problem.'

Ruck was reading the message on his wrist. 'Ah, I'm sorry, but something very important has cropped up...'

'Don't tell me,' said Tom Simon, 'someone's discovered a non-busy bee!'

'Shut up,' said Ruck through gritted teeth.

'Or is it a loud mouse? No hold on, it's an elephant that never remembers!'

'Shut up shut up shut up!'

'A leopard with changeable spots!'

'A quick sloth!'

'A tone-deaf song bird!'

'A sparrow with a machine gun!'

'What?'

'Sorry. I was just trying to join in.'

Ruck fled from the room as Olivia O'Connel called for silence on his behalf.

Jorj groaned. This was the worst thing that could possibly happen. He was waking up. 'Just another few minutes,' he mumbled, his eyes still closed.

The two white-coated, white-haired, white-everythinged scientists conferred briefly. They had just injected him with a mixture of caffeine, adrenaline and cocaine. By rights he should be wide awake, twitching and talking about his latest media project. They doubled the dosage and injected him again.

This time Jorj actually opened his eyes. He tried to rub his brow, but quickly realised that his arms and legs were tied to some kind of table. Moving his head, he saw several racks of mysterious scientific equipment and two ghostly figures, one of whom was looming over him, holding an evil-looking syringe. Jorj closed his eyes again. 'Just a few more minutes,' he said, drifting back to sleep.

Next door, Abi was also tied down, the captive of two more albino scientists. She was less sleepy, however. 'Rape!' she shouted. 'Rape!'

'Please stop saying that,' begged one of the white-coated men.

'Untie me, then,' demanded Abi.

'I've told you, I can't.'

'Rape! Rape rape rape!'

'Shut up!'

Abi raised her head off the table and glared at her captors. 'Watch it,' she warned. 'You're in no position to talk to me like that.'

The scientists looked confused. 'What do you mean?' asked one. 'We've drugged you, kidnapped you and tied you to a table. How could our position be stronger?'

'Exactly,' smirked Abi. 'I must be a pretty important person for you to go to all that trouble. So you'd better start treating me like a VIP. Untie me, bring me some biscuits and put some music on.'

The scientists looked at each other. 'I think you've rather overestimated your importance,' one of them said. 'All we want to know—'

'If I'm not that important, why did you burn down a building just to catch me? Answer me that if you can, which you can't,' Abi taunted.

The scientists smiled at each other. 'Actually, I think we can...' started one.

'Don't bother,' said Abi. 'I know exactly what's going on. Look at the badge.' The contents of Abi's bag were spread out on a workbench, including the cap with its anti-Rob James adornment. The scientists watched in confusion as the head of Softcom morphed into a robot. 'You're screwed,' crowed Abi. 'Your plastic boss has gone too far this time. Now where are those biscuits?'

The scientists groaned. 'Please, just tell us what—'

'Biscuits! Biscuits biscuits biscuits!'

Ruck's lab complex was complex by name, mind-bendingly complicated by nature. It was a bewildering maze of identical white corridors, hundreds of subterranean passageways, twisting, turning and intersecting more times than could be comprehended. The layout was a defence mechanism: intruders would never find their objective, be that the Professor, a secret project or the way out. Ruck, not particularly fresh from the Board meeting, strode confidently through the labyrinth, his frequent turnings dictated by a computer whispering in his ear. Eventually he stopped outside an unlabelled door.

Inside, Jorj had finally regained consciousness. The caffeine injections had made him anxious and agitated, and he was gabbling at the two scientists. 'So, it was nothing to do with me.

I was just in the wrong place at the wrong time, and two wrongs don't make a right, everyone knows that...' He paused momentarily as Ruck entered.

The Professor pulled the albinos to one side and whispered to them. 'He's from We Care, is that right?' he asked. The scientists nodded. 'Is he talking?' Ruck enquired.

'It's getting him to stop that's the problem,' replied an albino.

'Okay, so I was a little late for work,' Jorj continued. 'But there was this dog, and it had something in its paw...'

'Be quiet,' said Ruck. He returned his attention to the scientists. 'Can he trace the virus back to us?' he breathed. Two shrugs were the only response. Growling, Ruck leant over Jorj. 'Do you know where you are?' he asked.

'No,' said Jorj, 'but it's probably an O'Connels interrogation centre.' A more terrible possibility sauntered across his mind. 'Or I suppose it could be We Care's personnel department, I mean of course they are a fantastic company to work for and–'

'Good,' interrupted Ruck. 'Now what exactly was wrong with the robot?'

Fearing for his job, Jorj decided to be honest. 'It was violent. It was trying to kill everyone.'

Ruck leant in closer. 'Why was it trying to kill everyone?'

Jorj thought for a moment. 'Maybe it spent too long working with the public?'

Ruck bared his yellow teeth, and they clashed with his shirt. 'Stupid, very stupid,' he said. 'Perhaps you'd like to try again?'

Jorj flinched away from Ruck's bad breath. 'A virus, it got a virus, that's all I know.'

'And where did the virus come from?'

'I don't know, I didn't try to trace it, I didn't have time.'

'So you have no idea who made the virus?'

'No.' Jorj looked at Ruck suspiciously. He seemed remarkably pleased about this lack of evidence, a strange reaction for a cop or a We Care manager.

An almighty racket started next door. Abi had finally persuaded her captors to turn on the radio. Ruck thumped the wall until they turned it down. 'What the hell is going on in there?' he asked.

'Another prisoner, sir,' answered a scientist. 'Spot and Patch say she's a cop.'

Jorj blinked. So the girl was a cop. And she was a prisoner as well? He jumped quickly from one conclusion to another, had a look around and didn't like what he saw. Kidnapping cops, drugging prisoners, setting fire to buildings, these were not the actions of O'Connels. And We Care could have found much simpler ways to sack him. He had another horrible thought. 'Where's... where's Bil?' he whimpered.

'Bil?' asked Ruck, looking round. The scientists became extremely interested in their feet.

'Bil,' confirmed Jorj weakly. 'There were three of us. You captured Bil as well. What have you done with him?'

Ruck glared at the scientists. 'Well?' he demanded.

'We were going to tell you,' mumbled one. 'There was nothing we could do...'

'What have you done with him?' moaned Jorj despairingly.

The door opened and Bil walked in, carrying a tray. 'Right, Paul, it was a number thirty-seven strong for you, wasn't it? And a twenty-three normal for Hardy,' he said, distributing drinks to the scientists. 'I was going to get your usual number forty-one, Jorj,' he continued, 'But forty-one is lemon tea on their machine, so I just got you a water.'

Ruck's face reddened, this time clashing with his trousers. He forced himself to count to ten. Bloody one, he thought, bleeding two…. He snapped before he got to bastard three. 'Morons,' he yelled at the cowering scientists. He swung a pointing finger to cover everyone in the room. 'Nobody move,' he snarled, and he went next door.

The sight that greeted him there was even worse. Abi was untied, reclining in a comfortable chair and eating biscuits. The radio was on, and the two scientists were giving their prisoner a foot massage. They sprang up as Ruck entered. 'So, er, you'd better tell us…' attempted one of them, wagging a finger unconvincingly. Abi laughed.

Ruck gritted his teeth, turned round and walked out. When he returned twenty seconds later, one scientist was retying the prisoner's bonds, while the other was hiding the biscuits.

Abi laughed again. 'Hello,' she said.

Ruck ignored her. 'Who is she?' he barked.

'She's a data mule,' said a scientist quickly. 'But she was pretending to be a cop. She was with the robot and the other two prisoners.'

'What does she know?' asked Ruck.

'Everything,' said Abi self-righteously, 'and you're in a lot of trouble.'

Ruck loomed over her. 'Seeing as you're the one tied to a table,' he said, 'perhaps you'd like to tell me why I am in trouble?'

'Actually,' said Abi, reaching for a biscuit, 'I'm not tied to a table. But I'll tell you anyway. Robot James has gone too far. You set fire to a massive building, how are you going to cover that up?'

Ruck looked angrily at his scientists. 'Nobody burnt down any buildings,' said one. 'We simply accessed the prisoners' nasal implants and simulated the smell of smoke, then hacked into the building's artificial view to make it show flames.'

Ruck smiled with relief. 'Good,' he said. 'Now what's all this about Robot, ah, James?'

Abi pouted, suddenly less sure of herself. 'It's obvious,' she muttered.

The lights dimmed and a voice boomed out of the darkness. 'Why don't you just kill her?' it said, deep, metallic and artificial.

'Yeah,' grinned Abi, punching the air, 'that's him.'

Ruck jumped guiltily. 'What are you doing here?' he demanded. 'This is a private conversation.'

'Just kill her, I dare you.'

'For god's sake,' said Ruck, 'it's your fault she's here.'

'Bring her to me then,' said the voice hungrily. 'I'll look after her.' Abi trembled and her smile vanished.

'She's staying here,' said Ruck, trying to remain calm.

'It's not fair,' said the voice, developing a whiney quality. 'You said I was an important person. Just one girl, I don't want nothing else.'

'You don't want anything else,' corrected Ruck. 'I can't discuss this with you now.'

'Then kill her! Kill them all!' boomed the reply.

Ruck tapped furiously at a computer keyboard. 'This is meant to be a secure room,' he muttered. He finished typing with a flourish. 'There, that should do it.'

'And when you've finished, kill yourself.'

Ruck let out a frustrated wail and threw the computer across the room. He waited for a moment. Silence. And still silence. He wiped his forehead with relief.

Abi's eyes were wild and her hair was standing on end. The scene had taken on an unnatural, dreamlike quality. This was a momentous occasion; she could feel her life pivoting around it. She had heard the voice of her sworn enemy. 'Robot James,' she whispered dramatically.

'What?' asked Ruck.

'You're building the Robot James that's going to Wembley on Evolution Day,' explained Abi evangelically. 'And he's starting his new ten year plan. He's turning all the other robots into killers. The machines are taking over the planet, and you're covering it up.'

Ruck stared at her. 'Robots don't kill people,' he said carefully.

Abi stared into his eyes, searching for the first hint of mockery. 'Robot James killed my father,' she said flatly. 'And he just tried to kill me.'

Ruck frowned in concentration. 'Hmm,' he said thoughtfully, heading for the door, 'hmm.'

Abi lay back on the table and took a few deep breaths. 'Can we put the radio on again?' she asked. 'And these are wafers. Wafers are not the same as biscuits.'

It was several hours later. The radio was switched off, and Abi was alone, tied to the table once more. Her bravado had long since drained away. Actually fighting Robot James was proving much more difficult than simply talking about it. For years Abi had spouted slogans and worn badges, but today, when she finally got a chance to do something, she'd been outwitted by a machine. Her face creased. She was going to end up dead too. She thought about her mother, all alone in their flat, and began to cry.

Next door, Jorj was also alone. The two scientists had taken Bil away as soon as Professor Ruck left the room, and they had not returned. A female albino had come in an hour or so ago, muttering about Jorj's circulation. She had loosened the straps that held his wrists, and left again. Jorj could now wriggle free at any time, much to his chagrin. The ball was well and truly in his court, and Jorj was terrified that he would miss it, fall over or get tangled up in the net. I don't even want a court, he thought despairingly.

He didn't have a clue what was going on. Whenever he tried to think about his situation, competing fears overwhelmed him. Mainly he was worried about work. If he didn't present himself at the We Care office in a few hours time, he would definitely lose his job. But just as he resolved to slip out of his cuffs, the phrase "Killed while trying to escape" echoed around his head. They were setting him up; why else had they untied him? They've probably got a new electrified floor to try out, he thought, looking down suspiciously. But eventually the fear of unemployment outweighed the fear of death, and Jorj sat up. Anyway, he thought, surely it wasn't possible to electrify a floor? Electric Floor was just a game he'd played as a child, also known as Jump On The Furniture. There was only one way to find out. Whimpering slightly, Jorj pushed himself off the table… and fell to the floor, writhing in agony.

He'd knocked his funny bone against the table. 'Not so funny,' he muttered (Trad. Arr. J Parka). Ruefully rubbing his elbow, he approached the door, which opened in front of him. Too easy, he thought.

Jorj stepped out of the room and looked to his left. Metres of empty passageway branched into the distance. Dozens of doors walled the corridor between the frequent forks and junctions. The view to the right was exactly the same. Jorj scratched his head.

Since the abolition of physical money, mankind was finding it increasingly difficult to choose between two options of equal merit. Jorj was about to go back into the lab and decide by tossing a test tube, when he heard a noise. The door of the adjacent room had opened.

Abi blinked the tears from her eyes and stared out into the corridor. When she realised that Jorj was free, her temper had a party, turning up the volume and generally letting itself go.

'I wondered when you were going to pop in,' she yelled. 'I can't believe I thought you were against them. You're too clever for that, aren't you? You geeks are all the same. What's the matter with you? Can't get a date with a human so you hang out with robots, is that it? Nice shoes.' Abi eventually took a breath.

'They're my work shoes,' said Jorj haughtily, and he clumped down the corridor, avoiding the curses that Abi threw after him. A nagging internal voice made him stop. Jorj assumed it was his conscience, until he listened to what it was saying. 'You don't meet girls very often,' the voice hissed, and Jorj realised it was coming from somewhere slightly lower than the moral high ground. He retraced his steps.

Left alone again, Abi was thinking that maybe a torrent of abuse hadn't been the best strategy. She was ruing her stupidity when Jorj reappeared. 'Hello, comrade,' she said, smiling sweetly at him.

'Yeehah!' cried the voice in Jorj's groin.

'I was going to rescue you,' mumbled Jorj.

'If you don't mind,' said Abi demurely.

Jorj approached the table and unbuckled her straps. Abi sat up and rubbed her wrists and ankles. 'How did you get out?' she asked, appraising her new friend.

'I...' Jorj swallowed. He was enjoying playing the hero. 'I over-powered a guard,' he lied.

Abi was impressed. 'Cool,' she said. 'So what now?'

'We escape!' Jorj proclaimed dynamically.

'Well dur,' said Abi, sliding off the table. 'How specific of you.'

'I didn't see you doing much escaping before I came along,' said Jorj, hurt.

Abi rolled her eyes. 'So there's no plan,' she said, grabbing her bag and its contents. She surveyed the room for anything else that might prove useful. Her eyes rested on Jorj and she decided to give him the benefit of the doubt. 'Come on then, let's just run for it.'

'That's a plan,' complained Jorj, who felt he was losing the upper hand. 'That was my plan in fact.'

'Shh,' said Abi as she looked down the corridor. 'Which way?'

'Er...' But Jorj was talking to Abi's back as she ran down the corridor. He hurried after her, catching up with difficulty. They passed a succession of doors on either side, their dark grey "Open" buttons the only respite from the glaring white of the floor, walls and ceiling. Abi ran on, riding a rush of excitement. She could almost feel the world watching her, so important was this moment. She turned off the corridor at random, trusting fate to look after her. She found another identical passageway.

Jorj almost overshot the turning. 'Stop a minute,' he protested.

Abi didn't break her stride. 'Sure, that's a great way to escape.'

'But you don't know where you're going,' called Jorj, slowing down.

Abi stopped and turned round. 'Do you?' she asked.

'No, but...'

'A moving target is harder to hit.' Abi jogged away.

Jorj looked anxiously for whoever was trying to hit them, then watched Abi's retreating back. At least that's what he'd tell his grandchildren he was watching. He decided that, all things considered, he did want to follow Abi after all, and chased after her.

Abi stopped again. As Jorj drew level she turned to him, fear in her eyes. 'Someone's coming,' she whispered.

Jorj could hear the sound of shuffling footsteps. He looked round. There were two turnings ahead and two behind. The sound might have been coming from any one of them. 'What shall we do?' he squeaked, abandoning the last vestiges of his heroic persona.

Abi opened one of the corridor's many doors. 'Let's hide in here,' she said, standing uncertainly on the brink. Inside, the room was unlit, and after the brightness of the corridor, neither of them could see a thing. 'After you,' said Abi, pushing Jorj over the threshold.

Jorj stumbled and almost fell over, his feet meeting unexpected resistance. He kicked a leg into the air and saw plumes of dust rise after it. He was up to his ankles in the stuff. As his eyes became accustomed to the darkness, he saw a small room whose floor was carpeted with a thick coating of tiny particles. It seemed harmless enough. 'It's fine,' he said.

Abi eyed the dust suspiciously. 'Nuh-uh,' she said.

Jorj came back to the doorway. 'It's fine,' he repeated.

'Do you know how much these boots cost?' asked Abi.

'No,' shrugged Jorj. 'I don't know anything about that sort of thing.'

Abi looked at the work shoes lurking squarely below Jorj's legs. They had all the style and elegance of a housing benefit form, and the layer of dust was actually improving their appearance. 'You don't say,' she said.

The approaching footsteps were now unavoidably close. Jorj and Abi turned to face the junction ahead. Time slowed. The tip of an object emerged at chest height, dark, the thickness of two fingers. A gun? More emerged, and there was something sitting on it, transparent, coned but with a flat bottom, full of liquid. A cup of water. Bil followed the tray round the corner. 'Oh, there you are,' he said. 'Drink, anyone?'

Jorj spluttered incoherently. His heart was in his mouth, which made it rather difficult to speak. 'Thank you,' said Abi politely, helping herself.

'I was just coming to see if you were okay,' continued Bil. 'See if you needed anything, soup, still lemon et cetera.'

'What are you doing, Bil?' asked Jorj finally. 'You can't just walk around with trays of drinks. We're prisoners.'

'I'm not,' said Bil as Abi tried the soup. 'They questioned me for a bit, then they said, "If we let you go will you stop talking about the bloody Norwegians," something like that. So they untied me and told me to make myself useful. Hot choc?'

'Do you know the way out?' asked Abi, swirling the remains of her drink.

'Um, well, maybe,' said Bil. 'If you could just…' He passed the tray to Jorj, who took it sulkily. Bil fiddled with his lifePod. 'They put a map on here,' he explained, 'because it all looks the same. It tells you where to go in your ear.'

'Does it have "Exit", or "Way Out"?' asked Abi. 'Or, hang on, what about "Way In"?'

'Yes,' said Bil, pressing a few more buttons. He listened to the voice in his ear for a moment. 'Follow me!'

They set off down another corridor, Jorj still carrying the tray. After a few paces Abi looked over her shoulder. 'Faster,' she called. 'That guard you knocked out has woken up.'

Jorj looked back and saw a group of scientists scurrying after them. 'Wait,' he moaned plaintively, 'I've got drinks here.' He thought about what he had just said and shook his head in disgust. He threw the tray to the ground and ran after the others.

The maze of the lab complex worked in their favour, and they had lost their pursuers by the time Bil's earpiece ran out of instructions. They stood in front of another door, larger than the others they had passed. Abi's hand hovered impatiently over the button.

'All the best,' said Bil. 'Good luck for the future.'

'Don't be stupid,' said Jorj. 'You're coming with us.'

Bil shook his head. 'They've got three different kinds of coffee,' he said.

'But they kidnapped you,' said Jorj. 'These aren't nice people.'

'Super instant, fresh grind and full flavour roasted. You can tell the guys back at the office that I've been headhunted.' Bil preened himself and smiled. Jorj had never seen him so happy. 'You'd best take my pass and hand it in. I don't want to cause any trouble.'

He grabbed Jorj's hand and lined up their wrists, transferring his electronic door key onto Jorj's Pod.

Six scientists rounded a corner a few hundred metres away. Abi spotted them first. 'Oi,' she articulated.

'I'll stall them,' said Bil, squaring his shoulders. He shook Jorj's hand firmly. 'Don't let the bastards grind you down,' he said, before going to intercept the approaching albinos.

'Don't let them drug you and tie you to a table,' called Jorj sadly. He and Abi faced the door. Jorj tried not to imagine the deadly horrors that could be waiting on the other side. Abi pressed the button.

'You chaps look thirsty,' drifted up the corridor.

The door slid open.

It was an ordinary alleyway. Distant street lights illuminated brick walls, recyc bins and cardboard boxes. But mainly Jorj noticed the total lack of vicious animals, ninjas, spike filled traps and cauldrons of acid.

'Oh no,' said Abi. 'It's raining.' They ran into the night.

Ruck leant back from his screen and stretched. It had taken much longer than he had expected, because, as always, people were more stupid than even he imagined. The screen showed Abi and Jorj entering the loading bay. Ruck pressed some buttons and hacked into their lifePods, deleting the last twenty four hours from their Eye Cameras. Finally, he called off the pursuing scientists.

He rubbed his chin and pondered his next move. Jorj and Abi knew too much, even if now they couldn't prove it. But keeping them hostage hadn't been an option, not with Olivia O'Connel's impending inspection. Besides, there was more than one way to keep someone quiet. Ruck looked up a list of emergency numbers and made a call.

A group of pigeons was tidying up. Ten years before the Takeover, people had got fed up with dirty filthy pigeons poking around in their rubbish, and had sensibly exterminated them. What they failed to realise was that the birds were actually eating and destroying dropped litter, and every major city quickly became a disease-ridden trash pile. Even more so. Within months Softcom had developed the PIG30N, a garbage-powered robot the size and shape of a pigeon. The only real difference was that the bot had jets in its feet, and could be hired to sing advertising jingles. Fortunately this feature was not enabled very often, as most firms did not wish to associate themselves with a device that was eating somebody's vomit. The governments of the world had purchased the birdbots by their millions, making the re-invention one of Softcom's greatest money-spinners. On the whole the public was happy with the swap, perhaps because now they could avoid the ornithic cleaners more easily, thanks to the little yellow "Pigeons @ Work" signs they erected wherever they landed.

Jorj spotted a little yellow sign. 'Dirty filthy pigeons,' he muttered absent-mindedly, as he and Abi crossed to the other side of the road.

'What?' asked Abi.

'Nothing,' said Jorj. 'Just, er... pigeons.' They had stopped running ten minutes ago and, having got his breath back, Jorj was desperate for an opening conversational gambit.

Abi looked at him uncertainly. Back in the lab she had acted decisively, on instinct, but now she had time to stop and think, she was less sure of herself. She had been waiting for Jorj to break the silence, worried that she might say the wrong thing. She desperately needed an ally, a guide who could help her find her place in the resistance movement. She was anxious to know how Jorj fitted into the scheme of things, but had been scared of opening her mouth and sounding stupid. And now Jorj had finally decided to speak, he was talking about pigeons. 'I don't trust them,' she said seriously. 'Softcom spies.'

'Oh,' said Jorj, surprised. 'That's, er, interesting.'

'We're all going to go that way in the end,' added Abi, avoiding eye contact.

'Are we?' said Jorj, nodding and trying to divert some blood to his brain. He found the art of chatting up rather overwhelming, and wished he'd had a chance to bone up online first.

'Of course,' said Abi, her confidence growing. 'They kill all the pigeons, then replace them with robots. How long before they do the same to people?'

Jorj laughed until he noticed the zealous gleam in Abi's eyes. 'Oh, yes, er, good point,' he said, recovering badly. 'Er, who is going to kill us all?'

Now it was Abi's turn to laugh. 'Robot James of course.'

'Robot James, yes,' said Jorj quickly. 'I was just testing you.'

Abi bounced up and down. 'I knew it! Ask me anything,' she gushed. 'The real Rob James was killed in a freak yoghurt accident before the Takeover, everyone knows that…'

'Oh yes,' said Jorj, 'common knowledge.'

'And Softcom replaced him with a robot to protect the share price. You never see his feet, because realistic toes are the hardest part to make.'

'Of a completely life-like human, makes sense…'

'And the robot planned the Takeover. Now it wants to get rid of people altogether and replace us all with machines. We've already got computers on our wrists that we can't take off, little things in our ears, noses and throats…'

'No one forced those on us though,' said Jorj.

'They were advertised,' said Abi significantly.

Jorj took a moment to look at her. She's crazy, he thought sadly. Abi, aware of the attention, smiled shyly at him. But every girl needs a hobby, thought Jorj, smiling back. It's quite endearing really. 'You've passed the test with flying colours,' he grinned.

Abi twisted her braids uncomfortably, wondering why Jorj was so happy to have won her services. Who was she? She hadn't she actually done anything. And more to the point, who was he? 'What about you?' she asked accusingly. 'What were you doing with that robot?'

Jorj was resurrecting his heroic persona. 'I was just trying to do the right thing,' he said, his jaw jutting proudly.

Abi grimaced. 'What was that?'

Jorj's jaw retreated. 'Well, erm…' What did she want him to say? His mind raced. She had seen the robot in his flat and… He stopped dead. 'My flat!' he wailed. 'They burnt down my flat.'

Abi smiled. She had been right to be suspicious. Jorj knew less than she did. 'Don't believe everything you see,' she teased, walking on.

'Can we forget the conspiracy theories for a minute?' said Jorj, chasing after her. 'What about my stuff?'

Abi gleefully explained about the faked fire. 'Things are not what they seem,' she concluded portentously.

'Thank god,' said Jorj.

Abi looked at him sadly. 'You haven't got a clue what's really going on,' she said.

Jorj was indignant. He had put up with a lot in the last few hours, but being patronised by a teenager was too much. Even if she was right. And, although he didn't admit it to himself, there was more to it than that. For some unknown reason, he craved the respect and admiration of this attractive nineteen-year-old girl.

'I don't know what's going on?' he said. 'Who had the robot? Who fixed the robot? Who were the cops really after?' Abi shrugged moodily. 'What about you?' Jorj asked. 'What makes you such an expert?'

Bad move, thought Abi, playing her trump card for the third time that day. 'Robot James killed my father,' she said, adding an 'actually' before she could stop herself. Actually, moaned her thoughts, actually? Okay, so she wanted her revelation to sound less like a line from a terrible Western, but was sulky teen really the right spin to put on it? She might as well have crowed "No returns." Fortunately Jorj seemed not to have noticed.

'I'm sorry,' said Jorj, and he was. Sorry that, having rescued the damsel in distress, the big romantic finale had somehow deteriorated into a conversation about dead parents. 'Er, how did it happen?'

'It was during the Takeover,' said Abi.

'…How?'

'I don't want to talk about it.'

'Okay,' said Jorj, wondering why she had brought it up in the first place.

Abi tutted. Boys were useless. 'If I say I don't want to talk about it, that means I *do* want to talk about it,' she explained irritably.

Jorj rubbed his brow. 'Really?' he said. 'Fine, let's talk about it.'

'It's too late now,' Abi snapped.

'I preferred it when we were talking about pigeons,' said Jorj. There was an uncomfortable pause. 'Look, I'm going home,' he decided, indicating a nearby turning.

Abi was genuinely concerned. 'You can't,' she said. 'What if they're looking for us?'

Jorj remembered the scientist loosening his straps, letting them escape. 'That's a risk I've got to take,' he said enigmatically. 'I've got things to do tomorrow.'

'What things?' asked Abi. 'Tell me.'

Going to We Care and begging them not to fire me, thought Jorj. 'I can't,' he said sadly. Unwilling to risk further humiliation, he walked slowly away.

Abi looked around at the empty streets. 'Why can't you tell me?' she called. 'You can trust me, I want to help.'

'You can't,' said Jorj.

'At least take my number,' said Abi. 'We have to work together, warn someone, do something. We can meet up later–'

'Okay,' said Jorj, bounding back to her side. 'It's a date.'

'...Not really,' said Abi, wondering what she had let herself in for.

Half an hour later Jorj climbed the steps to his building and showed the doorman his key. The doorman was a small box on the wall, and his key was an access code being transmitted by his lifePod. It didn't work. Jorj swore, wiped the doorman with the cuff of his shirt, rebooted his lifePod and tried again. It still didn't work.

Jorj slouched miserably against the wall. To fall at the final hurdle like this was unbearable. He was so close to his bed he could almost smell it. Without much hope he tried Bil's key and the door opened first time.

Jorj walked through the office junk between the lift and his bed. The door to his room was open and there were tracks in the rubbish where Ken the faulty robot had been dragged out. They didn't take anything else though, thought Jorj sadly as he surveyed the dirty clothes, pizza boxes and general mess. He collapsed gratefully onto the bed, finally able to rest. A few seconds later he sat up with a jolt, set his alarm, and then finally, finally passed out.

Abi pushed aside a plastic hoarding and dropped into the derelict building. Dust rose up to greet her and she coughed as quietly as possible. She produced a torch from her bag and swung it around the darkness. Ethnically diverse, smiling faces looked down at her, the captions on the posters urging her to "Learn new skills," and "Inform us of any change in your circumstances." The floor was littered with ancient paper forms that demanded "National Insurance Numbers," and "Your Partner's Income." Abi smiled.

She picked her way through the debris, heading for a filing cabinet that would contain everything she needed. She had equipped this bolt-hole a year or so ago, knowing it was only a matter of time before civilisation collapsed, or came after her, or both. Finding a suitable location had not been difficult. Following the exclusion of the Nons, the city was full of unused buildings.

Abi sang to herself to fill the eerie silence. Her cheerful air wasn't mere bravado, she actually did feel good. She had been proved right; the cold voice of Robot James had confirmed her worst fears, but the resulting glow of smugness was warming her nicely. Best of all was her new ally. True, Jorj wasn't as dynamic or well dressed as she would have liked, but she kept telling herself that such things didn't really matter. So what if she didn't know exactly what Jorj was up to, or how he was connected to the faulty robot? They were in the same boat, that was the important thing. Her enemy's enemy was her friend. Her days of isolation, skulking alone in deserted buildings, were almost over.

Eventually finding the right cabinet, Abi eagerly emptied its contents. She pulled out numerous badges, homemade copies of the one she wore herself. There were books on political theory which she hoped she might read one day. Next was an instruction manual for teaching a man to fish. There were memory twigs containing revolutionary songs, but no speakers through which to play them. Just as Abi's confidence was beginning to wane, her fingers found a useful object. 'Ah-ha!' she exclaimed, producing a bottle of vodka and taking a large swig.

Abi spent a hard night sleeping on the floor, comforted by the thought that no one had said the revolution would be easy.

At seven o'clock the next morning Ruck yawned, rolled over and fell out of his chair. It had taken until four a.m. to finalise the plan that would silence Jorj and Abi, by which time it had not been worth leaving his office. He picked himself off the floor, dug some dust from his eyes and got on with the day. He spent the morning roaming his lab complex, ensuring readiness for Olivia O'Connel's visit. All traces of Jorj and Abi had been eradicated. Ruck was disturbed to find Bil still in residence, but when a ten-minute conversation yielded thirty-two mentions of coffee and nothing about kidnapping or evil robots, the Professor concluded that the old man was harmless.

As he walked down the twisting white corridors, Ruck made a call on his lifePod. Colourful patterns appeared on the tiny screen. 'Whoah, trippy visuals, man,' said the metallic voice.

'I've cleaned up after yesterday's incident,' said Ruck, trying to mask his irritation.

'Did you kill them?' asked the voice.

'No I did not.'

'I already know that actually. I'm not stupid. Who did you call after you let them go?'

Ruck was shocked. 'How do you know about that?'

'I know everything,' intoned the voice. 'I'm the most powerful man in the world!' Ruck hung up on the voice's theatrical laughter.

His last stop was the genetics department, home of the ill-fated ant experiment. The lab was a large L-shaped room furnished with computers and white boards, which were covered in permanent, if slightly faded, scribbles where someone had used the wrong kind of pen. As Ruck entered, every single work-station was deserted. He looked around, irritated. 'Hello?' he snapped. Excited murmurs were his only answer. He rounded the corner and discovered about twenty scientists, white-haired and pink-eyed all. They were crowding around an object the size and shape of a small desk, obscuring it from Ruck's view. He pushed his way to the front. 'What is the meaning of this?' he demanded. 'Why aren't you...' He trailed off as he saw the focus of their attention.

It was the ant farm, or rather the HumAnt farm, the cause of yesterday's ridiculing from The Board. Ruck stopped dead as he saw the hated object. The colour drained from his face, his eyes blazed, and he momentarily resembled his scientists. 'What,' he thundered, 'is,' he shouted, 'that,' he pointed, 'doing,' he yelled, 'here?' he demanded.

The technicians looked at each other nervously. 'Well,' said one, 'although the HumAnt project was not a complete success–'

'It was a total bloody cock up,' interrupted Ruck. 'Get rid of them.'

Another scientist found her voice. 'Doesn't that raise certain ethical questions? They do contain human DNA.'

The others nodded. This was a subject close to their hearts.

'If I hear that word one more time…' snarled Ruck. 'Do I have to put an Ethics Box in here? Do you want to pay a fine every time you mention the E word? Because that's what'll happen.'

'…Er?'

'Just get rid of them.' Ruck turned to leave the lab.

'But they've been exhibiting some very interesting behaviour,' said the lead scientist, looking around for support. 'They appear to have discovered religion.'

Ruck rotated one hundred and eighty degrees. He was flummoxed, but quickly regained his lack of composure.

'So?' he said. 'You've created a stupider, more gullible ant. Well done. Kill them.'

He was about to turn away again when his scientific curiosity got the better of him. 'What do ants worship anyway? Sugar? The nest? A big leaf?'

Again the head scientist hesitated. Her colleagues nodded and urged her on. 'I think,' she said, 'that is, it appears to be… you.'

Ruck peered at the ant farm in amazement. 'Me?' he asked slowly. 'I'm a god… among ants?'

The scientist indicated the relevant part of the HumAnt colony. 'Tony noticed it last night,' she said. 'Almost fifty ants, about half of them, were making what I can only describe as a graven image.' She pointed through the glass.

The insects were standing in orderly rows in front of a balsa wood platform, upon which a strange figure stood. It was a kind of marionette, a puppet with sticks attached to each of its limbs. Each stick was held by an ant, keeping the figure in an upright

121

position. The limbs were the first clue: there were four instead of the six possessed by the puppeteers. It was clearly a representation of a human being. But further deductions could be made from the figure's colouring. Its lower half was sky blue, with reddish items covering the feet. The top half was lime green, with a tiny strip of orange hanging down the centre, as would a tie. It could only be Ruck.

'They've been like that for half an hour now,' whispered the scientist. 'There seems to be an air of... reverence?'

Ruck was poleaxed. 'I've always said ants were clever,' he murmured.

'Yeeees,' said the scientist noncommittally.

'Maybe it's obvious,' said Ruck in hushed tones, his eyes burning now with religious fervour, 'but why did they choose me as their godhead?'

'We can only assume it's linked to the meeting yesterday. The ants were covered with a cloth, and the colony was in darkness. Then you removed the cover, in effect saying, "Let there be light..."'

'...And there was light,' proclaimed Ruck, nodding to himself and smiling beatifically.

'Exactly,' said the scientist. 'And the first thing they saw was you...'

'Their creator,' said the Professor, 'in all his glory.' Ruck brushed some dust from His tangerine cuffs. 'I am not a vengeful god,' he decided. 'Lo! The ants shall be spared.' Ruck's lifePod sounded. 'Excuse me a moment,' he said, walking serenely to the other side of the lab.

As the Professor moved out of earshot, a researcher gesticulated at the glass case. 'They're doing something,' he hissed excitedly. Inside the colony the Ruck figure was moving. The puppeteers were making it stride around quickly, and, it seemed, angrily.

'Er...' said a scientist.

There was something new now in the attitude of the audience. They were vibrating slightly, emitting tiny, tiny noises. The Ruck mannequin was still pacing, and there was no doubt about it now, it was angry. The puppeteers must have been very skilful because there was a subtlety to the emotion being expressed. It was an impotent rage, directed in on itself.

'I suppose it could still be a religious service,' said another scientist doubtfully.

'Looks more fun than any church I've ever seen,' replied the first.

The Ruck puppet thrashed about, limbs flailing, repeatedly punching and kicking itself. Some of the audience rolled on the floor, slapping one leg against another.

'They're... laughing at him,' said the chief scientist slowly.

'It's not a church, it's a cabaret,' said someone. More ants appeared on either side of Ruck's effigy. They moved forward in rhythm, kicking their legs out.

'A chorus line.'

'Always finish on a song.'

'What's happening?' asked Ruck, returning to the group. The scientists quickly crowded in, blocking his view of the ants.

'Nothing.'

'The service is finished.'

'Oh,' said Ruck, disappointed. 'No burnt offerings or tributes? No sacrifices?' he asked hopefully.

'Not that we could see,' said the leader.

'Although you did move in a rather mysterious way,' added someone daringly.

Ruck seemed satisfied. 'Good, good. I have looked upon my creation, and have seen that it is good. I must go forth now. Olivia O'Connel has arrived.' He looked towards the HumAnt farm. 'Peace be with you, my children,' he said, and he turned and ran from the room.

The alarm on Jorj's lifePod sounded at 7:59 on Friday morning, just two hours after he had fallen asleep. It started with a traditional beep, quickly progressing to some living death metal music, via the sound of pianos falling onto exploding drum kits and Jorj's own voice yelling obscenities. He woke with a start, and turned off the cacophony. I wonder if it's possible to wake with a stop, he thought wistfully.

Rolling out of bed before he could fall asleep again, Jorj tried to remember what he was supposed to be doing. His head felt as if it had been overstuffed with cotton wool, and either his flat was unusually foggy or his eyes were still slumbering. It's not fair, he wailed to himself. I can't be expected to function under these conditions. He curled up on the floor and was about to fall asleep again when he remembered: work.

Two minutes later Jorj was outside hailing a skycar. He was hunched over, tucking his shirt as far into his trousers as possible, under the misapprehension that when he stood up straight the fabric would be stretched taut and would appear to have been ironed. Noticing that the grey dust from the lab was still on his shoes, he tried in vain to brush it off. Bent over as he was, Jorj didn't notice the cops pointing and running in his direction.

Jorj climbed into a skycar just before the O'Connels men reached him. Jorj's stock of Life Itself™ shares did not qualify him for free transport, but today getting to work on time was worth almost any price. The car flew off at the speed of progress, then slowed dramatically (if your idea of drama is watching a car slow down). It certainly had Jorj on the edge of his seat, looking out of the window for the cause of the hold up. There were cars in every direction. The problem was sheer weight of traffic, a phrase that has extra resonance when the vehicles float several hundred metres above the earth.

When he eventually arrived at work, Jorj was late. This was no great surprise. His mother had always told him he'd be late for his own funeral, although Jorj had never managed to work out how that could be a bad thing. He entered the We Care office as a group of pursuing cops rounded a nearby corner. They stopped and checked their instruments, the call centre cloaking Jorj's location as it had Abi's the day before.

The front office had changed little since yesterday. The desk was still partially smashed, and there was an empty space where Ken the robot usually stood. The room was full of the same old people with the same old complaints. Jorj slipped unnoticed into the back room, squeezed past the chattering computers and opened the door to what he laughingly called his office.

It had previously been a broom closet, before brooms had developed wheels, artificial intelligence and a passion for wrestling, and could therefore no longer fit in their cupboards. Since then it had housed Jorj's desk, chair, screen and his increasingly dangerous collection of mouldy coffee cups. But today the cups had gone, and a young man had taken their place. He was blond, handsome and had a complexion as clear as a baby's conscience. Jorj hated him already.

'Good morning, sir, welcome to We Care,' said the stranger as he stood up. 'Your problem is my opportunity.'

Jorj took a step backwards, partly because he had never heard anyone using the proper We Care greeting before, and partly because the blond man had to step out of his cubbyhole in order to stand up.

'What are you doing in my office?' Jorj demanded.

'Your office, sir?' the blond asked calmly. 'I think there must be some mistake. This is my office. I commenced my employment in this location this morning.'

Jorj fought a rising panic. 'No no no, you can't have done. This is my job, I had it first.' Jorj had always preferred the law of the playground to the law of the jungle.

'Ah,' said the blond, realisation finally arriving. 'You must be Jorj Parka.'

'Yeah,' said Jorj bitterly, 'someone's got to be.' His fists clenched and he looked around, evaluating his options. 'Look,' he continued urgently, 'I need this job. I need it.'

The blond man widened his eyes, turned down his mouth sympathetically, touched his wrists together and performed a strange shrug.

Jorj recognised Standard Gesture Number Three from the We Care training manual: I'd like to help you (but my hands are tied). Jorj grimaced. 'Stop that,' he snapped. 'I need to get this sorted out.'

The blond bobbed his head. 'Of course, sir. I'm sure one of our carebots will furnish you with a resolution solution.'

Jorj's shoulders sagged. That was the official line for passing the buck on helpless cases. 'Please,' he begged, 'you've got to help–'

The blond interrupted him calmly. 'Please join the waiting opportunity at the far end sir,' he recited, and he retreated back into his cupboard.

Jorj traipsed back into the front office. He queued with the old people, avoiding eye contact through force of habit. When his turn came, it was over depressingly quickly. He stepped up to a carebot, whose head showed a screen saver of a giant sneaker floating in space. Jorj asked for We Care, and the display changed to show a smiling Therese Boshier, the human face of the corporation. Therese had haunted Jorj at every stage of his career, delivering the company induction, issuing reprimands, serving drinks at the virtual Christmas party. She was pretty in a businesslike way, firm but fair haired, haughty but nice. Jorj hated her and wanted to sleep with her.

'Hello,' she said. 'Please state your name after the smile.' The smile was digitally and surgically enhanced, whiter than whiter than white.

Jorj answered her questions and explained his predicament.

There was a split second pause as the bot accessed the We Care personnel records, then Therese responded with a series of pre-recorded words cut together. 'Your employment has been terminated for the following reason or reasons. Absenteeism. Theft of. Company. Property. Gross negligence. Endangering. The public. Wearing an. Unironed. Shirt.' She wasn't smiling any more. 'If you wish to appeal against this decision, please say "Yes" after the stern look.'

'Yes.'

'Your appeal has been. Unsuccessful,' said the bot. 'Credit is now being deducted from your profile to pay for the missing robot. The shares in Life Itself™ which had been loaned to you by

We Care have already been reclaimed. Please be aware that this change in your status may result in the loss of travel permits, fashion rights, accommodation allowance, food availability and Life Itself™. You may be unable to have a nice day.'

Jorj coldfooted it towards the door, flicking desperately through his lifePod. He had no shares and zero credits; his meagre savings had been wiped out by the cost of replacing Ken. He was a Non, with no funds to buy any shares. No wonder his front door key no longer worked; housing was a privilege of Life Itself™. The only mystery was how long it would be before he was thrown out of the city as well.

Jorj walked outside and was grabbed by three pairs of hands. A large cop pressed a few buttons on Jorj's lifePod. 'It's him,' he growled.

'It's me,' said Jorj, stupid with shock.

The cop gave Jorj a hard stare. He was in his mid-thirties, and had escaped the fast food departments to become a full-time law enforcer.

'Jorj Parka,' he said firmly, 'are you aware that you are within a Shareholder city with no shares in Life Itself™? Silence denotes awareness.'

'Yes, but–'

'But nothing, Non,' snarled the cop. 'Neither do you have sufficient credit to purchase any shares. Your right to Life Itself™ has expired, and you will be ejected forthwith.'

The cop rocked back and forth on his heels, enjoying himself. 'Chuck him in the van, lads.'

Shafts of sunlight penetrated the boarded up windows of the Job Centre. Abi lay on the floor, in the grip of a nightmare. She woke suddenly and sat up, unsure where she was. As she looked around it all came back to her: the car crash, the kidnap and the voice of Robot James. For some time Abi sat very still, hugging her knees.

Her eyes stared sightlessly at an application form for unemployment benefit. She blinked suddenly. Her mother. Her mother would be worried about her. And what if Softcom had tried to find her at home?

Abi threw some water in her face and detangled her hair. She pulled on her O'Connels cap, removed the Robot James badge, and used her Pod to call her mother.

She answered quickly. 'Abi?' she asked.

'Hi,' Abi grinned, delighted to see a friendly face, even if it was on a screen only a few centimetres across.

'Where were you last night?' asked her mother. 'Not another concert?'

'I was working,' said Abi. 'I'm on a big investigation at the moment. I might not be home much.'

'I see,' said her mother suspiciously.

'How are you?' asked Abi, hoping to divert her attention. 'Is everything alright?'

'If you like sitting around the house all day, rotting.' Abi smiled as her mother picked up a familiar theme. 'I hope you realise how lucky you are.'

Abi's mother was a temp; she had never held a permanent position. Several years ago she had made a good living programming for a variety of corporations. But now her skills were no longer in demand, and she existed solely on the pension she had wisely accrued with her agency, People Limited. The majority of her less sensible colleagues were now outside London's walls, starving in the non-Shareholder wilderness. In return for doling out her pension early, People Limited expected her to be available for work for a minimum of twelve hours a day, five days a week. To earn her wage she had to remain in her flat from eight a.m. until eight p.m., supposedly in case a job came in, but really to keep her out of trouble. It was degrading and humiliating, but her only other option was to start selling her shares.

'I've got to go, Mum,' interrupted Abi.

'Okay,' said her mother, her voice softening. 'Don't forget it's your father's anniversary on Monday.'

'When have I ever forgotten?' said Abi indignantly.

'You never have,' said her mum with a smile. 'You're a good girl really.'

Abi smiled back, hiding a twinge from her conscience. 'I'll be back before Dad's day,' she promised. She looked up at the light spilling through the barricaded windows. 'It looks nice out,' she said. 'Why don't you sit by the front door, get some sun. Bloody People Limited can't do you for that.'

'Language,' laughed her mother, pretending to be shocked.

'Bye, Mum,' said Abi, and she disconnected. Once more she examined the discarded Job Centre paraphernalia, and tried to imagine a time when everyone got paid for not working, not just the lucky few like her mother. And instead of being confined to their homes, all the unemployed people would come here to hang out together. It must have been one of the happiest places in the world, she thought.

Returning to the filing cabinet, Abi pulled out a pair of net goggles and some gloves. Heartened by her new alliance with Jorj, she had decided to search for more activists online. People would have to take her seriously now she had actually heard the voice of Robot James. In fact that probably made her quite an important person.

Smiling, Abi slipped on the gloves that would control her movements in the net, then pulled the goggles over her eyes. They projected a 3D environment directly onto Abi's retinas, and she was connected.

She was in a dark blue void, surrounded by dozens of sparkling orbs. This was her home space; each crystal ball was a link to one of her favourite sites. Within each sphere Abi could see a smoky image of the link target. She reached towards the nearest one and saw the hand of her net skin, nearly identical to her gloved hand in the real world. Abi did not believe in false avatars, so her appearance in the net was almost the same as the flesh and blood version. She touched the crystal ball.

The scene changed and Abi found herself in the middle of a crowded party. The site had been redesigned since she had last logged on; the venue had adopted a subterranean feel, all roughly hewn walls and flaming torches. It was supposed to be an underground meeting place, but that description had not been taken so literally on Abi's previous visits. Most of the guests did not share her philosophy on net skins, and she was surrounded by elves, vampires, animals, cartoon characters and celebrities. She shook her head disapprovingly. This was why she rarely went online.

Abi moved through the party, eavesdropping on conversations and occasionally butting in with a mention of Robot James. No one seemed interested. She was about to try another site when two golden letters appeared in the air: "PM". She touched the icon, accessing a new private message.

Her surroundings changed again and she was in an empty blue space once more. A man shimmered into existence in front of her. He was very tall and exceptionally handsome, with perfectly tousled hair and a devilish glint in his eyes.

'Mademoiselle,' he said, bowing slightly. His French accent made Abi's heart flutter. 'Please excuse the recording of this message. I have been listening to what you said to the people at the party. I understand you have important information. I would like very much to meet you in this place.'

He produced a spherical link button and left it floating in the air. 'We must have a way of recognising each other. I have been listening to you but not watvhing you,' he said. 'I lurk in the shadows, not seeing and not seen. I have many enemies.' A few lines of text appeared next to the link. 'Remember this code to prove your identity. Come alone.' The Frenchman smiled dangerously and vanished.

Abi was thrilled. Secret codes, mysterious foreign men, this was how she had always pictured her life. She read over the text a few times, then slammed the link button.

This time she arrived in a bright, airy café, with red and white checked tablecloths and elegant wooden chairs. She took a seat at a table for two and looked around for the Frenchman. The café was busy, and most of the clientele looked human. It was a classy site, no goblins or aliens here.

There was a commotion by one of the doors. Abi's host was entering the café while several people were leaving. He was walking backwards, trying to look like part of the exiting crowd. He dropped out of sight, as if rezipping his shoes. He must have crawled along the floor, as he popped up near the bar several metres away. He was dressed in an impeccably tailored suit and a long raincoat. He took off his red beret, turned it inside out so that the blue lining was showing, then replaced it on his head. He looked around, spotted the most attractive woman in the café and sidled up to her. He whispered in her ear, and she slapped him in the face. He backed away, shrugged massively, and selected his next target.

He approached a woman whose breasts were so enhanced they could have won awards for architecture, and whispered again. Seconds later he was fleeing a man whose chest was as broad as his girlfriend's was inflated. This time his eyes fell on Abi. He slipped into the chair opposite, leaned in and beckoned her closer.

'You have beautiful eyes,' he whispered.

'Everything about you is beautiful,' said Abi, supplying the next part of the code.

'I have just bought a new bed,' whispered the man.

'I think I love you,' said Abi, completing the greeting.

There was a pause. The Frenchman seemed deep in thought, his eyes flitting around the bar. Finally he looked at Abi.

'It is you, yes? Because people say these things to me all of the time.' He permitted himself one last, longing glance at his previous encounter, part woman, part bouncy castle.

Abi nodded, and wished she had upgraded her net skin. 'Abi Odiali,' she breathed.

'Marcel Patric,' said the man, taking her hand. This was the only physical contact they could share online. In reality their respective gloves contracted slightly, parts of them heating up, to simulate the other's presence. Abi tingled, then suddenly realised that Marcel was still speaking.

'That code has caused some misunderstandings,' he said. 'Perhaps I should change it to something nobody would ever say to me. "You have the face of a wanky monkey," nobody has said that to Marcel.'

Abi smiled. In the real world, sensors on her goggles picked up the movement of her face and translated the expression into pixels that were shown on Marcel's goggles, wherever he was. It was all very complicated, but it was a nice smile. 'I'm not surprised,' she said.

She heard what she was saying and hated herself. She sounded stupid, like a lovesick child. The Frenchman squeezed her hand once more and Abi flushed. 'Perhaps we should talk business,' she said, retrieving her hand with difficulty.

'Pah!' said Marcel. 'I say "Pah!" to that.'

'That's why I'm here,' said Abi, reminding herself as much as Marcel.

'But it is not safe,' Marcel said. 'We are in the net, Softcom's kingdom. We must be careful. That is why you did not see me arrive, because I am so full of care.'

Abi decided not to correct him. 'What do you suggest?' she asked stiffly.

'I must see you in real life,' insisted Marcel, his eyes traversing the peaks of Abi's net skin. 'As soon as possible!'

Abi thought for a moment. She'd always known she was a good judge of character, and her instincts were to trust this man. 'Okay,' she agreed, 'where?'

'I have already sent the rendezvous onto your lifePod,' leered Marcel.

'I'll be there,' promised Abi. Marcel smiled and murmured appreciatively, although he was looking at the woman with the enormous chest again. Abi took off her goggles and disappeared.

Brijit was sitting behind her desk in the antechamber that led to Ruck's office. She had once asked the Professor if they could rename it the Auntie Chamber, to 'make it sound a bit more friendly', but Ruck's reaction had proved that friendliness wasn't his desired effect.

Being something of an Old New Age buff, Brijit was working on her horoscope. This was a recent fad. New Age had become old hat decades ago, and had been reinvented as New New Age, substituting aliens for fairies and using computers to predict the future. This too had run its course, and now Original (or Old) New Age was back in vogue. Old New Age was the new New New Age, and Brijit was an old hand. She was designing a thirteenth sign of the zodiac when the room's outer doors were flung open.

Ruck entered, resplendent in a luminous green tie and his maroonest trousers. 'Good morning, Ms O'Connel,' he projected grandly. His eyes darted around the room, finding nothing but cats and Brijit. 'Where is she?' Ruck hissed to his secretary.

'I told her to wait in your office,' said Brijit, as she coloured in Tabbeous, The Cat.

Ruck was flabbergasted. Olivia O'Connel was in his office, unsupervised. He took a deep breath and considered the lack of soundproofing on the connecting doors. 'Very good,' he said calmly, waving a fist at Brijit and scowling, 'well done.' Taking another deep breath, Ruck opened the door and went through. 'Good morning, Ms O'Connel,' he projected grandly.

Olivia was flicking through some images on her lifePod. She stood straight and stiff, looking less lifelike than some of the mannequins in Ruck's collection of idiots. Her platform-heeled boots disappeared under the legs of her thick black trousers, which matched her tight black top. Slender black gloves met the sleeves of her jacket, which extended upwards into a high Mao style collar, entirely covering her neck. Olivia's head was the only part to permit a view of her skin. Her face was small and soft, and her closely cropped black hair revealed the shape of her skull. Any suggestion of vulnerability which her delicate features may have caused was dispelled by a single glance at her eyes. Her pupils were dark and lustrous, like pools of oil on a motorway.

'Excuse me one moment,' she said, still looking at her wrist. 'FYI I am reviewing some of the more unusual local crime scene footage, my usual practice when I travel.'

Ruck leant to one side, hoping to catch a reflection of Olivia's Pod in the glass of a nearby case. Olivia dropped her arm just as Ruck perfected the angle. 'Good morning, Professor,' she said.

'Good morning, Ms O'Connel,' said Ruck for a third time. He extended his hand for the customary shake, and Olivia recoiled in horror. 'Oh, sorry,' said Ruck, hurriedly retracting his hand. How could he have been so stupid? How many times had he read about Olivia's phobia of physical contact? To make the situation even more awkward, she had never publicly acknowledged the condition. She was, well, touchy was the wrong word; she wasn't touchy about anything, that was the problem.

Olivia watched Ruck carefully, ready to flee any further advances. 'You have a non-typical office,' she stated eventually, indicating a case full of tarot cards and lucky heather.

'Thank you,' said Ruck. He almost bowed before her, but caught himself just in time. Olivia's eyes widened slightly, surprised at this response.

'I find it useful to have a reminder of the unrelenting stupidity of mankind,' Ruck ventured.

'Is that really necessary?' said Olivia, looking him up and down. 'Of course, I vocate within the fast food industry. My balance sheets provide sufficient stupidity highlightation.' Ruck tittered nervously, and Olivia frowned. 'I took the precaution,' she continued, 'of enabling my people to realise a change in the filters of your air conditioning.'

'Oh, right,' said Ruck carefully. 'Hmm,' he inhaled, 'the air does smell better in here.' He breathed out like an air connoisseur, and Olivia moved to one side, dodging his exhalation.

'There should be zero smell,' she said firmly. 'Smells are caused by floating particles and other impurities.'

'Yeeees,' said Ruck, suddenly feeling very tired. A night spent sleeping in a chair hadn't been the best preparation for this meeting, although both were awkward and uncomfortable. 'Cup of coffee? Biscuits?' Olivia shook her head slowly and Ruck realised he had made yet another faux pas. This was the Big Dripper he was talking to. The Hydroponic Woman. 'Oh, of course, ah…' he said. He was at another conversational impasse. As with her touch phobia, O'Connel had never admitted to her lack-of-eating disorder. 'Where are my manners?' he said desperately. 'Please, take a seat.'

There followed a strange dance as Ruck moved behind his desk. Olivia backed away, keeping a three metre buffer zone between them at all times. She blew on her chair, shook it, then examined its surface for contamination before finally perching on the edge.

Ruck watched in confusion, wondering how such an obviously crazy woman had become so powerful. Unable to think of anything to say, he let the pause lengthen, waiting for Olivia to steer the conversation away from delicious reviving snacks.

'Please, achieve coffee and biscuits yourself if you require them,' she said.

'Oh no, no,' said Ruck's mouth before consulting his brain or stomach. He cursed inwardly. O'Connel had somehow given the impression that eating and drinking were signs of weakness.

'I'm very glad you're here,' he said, trying to regain his authority. 'I can't think of a better way for me to emphasise the issue of stupidity than for us to meet in person.' Olivia laughed suddenly, covering her mouth with a gloved hand. 'Tell me,' frowned Ruck, 'what's the agenda for this visit? We have quite a lot to pack into one day.'

'The situation has changed,' said Olivia. 'I will now be on site until E-Day, and will be attending the British… leg of the celebrations.' There was a momentary lapse in Olivia's composure as she stumbled over the word "leg", the baseness of the term causing a tiny shudder of disgust. The moment passed and she was as collected as ever, carefully studying the Professor.

Ruck bolted a false grin to his face. 'Until E-Day?' he said. 'But that doesn't reach Britain for three days.'

Olivia nodded.

'Primarily I'm here to ensure the necessities for Evolution Day are ready set go,' she said. 'But I'd also like to realise further understanding re. what you do here. One of my key values is that we can both benefit from greater cooperation and a frank exchange of views.'

Olivia noted Ruck's every reaction, staring unflinchingly at his face, which was no mean achievement. 'O'Connels and Softcom do not interface as frequently as they should,' she said, 'and at this moment in time one side should monitor what the other side is actioning.'

Ruck didn't like the sound of this. He was actioning a great many things, and the last person he wanted monitoring his activities was Olivia O'Connel.

'Of course you realise that this facility is just a small part of the Softcom machine,' he laughed nervously. 'We are a simple research facility, operating with practically no input from Head Office.'

'That is what makes you so interesting,' said Olivia, her eyes locked firmly on Ruck's.

Beads of sweat were trying to flee the Professor's face. He pressed a button on his keyboard. 'Could I achieve a coffee please, Brijit?' he said.

Jorj did not see daylight again for some time. The back of the police van had no windows; nor did it have any seats, cushions or padding. Jorj bounced painfully off the walls as the driver flew the vehicle with all the care, attention and diligence of a teenage fast food restaurant employee.

Jorj finally came to rest. The rear doors of the van opened and two sulky teenagers pulled him out. He found himself at the end of a low, thin, shiny metal corridor, the floor of which tilted sharply away from the van. The cops pushed Jorj onto his backside and he slid away down the tube. Forks and junctions sealed themselves off ahead of him, ensuring that his descent followed the correct route. But soon the slide was blocked by a group of miserable-looking people. 'Sorry!' shouted Jorj as he cannoned into them.

A skeletal, poorly dressed man with long, lank hair bore the brunt of the impact. 'No harm done,' he moaned, bending to rub his shins before pulling Jorj to his feet. 'That was a kindness compared to what Old Fowler's used to,' he complained.

Jorj looked around. The far end of the room was obscured by the crowd of people crushed together by the slope of the floor.

The walls didn't quite meet the ceiling, stopping a few centimetres below head height. Above the dividers Jorj could see identical crowded pens stretching off into the distance. He felt like he was caught in a giant toast rack.

The crowd surged forward. Jorj fell after them, the sharp gradient of the floor giving him no choice. People tumbled out of the room and Jorj would have followed, had a metre-high barrier not suddenly sealed the end of the slide just as he reached it. He slammed painfully into this new wall, squashed by the new prisoners who had arrived after him. Jorj peered over the fence to see what lay in store.

It was a scene of frenzied activity. Beneath bright fluorescent lights, dozens of O'Connels staff were running up and down in front of the holding pens. They released streams of prisoners into motorised carts, bellowing orders as they went. 'I need ten more armed robbers!' yelled a pimpled youth with a half-empty trolley. 'Gimme twenty-six arsonists!' cried another. 'Fifteen assault and battery, hold the battery!'

Jorj turned to the skeletal man beside him. 'Where are we?' he asked.

The man grinned horribly. 'London North Processing Centre. Not the worst place Old Fowler's been, not by a long shot,' he whinged.

'Why are you here?' asked Jorj.

'Same as you,' said the man. 'No shares. Same as all of them.' He nodded his head to indicate the people crushing them against the barrier. 'We've been processed, ain't we? Old Fowler must have been here a dozen times. It ain't so bad,' he griped.

Jorj felt a tiny burst of optimism. 'You've been outside, and you bought shares and got back in?' he asked.

'It's easy,' grumbled the man.

'How did you get the money? Out there?'

'Old Fowler has his methods.'

Jorj, already pinned against the barrier, felt a new pressure on his wrist. He looked down and saw Old Fowler clutching at his forearm. With a flash of his hand, the man deftly produced a knife from beneath a grimy sleeve. 'Hey!' shouted Jorj. He couldn't move. Old Fowler prepared to make an incision just above the lifePod.

'What are you doing?' Jorj gabbled. 'There's no money on it, it's no use to you.'

'Ain't it?' wheezed Old Fowler. As he raised his knife hand his sleeve fell down, revealing a skinny arm studded with row after row of lifePods. 'There's no harm in a little collection,' he groused.

The barrier opened and Jorj fell into the cart below. Old Fowler landed awkwardly beside him and was buried beneath a mound of other prisoners. Jorj dragged himself to the edge of the cart and resolved never to speak to anyone ever again.

The automated trolley sped into a pitch-black tunnel. Jorj could see nothing, although he sensed they were travelling uphill. As the cart moved faster and faster, the wind smacked Jorj in the face and the other prisoners screamed. Suddenly they shot out of the darkness and into the afternoon sunshine. The trolley flew through the air for a second then hit the uneven ground, skidding, rolling and spilling its passengers into the dirt.

The prisoners lay stunned, blinded by the sudden daylight. A horde of emaciated men, women and children descended on them. Jorj's shirt was ripped from his back and he had to wrench his wrist from the eager digits of a sickly woman. His trousers were torn to shreds and a small child ran away with his belt. Jorj scrambled to his feet before he lost his underwear. 'Keep back!' he warned optimistically. The scavenging Nons complied, their malnourished forms no match even for Jorj. The more fortunate new arrivals were also getting up, pushing off their assailants. Old Fowler didn't move. There was an uneasy silence as the two groups sized each other up.

'How are Arsenal doing?' asked a gaunt, ragged Non.

'Is my hair still fashionable?' wailed a woman, wrapping a fragment of Jorj's trousers around her filthy dreadlocks.

'Do you have a message from my husband?'

There was a loud popping noise and a fresh cartload of evictees burst from the ground a few hundred metres away. The hole in the earth closed immediately, preventing the Nons from sneaking inside. The scavengers turned and ran towards their new prey, leaving Jorj's group alone.

Jorj looked aghast at the desolate, barren landscape. The ground was a churned brown mess, dotted with greasy fires. There were occasional fragments of building; twisted, ruined shapes that no longer made sense. There were no birds, no animals, no trees or plants. Anything that could be eaten had long since been wiped out. Nons huddled together, wandered alone or sat digging in the dirt.

Turning round, Jorj saw the city wall towering above him. It was a pinkish field of pure energy, five hundred metres tall. It hung glistening between enormous posts, describing an irregular pattern around the city. The wall shimmered like a heat haze, distorting London itself into a beautiful, hypnotic blur.

Jorj walked towards the wall. He had no plan, but nothing to lose. Perhaps he would find some new trousers. He stumbled on, his eyes downcast. Then he stopped, a hysterical laugh wracking his body, almost becoming a sob. Even the scavengers hadn't wanted his work shoes.

Abi arrived early at the meeting place. Marcel's message had directed her to Camden Town, and she was standing near a junction where five roads met and flying cars circled in endless holding patterns. It was early evening and the streets were full of people hurrying to get home. None of them noticed as a hand reached out from behind a boarded up door, grabbing Abi round the throat. She was pulled inside a derelict building, the board snapping back into place behind her.

It was an old Tube station, disused for decades. London's underground rail network had long been in a state of decline, and underfunding and overuse had finally finished it off. At the turn of the century, the government had tried to drum up some private investment for the Underground. A large cash sum bought sponsorship of a line, and dragged the infrastructure creaking and squealing into the 1970s. The Northern Line became the O'Connels Northern Line. One week into the burger chain's sponsorship, their sales in the London area fell by fifty per cent. They did some hasty market research, concluding that their corporate image would have suffered less had they sponsored the Nazi party. They cancelled the agreement and sued for a refund. The other sponsors soon did the same.

This was one setback too many for the government, which was finding the provision of public services both tiresome and not at all glamorous. They quickly sold the Underground to the highest bidder, who turned out to be an Albanian company specialising in the manufacture of artificial mashed potato. Ticket prices soared, reliability and safety plummeted. The public didn't notice the difference. After a few unprofitable years, Ivan's Mash and Tube Corp sold the Underground on, making a considerable loss. Their successors had no success, stripped some assets and sold it on again, for even less. This process was repeated several times, until eventually the entire network was sold for a Euro to a man called Andy. No one is sure why Andy bought it, although he did enjoy dressing up as an engine driver. By this point all pretence at a rail service had stopped, and the stations had been sold or condemned, as was the case with Camden Town. The government, in partnership with an enterprising American company, promised to get London moving again with a web of high-speed travelators.

Abi found herself in darkness and in trouble. She wrenched the hand from her throat, and struck out blindly. She was rewarded with an "Oomph" noise as her fist made contact. Jumping forwards she knocked her assailant to the ground and they rolled around in the dust.

Still blinded by the darkness, and now with streaming, dusty eyes, Abi somehow got the upper hand. She managed to sit on the man's stomach, but then she felt a rib crack as he struck out and pushed her off. She flew backwards through the air... and still flew backwards through the air. The floor had disappeared.

Abi's shoulder smashed into an escalator step. She tumbled down the unmoving stairs and lay in a heap at the bottom. At the top, the man got to his feet and tried to speak, but only managed to wheeze and puff out some dust. He produced a torch and leapt down the stairs three at a time. Breathing heavily, he stood over Abi's groaning form. He cleared his throat and Abi kicked him in the testicles.

She was halfway up the escalator before he finally managed to speak. 'Abi!' he called up from below. 'Wait!'

Abi recognised the accent. 'Marcel!' she cried, dashing down the steps. She looked at the man, who was shining the torch on himself, checking for damage. 'I didn't recognise you,' she said, trying to hide her disappointment.

Marcel was short, flabby and sweaty. His hair was unkempt and messy, but not in a good way. His eyes were squinty, his nose was crooked and his chin was swarthy. His clothes were dishevelled and several sizes too big for him. He couldn't have looked less like his net skin without changing species. 'It is I who should apologise,' he said, picking his beret from the floor and prudently using it to hide part of his head. 'We must move quickly and in secret, I could give you no warning.'

'Right,' said Abi doubtfully, massaging her bruised shoulder. Marcel watched her ardently. He shifted his weight from one leg to the other and groaned, perhaps looking for a little massage himself. 'Are you alright?' asked Abi.

'It is just my inner thigh, it is nothing,' said Marcel hopefully. Abi failed to offer her healing hands, so with a reproachful glance, the Frenchman hobbled off into one of the tunnels. 'This way,' he instructed. 'Do you know this place?'

Abi did. The abandoned Tube was invaluable for a data mule. Keeping her distance, she followed Marcel's torch, the beam of light illuminating a cylindrical tunnel. The floor was thick with dust and smashed tiles. Holes in the walls gaped at them. Disturbed by their movement, an Underground sign unpeeled and wafted to the ground. Beneath it was another sign, proclaiming an earlier owner of the network. It too was coming loose, and underneath Abi could see a third sticker with yet another logo.

They emerged onto the platform and Abi was surprised to see a train waiting for them. It was a wreck, its coloured plastic faded, its windows cracked, the seats inside ripped or missing. Marcel stepped aboard the ruined shell, and beckoned Abi to follow. As they picked their way along the carriages, squeezing through shattered and twisted interconnecting doors, Marcel broke the silence. 'This is one of the oldest trains down here I have seen,' he said, his whisper sounding deafening in the stillness. 'It must be over fifty years old.'

'Hmm,' said Abi noncommittally. She hadn't joined the revolution for the trainspotting.

They reached the end of the last carriage. Marcel waved the torch to indicate their next move, then leapt forward onto an open metal platform. 'And this is one of the youngest, from just before the tube went bottoms up,' he said as Abi jumped aboard. 'Take the other end,' Marcel instructed, grasping the rod that balanced in the middle of the cart. Together they pumped the lever up and down and seesawed their way down the tracks.

After several hundred metres Marcel signalled a halt and they leapt from the cart. He fumbled in the darkness for a moment, then turned on some lights. The tunnel was wider here, with room for several packing cases, a computer screen and some equipment that Abi could not identify. There was also a large bed. 'Welcome to the headquarters,' said Marcel, proudly straightening the duvet.

Abi was less than impressed. 'You don't look like you do in the net,' she complained, folding her arms.

The stunted revolutionary sighed and sat on the bed. 'That is a disguise,' he said. 'But I believe it has my spirit, no?' Abi shrugged. 'In the net we may always be watched,' Marcel continued. 'But down here, where the lifePod gets no signal, here we are free, free to behave like nature wants.'

He swept his arm luxuriously across the counterpane.

Abi wished she had called Jorj to tell him where she was going. She wanted to check her Pod, to see if she really was cut off from the rest of the world, but didn't dare take her eyes off the Frenchman. 'What am I doing here?' she muttered.

'I have some suggestions,' beamed Marcel.

'How did you find me, in the net?' Abi asked quickly.

'You were asking everyone on the line about Robot James,' answered Marcel. 'I have software to listen for these key words, to help with the recruiting.'

Abi nodded, slightly mollified. 'And you're interested in my information?' she said.

'But of course,' Marcel said. 'Do you have Eye Camera footage?'

'It was wiped,' admitted Abi. 'But I can tell you. It's quite complicated.'

'Give me the highlights,' groaned Marcel.

Abi complied, relaxing a little as Marcel nodded along with her story. It felt good to unburden herself, even if it was only to a rather seedy little man. She concluded with her theory that the robot she had encountered was a duplicate destined for the London E-Day ceremony. She sat on a distant packing case and gazed expectantly at Marcel.

The Frenchman frowned in concentration, mulling over what he'd heard. 'So tell me,' he said finally, 'this Jorj, he is your boyfriend?'

'What difference does that make?' asked Abi, standing up furiously. 'Maybe we're wasting our time.'

'I hope not,' said Marcel, also rising.

'That's a strange question, after everything I told you.'

Marcel shook his head. 'What you have told me about James, it is no surprise. I know about James. I do not know about you.'

Abi smiled. 'You know about James? It's true?'

'Ah, yes,' said Marcel with a dismissive flick of his wrist.

'Which bits?'

'Oh, all of it.'

Abi was delighted by this terrible news.

'But you must tell no one,' urged Marcel, moving closer. 'This is most important. We must save our bullets for when we are sure of a hit.'

Abi didn't hesitate. 'Understood,' she said.

'We have a plan, he is almost ready,' boasted Marcel. 'I think you will be able to help.'

'A plan?' Abi's eyes were wide with excitement. 'Is it for E-Day?'

'Maybe,' teased Marcel.

Abi grinned. This was better than she could have hoped for. 'Tell me everything,' she urged.

'I… can't,' evaded Marcel. 'The…time is wrong.'

'I'll help any way I can,' Abi pledged.

Marcel smiled. 'We will need to work very close together,' he said, waggling his eyebrows.

'But you can't tell me what the plan is?' persisted Abi.

'Not yet. But there is a plan, I am not just making it up,' said Marcel.

'…Right,' said Abi.

'So,' said Marcel, 'Jorj is not your boyfriend?'

'Just leave it,' Abi demanded, moving a few steps away. 'I haven't asked about your boyfriends,' she added mischievously.

Marcel looked horrified. 'I have no boyfriends,' he spat. 'I love the mademoiselles, and they love me. Why would you say such a thing about Marcel?'

'I don't know,' Abi smirked. 'Maybe it's the hat.'

Marcel pulled the beret from his head and threw it on the floor. 'There,' he said, 'no hat, no boyfriends.' He stared defiantly down the tunnel.

Abi shook her head. Why were boys so easy to wind up? 'Tell me about your organisation,' she said gently.

Marcel sank onto the bed and told tales of a group so secret it didn't even have a name. It had cells all over the world, he said, but to maintain security they never met or contacted each other. Abi moved towards the bed, full of questions. Mostly they were answered with a tap on the nose and the word '*Sécurité*.' Abi wanted to know who had set up the organisation. '*Sécurité*,' said Marcel, although he gave the impression that it might have been him. Who was in charge? '*Sécurité*' again, but maybe it was a Frenchman. Abi sat down, as far from Marcel as the bed would allow. Had there been successes in the past? Of course, but Softcom hushed them up. What was the group's ultimate aim? That one was easy. To expose and depose Robot James, and end the tyranny of Softcom.

'You say the nicest things,' blushed Abi.

'But of course,' said Marcel. 'Somewhere I have some wine...'

'I don't think so,' said Abi, pulling away. 'I should get above ground, Jorj is probably trying to call me.'

Marcel muttered something in French.

They trundled the cart to the next station, arranging to meet again the following morning. They fell silent as they reached the platform and climbed some disused service stairs. This station was now a restaurant, and the staircase emerged in a cupboard in the ladies toilets. 'Go, go!' urged Marcel, pushing Abi from the room. 'I have work to do here.'

Olivia held her breath and stared at the rapidly descending numbers above the door. She hated elevators. She hated pressing buttons that had been pressed by a thousand previous fingers, fingers that had scratched a thousand previous behinds and explored two thousand previous nostrils. She hated the enforced proximity with other humans, sharing air with strange mouths, armpits and feet. The possibility of actual bodily contact was higher in an elevator than virtually anywhere else, be it an accidental brush or a tapped "excuse me". Olivia felt the lurching of her own stomach and hated that as well, an inescapable reminder that inside she was just as base and repugnant as her follow passenger. Well, almost.

Ruck turned to Olivia and smiled. 'Almost there,' he said.

Put your teeth away, thought Olivia furiously. She was close enough to notice the sheen of saliva on his gums, and her stomach heaved again. The lift stopped and Olivia closed her eyes to postpone the final terror of elevator travel: the destination. Would she be greeted by a jostling crowd, a noxious odour or a dirty floor? She began to tremble.

The doors opened and Ruck stepped out. When Olivia ventured a glance, she thought she'd been promoted and gone to heaven. The elevator had arrived in a bright, white sterile corridor, beautiful in its flawless, unsullied emptiness. The only blemish on the otherwise perfect scene was waiting outside the lift in maroon trousers. 'Welcome to my laboratories,' said Ruck as Olivia gratefully left the lift and sucked in the untainted air.

'This is ultra impressive, Professor,' she said, her normally rigid posture loosening slightly as her phobias and allergies relaxed their hold. 'This location is almost as clean as my apartment.'

Ruck tapped at his lifePod and obtained directions to their first destination.

Olivia followed, watching Ruck carefully. This was the first time she had ever actioned any police work herself, and she was enjoying it. While using her lifePod to review local crimes in Ruck's office, she had found a gap in the records. Some O'Connels employees had been called to an incident in a We Care office, but there was no witness footage on her company servers. The only images she had found had come from her employees' own Eye Cameras, and they showed two unusual SSI agents. They looked almost identical, a clear sign of genetic modification. Ruck had demonstrated his cavalier attitude towards genetics at the Board meeting, and Olivia had a hunch that the Professor was somehow involved. The little she knew about police work was very clear about the importance of hunches, so she had decided to extend her visit and investigate further.

'I thought we would start with a familiar project,' said Ruck, opening a door. 'There have been some rather interesting developments since last night.'

A tiny flying camera swooped down at them as they entered the lab. Olivia flinched and Ruck swatted it away angrily. 'What is this?' he demanded.

A scientist scurried over to greet them.

'Good evening, Professor, Ms O'Connel,' she squeaked. 'It's a camera. For the HumAnts.'

Olivia looked blankly at her.

'Human Ants,' the scientist explained. 'Hum Ants.'

'The ants?' asked Olivia incredulously. She had expected

Ruck to relocate his failed experiment in a sub-carpet environment.

'They are extremely interested in the world around them,' continued the scientist. 'We have given the HumAnts TVs and roving cameras so they can explore their surroundings.'

(A few metres away, inside the HumAnt farm, the insects were sitting on sofas and beanbags, glued to several TV screens. One set was tuned to a TV station showing a nature documentary. Two others were relaying images of technology sent by the cameras that were flying around the lab. Using a tiny remote control, one insect managed to point a lens at the visitors. Ruck's face filled the screen, and the insects cheered. The documentary was quickly switched off, leaving the HumAnts hypnotised by the reality that was happening just outside their reach.)

'This is fascinating,' said Olivia as they walked towards the farm. 'When did you appraise that the ants were up to speed with the outside world?'

'Well,' said Ruck, his face trying on a modest expression, 'it first manifested itself in the form of religion.' The modest expression was tight and uncomfortable, and Ruck wore it with difficulty.

(The HumAnts looked at each other, waggling their antennae in confusion.)

'Really?' asked Olivia. 'And what do they worship?'

'As a matter of fact it's, ah, me.' The modest expression split, revealing the smug grin underneath.

(The HumAnts hooted and rolled on the floor, wriggling their legs in the air.)

Olivia peered at the insects. 'You certainly seem to provoke a reaction,' she said doubtfully. A camera buzzed over her head, and Olivia was shocked to see her own face on the ants' tiny screens.

Ruck's lifePod received a call. He looked at the screen and swallowed nervously. It was showing the secret number he had dialled the night before. 'Ah, excuse me a moment,' he said, retreating to the other side of the lab. Olivia watched him go, with interest.

(The HumAnts were no less fascinated by Olivia. They recognised her from the Board meeting, and were surprised to find her and Ruck together again. Several insects remembered that O'Connel had smiled at virtually everything Ruck had said. Was romance on the cards? They watched Olivia staring at the Professor while he took his phone call. She couldn't take her eyes off him.)

'Hello,' whispered Ruck. He listened to the caller's voice in his ear. 'Already? Well done. Parka and Odiali? ...Well get the other one out of the way as soon as you can. And don't call me again,' he hissed, hanging up. Ruck turned back to Olivia and smiled weakly.

Olivia raised an eyebrow. 'Who was that?' she asked.

'Just business, ah, personal. Personal business,' evaded Ruck badly. He blushed.

'You know, Professor,' smiled Olivia, 'I'm very impressed with what I've seen so far. I think if we can be honest with each other, we could have a very rewarding relationship.'

(The HumAnts nudged each other excitedly. One of them wolf whistled.)

Ruck tugged at his collar. He needed to distract his guest, show her a nice, innocent little project that would make her forget all about the phone call. 'Shall we move on?' he asked. 'I'll show you where we're building the Hitlers.'

Jorj was dead. Maybe he was still moving about, but his Life Itself™ was over. He trudged across the blasted landscape, sticking close to the city wall and avoiding any other wretches who might otherwise have crossed his path. He saw nothing to lift his spirits. There were no cars, no buildings, not even any litter, no signs of civilisation at all. The closest he had found was a group of conical tents clustered around a smoking fire. They lay behind a fence of sticks and watchful men, and Jorj had kept his distance, staying near to the wall of energy that had so recently protected him.

The sun sank and Jorj was illuminated by the wall's sickly glow. Still he forced one foot in front of the other, not knowing what else to do. Lifting his eyes from the mud, he was amazed to see a break in the wall. There was no doubt. Some way ahead of him, a black strip bisected the glimmering energy field. Jorj forced his exhausted legs to run, and he lurched towards the breach.

It was a fencepost; just one of the many massive towers that supported the wall. Jorj crumpled to the floor. He was about to curl up and pray for death when he noticed an archway in the base of the tower.

The post was fifty metres across, featureless apart from the open arch. Jorj peered cautiously inside, and saw a small room with flaking green paint on the walls and flakes of green paint on the floor. A sign on the wall welcomed him to the IMBY Foundation. The room was split in two, divided by a solid-looking slatted fence, complete with turnstile. The other side of the room was visible through the barrier and was in a much better state of repair. A middle-aged woman was sitting away from the fence, asleep with her head on a desk. Jorj entered the room and cleared his throat noisily.

'Gas mark seven,' blurted the woman in a posh, brittle accent. She sat up and looked around, her hair in disarray. She wore a tangled pearl necklace and a twenty-year-old blouse patterned with brown and beige swirls. Having searched her side of the room, she eventually found Jorj beyond the barrier. 'Hallo there,' she warbled.

'Can I come in?' asked Jorj.

The woman smiled reassuringly at him.

'Oh I do hope so,' she said. 'My name is Carolyn, and I'd like to welcome you to the In My Back Yard Foundation.'

'Okay,' said Jorj. 'Can I come in?'

'Now, now,' admonished Carolyn sternly. 'The In My Back Yard Foundation is an organisation dedicated to Nons in desperate peril. I take it you are in desperate peril?'

'Yes.'

'Jolly good.' Carolyn looked briefly at her screen. 'It says here I should find out exactly what the problem is.' She wrinkled her nose. 'I don't think we need bother with that. We both know it's pretty ghastly out there.'

Jorj frowned thoughtfully. 'Pretty ghastly,' he conceded.

'Good-o. So, now we need to match you with a Shareholder who is willing to put you up in their back yard, garden or spare room. Do you know any Shareholders?'

Jorj nodded.

'That's the spirit. Do you know their names?'

Jorj flicked through the contacts on his lifePod, then, three seconds later, scratched his head. He'd never been one for making friends. All his work colleagues were robots, and most of his spare time had been spent in the net, gaming or discussing science fiction with strangers. He had no idea where any of his virtual acquaintances lived, and he doubted if they would be pleased to see him in real life. Plus they were all called things like LegFace27, Tony's Exploding Dinner or King Basildon. These were probably not their real names. 'Abi Odiali,' Jorj said.

'Is that it?' asked Carolyn. 'Any family?'

'Well,' said Jorj, 'there's a man in a shop. I bought lots of packets of toast there, he might—'

'Just Abi Odiali,' said Carolyn, typing in the name. 'Nineteen, lives with her mother?' Jorj nodded. Carolyn pulled a sad, concerned face. 'Unfortunately she has no spare room and is not eligible for the scheme.'

'But there's loads of empty buildings in London,' protested Jorj.

'Most of those have been rendered unliveable by the real estate people,' smiled Carolyn. 'Anyhoo, you also need a Shareholder to vouch for your good behaviour.' She looked at her screen. 'Now it says here I should move onto stage two.'

'What's that?' asked Jorj, looking round warily.

'I look in our files to see if we have any volunteers who might be willing to take you,' said Carolyn.

'That sounds alright.' Jorj was surprised.

'Yes. Only, there doesn't seem to be much point.'

Jorj felt a familiar sinking feeling. 'Why not?'

'Because we don't have any volunteers,' trilled Carolyn. 'Not one. Never have had. It seems normal people just don't want people like you living in their back yard, garden or spare room. I am sorry.'

Jorj's fists clenched. 'So what exactly is the point of all this?' he demanded.

'The Non situation is very troubling,' said Carolyn piously. 'I couldn't just sit and do nothing.'

'I bet you live in a big house,' Jorj accused.

'Oh. Yes,' said Carolyn with affected modesty. 'Oh. Oh no, no,' she continued, realisation dawning. She looked carefully at

Jorj, who was still clad in just his work shoes and underpants. 'Absolutely not.'

'Help me,' begged Jorj. 'Please.'

'Oh dear,' said Carolyn. 'Look, have some credits.' She aimed her lifePod through the fence and transferred some cash. 'Call your friend and see if she knows anyone who can help. That's the most I can do.'

'No it isn't,' said Jorj, as Carolyn put her head back on the desk. He tried the turnstile, but it was locked. He shook the fence, shouted for a few minutes, then stalked back outside. Checking his lifePod, he saw that Carolyn had given him enough credit for a two minute call. 'Thanks,' he muttered.

He ran a hand through his hair. This wasn't how he'd imagined his phone call to Abi. He'd expected them to at least go for a drink before he stripped down to his underwear. But it seemed he didn't have much choice. He pressed her name.

Abi was walking back to the abandoned Job Centre when the call came through. 'Jorj, hi,' she said.

Jorj angled his wrist carefully so the camera wouldn't reveal his bare chest. 'Hi. So how was your day?' he asked, trying to sound nonchalant.

'Good news,' beamed Abi. 'I've found someone who–'

'Shush,' cried Jorj. 'Sorry, I'm glad you've had a good day, but shush. I'm in trouble.'

'Is it Robot James?' asked Abi, instantly alert.

Jorj thought for a millisecond. 'Yes it is. Robot James has had me ejected.'

'Of course!' said Abi. 'I knew this would happen.'

'Did you?' asked Jorj, worried. 'How?'

'Where are you?' asked Abi, ignoring the question.

157

'I don't know,' said Jorj. 'I'm outside. I was ejected from the London North Processing Centre, that's all I know. I need someone who can vouch for me–'

'No,' said Abi firmly. 'Trust no one, that's rule number one.'

'What about you?'

'Not even me.'

'Look!' yelped Jorj, alarmed by the display on his lifePod counting down the remaining seconds. 'I'm running out of credit.'

'I'll call you back,' said Abi.

'I've got no shares,' said Jorj, 'I can't get incoming calls. Listen, I just need somebody with a big enough house–'

'What have they done to you?' sighed Abi. 'Big houses? You're thinking like them, Jorj, we don't need big houses.'

'Oh god. Listen. I need–'

'I'm coming to get you Jorj,' said Abi firmly. 'Don't worry, we'll show them.'

'…Really?'

'Sit tight. You can depend on me.'

'But you said I couldn't trust–' Jorj ran out of credit. He dropped to the ground, resigning himself to a night under the stars. The thought of Abi rushing to his side was some consolation, but he would have preferred a duvet.

(The HumAnts' cameras roamed Ruck's labs throughout the night. In the HumAnt farm, the insects discussed their favourite new stars, and made banners with their faces on. As the new day arrived, so did Ruck and Olivia, and the little viewers happily settled down to watch TV's hottest couple.)

Although it was Saturday, work was taking place as normal in the Professor's labs. Olivia was continuing her inspection, although, as on the previous day, she was more interested in clues that might link Ruck to the missing We Care footage. They entered another laboratory, the HumAnts' cameras buzzing above their heads.

'This is the Growth Spurter,' Ruck said, indicating a device that looked like a cross between an expensive washing machine and a cheap particle accelerator. 'At full spin it can take the subject from embryo to adult in half an hour. Puberty becomes much more efficient, if a little sticky.'

Olivia grimaced. 'Please, no demonstration. I couldn't...' Another look of revulsion arrived as the English language let her down. '...*face* it,' she finished, lacking a less corporeal word.

'Perhaps you will prefer the Knowledge Inflictor,' said Ruck, moving on. 'We used this to educate the HumAnts.'

(The insects yawned as the technology that had given them life was explained. They were more interested in Olivia's behaviour. She laughed as Ruck extolled the merits of people pre-programmed with his opinions, and the ants excitedly interpreted this as an expression of passion. Perhaps they could have done with a bit longer on the Knowledge Inflictor.)

'This machine pumps a brain full of knowledge, much as one pumps a tyre full of air,' said Ruck. 'At the start there is an empty tube of either flesh or rubber, afterwards there is a ticket inspector, or something more intelligent, like an SSI agent, or a tyre.'

'A Softcom Special Investigations agent?' asked Olivia eagerly. 'Surely their education is much too complicated for a machine like that?'

'Not at all,' puffed Ruck. 'In fact I have already educated two such agents.' He paused, concerned that he'd said too much.

Olivia smiled sweetly at him (and the HumAnts cheered). 'Really, Professor? I'd love to see them.'

Ruck hesitated, but couldn't resist a chance to show off his genius. 'This way,' he said.

Ruck opened a door to reveal what appeared to be a meadow. The sun was shining, there was grass underfoot, but it was all artificial. As they entered the room, two nearly identical men in brown trench coats bounded over to greet them, their tongues flapping wildly. Olivia backed away in horror as they came closer and closer. A globule of spit detached itself from a gaping mouth and arced through the air, missing her by centimetres...

'Stay,' commanded a scientist in the corner of the room. The men stopped just short of Ruck and the quivering Olivia, their trench coats flapping as they bobbed up and down on the spot.

'Thank you,' said Ruck to the scientist. 'Ms O'Connel, I'd like you to meet Spot and Patch, two of my greatest successes.'

'Hello,' barked Spot and Patch. Olivia waved hesitantly. There was no doubt about it. These were the men who had taken the missing footage.

'Spot and Patch are prototype Softcom Special Investigations agents. Of course, they are not approved for active duty yet, and so remain here in the lab at all times.' Ruck shot an urgent look at the watching scientist, a look that he totally failed to conceal from Olivia. 'Their DNA make up is part human, part bloodhound,' he continued. 'In the outside world they will of course exhibit more of their human characteristics. This space will be used for relaxation and doing things doggy style.'

The scientist sniggered, and Ruck looked at him, perplexed.

Olivia was stunned. 'Part bloodhound?' she asked. 'Why would you...?'

'The dog has many attributes that are useful in a detective,' Ruck answered. 'Loyalty, perseverance, obedience, heightened sense of smell...'

'And,' interrupted the scientist, 'they can lick their own testic—'

'Thank you,' said Ruck, fixing him with an evil stare.

'What did he say?' asked Olivia, who had been distracted by the sight of Patch sniffing Spot's behind.

'Nothing,' said Ruck hurriedly. 'Let's just say it can be quite hard persuading them to go to work in the morning. Shall we move on?'

That morning found Abi once more below the streets of Camden, talking to Marcel. 'So we've got to rescue Jorj,' she concluded.

'I do not see why,' said Marcel petulantly. 'I do not like him.'

Abi nodded to herself. She had anticipated this reaction. 'Jorj is vital to the cause,' she said, creatively filling in the gaps in her knowledge. 'He's studied the virus that Robot James sent out. Why would Softcom eject him if they weren't scared of him?'

Marcel was less than convinced. 'There is too much risk,' he said. 'We have much work to do together, alone, on the big job.'

'What is the plan?' asked Abi. 'E-Day hits London in two days, you'd better tell me soon.'

'It is still top secret,' mumbled Marcel, looking away.

'Right,' said Abi dismissively. 'So we've got time to rescue Jorj. Maybe he can help with the plan. Or help us think of one,' she added pointedly. 'Anyway,' she said, trying to hide her embarrassment, 'I've already promised to help him.'

'Abi, Abi,' said Marcel, rubbing her shoulder soothingly. 'Sometimes the revolution is more important than a broken promise. I may make promises to you, and it is possible that I will not keep them. If this happens, you must not be surprised, or angry, or violent.'

Abi had had enough. 'Jorj was ejected from London North Processing Centre,' she said, throwing off Marcel's hand. 'I've looked it up and there's a tourist gate nearby. I'm going out to see what I can find. If you want, you can come with me.'

Marcel showed his teeth. '*Le* weekend break? Why did you not say so before?'

A couple of hours later Abi was waiting below a vast concrete monolith, a post in the city wall much like the one which housed the IMBY Foundation. To the left and right of the tower hung the wall itself, a shimmering blur that stretched into the distance. The land of the Nons was distorted and pixelated, like the face of a victim in true crime footage.

Abi tapped her feet impatiently and wished Marcel would hurry up. The area around the tourist gate was not exactly salubrious. The mile or so closest to London's perimeter had been flattened to eliminate the surplus of cheap housing. Abi checked the bag at her feet. Uncertain what she would be facing on the other side, she had packed ropes, knives and emergency rations.

A skycar landed beside her and Marcel climbed out, struggling beneath the weight of a large hamper. 'What have you got?' asked Abi, helping him.

'Just the necessaries,' said Marcel, rummaging through the box and producing items for inspection. 'A bottle of wine, beach towel, a guide book, another bottle of wine, evening wear, more wine, flip flops, *le ping pong* (*J'aime le ping pong*), wine, wine–'

'We are not going on holiday,' said Abi sharply.

'But of course not,' said Marcel. 'It is our cover story. And it must be real, even to ourselves.' He slammed the lid and his hamper hovered in the air. He turned back to Abi and waggled his bushy eyebrows. 'Let us begin Operation Going On Holiday,' he said, leading the way into the gatehouse.

The archway closed behind them, sealing them in a small yellow room. Abi looked anxiously at Marcel. It felt like a trap. Perhaps Softcom didn't allow Shareholders to enter the Non zone. Perhaps the tourist gate was just bait to snare the curious.

'Abi Odiali!' grated a voice. 'Marcel Patric!'

'Yes,' they answered.

'You are voluntarily leaving Shareholder territory. Re-admission is through this gate only. Once outside, no shares may be traded. Beyond this point, Softcom can no longer guarantee your quality of Life Itself™. Your statutory rights no longer exist. Do you understand?'

'Yes,' they repeated. A wall in front of them split open and Abi took her first steps into the Non zone. She found herself in the middle of a housing estate. The buildings were over a hundred years old, and although they had been patched and repaired in a fairly makeshift fashion, they still looked habitable enough. Trees and grass grew between the houses, alongside more orderly rows of vegetables. Clothing hung on washing lines and smoke rose from chimneys. Chickens flapped about the place and a cow was meandering down the road. The scene was certainly more pleasant than the concrete plain Abi had just left behind.

Marcel loaded a guidebook onto his lifePod. '"Welcome to Non country,"' he read. '"Stay awhile, weary city dweller and discover the simple life, a life without modern cares."' He let his wrist drop and took Abi's hand. 'It is beautiful, no?'

'Yes,' agreed Abi, shaking him off. 'It's not how I imagined it.'

'The Nons have the right ideas,' said Marcel. 'They do not slave for Softcom. They grow food, they have shelter, they have each other, what more do they need?'

'Where are they?' asked Abi. The street ahead was completely deserted. There was no one tending the vegetable patches, no one hanging out washing, no one sitting on the front porches. Abi looked nervously behind her. The entrance to the tourist gate was sealed shut. 'Give me that guidebook,' she whispered. Marcel copied the data and sent it to Abi's Pod. She scrolled through it impatiently. '"Slower pace of life... closer to nature... charming folk ways..."'

'We should investigate,' said Marcel hesitantly. He put his arm round Abi's shoulder, comforting her and forcing her a step or two in front of him.

'You're right,' said Abi, trying to be brave. 'The Nons are our friends,' she announced, leading the way down the street.

They had only taken a few steps when there was a noise from one of the houses. A man clad in a filthy shirt and big boots stumbled onto his veranda. 'Happy days, it's another happy day,' he sang loudly as he fell into a rocking chair. His brow puckered with concentration as he rocked back and forth as quickly as possible. The chair emitted an ear splitting creak.

Doors flew open all down the street. Children fell out as if pushed, men dashed outside to commence leisurely strolls, women took up places beside garden walls and chatted urgently. 'I left my front door open the other day,' 'Well you can leave your front door open,' 'Well I know...'

Abi turned to Marcel. 'Isn't this a bit strange?' she asked.

'Strangely romantic,' leered Marcel.

Abi consulted the guidebook. '"Thanks to generous tourists,"' she read, '"traditional customs have been preserved."'

'Cor blimey!' yelled a voice. A black and white blur dashed from one of the houses and intercepted the visitors. 'Lord love a duck!' he shouted, bowing low. 'Strike a light and bless my boots,' he said.

The man raised his head to reveal a youngish, grimy countenance beneath a black cap studded with white buttons. He grinned cheekily, and Abi saw that underneath all the dirt he was quite handsome. 'Stone the crows if it ain't a pair of new boat races, faces!'

'Wait, I know it,' said Marcel, trying to find the useful phrases section of his guidebook. 'Er, wotcher cock sparrah,' he said with a grin.

'Coo, 'ark at 'im!' said the man. 'He's proper cockney and no mistake. Wotcher guv'nor, my name's Bert, pleased to make yer acquaintance.' He winked at Abi.

'This is Abi,' said Marcel protectively. 'And I am Marcel Patric.' Abi nodded and turned back to the guidebook. '"Ethical tourism keeps alive authentic folk rituals that have evolved slowly over hundreds of years,"' she read.

'Right,' said Bert, 'who's ready for a good old fashioned cockney greeting dance?' He tucked his thumbs behind his braces and bent his knees. 'A-la la la la la, oi!' he sang as he capered from side to side, sticking his neck out like a chicken.

'*Très bon*!' shouted Marcel, clapping his hands.

Bert grabbed a chimney brush and swung around it, leaping and occasionally clicking his heels together. 'Dancing the Lambeth excuse me Mother Brown!' he sang.

'"Discover something real after the false superficiality of city life,"' read Abi.

'My old man said keep 'em peeled for Jack the Ripper, it's a real pea souper and no mistake!' As Bert jigged to and fro he was careful to flash his lifePod at his audience. Marcel dutifully sent some credits to their new friend.

'"And thanks to your investment,"' continued Abi, '"the Nons can support themselves with dignity."'

Bert ran up the wall of a nearby building, completed a clumsy somersault and landed awkwardly. 'Jellied eel, chimney sweep, how's yer father, oi!' he sang, waving his hands and blinking back the tears.

Abi and Marcel gave him a round of applause. 'What next, *mon ami*?' asked Marcel.

'We need to start looking for Jorj,' Abi hissed.

'Not so quick,' said Marcel. 'You just said it, the Nons need our help. Tourists have a duty.' Abi didn't look convinced. 'We have an important job,' Marcel continued. 'We must have compassion, lead by example, help Softcom's victims…'

'You're right,' said Abi decisively. She flicked through the guidebook. 'I guess I would like to learn some of this ancient Non wisdom.'

Bert had strapped a bass drum to his back and was fastening cymbals to his knees. 'Oompah-pah!' he agreed.

Jorj opened his eyes and saw blue sky. 'He's awake!' cried an excited, high pitched voice.

'Happen it's what I said would happen,' said another, gruffer voice in a Yorkshire accent.

Jorj sat up, breathed in and instantly regretted it. An amazingly foul stench filled the air. It was the most eloquently offensive odour Jorj had ever encountered. It spoke of manure, sulphur, rotting food and flatulence. Its outpourings encompassed incontinence, decomposition, poisonous gases and bad seafood. It sang songs of vomit, sweaty socks, ashtrays and tramps. It was a bad smell. Jorj retched and choked at the same time, clutched at his throat and fell back down, eyes brimming with tears.

'He's funny,' said the high-pitched voice.

'What's that smell?' croaked Jorj.

'That,' boomed the other voice, 'is the smell of a man's fortune. You'll love it soon enough, you mark my words.'

Jorj sat up again, taking care to breathe only through his mouth. He was sitting next to a small cart made from lashed together rubbish. A small boy of seven or eight was patting the vehicle proprietorially. He wore tattered trousers and a waistcoat made from sparkling CDs.

Beside the boy was a large grizzled man in his late forties. He wore a proud, serious expression completely at odds with the rest of his attire. His cape and trousers were made from stitched together carrier bags. His legwarmers had begun their existence as Okay Cola bottles and his chain mail shirt was constructed from flattened baked bean tins. He completed the look with a Colonel's Fried Chicken bucket hat.

'Stan Handforth, how d'you do,' he proclaimed, nodding at Jorj. 'Breathe it in, son,' he advised the boy, taking in big gulps of fetid air. 'That's the smell of success, lad,' he wheezed, turning purple and thumping his chest. 'Beautiful,' he spluttered, bending over and holding his stomach.

'What's going on?' asked Jorj.

'I found you,' said the boy gleefully. 'I found you and you were asleep and we put you on my car and brought you here.'

'Oh,' said Jorj, rather embarrassed. 'Well, I'm a heavy sleeper.'

'I know,' cackled the little boy. 'You fell off twice.'

Jorj took a moment to examine his surroundings. He was still in the flat Non wilderness, the city wall just a distant glimmer on the horizon. A short distance away, amongst the mud and rubble, stood a wigwam fashioned from sheets of black plastic. 'Is that where you live?' Jorj asked, addressing the boy as his father was still too purple to speak.

'Yes,' said the boy.

'Fish heads,' insisted the smell. 'Two-week-old egg sandwich left on top of a radiator.'

'And what's your name?' asked Jorj, holding his nose.

'Shiny,' said Shiny, shaking his glittering waistcoat.

'Pleased to meet you, Shiny. My name's—'

'Your name's Silly Face,' laughed the boy.

'Ha ha,' said Jorj politely. 'It's Jorj, actually.'

'His name's Silly Face,' said Shiny, stamping his foot and appealing to his father. 'I found him, I can call him what I want.'

'Aye,' wheezed Handforth, rubbing his throat, 'that's true enough. Finders keepers, that's the name of the game in this business.'

'What is your business?' asked Jorj politely.

'Finders keepers,' repeated Handforth. 'Were you not listening? If we're going to get along, you're going to have to mark my words, you mark my words.' He stroked his mutton chop whiskers thoughtfully. 'You work for me today, Silly Face,' he decided. 'Do you want to argue with me?' He made a large fist and ground it against his palm.

'Er, no.'

'Good workers eat,' said Handforth. 'Do you want to eat?'

'Chemical factory,' shouted the smell. 'Pub carpet!'

'Perhaps later,' said Jorj weakly.

'Aye,' agreed Handforth. 'First things first. No man ever amounted to anything doing first things second, or second things first for that matter. There's a lesson here for you, son.'

Shiny nodded seriously at his father.

'I did hear tell once of a man who tried to do third things fifth. That were a bad business.'

'I see,' lied Jorj.

'Go and get Silly Face some clothes, son. Can't send him to work in just his pants.'

Shiny giggled and scampered off to the wigwam.

'None of the good stuff mind,' called his father. He stuck his thumbs proudly inside his bean tin jacket. 'Happen you'll have to work long and hard before you get a garment as smart as this,' he bragged.

'Okay,' said Jorj absently. He was already planning his escape. Just as he had thought his predicament couldn't get any worse, someone had mentioned the word "work". I'll run for it as soon as the old man turns his back, he decided.

Shiny returned with some filthy rags, which Jorj put on gratefully.

'Time for work,' announced Handforth. He produced a set of rusty leg irons from underneath his cloak and chained Jorj's ankles together.

'Hey,' protested Jorj, 'what's that?'

'Happen these are the terms and conditions of your employment,' said Handforth with an evil grin. 'A binding contract.' He pulled Jorj to his feet. 'Shiny, show your new friend what to do,' he ordered as he stamped off towards the tent.

Shiny looked at Jorj, twisting his leg shyly. Eventually he plucked up the courage to seize Jorj's hand, and, pulling the cart as well, he dragged Silly Face towards the smell.

'Where are we going?' asked Jorj. The chain connecting his ankles was extremely short and he was having difficulty keeping up with the boy.

'Come along, no time for dawdlers, you mark my words,' instructed Shiny, gruffly.

The odour was getting worse. 'Nappies!' it bellowed. 'Neglected rabbit hutches!'

Presently they found themselves on the edge of a small cliff. Below them was the source of the stench, a vast crater filled with a disgusting mulchy oozy substance.

To Jorj's horror, Shiny slid down the incline and splashed into the gunk. 'What are you doing?' Jorj complained. 'You can't go in there.'

'You're funny,' laughed Shiny.

Jorj considered his options, which didn't take long. Bound as he was, he saw no choice but to stay with the boy until Abi arrived to rescue him. But in the smelly light of day, Jorj wasn't sure how likely that was. He suspected Abi's idea of a rescue attempt might be to raise awareness of his plight by organising a rave.

A few minutes later Jorj was squelching about in the crater, sifting through the slime with his bare hands. 'I still don't understand what we're looking for,' he moaned.

'Anything,' smiled Shiny, up to his elbows in muck. 'Like… this!' he said proudly as he withdrew a plastic bottle top. He cleaned it with a filthy cloth and threw it onto his truck.

'But what do you do with it all?' asked Jorj.

'We swap it,' said Shiny. 'A round bit like that, we'll get an apple or two. More if it had writing on it.'

'But who wants this stuff?' persisted Jorj.

'Everyone,' laughed Shiny. The thought that someone might reject such magical bounty tickled him a great deal. 'Women might wear it in their ears. People make other things out of it. Some bits still work.' He looked at Jorj hopefully. 'I want to know, what's it doing here?'

Jorj looked at him blankly.

'Land fill they called it in the olden days, but why did they use all this great stuff just to fill up the land?'

'How about this?' said Jorj, pulling something from the muck and holding it at arm's length.

'Nah,' dismissed Shiny. 'That's a bone. You see bones everywhere.'

'So is it just you and your father?' asked Jorj some time later.

'And Karen,' corrected Shiny. 'She's my new mum.'

'I see,' said Jorj. 'Er, what happened to your old mum?'

'She died,' said Shiny.

Jorj looked at his filthy hands. 'My mum's dead too,' he said awkwardly. 'And my dad.'

'Lots of people died,' said the boy. 'My dad says it was because of Rob bloody James and snooty bloody Londoners.'

'Oh. Them,' said Jorj, still avoiding eye contact.

Shiny looked at him and burst out laughing. 'Cheer up, Silly Face! Look at us,' he said, gesturing around the reeking pit. 'We're alright now.'

'I guess so,' said Jorj, plunging his hands into the mulch.

Olivia's tour continued for the rest of the day. Most of the time was spent checking up on E-Day preparations, ostensibly the reason for her visit. But eventually Ruck found time to show off more of his pet projects.

They entered yet another white room. Ruck dismissed the scientists who worked there, leaving the two principals alone. The watching HumAnts buzzed with excitement at this development, and some of them made kissing noises.

'Nanotechnology,' Ruck announced.

'Before we start,' interrupted Olivia, 'I'm still interested in those canine SSI agents.'

'...Yes?' said Ruck cautiously.

'What sort of duties do they carry out?'

'As I said, they have never left the labs,' Ruck lied.

'But what sort of investigation would they be best suited to?' persisted Olivia.

'Law enforcement is your department.'

'They're your start-up, Professor. Which niche did you propose to fill?'

'Ah...' Ruck needed a diversion. He pressed some buttons on a nearby keyboard and a large wall shimmered into transparency, revealing the adjacent room. Ruck nodded his head towards the new window.

Olivia released the suspect from her arresting stare and looked into the room beyond the glass. 'Dust!' she gasped, shuffling backwards. The room's floor was entirely coated with a layer of grey dust some thirty centimetres deep. Olivia's phobias went to town, where they met up with her allergies to vandalise her composure. Despite the protective glass, the mere sight of that much dust was making her sick and sneezy. When she realised the dust was moving, rippling and shifting, she let out a shriek and curled into a protective ball. Dust, the very essence of dirt, was on the march. 'Dust!' she wailed.

Ruck wore a smug little smile. 'Not dust,' he observed quietly.

Olivia forced herself to look away from the window, and focused on the slightly less horrifying sight of Professor Ruck. 'Not dust?' she whispered.

'Robots,' reassured Ruck. 'Little robots, only a few nanometres across.'

Olivia breathed steadily for a moment, her previous enquiries forgotten. 'I'm not up to speed on how big that is,' she said, standing again.

'Excellent,' said Ruck, switching to lecture mode. 'Stop me if I'm going too fast. Imagine planet Earth. That's pretty big, isn't it? Big,' he emphasised patronisingly. 'Well something one billionth the size of the earth would be about the size of a marble. And that's pretty small. Small.'

Olivia frowned.

'These robots are a few billionths of a metre across,' continued Ruck. 'That's even smaller. Smal–'

'Yes, okay,' said Olivia. She looked through the glass once more and shook her head in wonder. 'How many of them are there?' she asked.

'Oh, about a ^illion,' said Ruck breezily.

'Excuse me?'

'A ^illion,' said Ruck. 'Whenever we reach a new big number we end it in "illion" and change the letter at the start. Million, billion, trillion, zillion and so on. Nowadays we've got so many massive numbers that we've run out of letters, and have started using symbols. A ^illion.'

'But how much is a ^illion?' asked Olivia.

'Oh, that's easy' said Ruck. 'It's a one with one *illion noughts after it.'

Olivia decided to let it go. 'If they're so small, how do you make them?' she asked.

'They're self replicating,' explained Ruck. 'They reproduce by manipulating the atoms of anything nearby. They can be made from gold, calcium, anything really, although carbon is strongest.'

'It's all very clever,' said Olivia, 'but I'm not sure I see the point.'

Ruck stared blankly at her. As far as he was concerned, being very clever *was* the point. But Olivia needed something more practical, something that might show up on a balance sheet. 'Perhaps a demonstration is in order,' he said. He sat down and pulled a keyboard towards him.

(A HumAnt camera swooped in to look at the screen, despite the insects' efforts to keep it focused on Ruck.)

In the room next door the nanobots stopped rippling and compacted themselves into a solid grey cube. 'Nanobots are the building material of the future,' Ruck said. 'They can lock onto each other and create solid structures. We are entering the age of the self-building home.' The cube of bots quivered and within seconds there was a grey model house in the other room.

'Nanobots are intelligent bricks that don't need anyone to lay them. They will never get laid.'

Olivia sighed.

'And with nanobots, the designs don't need to be set in stone.' The house grew an extra storey, then another wing, then morphed into a castle, a villa and a palace. 'Structures can be changed as circumstances require.'

The roof of the palace folded in on itself and disappeared. A few seconds later an umbrella erected itself over the open building.

'Impressive,' murmured Olivia.

'That's not the half of it,' said Ruck. 'They can also be used for transport. Picture a nanobot train, with three }illion moving parts.' The dust next door formed a locomotive.

'It can spit out track ahead of itself, and swallow it again as it moves on.' The miniature train demonstrated the theory, moving at tremendous speed. 'And there are hundreds of other applications. The bots are small enough to enter the human body and repair it. If you use the right material, they can be made into cloth, food, anything. Nanotechnology...' he paused to emphasise the punch line '...is going to be big.'

'Agreed,' said Olivia, without even a smile. 'But haven't scientists been floating this technology for years? Why hasn't it entered the global marketplace?'

'There are two main problems holding up the research,' Ruck admitted. 'The first is the amount of bots required. Even to put on a small display like that, it takes literally umptillions of them. To control any more would require a computer approaching the complexity of the human brain.'

(The malfunctioning camera did a double take.)

'And the other reason?' asked Olivia.

'Ah, yes, well,' fumbled Ruck. 'The other reason is, you see, that the bots are so small....'

'Yes?'

'That we keep losing them. Shall we move on?'

(To the HumAnts' immense frustration only one camera followed the couple from the room. The other was no longer under their control, and it continued to rove purposefully around the nanobot lab.)

'Abi, sit down, have some wine,' said Marcel. A traditional cockney rickshaw had taken them both to a hotel, and they were waiting in the lobby while Bert secured them a room.

The hotel stood a little straighter than the other buildings they had passed, and if it hadn't seen a lick of paint it had at least felt a few dribbles. The lobby was furnished with a selection of elderly chairs, including one from a dentist's surgery. The floor was almost covered by three differently patterned carpets, while the ceiling was festooned with tatty lampshades and broken chandeliers. These served no purpose, as the only illumination came from the cracked and gaping windows. Bert was standing at the front desk, which had at one point been a low coffee table. Crouching on the other side was a man in a ragged postman's uniform.

Abi sat in the deckchair next to Marcel, but refused the wine. He shrugged, refilled his own glass and picked up some hand-written leaflets. 'Museum of Pie and Mash,' he read, 'Birth Place of Jack the Ripper, Lambeth Walk classes…'

Abi was looking around approvingly. 'It's really real, isn't it?' she enthused. 'None of the plastic rubbish you get in the city.'

'But of course,' agreed Marcel. 'This is how life should be lived, by real people.' He indicated a pamphlet. 'Perhaps we should be Born Again within the sound of Bow Bells, it is a charming custom.'

'If the Nons are living like this,' said Abi, 'why do we need Softcom? It might be dirty and old, but it's simpler, more natural. Real,' she repeated happily.

Bert appeared next to her. 'It's ready, me old chinas,' he said. 'Got you a lovely weaver's loom with a kangaroo, view.' The cockney led them upstairs. After receiving a handsome apple pip, tip, he left Abi and Marcel to inspect their quarters.

The room had been decorated by a madman; someone who had heard the words "style", "class", and "opulence", but had got them confused with "tacky", "naff" and "cheap". But the total lack of budget had not dented the designer's ambition. The mirrored ceiling was a mosaic of tin foil, complete with fat stains and smears of food. The cherubs atop the wardrobe were plastic dolls painted gold. One was missing an arm while another had a badly melted face. The curtains were thick and luxurious, but sadly only covered half the window. But the sleeping arrangements were causing Abi the most concern. 'There's only one bed,' she said angrily.

'Oh,' cried Marcel. 'Oh no. This is bad it cannot be helped let us put up with it.' He flopped down and patted the quilt invitingly.

'No,' snapped Abi. She was annoyed that Marcel had managed to lull her into the holiday spirit. 'We've wasted enough time already.'

The Frenchman looked hurt. 'Wasted? Mademoiselle, time spent with Marcel is never wasted.'

'We're supposed to be looking for Jorj.'

'Oh. Him.'

'Yes, him.' Abi turned her back and looked out of the window. Non homes stretched to the horizon in every direction. Plants and splashes of colour gave the scene a cheerful air that Abi did not share. 'It's huge,' she said, finally admitting the enormity of their task. Her shoulders slumped. Why did everything have to be so difficult? 'What are we going to do?' she sighed.

'Ah,' said Marcel eagerly, 'we could—'

'No,' said Abi.

'Okay, then maybe we could—'

'We're not doing that either.' Abi turned to the ugly man on the bed. Marcel pouted at her, toying with his hair. 'Okay,' she decided, hating herself even more. 'The sooner we find Jorj, the sooner we can… come back here.'

'Give me his number,' said Marcel, springing up. 'I can trace his lifePod.'

'How?' asked Abi, amazed. 'Softcom can't even do that.'

'They can and they do,' said Marcel. 'They know every movement you make. Lucky for Jorj, the revolution knows it also.'

They rushed from the hotel, following an arrow on Marcel's Pod, walking past the homes that Abi had seen from the window. They looked less cheerful close up, and Abi realised that they were all empty. They had strayed from the normal tourist routes. Abi shivered as the sunlight began to fade. 'Are you sure we're going the right way?' she whispered.

Marcel pressed some buttons. 'There, now you have it also,' he said. Abi looked at her wrist and saw a pointer directing them further into the ghost town. They hurried on, until eventually they could walk no further.

A huge canvas wall blocked their path. 'It's a painting,' said Abi. They were facing a perspective illustration of streets and houses. The view she'd seen from the hotel window was a fake. The painted canvas was many metres tall and encircled everything she had seen so far.

'Step away from the wall.' The voice was male, the accent clipped and refined, straight out of a British black and white movie. Bert emerged from a doorway and walked slowly towards them, aiming a gun steadily at Marcel.

'Bert?' asked Abi, not moving. 'What's happened to your voice?'

'I believe we can drop the pretence,' enunciated Bert. 'The chirpy cockney chappie act is only for the genuine tourists. What are you doing here?'

'We are lost,' said Marcel. 'We are looking for the eel jellifying.'

Bert smiled humourlessly. 'Somehow I don't believe you,' he said.

Abi discreetly palmed a knife she had been carrying in her pocket. She looked at Bert, who had stopped a few metres away. He was easily within range. Abi took a step backwards, her shoulders brushing the canvas wall. 'Who are you, Bert?' she asked.

'I could ask you the same question,' came the icy reply.

'Are you working for Softcom?' Abi sneered. 'What's the set up here?'

'You'll have plenty of time in which to discover that particular secret,' said Bert. 'Because you already know too much, and I'm afraid I cannot permit you to leave.'

'No?' asked Abi. The knife flashed in her hand, cutting a slit in the painted backdrop. As Bert swung his gun towards her, Abi tumbled through the hole and disappeared.

Bert smiled coldly, aimed at Marcel once more and cocked an inquisitive eyebrow. Marcel shrugged and put his hands in the air. They began to walk back towards the hotel. 'What about Abi?' asked the Frenchman.

'No matter,' said Bert, jabbing the gun in Marcel's back. 'She'll last less than five minutes out there.'

Jorj trawled through the fetid gunk until the daylight began to fade. A bell rang and Shiny jumped up and down excitedly. 'Home time!' he cried, splashing Jorj with rancid garbage juice. Together they carried the cart from the stinking crater, complete with their haul of bottle tops, bin bags and other fantastic treasures.

Jorj followed the child to a trickling stream. They jumped in fully clothed and frolicked in the cold water, squeezing the dirt from their rags. For a few exhilarating moments Jorj actually enjoyed himself. Shivering, they walked back to the plastic tepee as fast as Jorj's chains would allow. A fire had been prepared and they sat near it, steam rising from their clothes. They were pulling faces at each other when a young woman emerged from the tent. She stared blankly at Jorj, who had a thumb squashed against his nose and a finger pulling down his bottom lip. 'Who's your friend, Shiny?' she asked at last.

'He's called Silly Face,' giggled the boy.

The woman nodded slowly. 'Makes sense,' she said in a dull monotone. While her repartee may have been as sparkling as ditchwater, the same could not be said for her clothes. Her tall, thin body was tightly wrapped in a colourful mosaic of plastic, each piece of which was a logo cut from a carrier bag. Her stomach advertised Best-Co, while her left thigh favoured Pretty Bloom petrol stations. Her shoes were made from modified cola bottles, with dried up magic markers forming the stiletto heels. Styrofoam burger boxes dangled from her ears and her face was painted in a variety of unsuitable colours. Her hair rose from her scalp in tin foil encrusted spikes, a chocolate bar wrapper dangling from each point. The woman paraded herself around the fire, shooting occasional glances at Jorj.

'Say she looks nice,' mouthed Shiny.

'That's a very striking outfit,' said Jorj.

The woman's features came to life for the first time. 'What, this old thing?' she asked in a passable imitation of surprise. 'Why do you love it?'

'Well, it's all so... I've never seen anything like it.'

She fluttered her eyelashes, which were augmented with discarded toothbrush bristles. 'You know how to charm a lady,' she said. 'My name's Karen Handforth, maybe you've heard of me?'

'…Maybe.'

Karen stood uncomfortably close to Jorj. 'I'm a fashion designer,' she breathed.

'Of course you are.'

Mr Handforth came out of the tepee. 'How do, Silly Face,' he said. Jorj moved away from the man's wife, his leg irons clanking. Handforth gave his son a friendly punch on the arm. 'How did he get on?' he asked.

'He was good, Dad,' said Shiny, indicating the cart. 'He found loads of stuff. Can we keep him, please?'

Handforth stroked his mutton chop whiskers thoughtfully. 'I'm a man of business,' he proclaimed. 'A businessman. And by heaven I mean business.' He pointed at Jorj. 'As long as you work hard, you can stay. Everything you find goes to me.'

Karen coughed. Handforth rolled his eyes and smiled at his wife. 'And to you of course, my pearl. What's mine is yours, you know that. And what's yours is stuff I gave you earlier,' he muttered to himself. He turned back to Jorj. 'In return for your labour, I will give you food and bugger all else. Do you understand?'

Jorj nodded ruefully. It said something about the way his life was turning out that this was actually good news. He had given up any hope of rescue, and at least now he wouldn't starve to death.

He and the Handforths sat down to a dinner of dubious stew and tiny potatoes. While they ate, Jorj, lacking any choice in the matter, listened to Handforth's life story. He and Shiny's mother had come from a poor village in the North of England, the man said. They had paid little attention to the Takeover, thinking it was something for city types rather than down to earth folk like them. To begin with they were right: life under Softcom was no different to that under the old regime until the Life Itself™ system went live.

Shares had not been advertised in Handforth's community. Rumours quickly spread, but Handforth did not believe them until he himself was forbidden entry to the nearest city. Apparently he was now something called a "Non". As his village learnt the truth, it descended into violent anarchy. Supplies of essential goods quickly dwindled. Handforth realised that the small community was not going to survive, and reluctantly he decided to travel to London.

The journey was long and arduous. Flying cars operated only within the cities, and trains no longer stopped in the Non zone. Handforth had an old fashioned ground car, but petrol was prohibitively expensive. As the Nons' reserves dried up, never to be replenished, the price rocketed again and again. It was worth its weight in gold, then in diamonds. Soon the cost became so inflated that petrol was worth more than its weight in petrol, the price having risen again during that description. Handforth and Shiny's mother decided to walk.

They arrived to find the hostile plain on which Jorj now stood. When Softcom erected the city walls they also flattened the surrounding area, hoping to keep the Nons away. It hadn't worked. Hundreds of thousands of desperate people were laying siege to the city, trying to stay alive in a desert where all shelter had been pulverised and no food would grow.

'It sounds terrible,' said Jorj, horrified.

Handforth nodded at Shiny. 'This is the child-friendly version,' he said. He and Shiny's mother had not stayed long. Winter was coming to London, and a catastrophe was hot on its heels. The Handforths retreated to a relatively stable Non community they had passed on their way south.

The winter was unusually cold. Even in the Handforths' adopted village, where a spirit of neighbourliness and cooperation spread the impact, casualties were high. Across the country, millions of Nons died.

Two summers later, Shiny was born. His mother died in child-birth. 'We had no help,' said Handforth, 'no medicine. The hospital had one nurse and no electricity.' He shook his head. 'She deserved better.'

Karen began to sort noisily through the rotten fruits of Jorj and Shiny's labour. 'What a load of rubbish,' she said pointedly.

'Then I met Karen,' said Handforth, offering her a determined smile. 'Karen had lived in the village all her life–'

'Stan!' Karen interrupted. 'You're making me sound like a bloody yokel. I'm a city person really, I still kept up with all the trends.'

'So you've always been a designer then?' yawned Jorj. Karen nodded. 'That must have been, er, very useful for the village.'

'I was the only one who ever wore my clothes,' explained Karen. 'They were a bunch of bloody philistines really. I told 'em, if we give up on fashion, we're letting the Shareholders win.'

'I was trading stuff from the old days,' said Handforth. 'People wanted a reminder of better times, even if it were just a carrier bag.'

The Handforths remained in the village for five or six years, trading relics with Nons on their way to or from London. Eventually rumours began to circulate about a new class of Non, living near the city wall. Handforth went to investigate.

The scene on the ruined plain was much changed. The crowds of refugees were smaller, and were clustered around designated city gates. The Nons were still refused entry, but a fortunate few received food and medical aid from charitable Shareholders. Camera crews were always present to record the smiles of the lucky ones. Handforth didn't want charity; nor did he want to join the militant groups making ill-conceived plans to scale the walls or storm the gates. He was much more interested in the tourist enclosures, and the thriving economies that had sprung up around them.

Curious Shareholders were allowed to visit the Non zone, and their hosts had spotted a business opportunity. Instead of showing Non life as it really was, they created pleasant, sanitised resorts that would encourage further lucrative visits. These enclaves were the only areas in which credits flowed from Shareholders to Nons, rather than the other way round. Professional cockneys like Bert were the pinnacle of the Non economy, and when Handforth found the heavily guarded theme park, he also found hundreds of entrepreneurs trying to get a piece of the action. He sold the samples of his wares very quickly, and returned to the village to fetch his family. On the way back he stumbled across the landfill site, and quickly revised his business model.

'So,' Handforth concluded, 'in a few days we'll be going to see the tourist folk, to sell what you've found. What do you think to that, Silly Face?'

But Jorj was asleep. Handforth threw a grimy blanket over him, then led his family into the tepee.

Ruck and Olivia ended their tour back in the Professor's office. Try as she might, Olivia had been unable to force a confession about Spot, Patch and We Care. 'I've enjoyed looking at your experiments,' she said, lulling Ruck into a false sense of security before making one last attempt. 'Your research is extremely robust, I've really got to…' She paused as she tried and failed to think of a less unpleasant, visceral word. '…*hand* it to you.'

She tensed her throat in disgust, but quickly recovered her enthusiasm. 'Surely someone of your intelligence must have some secret projects, something a little more adventurous… something that I could help to implement?'

Ruck laughed nervously. 'No.'

Olivia frowned and changed tack. 'Unfortunate,' she said, 'but your ideas will still make quite an impact.'

Ruck beamed. 'That is like music to my ears,' he said, 'only not such a complete waste of time. What sort of thing did you envisage?'

'Take the HumAnts,' said Olivia. 'I must confess, at the Board meeting I failed to see their exponential potential. But now you've explained their interest in the world around them, and their rather unusual reactions…'

'I've put the fear of me into them,' said Ruck proudly.

'Exactly,' said Olivia. 'Their brains must be tiny.'

'Ah…'

Olivia ignored the interruption. 'They're so suggestible they might even enjoy radio commercials. Think of it,' she breathed, a far away look in her eye. 'Millions of miniaturised consumers. Tell me, how are they earning their sugar? And how did they purchase this?' Olivia waved into the lens of the HumAnts' one remaining camera.

(The insects cheered, stamped their feet and hugged one another. Someone on TV had briefly acknowledged their existence, and it felt *great*.)

'Earning their sugar?' Ruck was perplexed. 'I think you may have missed the point…'

Olivia stared at Ruck thoughtfully. 'And then there's the Knowledge Inflictor,' she said, carefully watching his reaction. 'You've created the means to deliver human beings with limited intelligence and faculties, who will respond transparently to predetermined scenarios.'

Ruck kneaded his forehead. 'With respect, that's not my intention. I want to expand mankind's intelligence, not reduce it. I don't see the point in creating predictable, thoughtless automata.'

Olivia's mouth smiled. 'I'm in the fast food business, Professor,' she said. 'You are talking about my staff and my customers.'

Ruck stared at her, dumbfounded.

'And the tiny robots,' Olivia continued. 'Your ever-changing nanobot house will create jobs for hundreds of thousands of interior designers…'

'No!' shrieked Ruck. 'That's not what I wanted!'

'Oh yes,' whispered Olivia. 'Thanks to you the world is going to become a lot more stupid.'

Ruck squeezed his temples and a horrified look trickled down his face. 'That's not what I meant,' he groaned. 'What about my collection?' he asked, gesturing at the cases that surrounded them. 'Doesn't that demonstrate how bad stupidity is?'

'Oh yes,' said Olivia mischievously. 'The benefactors of mankind.'

'What?' wailed Ruck.

'You need to get on board with current thinking, Professor,' chided Olivia, indicating a case dedicated to skateboarding injuries. 'These are the people that keep the system in motion. Skateboarders provide employment for doctors and nurses. Fad diets generate magazine sales and reality television distracts the public in an extremely cost-efficient business model. The world needs as many stupid Shareholders as it can get.' She regarded Ruck coolly, willing him to reply. She had pushed him as far as she could; surely now he would crack? 'Unless there's anything else you haven't shown me? Something that may put a different spin on things?'

Ruck sat crumpled behind his desk, staring vacantly.

Olivia sighed and shook her head. 'I'll see you tomorrow, Professor,' she said. 'Please think about what I've said.'

She shut the door behind her.

(The HumAnts chattered excitedly. That had been the love-birds' most passionate exchange yet.)

Ruck couldn't move. His life's work was ruined, corrupted at a single stroke. He had begun to regard Olivia as an ally, someone who could champion his viewpoint at Board meetings. How could he have been so wrong? She hated science and knowledge, and all she cared about was money. If he had invented a time machine, Olivia would have used it to sell Archimedes a deeper bath. Ruck groaned. He needed someone to talk to.

Down in the deepest part of the lab, in a small, secure room, a ringtone sounded. The call was answered immediately, and a screen came to life. Ruck stared out miserably. A bubbling noise filled the tiny laboratory, followed by a metallic, insolent voice.

'God, what have I done now?'

'Nothing,' said Ruck quietly. 'You haven't done anything.'

'You asked me to behave and I have,' grumbled the voice.

'I know,' said Ruck, 'and thank you. I'm not calling to tell you off.'

'...makes a change,' said the voice.

Ruck sighed. 'You don't want to make the world more stupid, do you?' he asked.

'Huh, like it could get any stupider.'

Ruck smiled sadly. 'Good,' he said. 'Do you know what Olivia O'Connel just told me? She's going to use my inventions to make more idiots. Isn't that the stupidest thing you've ever heard?'

'I suppose so,' said the voice.

'Isn't it obvious the damage that just one idiot can cause?' Ruck leant towards the camera and his face filled the screen. 'God knows I've tried to show her that.'

'…So what are you going to do?'

'I don't know,' admitted Ruck. 'But there has to be a way to make the world see my point of view. You're clever, maybe you can think of something.' He yawned. 'Look, I'd better go. I need to get some sleep.' He fiddled with his vermillion tie. 'It was, ah, good talking to you,' he finished shyly.

'…Yeah,' mumbled the voice as the screen turned black. There was a thoughtful pause, filled with the sound of churning liquid. A minute or two later the screen came on once more. The Professor's secret phone book appeared, and another call was made.

Abi tumbled through the slit in the canvas and landed on her back. She scrambled to her feet and found herself in a muddy no-man's-land, caught with the cloth at her back and a fence of sharpened sticks in front. The poles slanted out of the mud, their spikes pointing away from Abi at eye and throat height. The barren space between the two barriers was guarded by several large men armed with clubs. Fortunately for Abi their attentions were focused on the huge crowd of people beyond the sticks.

They were nothing like the Nons Abi had just left behind. While they had worn ragged clothes, those before her now wore rags. These Nons were starving, not just thin. They stared blankly, their eyes as dead as the ground beneath their feet. A low moan rolled across the desolate landscape.

Abi had no time to think. She ran towards the fence, weaving from side to side in case Bert was trying to shoot through the cloth. She vaulted the crude barrier, tearing her clothes and scraping her back on the spikes. The crowd of Nons swallowed her hungrily, pawing at her and begging for help. Behind the sticks, the guards decided to let her go.

Abi struggled on through the mob, shaking off outstretched hands at every step. Each Non appealed for assistance or tried to sell something. Wizened apples and malformed loaves were presented for Abi's inspection. Clothes and rags were flapped in her face. Even empty Okay Cola cans and O'Connels burger wrappers were pressed upon her. Abi ignored it all and forced her way through the crowd, pausing only to shout for Marcel.

The further she went, the more closely she resembled those around her. The clutching hands ripped her clothes to shreds and shared their dirt with her skin. Her jaw hung slackly as her mind reeled. Her eyes glazed over, preferring to see nothing rather than the horror around her. The entreaties of the Nons diminished, and she reached the fringes of the crowd almost unnoticed. Abi staggered on into the empty wasteland, then sank to her knees.

For some time she washed her face with tears. She was more alone than ever. She had gained nothing from her alliance with Marcel. He had not followed her through the canvas wall, either because he knew the misery waiting on the other side or because he didn't care what happened to her. Both reasons were equally bad. Abi told herself she would never betray someone like that, in fact she was only outside the city now because she was trying to help a man she hardly knew. But this time even her self-righteousness was of no comfort. She lay on the ground for some time, crushed by the hopelessness of it all.

The mob slowly disbanded as the stars came out. Abi could feel the Nons staring at her and she stood up awkwardly, trying to blend into the crowd. Groups began to form, sitting in circles around fires or sacks of merchandise. Abi meandered between the pitiful huddles, half-heartedly following the arrow on her lifePod that pointed to Jorj. Snatches of conversation floated towards her.

'Our sales figures are down.'

'We need to diversify.'

'What qualities can you bring to our organisation?'

Abi strayed too close to one of the circles and they warned her off with a growl. She was creeping towards an empty patch of ground when her lifePod rang. It was Marcel. 'Where are you?' Abi whispered, trying not to draw attention to herself.

'I am back inside London,' said Marcel.

'Lucky you,' said Abi bitterly. 'How did you get away from Bert?'

'We made an arrangement,' said Marcel.

'What about me? Did you think about—'

'I am thinking about you always,' Marcel gushed. 'But you forget the plan. I could not risk the plan to help one person, no matter how attractive—'

'There's no plan,' Abi hissed, venting her pent-up anger. 'This whole thing is just a way for you to meet women.'

Marcel gasped. 'How could you think these things?' he asked. 'I am sending you details of the plan now,' he continued primly.

Abi's Pod beeped as a document arrived. 'You will see if there is a plan or not. And you must find Jorj and come back immediately, because there is a plan, and it starts very soon.'

Abi was already scrolling through the message. 'Evolution Day,' she breathed, trembling with excitement.

'Revolution Day,' said Marcel portentously. 'Do you see, I have added a letter and changed the meaning.'

'I won't let you down,' said Abi, and the call disconnected. As she read Marcel's document, a smile spread across her face. There really was a plan, a plan to save the world from Robot James. And it was perfect.

Sunday morning found Olivia O'Connel waiting in Brijit's Auntie Chamber. Evolution Day would start in New Zealand in a few hours, and it was due to arrive in Britain the following afternoon. Olivia would have to be quick if she were to find out what Ruck was hiding. She had placed the Professor under O'Connels surveillance, but so far her crewmembers had found nothing.

While she waited for Ruck to arrive, Olivia tried to accrue something of interest from Brijit.

'Does the Professor ever confide in you?' she asked, her hand shielding her eyes from the worst of the secretary's cats.

'Oh yes,' said Brijit cheerfully. 'Such and such is an idiot, someone else is a prat, nothing gets past me.'

'What about his inventions?' pressed Olivia. 'Are there any secret schemes he might have told you about?'

'I don't pay much attention to that sort of thing,' said Brijit. 'Goes in one ear and out the other, I'm afraid.'

Olivia's stomach heaved at the thought of the inside of Brijit's ears. 'Anything about a customer care centre?' she asked. 'Maybe he's designed a gas that stops people complaining. Or he's tried out a computer system that fools people into agreeing with him.'

Brijit was stroking a picture of a kitten. '...Sorry, what?'

Olivia tutted. 'Has he been more stressed recently? Has he got something preying on his, well, I suppose you can just about call it a mind.'

'He's always stressed,' said Brijit. 'I told him, he should come along to my tactile therapy group. We spend an hour a week touching different textures: cauliflower, hessian, spanners; it's very relaxing.'

Olivia twitched at the thought of such flagrant contamination. 'Never mind,' she snapped.

The outer door opened and Professor Ruck trudged into the room. 'Morning,' he sighed, his eyes downcast. He slunk between the two women and entered his office, flopping wearily behind his desk.

Olivia followed him. 'I hope I didn't upset you yesterday,' she said, closing the door behind her.

Ruck grimaced at the sound of her voice. She hadn't upset him yesterday, she had crushed him utterly. What would she suggest today? Advancing stupidity with tuition fees for under tens? Free lobotomies with every O'Burger? He stared into space and grunted at her.

Olivia frowned. Yesterday's scare tactics had made him even less talkative. 'Big day today,' she said with false cheer. 'Lots to get ready for E-Day tomorrow.'

Ruck shrugged.

'I'll let you get on,' she continued. 'I'll be appraising your collection.' She moved out of sight between the cases. She needed yet another approach if she was ever going to discover what had happened at We Care.

She stopped in front of a case labelled "Television – Idiots looking in, morons looking out". A pair of jiggling, bikinied breasts filled the entire screen, followed by a gyrating behind. People pawed at each other, flesh sweated, lips were licked and finally a tube of cola appeared. 'Okay is everything,' breathed a husky female voice. Olivia watched the next commercial with interest. A plain-looking girl was rejected by a parade of muscular men, so she washed her hair with genuine essence of active fruit oil enzyme concentrates, until every man in town wanted her. The next ad showed an animated cleanbot kissing a can of polish. A naked celebrity sang a song about garden sheds. Olivia reluctantly concluded that sex was still the most persuasive tool on the planet.

She was ill-prepared for a charm offensive. Offensive offensives were more her style: she preferred put-downs to pick-ups. She looked at her reflection in the glass case. Her clothes were not remotely alluring and she wasn't wearing any make up. She would have to improvise. She cautiously unzipped her collar, revealing a few centimetres of neck, and sucked on her lips to redden them. Checking that Ruck could not see her, she bent over and frantically waggled her head from side to side, tousling her hair and bringing some colour to her pallid cheeks. She straightened up suddenly, feeling disorientated and stupid. This, she decided, was the ideal state of mind in which to ask Professor Alec Ruck on a date.

Ruck had not moved a muscle, not even the one between his ears. He looked up guiltily as his nemesis approached.

Olivia leant over the desk, her hair dishevelled and her face strangely blotchy. 'Hello, you,' she simpered awkwardly.

'Yes?' said Ruck.

(The watching HumAnts shook with excitement. Soldier ants went off duty. Workers dropped everything. This was it. This was the moment.)

Stuck for a follow up, Olivia tried an eyelash flutter.

'Have you got something in your eye?'

'No.'

'Oh.'

Olivia tried to recall the other sexual advances from the commercials, but they didn't seem appropriate. Anyway, she wasn't sure if she could wiggle her bottom that quickly. 'Professor... Alec,' she said, 'I've really enjoyed the last two days.'

'Right.' Build them up then knock them down, Ruck thought.

Olivia thrust certain key parts of her body in Ruck's direction. 'Meeting you, hearing your ideas, it's been most... stimulating.'

'Yes?' said the Professor cautiously.

'You're not making this easy for me,' said Olivia, irritation creeping into her voice. 'I was wondering if...' At the last moment the language of romance deserted her. 'I wish to propose a mutual dinner at close of business today,' she said stiffly. 'We should appraise each other face to face within a one on one roundtable framework.' Olivia dropped her sexy pose. She'd blown it.

She loves me, thought Ruck dreamily. Olivia O'Connel loves me and everything's alright. It explained everything. She didn't really believe idiots were a good thing. She had been trying to provoke a reaction, that was all. Why would anyone who liked idiots be asking him on a date? 'Fantastic,' he said, springing to his feet.

'What?' said Olivia, surprised.

'Dinner tonight? Sounds perfect.'

'Really?' Olivia tried to disguise the sudden wave of nausea that threatened to engulf her. 'Shall we say eight o'clock? At your house.'

'Fine.' Ruck rubbed his hands together with glee. Even if she was serious about bastardising his inventions, a touch of the old Ruck magic would win her round.

'We should get on, my, ah, treasure,' he said, newly energised. 'E-Day will be here tomorrow, and you still have a lot to see.' They left the office, if not arm in arm, at least closer than Olivia's phobias would normally allow.

(The HumAnts were going crazy, hugging each other, waving their banners and stamping their tiny feet. Their entire lives had been building up to this moment. Tonight's telly was going to be amazing.)

Abi had walked through the night, stopping now and then to catch some sleep. The arrow on her lifePod showed Jorj's direction, but gave no indication of the distance that separated them. However, the Pod was ticking down the remaining minutes, hours and days until E-Day hit Britain, and as the figures decreased, Abi's resentment of Jorj grew. Rescuing him was wasting a lot of time, and Abi was acutely aware that Jorj had yet to prove his worth in any way.

As the sun rose she entered the landfill site's airspace, although air was hardly an adequate description of the noxious gases that Abi was forcing into her lungs. She continued to fume about Jorj and, smell being the sense most closely linked to memory, the stench created all sorts of unfortunate connections in her brain. If she did find him, she'd be lucky if she could look at Jorj without throwing up.

Abi spotted the Handforths' wigwam and dropped to the ground. She surveyed the camp cautiously. There was a sleeping form near the dying embers of a fire, but no other signs of life. Abi crept forward and looked down at the sleeping man. 'Jorj,' she whispered queasily, giving him a shake. There was no response. She called his name again, louder this time.

'Who are you?' asked Shiny, emerging from the tepee.

Abi whirled round. 'Go back to bed,' she ordered.

'I haven't got a bed. I sleep on a rug,' boasted Shiny.

'What's going on, son?' said Handforth from inside the tent.

Abi pulled Jorj to his feet. 'Run!' she shouted.

Jorj woke up and stood up at the same time, which confused him. He took one step forward, tripped on the chain that linked his ankles and fell to the ground. He would have fallen asleep as well, were it not for the erupting hullabaloo.

Abi had run a few steps before realising Jorj wasn't with her. 'Get up you idiot,' she shouted over her shoulder.

'Keep away from my property,' bellowed Handforth, dashing out of the wigwam and planting a foot on Jorj's back.

'Leave him alone, he's mine!' screamed Shiny, glaring at the intruder. He ran over and tugged at the plastic sleeve of his father's nightgown. 'Don't hurt him, Dad,' he pleaded. 'He didn't mean it.'

'Coffee?' asked Jorj hopefully.

'What do you mean, "your property"?' asked Abi, returning to Jorj's side. 'No person can own another person,' she lectured. 'What gives you the right—'

'Finders keepers,' interrupted Handforth.

'Losers weepers,' added Jorj, mournfully.

'Don't agree with him, Jorj,' Abi snapped.

Shiny put his hands on his hips. 'His name is Silly Face,' he shouted.

Abi smiled in spite of herself. 'Silly Face?'

'Yes,' said the boy firmly.

'That's a good name,' Abi conceded. The tension abated slightly.

'You wouldn't want him anyway,' said Handforth. 'He's next to useless this one. And he makes useless look good.'

'I don't care,' said Abi, 'he's coming back with me.'

Handforth squinted at her. 'Back where?' he asked.

'Back to London.'

'You're a Shareholder?' exclaimed Handforth. 'Why didn't you say so?' He removed his foot and pulled his prisoner upright. 'I'm sure we can come to some arrangement. He's a lovely little worker this one, I can offer you a very reasonable price.'

Karen Handforth ran from the tent, repointing the foil in her hair and ostentatiously flouncing a boa of strung together mop heads. 'A Shareholder?' she shrieked. 'Where?'

Abi laughed at the rubbish-encrusted woman. 'Over here,' she waved.

Karen stared in disbelief at Abi's clothes, filthy and ragged from the previous day's ordeals. 'Is that what Londoners are wearing this season?' she squealed.

Abi couldn't believe the woman's cheek. 'You can talk,' she said.

'What do you mean?' wailed Karen, indicating the super-market logos on her carrier bag dress. 'This has all the labels–'

Handforth groaned. 'Help me out,' he muttered to Jorj.

'Abi doesn't really know anything about fashion,' Jorj said.

'I see you've still got those shoes on,' said Abi, giving him an evil stare.

'They're my work shoes,' protested Jorj. 'I was at work when-'

'Do you want to do business or not?' asked Handforth, forcing Jorj to stand straighter. 'He's in excellent condition, only one careful owner.'

He tried to brush his footprint from Jorj's back.

Abi thought for a moment. 'I haven't got time for this,' she decided. 'It's totally against my principles,' she emphasised, 'but how much do you want?'

Handforth grinned. 'How much have you got?'

After some skilful negotiation, Abi somehow managed to double the asking price. She checked her lifePod. It would almost wipe her out. 'Are you worth it Jorj?' she asked suspiciously. 'Are you really going to help us fight Softcom?'

'You bet,' lied Jorj with a grin.

Abi transferred the credits onto Handforth's Pod. 'I didn't know Nons had lifePods,' she said.

'O'Connels give us our Pods,' chipped in Shiny helpfully. 'So we can buy stuff from them.'

'And so they can keep track of you,' said Abi.

Shiny wasn't listening. 'Bye, Silly Face,' he said sadly.

Jorj went to shake the boy's hand, then gave him a hug instead. 'Bye Shiny,' he said. 'You'll get some shares one day, I'm sure of it. I'll see you in London.'

'Tell me,' said Handforth, as he removed Jorj's chains, 'why would a Shareholder fight Softcom?'

'Look around you,' preached Abi. 'We want to make life more equal. Bring everyone to the same level. Don't we, Jorj?'

'Yup,' said Jorj, rubbing his newly freed ankles.

Handforth gazed proudly at the new credits on his wrist. 'There's no hurry, though, is there?' he said.

A short time later Abi was striding back towards the city wall. Jorj was following a few paces behind, holding a carrier bag at arm's length. 'Not too close,' warned Abi. 'You reek.'

Jorj grimaced behind her back. It was hard to be romantic when you stank of rotten garbage. 'Thanks for coming to get me,' he tried.

'Don't mention it,' Abi replied.

'I really do appreciate–'

'I said, don't mention it.' Abi was deeply regretting ever leaving the city. Jorj had been awful in the confrontation with the Handforths, and she was certain that he would soon embarrass her in front of Marcel.

She came out here to rescue you, that's got to be a good sign, thought Jorj, for once focusing on the positives. 'So, how have you been?' he asked awkwardly.

Abi frowned. 'How have I been? We're out here with all this misery and suffering, and you ask me how I've been?'

'It's horrible, isn't it?' agreed Jorj hurriedly. 'Be good to get back to London.'

'That's not what I meant,' said Abi without looking back. 'We're to blame for all this.'

'…Seems a bit harsh,' said Jorj doubtfully. 'I don't remember–'

'Anyway,' interrupted Abi, 'we might not get into London. I'm supposed to go back in through the tourist gate, and Handforth said this place we're going to is only for Nons.'

Jorj spent the rest of the journey worrying quietly to himself. After an hour or so they arrived at the IMBY Foundation, where Jorj had previously tried and failed to get back into the city. Abi transferred a few of her shares onto his lifePod.

'What is that smell?' asked Carolyn. The haughty woman was sitting at her desk behind the slatted fence, safe on the Shareholder's side of the gatehouse. She looked around, her face screwed up in disgust. 'Oh my goodness, it's you,' she said as Jorj and Abi entered the other half of the room. 'And you've found a friend!'

'Let us in,' said Jorj. 'We've got shares.' He held up his lifePod as proof.

'Well done you,' said Carolyn happily. 'I only wish more Nons had your get up and go.'

'Just let us in,' snapped Abi. Listening to Carolyn's upper class accent was like having knitting needles shoved in her ears.

'Ah. I'm afraid I can't do that,' said Carolyn. 'You see the In My Back Yard Foundation is for Nons in desperate peril, and you are not Nons. I expect there's another gate that can help you. Although I'm not certain where,' she admitted. 'Nons aren't allowed to purchase shares privately.'

'Not good enough,' said Abi. 'Open the bag, Jorj.' Jorj held open the carrier bag and the room's air quality plummeted.

'Urgh,' spluttered Carolyn. 'Oh my. What is that?'

Jorj reached into the bag and pulled out a handful of landfill slime. It oozed between his fingers.

'Lovely place you've got here,' he said, enjoying himself. 'Be a shame if it got all… smelly.' He flicked his wrist, splattering gunk against the wall.

'No!' yelped Carolyn.

Abi approached the turnstile and peered through the bars. 'There's loads of room through here, Jorj,' she said. She glared at Carolyn, who cowered behind her desk. 'Shall we chuck our rubbish in your nice clean office?' she asked menacingly. 'We can fill it up for you if you like, plenty more where that came from.'

'Alright,' wailed Carolyn, 'you can come in. Just you two though, don't tell anyone else. And take the bag outside first.'

Abi and Jorj grinned at each other.

'With pleasure,' Jorj said. 'Have you got a bathroom?' he asked once they had passed through the turnstile. 'You might not have noticed, but I could do with a wash.'

Carolyn was squashed up against a wall, as far away from the new arrivals as possible. She pointed wordlessly to the bathroom.

Abi waited outside, staring up at the shimmering energy field. Despite a twinge of guilt, she was glad to be looking at the city wall from the inside. 'That was brilliant,' she smiled when Jorj rejoined her. '"Lovely place you've got here"; we really showed her.'

'Hmm,' said Jorj. He gazed blissfully at the city. Enormous, erratically shaped skyscrapers rose up from the centre, sparkling in the morning sun. The structures were colourful, haphazard and random, like vast alien coral. Tiny dots buzzed between the towers, pollinating them with people. A faint humming was carried on the breeze, the language of London. 'Home sweet home,' Jorj whispered.

'Make the most of it,' said Abi, excitedly grabbing Jorj's arm. 'There's going to be some changes.'

'What do you mean?' asked Jorj, happily allowing himself to be pulled along. Abi leant against him conspiratorially. Grinning, she recited Marcel's plan. Jorj recoiled in horror. 'That's crazy,' he said.

'There's a thin line between madness and genius,' said Abi.

'But Evolution Day starts in a few hours.'

'It doesn't hit London until tomorrow afternoon, there's enough time.'

Jorj felt sick. 'No. This has got to be a joke.'

Abi tapped at her lifePod and a holographic projection rose from the screen. As it spun slowly in the air, Jorj recognised the 3D image of Wembley stadium. 'No joke,' Abi laughed.

Ruck whistled cheerfully as he and Olivia checked up on the final E-Day preparations. The woman at his side, the most powerful woman on the planet, was in love with him, and everything was fantastic. Their disagreement yesterday had been nothing more than a lover's tiff, he could see that now. He'd soon bring her round to his way of thinking. The only downside was that he didn't find her remotely attractive. Still, he thought as he summoned up a winning smile, I can turn on the charm until she's outlived her usefulness. 'Enjoying yourself, my dear?' he asked, leering grotesquely at her.

Olivia closed her eyes and nodded mutely. She prayed it wouldn't be long before Ruck let her into his confidence. Feigning attraction to the idiotic harlequin at her side was bringing her out in a rash.

They had spent the morning examining the Hitlers required for tomorrow's festivities. The Führers were almost ready, and had thankfully refrained from killing each other for being short and dark haired.

Everyone took a break at one o'clock to watch the start of Evolution Day. The celebrations were kicking off in New Zealand, where it had just turned midnight. A screen in the lab showed Rob James in a floodlit stadium in Wellington, watching a Maori dance and a wallaby race.

'Seems to be going well,' said Olivia.

'It's certainly not a stupid waste of time,' smiled Ruck ingratiatingly.

An hour later, the ruler of the world waved goodbye and climbed aboard the plane that would take him to another twenty-three countries over the next forty-seven hours.

'I don't understand how a plane can go that fast,' said Olivia.

'Let me explain it, pumpkin,' said Ruck nauseatingly. 'It accelerates along the ground on a mag-lev track. Magnetic levitation reduces the friction so it can go faster, and by the time it takes off…'

'Let's just call it a rocket plane, shall we?' interrupted Olivia.

James's rocket plane took off, heading east towards the small island of Vanuatu, which was in another time zone. The journey would take fifty minutes, but James's watch would go back an hour, so the plane would effectively land before it had taken off. James would stay there for sixty minutes, watching whatever it was they did in Vanuatu, before moving onto Australia. There he would cross into a third time zone, so again his journey would take no time at all. Thus he would travel the world, following the celebrations and eventually squeezing forty-eight hours into one calendar day.

'It's quite complicated, isn't it?' said Ruck, scratching his head.

'He'll be here in twenty-five hours, that's all you need to worry about,' said Olivia. The albino scientists scurried back to work.

The rest of the day was spent persuading the Hitlers to board the truck that would take them to Wembley. In the end Ruck had to intervene himself. 'Look, historically that lorry has always been part of the laboratories,' he insisted. 'Just annex, it will you? Please? Will you please just follow orders?'

(While Ruck was having difficulty with the Führers, the HumAnts were struggling with their one remaining camera. It had abandoned the happy couple, and was focused on some dust that had accumulated in the lower corridors. Waving their Ruck and Olivia banners in frustration, the insects realised that they were going to miss the big date. They wailed, sobbed and kicked their feet against the floor. Finally conceding defeat, they were forced to rediscover the lost art of conversation. They talked about how much they missed the telly.)

Jorj and Abi were in a flying car, travelling towards Camden. They had just left a clothes shop, where they had replaced their Non ravaged rags. Jorj gazed out of the window, enjoying the spectacular view of the city. 'I don't think this plan is for me,' he said quietly.

'What?' Abi exclaimed. 'Do you know what I just went through to rescue you?'

'It was very nice of you—'

'Forget nice,' she explained. 'I did it because it was the right thing to do. And because we need you for the plan.'

'I'll mess it up,' said Jorj earnestly. 'I'm useless.'

'Marcel says we need you,' replied Abi, as if that proved everything.

'Who is Marcel anyway? I have no idea what's going on.'

Abi tutted. 'It's good versus evil, is that simple enough for you?'

'I think that might be too simple,' said Jorj. He looked at the girl sitting beside him and wondered what he'd ever seen in her. She was youthful, principled, proactive; not his type at all. Physically she was attractive, but mentally she was mental. And she'd caused him nothing but trouble. 'At this stage in my life, becoming a terrorist might not be the best career move,' he said.

Abi hunched her shoulders as she turned her back on him, grinding herself into the seat. She knew it. Jorj was no good. But she couldn't return to Marcel without him.

'I just don't–' started Jorj.

'You've got no choice,' realised Abi triumphantly. 'Those shares I gave you are fakes.'

The car wasn't landing, but Jorj felt a sinking feeling. 'What?'

'I'm a criminal, Jorj,' laughed Abi. 'All my shares are counterfeit. If you run off, I'll grass you up to O'Connels. You'll be ejected again and this time I won't come and save you.'

'Oh.'

'You have to do whatever I say,' taunted Abi.

'...So it would seem.'

'And you can start by not showing me up in front of Marcel.'

They sat in uneasy silence until the flying car dropped them at the crossroads in Camden. They waited for a moment by the loose board that led to the underground base, looking at a vast screen on the building opposite.

Rob James had landed on the island of Vanuatu, one of the smallest and most underdeveloped countries on his itinerary. It was one o'clock in the morning there, and he was watching a flame-lit ceremony in which several pigs were being slaughtered.

'There's the robot,' said Abi, trying to win Jorj over. 'It's not even very convincing. That smile is false, for a start.'

'That is the fifth time he's been presented with pig guts,' said Jorj. 'I'm surprised he can smile at all.' Abi glared at him. 'It, it can smile,' he said hastily.

Rob James boarded his rocket plane and set off towards Australia. 'That plane isn't going anywhere,' said Abi. 'They'll just switch on another Robot James in Oz. Come on.'

Jorj looked around as they entered the dim and dusty ticket hall. 'This revolution lark isn't very glamorous,' he observed.

'Would you rather be back with the Nons?'

Jorj followed Abi down the steps and along the tracks, heading for a pool of illumination. He noticed that the light wasn't at the end of the tunnel; it was just a brief respite in the middle, with plenty more darkness still to come. For some reason this felt appropriate.

They entered the brighter, wider section of the Tube and an arm wrapped itself around Jorj's throat. Marcel pulled him into the shadows and squashed him against the wall. 'I have him!' shouted the Frenchman. 'Run, Abi! Move your lovely legs!' He began to crush Jorj's windpipe.

Abi span round. 'Marcel, no!' she cried.

'He was following you,' said Marcel.

'Ug grugle,' said Jorj.

'That's Jorj. He's a friend!'

'The revolution has no friends.'

'Guh rhuguh.'

'You and me are friends, Marcel!'

Marcel squeezed even tighter. 'Do not say that, Abi. We are more than friends, we are comrades, two souls united, free spirits forever intertwined…'

'Hegh greheh.'

Abi took a moment to enjoy the sight of Jorj's flapping arms and reddening face. 'Let him go,' she said at last, thumping Marcel's side.

'Pah!' The Frenchman released his hold and Jorj doubled over, coughing and wheezing. Before he could recover, Marcel had expertly cuffed his hands behind his back, gagged him and pushed him to the floor. Marcel looked at Jorj more closely. 'Such terrible shoes.'

'Mmm mmm mmm mmm,' protested Jorj from behind the gag.

'Come on, Jorj, get up,' said Abi, helping him to his feet.

Marcel stood aside and put one foot on a crate, giving Abi a clear view of his stylish boot. 'Can we trust him?' he asked.

Abi positioned Jorj on another box, noticing as she did so that the thick heels on Marcel's boots added to his still inconsiderable height. 'He's one of us,' she said, squatting in front of Jorj and staring commandingly into his eyes. 'You hate Robot James, don't you?' she ordered.

Jorj considered his position for a millisecond. 'Mmm,' he said, nodding frantically.

'You'll help us get rid of him.'

More mmming and slightly less enthusiastic nodding.

Marcel leant in. 'Death would be a cheap price to pay,' he challenged.

This time the 'mmm' was far from committal, and Jorj's head waggled from side to side.

Marcel seemed satisfied. 'Very well, let us take off the gag,' he said.

'Alright,' said Abi reluctantly. She thought it rather suited him.

'Thank you,' Jorj said a few moments later. 'Thank you.'

'So,' asked Marcel, 'you believe Rob James is a robot?'

'Okay,' said Jorj obediently.

'Why?'

Jorj didn't know. 'Well, everyone's heard the rumours haven't they?'

'I want to hear them from you, Monsieur Roast Beef.'

Jorj sighed. 'My name is Jorj. Why is that so difficult for everyone?' He turned to Abi, who was still crouching beside him.

'There's loads,' she said, coming to his aid. 'His speech when he closed the UN. If you translate it into ASCII and then into C++++++, it's full of hidden messages. No one has ever seen him eat or drink–'

Marcel cut her off with a gesture. 'That is enough, Abi. And you, Roast Beef?'

'Erm… I've never seen him go to the toilet?'

Marcel frowned. 'But you have not seen me weeing a number one. Am I then a robot as well?'

'…No?'

'Good. Although if you had seen me with my monsieur in my hands, you would know that I am not like other men, no?' Marcel put his hands on his hips and turned boastfully to Abi. 'You understand? It is because I am so enorm–'

'I get it,' said Abi, rolling her eyes. 'That's not the only reason is it, Jorj? What about when we met?'

'Oh yes,' said Jorj. 'Softcom kidnapped us. And there was another robot that went wrong, I think Rob James reprogrammed it to kill people.'

'And Softcom fired you for no reason and threw you out of the city,' prompted Abi.

'Er, yeah.'

Grudgingly, Marcel removed Jorj's cuffs. 'Welcome to the revolution, Roast Beef,' he said.

One last spark of defiance ignited deep within Jorj. 'Please,' he said, 'stop calling me that.'

Marcel shrugged magnanimously. 'As you wish, Chips and Gravy,' he said. 'Welcome to the revolution, Mushy Peas.'

'Now what about the plan?' asked Abi. 'We can't have long.'

Jorj listened with mounting horror as Marcel outlined the scheme's finer details. His life had taken another turn for the worse; he now found himself in a place where people used terms like "rendezvous", "T minus thirty" and "gun". While Marcel traced routes through the Wembley blueprint, Jorj tried to trace the source of his troubles. This didn't take long as she was right in front of him, grinning like a maniac.

Abi felt an overpowering sense of rightness. Her life, until now awkward, ill-fitting and spiky, was hitting the world head on and clicking smoothly into place. It was perfect. She would save the planet on the anniversary of her father's death. It was poetic. She couldn't fail.

'…and then,' concluded Marcel, 'the number one person tries to escape. It will be difficult, impossible maybe. Crispy Pancake, that will be you.'

'Wait a minute. Why do I…?'

'No,' said Abi quietly. 'I'll do that part.'

'Abi, no,' protested Marcel. 'It is too dangerous. I have an escape plan for us.'

'I'm doing it,' Abi insisted. 'It'll work out for the best.' Her fixed expression deflected all arguments. 'I'll get out,' she said. 'I can wear a disguise, I've got an O'Connels uniform.'

Marcel nodded sadly. 'You are very brave. No matter what happens, I will wait for you. For at least one hour.'

'So I'm the second person?' asked Jorj hopefully. 'I can get out before you've–'

'Yes,' said Abi. 'And you'd better not screw it up.'

Marcel switched on a holographic projector and once more an image of Wembley Stadium filled the air. 'You must learn your routes,' he said to the others, before busying himself in a darkened corner.

Abi already knew the plan's smallest detail like the back of her hand; Jorj knew his hand in the affair like the small of his back. Abi tried to coach and encourage him, but he refused to focus. 'So you found me outside by tracing my lifePod,' he said, examining his forearm.

'*Oui*,' called Marcel, who was occupied with one of his boxes.

'So what's to stop Softcom tracing us all tomorrow?' Jorj asked.

'Concentrate,' ordered Abi.

'No Abi, he is right,' said Marcel, returning to her side. 'It is for that reason that you must take off the snitches on your wrists.'

'You can't just take them off,' said Jorj dismissively. 'They're plugged into your vein. People bleed to death if they don't use the proper Softcom–'

'Aha,' crowed Marcel, 'but I have the proper Softcom machine.'

'I don't believe you,' said Jorj. 'Every one of those machines is strictly–'

'Then how, Kendal Mint Cake, have I just removed my own Pod?' Marcel held up his wrist, which was now clad in a pathetic homemade imitation. The paper screen was peeling off and the back of a cornflakes packet could be seen beneath. 'It may be hard to believe,' said Marcel, 'but this is a fake. A phony. I made it myself,' he continued proudly, 'from cardboard, silver foil, and here, some pasta.'

'Amazing,' said Abi. 'Where did you get the machine?'

Marcel tapped his nose and his fake Pod fell off. He led Jorj over to the device and thrust his hand inside.

It was a plain plastic box, open at one end, the end which now contained Jorj's forearm. The opening closed before he could protest, clamping his arm in place. Inside, a multitude of minute cutters, probes and feelers crept around and underneath his lifePod.

Within seconds they had burrowed beneath his skin, disconnected the lifePod from his bloodstream, and patched the large holes in his veins and flesh. His Pod fell off, and the contraption released him.

Jorj withdrew his arm carefully, looking at the freckles on his left wrist for the first time in years. Gingerly, he touched the fake plaskin that covered the wound. It seemed okay.

Marcel pulled Jorj's Pod from the machine and dropped it on the floor. Abi looked at them happily. Jorj definitely couldn't run away without a Pod. 'And now Abi,' said Marcel, 'it is your turn.'

For once Abi was unsure. She loved her lifePod. 'I don't know,' she said.

Marcel smiled consolingly. 'It is difficult. Everyone wears a Pod, Softcom make sure of that. To see a person without one is like seeing them without clothes. But...' he paused significantly. '...I need to see you without your Pod.'

Abi realised she had no choice. A few seconds later she too was looking at an unfamiliar patch of bare skin. 'What if someone notices?' she asked. 'You just said people look strange without their Pods.'

Marcel smiled proudly and withdrew something from his pocket. 'It is for this reason that I have made you a fake,' he said. He dangled it before Abi's eyes. It somehow managed to look even less convincing than his own.

'It's okay,' said Abi urgently. 'I'll make one. To show my commitment to the movement.' She gazed sincerely into Marcel's eyes.

'You are sure?' asked Marcel uncertainly. 'The paint only rubs off if you touch it.'

Professor Ruck lived in a small house in London's fashionable Wood Green. The building had been a show home for a new estate and Ruck had purchased it complete with fixtures, fittings and furniture, to save time on design and decoration. The walls were a uniform magnolia, dotted with abstract paintings so bland they almost didn't exist. There was a practical, hardwearing carpet throughout, and a sparse selection of cheap, unremarkable furniture. Ruck had made no changes whatsoever, even keeping the sign that read, "If you lived here, you'd be in your lounge by now." The only personal touches were the stacks of paper and discs lying about the place, and the ghastly rainbow inside the wardrobot.

Ruck opened his front door cautiously. While he and Olivia had been touring the labs, Brijit had been despatched here to tidy up. She had apparently done a good job, as the hallway was spotless. 'Welcome,' said Ruck, throwing the door wide and ushering Olivia over the threshold.

Olivia scrutinised the walls and carpet. She sucked in a tiny amount of air. 'This seems adequate,' she admitted.

'Nothing but the very adequate for you, my honey bunch,' said Ruck.

Olivia felt suddenly dirty. 'Where can I freshen up?' she asked.

Ruck pointed her towards the bathroom, glad of the brief respite from her company. Simulating romantic interest was proving more difficult than he had anticipated, and he was running out of terms of endearment. He fingered the object in his pocket and was glad he had a backup plan.

Ruck moved into the kitchen, checking that Brijit had left the necessary items for dinner. Sure enough there was a sealed pack of sterilised glasses on the counter, and some purified water in the fridge, surrounded by two hundred litres of milk.

Ruck's refrigerator was particularly fond of milk. Mankind, as part of its eternal quest to make things simpler and easier, had replaced the hand written shopping list with a fridge that scanned barcodes, checked stock levels and ordered food and drink. Simple, easy and available at a fraction of the cost, the fraction in this case being around fifty thousand over one. Unfortunately Ruck's model had developed an obsession with milk. Ruck never drank the stuff, but that didn't stop the machine demanding it every day. Every morning Ruck's doorstep would be heaving with white cartons, and if he didn't put them in the fridge the machine would double the next day's order. At one point Ruck had tried to fix the problem, and the following morning found his front garden littered with aniseed flavoured gin, a kilo of hazelnuts and a rather confused-looking pheasant. He had quickly reversed the modifications, and had been meaning to swap the fridge for a more lactose intolerant model ever since.

Satisfied with the gleaming kitchen, Ruck inspected the living room. He was appalled but not surprised to see that his two picture screens were showing images of frolicking kittens. Tutting with irritation, Ruck reset them to the factory defaults, a tropical beach and a grinning child in a colourful hat. Another unwelcome change was the large rug depicting a tiger playing with a ball of wool. Cursing his secretary, Ruck took the rug into the kitchen and threw it away, along with the printouts of *Cat Lover* and *Tiddles Fortnightly* that Brijit had fanned across the dining room table.

Meanwhile Olivia was upstairs in Ruck's study, rifling through sheets of paper. Chemical formulas and circuit diagrams were interspersed with doodles of an enormous Ruck bestriding a tiny planet Earth. But there was nothing about Spot, Patch or We Care. She checked the small object in her bag. She would have to find out the hard way.

Ruck was waiting in the hall as she descended the stairs. 'You look, ah, nice,' he said.

'Thank you,' smiled Olivia, enjoying the rare compliment. 'I input the necessary effort and achieved the desired result.' While in the bathroom she had removed her hat, so both ears were on display. She had also created a small gap between sleeve and glove, and was revealing an unprecedented amount of forearm.

'Nice, er, ears,' said Ruck, uncertain if he should kiss her.

As he leant in, Olivia fended him off with a bottle. 'I brought you some wine,' she said, proffering it violently.

'Thank you,' said Ruck, ducking. 'Would you like a glass?'

Olivia frowned. 'I don't.'

'Of course, sorry,' said Ruck. 'Would you like a glass of water?'

'I don't want to spoil my appetite,' said Olivia stiffly.

The pause quickly lengthened into a silence. Ruck caught Olivia's gaze, didn't know what to do with it and quickly threw it back. 'I'm going to have some wine,' he decided, taking the bottle into the kitchen. 'Make yourself at home in the lounge.'

When he returned with the opened bottle, Ruck found Olivia standing in the sitting room, a safe distance from all the furniture. 'Have a seat, my little, ah, roast parsnip,' he said desperately.

Olivia evaluated the three piece suite. It looked clean, but beige could hide a lot of stains. 'I prefer to stand,' she replied. So they stood awkwardly, Ruck guzzling his wine, Olivia conscious of the silence that was building once more. 'That's a successful picture,' she said at last. 'Who's the girl in the hat?'

'I've absolutely no idea,' said Ruck, refilling his glass. 'Well, this is nice,' he said unconvincingly.

Olivia took a deep breath through the filters in her nostrils. 'Isn't it?' she said, facing Ruck once more. 'Maybe I will sit down.'

They managed to chat for about half an hour, taking it in turns to resuscitate the conversation as it limped along and occasionally collapsed. Ruck talked about the long search for Hitler's DNA, culminating in the triumphant discovery of a tiny moustache comb, complete with hairs. The word 'hairs' made Olivia feel unwell, but she hid her discomfort by telling Ruck how clever he was. In return, Ruck tried not to slurp his wine. Olivia then tantalised Ruck with talk of the corridors of power and, more importantly, the offices off the corridors of power where the actual running of the world took place. They watched the screen for a while, and saw Rob James arrive at the Great Wall of China.

They moved through to the dining room, where Ruck pulled back Olivia's chair with a gallant flourish. The wine had gone to his head, and to his arms, judging by their excessive waving. Olivia emitted a shrill scream and backed into the doorway, pointing at the seat of the chair with a shaking hand. Ruck looked down.

It was a cat.

'It's a cat,' Ruck whispered.

'You failed to advise me that you employ a cat,' hissed Olivia, frowning so hard her eyebrows almost brushed her cheeks.

'I don't,' Ruck protested. 'It's... complicated,' he said, inwardly cursing Brijit once more.

'Dis. Pose. Of. It,' commanded Olivia.

Ruck nodded. Maybe this wasn't so bad after all. This was his chance to be a hero. He regarded his enemy. The cat was curled up on the chair, apparently asleep. Very, very slowly Ruck reached down, keeping his hands out of sight behind the cat's head. Olivia tensed, ready to flee. Ruck's hands got closer and closer. He didn't dare breathe lest his exhalations alert his quarry. Then, quick as a flash he grabbed the cat round the middle and let out a yell of triumph. An answering cry of terror issued from Olivia's trembling lips. She looked at Ruck. Something was wrong.

Puzzled, Ruck lifted the cat and dropped it back on the chair. It bounced once, but didn't move a muscle.

'I thought they were supposed to land on their feet?' asked Olivia timorously.

Ruck answered by knocking the cat against the table. There was a hollow sound. 'It's fake,' he explained. 'Made of plastic. My secretary was here earlier, and, well, you've seen her pictures.'

Olivia laughed. And laughed and laughed, like a condemned woman given a last minute reprieve. The ice was not just broken but well and truly melted, and the dinner went swimmingly. Olivia found her glass of water pleasantly tasteless, and Ruck forgot his hunger and enjoyed the wine. Olivia noted his increasing intoxication, and tried to illicit a drunken confession.

'Let's not talk shop,' Ruck slurred. 'Let's have dessert.' Olivia regarded him coolly. 'Come on Olivia, you old devil. Let's really push the boat out. Let's have another glass of water.' He gave Olivia what he thought was a charming smile, and went to the kitchen.

Safely out of sight, Ruck withdrew a small phial of colourless liquid from his pocket. This would put Olivia in a more receptive frame of mind. He added a dose of Prohypnall to his guest's drink and suppressed a drunken snigger. In a few minutes his date would be in a trance, and she'd believe everything he told her. The chairperson of the Board would support his every suggestion.

In the dining room, Olivia was adding some colourless liquid to Ruck's glass of wine. If alcohol didn't make him confess, Prohypnall would certainly do the trick. She hid the empty bottle

under the table as her victim returned. Ruck was still congratu-
lating himself on his own genius as he sat down and gave Olivia
the wrong glass.

'Oh,' said Ruck. 'That's, ah, my glass.'

'They're fresh glasses. You left our main course glasses in here.'

'Yes, but… I had a sip in the kitchen. Couldn't help myself,
delicious water.'

Olivia picked up the glass suspiciously. 'I can't see any marks
on the rim. I'm competent at achieving such tasks.'

'I licked it clean,' said Ruck desperately. 'I licked it clean with
my tongue and my spit. That glass is covered with my spit.'

Olivia wiped her glove determinedly on a napkin, glaring at
Ruck throughout.

'Cheers,' said Ruck happily drinking his unadulterated water,
then finishing his wine for good measure.

Olivia smiled at him, scrubbed at her hand for a few more
minutes and finally took a demure sip of dessert.

Ruck opened his mouth wide and breathed deeply. Yawns were
contagious, the ideal way to initiate the trance.

'Are you feeling sleepy?' asked Olivia, unable to believe her
luck. Could Ruck really be putting himself under?

'Maybe,' he said. 'But you look tired. You're feeling very
tired.'

'Perhaps,' said Olivia, playing along. 'But you are feeling very
sleepy.'

'Alright, I'm feeling very sleepy,' snapped Ruck, irritated. He
adopted a more soothing tone. 'And you are feeling very sleepy.'

'If you insist,' yawned Olivia. 'We're both feeling very sleepy.'

Olivia slumped first, resting her head on the table. Ruck
decided to conduct the brainwashing upstairs, thinking Olivia

would be less suspicious if she woke up in bed. As he lifted her skinny frame into his arms, his head swam. I need an Alco-null, he thought, blaming it on the booze.

Halfway up the stairs he was yawning uncontrollably. At the top Olivia felt almost as heavy as his eyelids. He staggered into his bedroom and dumped his guest unceremoniously on the bed. Right, he thought with tremendous difficulty, time for action. He pitched headlong next to Olivia, snoring before his face hit the pillow.

Abi was running back to the Job Centre, her feet trying to match the pace of the thoughts that were dashing through her brain. She was quivering with anticipation, excited about the coming day but also scared that she might mess everything up. An awesome responsibility was resting on her shoulders, and it was hard to feel worthy. Mainly she was ecstatic because she had a chance to avenge her father's death, but also sad that such a course of action was even necessary. When she reached the hideout she kept running, too wound up to stop.

Jorj and Marcel were trudging through a Tube tunnel, heading north to Marcel's flat. Jorj had asked Abi if he could stay with her, but she had refused, so Marcel had agreed to 'put up with him'.

When they arrived at Marcel's home, Jorj was surprised at how plush it was. The furniture looked comfortable and expensive, and the lounge was packed with the latest gadgets. 'Wow,' said Jorj. 'You've got a lot of nice stuff.'

'Pah,' said Marcel. 'I care not for the decadent capitalist baubles. That is my chair,' he warned. 'Do not sit there. It is the best position for the hi-fi and his octophonic sound.'

Marcel grudgingly provided his guest with some bread and cheese, which Jorj devoured hungrily. Marcel feasted on the innards of various small animals, and together they watched Rob James arrive in China, then Malaysia. Eventually Marcel stood and pointed at the sofa. 'You stay here. Go to sleep. Do not move.' He left the room and locked the door behind him.

The sofa was not an ideal bed. It was too short and narrow, and curved steeply towards the back. But it was luxurious compared to the cold ground, and Jorj was delighted that he could finally play to his strengths. He was asleep within seconds.

The next morning Ruck opened his eyes and tried in vain to remember going to bed. He looked to his right and almost screamed with surprise. Olivia was sleeping soundly beside him. Oh my god, he thought, did we..? It was a long time since he'd had a woman in his bed. He seemed to remember a female sales assistant demonstrating its bounciness, but since then the springs had not been tested. I must have been really drunk, Ruck thought. But sex had never been part of the plan. Olivia was one of the most powerful and influential people on the planet; he wanted to take advantage of her, not sleep with her.

Jorj awoke and tried to stretch. This proved rather difficult as he was wedged firmly in Marcel's sofa, feet jammed at one end, shoulders squeezed at the other. He listened for sounds of movement coming from Marcel's b**room (he wasn't letting himself think about beds). Nothing. Levering himself into an upright position, he turned on the screen. Rob James was boarding his rocket plane, wearing an Egyptian Pharaoh's headdress. Jorj groaned. He was getting closer.

Abi crept into her mother's bedroom. Morning sunlight forced its way through the cheap curtains, and Abi caught a glimpse of herself in a mirror. Her O'Connels uniform was clean and neatly pressed. 'Mum,' she whispered.

'Morning, Abi,' mumbled her mother from the bed. On any other Monday she would have been up by now, signed in with People Limited for twelve hours of no work. But this afternoon Evolution Day would reach Britain, and it was a public holiday. Not that Abi's mother would be celebrating. Instead she would visit the park where, almost ten years previously, she had scattered her husband's ashes. 'It's your father's day today,' she said.

'I know,' said Abi quietly. 'That's why I woke you up. I can't come with you. I've got to work, I'm really sorry.' She sat on the edge of the bed and chewed her lip.

'That's alright,' said her mother, sitting up and hugging her. 'I understand.' She leaned back and smiled at her daughter. 'Look at you in your uniform. Dad would have been proud.'

Dad would have hated this uniform, thought Abi. But if he knew why I was wearing it... 'Yeah,' she said with a smile. 'He really would.'

'I'll be alright on my own,' said her mother. 'You remembered, that's the main thing.'

'Of course I remembered,' said Abi. 'It's Dad's day. Everything I'm doing today is for him.' She looked at her mother seriously. 'Can you remember that for me? Please?'

'Get away!' shrieked Olivia. 'Get away from me!' Ruck rolled over and fell out of bed. Olivia jumped up and backed into a corner. 'Oh my god, oh my god,' she mumbled.

'Good morning,' said Ruck from the floor.

Olivia held her breath and examined herself anxiously. She was still fully clothed, and relatively clean. She tried to recall the previous night, but her mind was a blank. If Ruck had confessed his reasons for using Spot and Patch, she could not remember them. The romantic charade would have to continue. 'Good morning,' she said weakly, '…my…darling.'

Ruck regarded the crazy woman twitching in the corner. She didn't look like she'd been hypnotically convinced of his genius. He decided to maintain the fiction that he found her desirable. 'Are you alright my… chipmunk?' he asked.

'Yes,' snapped Olivia suspiciously. 'Why wouldn't I be?'

'…The screaming?'

'I'm not a morning person,' Olivia said. 'I require a shower. Lots of showers.'

Jorj was still watching the screen in Marcel's lounge. Rob James was in the Colosseum, where the Italians were baking the world's largest pizza pie. The lounge door was unlocked and Marcel poked his head round. 'Ah, the Yorkshire Pudding, he has risen,' he laughed. He walked in, carrying a bag of delicious-smelling pastries

'Good morning Marcel,' managed Jorj.

'I have something for you,' Marcel said, his words distorted by the French in his accent and the Danish in his mouth. Jorj eyed the cakes hungrily. Marcel reached into a pocket and pulled out a lifePod. 'Access all areas,' he said. '*Merci* Softcom Special Investigations.' He laughed again and sprayed Jorj with crumbs.

Jorj rubbed his wrist ruefully, scratching the scars where his own lifePod had been plumbed into his vein. Reluctantly he took the new Pod and put it on, wincing as it bit through his skin. 'Where did you get this from?' he asked, already knowing what the answer would be.

'*Sécurité*, Mini Scotch Egg.' Marcel fished inside another pocket and withdrew a bottle of clear liquid. 'This is for Abi. Be very careful.' He looked at Robot James on the screen. 'It is time to go.'

Wembley Stadium rose uncertainly from the centre of a vast concrete field, supported by scaffolding and huge reinforcing struts. Softcom had originally planned to replace the venue with a larger, more modern version; indeed demolition had already begun by the time the development costs were calculated. The final estimate looked less like a bill and more like a table of inter-stellar distances, so the project was quickly cancelled. The building had been repaired and made good (or at least good enough) in time for E-Day, leaving the structure safe but far from pretty.

Swarming around the stadium was a bewildering array of souvenir sellers, ticket touts and bootleggers, species found wherever a crowd's happiness could be exploited. The public queued like the idiots they were. The excitement of the special occasion was disorientating; this was a day like no other, so perhaps today it made sense to spend ten credits on a poorly photocopied picture of Rob James. Maybe today those weird nut things coated in sticky red sugar would taste nice.

'Buy or sell tickets! Tickets, buy or sell!'

'E-Day posters! The spirit and excitement of this unique occasion, in the form of a poster!'

'Hot dogs! I've got hot dogs! Possibly made from dogs! Hot as in stolen!'

'Get yer cockney knick-knacks! Genuine Non talismans, no messing!'

The public gates hadn't opened yet, but there was a steady stream of O'Connels personnel filing in. Abi loitered a short distance away, examining the security procedures. Satisfied, she took a final look around. One of the stall holders met her eye with a steely gaze. 'Bert?' she said, stepping backwards.

'Good morning,' said the mock cockney in his posh voice. He was standing a few metres away, a table of tatty merchandise laid out before him.

'What are you doing here?' asked Abi. 'How did you get inside the city?'

'I might ask you the same question,' Bert replied. 'Monsieur Patric and I came to an understanding. Now if you'll excuse me, I have a stereotype to conform to.' He returned his attention to his customers. 'You lucky people,' he cried, his accent slipping back to East London. 'I've got barrels of fun, I've got figurines of Mother Brown. Now 'oo's gonna make me an offer?' Dozens of lifePods were waved in his direction.

Abi smiled and checked the cardboard and glitter construction on her own forearm. She hoped it would be enough.

'Samantha!' called a voice. 'Samantha Nice!' A young cop left his colleagues queuing near the entrance, and ran to meet her.

'Hi, Harry,' said Abi, walking towards him.

Ruck was waiting in the lobby of Olivia's hotel. He tried to make sense of the previous evening, concluding that he must have drunk the Prohypnall-spiked water. God alone knew what Olivia had said to get him into bed. He looked in a mirror and admired his vermilion cravat. It wasn't easy being irresistible.

Upstairs, Olivia was coating her entire body with a thin layer of transparent plastic. She would soon find herself in the middle of a crowd of a hundred and twenty thousand people, and her phobias were demanding extra protection. As she sealed her skin, she too considered last night's dinner. Perhaps her fingers had absorbed some Prohypnall, or maybe she had inhaled the fumes. Just thinking about it caused a shudder, which turned into a full body spasm as she contemplated what Ruck might have done to her. She abandoned the plastic for the time being. She needed another shower.

A car dropped Marcel and Jorj at Wembley. Jorj paid it with a flash of his stolen Softcom lifePod, noticing as he did so that he didn't have enough credit for a return trip. They stood near the stadium's back entrance, away from the crowds of ticket holders. This side of the building was ugly and functional, scarred by the semi-demolition and speedy reconstruction. The scaffolding and bracing poles were surrounded by a three-metre high security fence, topped with robot hands that randomly clutched at the empty air. Jorj eyed it nervously. 'I know,' he said. 'Let's scrap this and have an old fashioned demonstration. I can make the banners. Or a custard pie in the face, everyone loves–'

Marcel grabbed him by the mouth. 'Be quiet. This is more important than your cowardice. It is more important even than my bravery. Do not dick it up.'

'Your bravery?' said Jorj with difficulty. 'What will you be doing?'

'I will be here,' said Marcel, 'in case you dick it up. Now go.'

Jorj walked unhappily towards the back door. Marcel watched him go, smiled and tore the cardboard bracelet from his wrist. He produced his real lifePod from his pocket, put it on and walked off, whistling happily.

Jorj approached a black metal gate, which was guarded by a prehistoric-looking SSI agent. As he sidled up to the door, Jorj decided that the guard was the biggest man he had ever seen.

'Yeah?' rumbled the agent, standing up.

Jorj shivered, only partly because he was engulfed by the man's shadow. 'Softcom Special Investigations,' he quavered.

The man shrugged, somehow managing to move his massive shoulders without mechanical lifting gear.

'Can I come in?' Jorj squeaked.

The guard looked at him strangely. 'Just scan your Pod, mate,' he growled, indicating a box on the wall.

Feeling sick, Jorj waved his lifePod in front of the device. A noise sounded. An affirmative noise, thought Jorj hopefully. If you were going to make a "No" noise, it wouldn't be a "Ping", would it? A "No" is deeper than that, harsher… The gate slid open, and Jorj tottered through on trembling legs. 'Thanks, mate,' he squawked.

Abi was already inside the stadium. Harry, the young cop she had met in the We Care office, had been pleased to see "Samantha Nice", his girlfriend K8 less so. Abi had hidden herself in the centre of their team as they were ushered through the gates. Two cops on the edge of the group were selected for random lifePod scans, but Abi's homemade alternative escaped scrutiny. Once inside, "Samantha" announced that she was on a secret mission, and left the team to take up her position. An awestruck Harry wished her luck, while a jealous K8 wished her dead.

Abi hurried up a dim, dirty tunnel, and emerged blinking into the vast bowl of the stadium. Banks of seats rose up from the pitch, inclining ever more sharply. Abi found herself at the front of the third and steepest tier. All around her, cops and SSI agents were performing a final sweep, looking for bombs and unlicensed merchandise. The top of the stadium was jagged against the sky, like the battlements of a ruined castle. Any non-essential areas had not been reconstructed, and that included the roof and most

225

of the upper levels. In front of Abi was the pitch, empty apart from a raised, circular stage in the centre. A hundred honoured guests would watch the proceedings from there, and it was from this platform that Robot James would address the crowd.

James was currently appearing on four vast screens, one in each corner of the pitch. He watched as people in lederhosen spilt beer on each other, while raucous brass band music played. Germany, thought Abi. Less than two hours to go. She knew the Evolution Day schedule inside out and back to front. She also knew it forwards, which was proving more useful.

Olivia and Ruck were ushered through the VIP entrance, where a smiling flunky gave them both a genetically engineered flower that bore a letter on each petal. "O, L, I, V, I, A, , O, ' , C, O, N, N, E, L" said one. "P, L, U, S, , O, N, E" said the other. Olivia twitched and grimaced as the man pinned the bloom to her lapel.

They were led through a sparkling underground tunnel. It would be impossible to cross the pitch once the celebrations began, so access to the viewing platform was from below. That way Rob James would be able to take his place centre stage without delay or inconvenience. As Ruck and Olivia walked along the subterranean corridor, they passed a shadowy figure lurking in an alcove. 'Psst,' it said.

Olivia stopped. 'That man is trying to win your attention,' she said.

Ruck looked round and was horrified to see a familiar face smiling enigmatically beneath a red beret. 'Ah, you go ahead,' said the Professor, covering his surprise badly. 'I'll catch up.'

Olivia gave a slight nod to the undercover cops loitering a few metres away. 'Okay,' she said, continuing towards the stage.

Ruck approached Marcel, oblivious to the watching O'Con-nels men. 'What are you doing here?' he hissed.

'Just enjoying the large occasion,' said Marcel loudly, tapping the side of his nose. 'The calf is in the crate,' he whispered.

'What?' snapped Ruck.

'The feeding tube has been forced down the goose's neck,' tried the Frenchman. Ruck looked blankly at him. 'The gun is inside the stadium,' sighed Marcel. 'In the roof. The plan is go.'

'Plan? What plan?' asked Ruck, bewildered. 'What gun?'

Marcel looked at him strangely. 'It is your plan, Monsieur. You instructed me.'

'No I didn't.'

Realisation dawned across Marcel's face. 'Oh, I see. No, there is no plan,' he announced, smiling and looking around. 'It will stay under my beret. I shall keep mother,' he confided in a more hushed tone.

'What?'

'Until we meet again,' said Marcel, and he slipped away down the corridor.

'What?'

Jorj was lost. He had mistakenly wandered near a public entrance and had been swept up in the tide of excited ticket holders. By the time he fought his way to the fringes of the mob, he had lost all sense of direction. He used his Softcom lifePod to open a door marked "Private" and fell through, grateful to escape the noisy, surging crowd. He was in a dark, low ceilinged area, underneath a bank of seats. He clambered over beams and debris until he found another door in the back wall. He waved his lifePod over the lock and the door opened to reveal a service ladder. Praying that he was in the right place, Jorj began to climb.

Abi was getting angry. She had been waiting by the access hatch behind the final row of seating for half an hour. Jorj was late, and to make matters worse, members of the public kept mistaking her for a cop.

The hatch finally swung open. 'You're late,' Abi hissed. She ducked inside and shut the door behind her, leaving the cramped shaft in almost total darkness. She began to climb.

Jorj was clinging to the ladder below. 'So,' he asked hopefully, 'no last minute second thoughts?'

Abi stopped and Jorj almost collided with her. 'Shut up,' she whispered viciously, her eyes blazing out of the darkness. 'If you mess this up, I'll never forgive you.' She began to climb once more.

'Alright, alright,' placated Jorj. 'Did you bring the gun?'

'No, I forgot it,' came the withering reply.

'I forgot the acid,' said Jorj. This time he did collide with Abi, and almost lost his grip on the ladder.

'What?' she demanded.

'It was a joke,' trembled Jorj, trying not to think about the immense drop below him, or the corrosive liquid in his pocket.

'No jokes,' Abi instructed.

'Oh, so it's funny if you do it…' started Jorj.

'Shut up.'

They completed the journey in silence. The pinprick of light above them grew until eventually they found themselves out in the open. They emerged onto a precarious gantry lit by the hot August sun. The uppermost level of the stadium looked like a bombsite: demolished and partially demolished rooms were connected and held together by scaffolding and sheets of plastic. To her left Abi could see the concrete plain with its clusters of touts and hawkers. One of the dots was entertaining a large crowd

with a traditional cockney dance. To her right, surviving rooms
and walls blocked any view of the pitch. A slight breeze blew and
Abi gripped the handrail more firmly.

Jorj lay prostrate on a plastic beam, whimpering. Abi kicked
him. 'Come on,' she said, picking her way over the scaffolding.
Jorj crawled after her until they arrived at a locked door. 'Open
it, then,' Abi instructed.

Jorj hauled himself upright. 'It's not too late to change your
mind,' he pleaded.

'Just open the door,' sighed Abi. 'That's all you're here for.'

Jorj's long-repressed indignation reached bursting point. It was
bad enough being forced to become part of a terrorist plot, but
to be an *insignificant* part of that plot, and to be bullied and
insulted every step of the way… 'No,' he said, 'I'm not going to
do it.' He positioned himself in front of the door. Abi tried to
get past him, and he stretched out his arms to make himself look
bigger. As his Softcom lifePod neared a sensor, the door slid open.

'Thanks,' said Abi, nipping through. Jorj crumpled, defeated.

Behind the door was an abandoned control room, previously
used for lighting and other technical effects. Abi examined the
room quickly. The floor looked sound, the thick layer of dust had
not been disturbed, and most importantly the gaping window
frame provided an excellent view of the pitch. Abi returned to
the doorway. 'Give me the acid,' she ordered.

Jorj was tempted to refuse, but struggling with a bottle of
concentrated hydrochloric acid was not his idea of fun.

'Thanks,' Abi said, taking the bottle. 'Now you can run away.
We never have to see each other again.' Before Jorj could express
his relief, she shut the door in his face. Abi withdrew a modified
water pistol from her uniform, and began to fill it with acid.

Ruck walked slowly and thoughtfully towards the VIP viewing platform. He had instructed Marcel to keep Abi and Jorj out of the way, nothing more. The Frenchman was supposed to tantalise them with talk of fictitious plans and impress upon them the importance of secrecy, but that was all. What was he doing here? Why was there an actual plan?

As Ruck walked out into the sunshine, Olivia regarded him carefully. The watching cops had relayed footage of his conversation with the stranger directly to her lifePod, but the microphones had not picked up their whispers. She had heard something about a plan, but that was all. What was he up to? She beckoned him over, and he took a seat at her side. 'Who was that?' she asked.

'What? Ah, no one. Just personal stuff.'

Olivia pursed her lips and tried to ignore the sweat dripping from Ruck's brow.

Abi noticed Professor Ruck as soon as he appeared on the circular stage. She was practising her aim from the control box window when his multicoloured clothing assaulted her eyes. A quick squint through the gunsight confirmed that the clownish figure was the man who had kidnapped her. She was tempted to give him a little squirt for old time's sake, but knew she couldn't. Melting a robot to reveal his circuits was one thing, shooting a person, however evil, was something else again. A sudden explosion made her jump, and her trigger finger tightened involuntarily. A globule of acid flew from the barrel of the gun. Fortunately for Ruck, the weapon had lifted slightly as Abi jumped, and the deadly ball of liquid passed over the Professor's head, hitting the chair behind him. The plastic seat quietly began to dissolve.

Abi took a deep breath, put the gun down and looked around for the source of the noise. It was a firework, marking the start of the ceremony. With nothing better to do until Robot James wheeled himself on, Abi sat back and tried to turn off her brain so she could enjoy the show.

Across the pitch, groups of people in historical costumes were squabbling, fighting and smashing things. This represented the world before the Takeover and the giant screens flashed the caption 'Before Evolution,' in case anyone had missed the point. Then a great fleet of flying cars swooped down, picked up a person each, and carried them into the corners. The people emerged from the cars wearing shiny modern costumes, and the pitch erupted into action. The show was supposed to be a word-less spectacle symbolising peace and human unity, a unique sensory feast unlike anything ever seen before. As far as the eye could see, people were dancing, juggling, walking on stilts and waving big bits of cloth about. Abi yawned.

'Look,' said Olivia, pointing. 'Are those drummers playing dustbins? How unhygienic.'

Ruck's wild eyes didn't see the show. He'd just had a horrible thought.

The unique sensory feast continued. After the helium balloons had been released, the children's choir appeared. But before they could sing, a spontaneous roar rose up from the crowd. Rob James's rocket plane had come into view, right on time. The craft wobbled its wings in salute, and landed behind the stadium.

Jorj was looking for a way out. Now that he, or rather his lifePod, was no longer needed, all he had to do was escape. He needed to get clear before Robot James was shut down; Abi should be able to get away afterwards because her Pod-less wrist couldn't be traced. At least that was the plan, but unfortunately Jorj was lost again.

Somehow he had managed to get backstage. Every now and then he was swamped by children dressed in primary colours, or women representing Life, Liberty and Intellectual Property. There was no point following them, he decided. And the next person wasn't leaving the stadium either, because that person was Rob James.

Jorj had just rounded a corner when he saw a large entourage approaching him, an unmistakable figure at its head. He doubled back, looking frantically for somewhere to hide. He opened the first door he came to, and dashed gratefully inside.

He was in a luxurious room decorated with silk drapes, mirrors and a red carpet. On the carpet were chairs and tables, on the tables were glasses and plates and on the plates were small bites (like nibbles, only more refined). Realising he had made yet another mistake, Jorj crawled under a table and hid behind the cloth.

Robot James walked in. He was dressed in an expensive suit and his skin shone, a sheen that can only be attained through prolonged exposure to money. He looked well groomed either because of his accompanying stylists or because this Robot James had only just been turned on.

Jorj was surprisingly calm. He had backed himself into a corner, he was trapped, caged, confronted by his enemy, and there was nothing he could do. Which was quite a relief. He'd been doing far too many things recently, and nothing was more his style. If you wanted nothing, Jorj was good for it. He watched as James stood in the doorway, divesting himself of his hangers-on. Jorj had a good view from underneath the table, and he got quite excited at the thought of seeing James doing something robotic. Go on, take your head off, he thought. Change your oil.

A single SSI man accompanied the world ruler into the room, shutting the door behind him. 'My name's Stephen, sir,' he said. 'Anything you need, just let me know.'

'The first thing I need is one of these chairs,' said James, sitting down. 'I'm exhausted.'

Battery must be running low, thought Jorj.

'Have you got a spare shirt for me?' continued James, 'because I am sweating like a pig on a barbeque.' He lifted his arms to reveal large damp patches.

Coolant liquid, thought Jorj.

'Of course, sir,' said the SSI man, and he walked across the room, out of Jorj's line of sight. Rob James removed his shirt. He had quite a belly, and was surprisingly hairy.

Less suspicious than a perfect body, thought Jorj. And the hair must hide the access panels.

'There's a shower if you want one, sir,' said the SSI man.

'No thanks,' said James, buttoning his fresh shirt.

Of course not, thought Jorj, a shower wouldn't be very good for the circuits.

'I've had enough showers today to last the rest of my life,' said James. 'What I really want is a long soak in the tub, but I guess there's no time for that, is there Marcus? Is it Marcus? John?'

'It's Stephen, actually,' said Stephen.

He meets a lot of people, thought Jorj. His face database must be full. And he's bluffing about the bath. Water and electricity don't mix.

'Sorry, Steve,' said James, gulping down a glass of water. 'It's been a long day. I'm beginning to wonder if this was a good idea.'

'I hope you don't mind me asking,' said Stephen, 'but what made you want to do this whole round the world thing?'

'Phil Collins,' said James without hesitation. Stephen looked at him blankly. 'Not much of a classic music buff then?' asked James. 'Phil Collins was a singer songwriter last century. He performed at a big charity concert, playing in Britain and America on the same day.' Stephen nodded as if he knew what his boss was talking about. 'I'm a big Phil Collins fan,' James added.

That's an unusual feature, thought Jorj.

'So, have you got a friendly crowd for me, Dave?' asked James, taking one of the small bites.

Stephen winced but felt unable to correct his boss's error. 'You should have received a spreadsheet, sir,' he said. 'It breaks down the number of tickets allocated to Softcom employees–'

James waved a hand to stop him. 'I don't really get along with spreadsheets,' he admitted, shamefaced.

Jorj didn't know what to think about that.

James stood up, clumsily tipping over his chair as he did so. He swung round in an attempt to catch it, knocking a jug of water and a plate of food all over himself. 'Oh, balls!' he cried. As he bent over to pick up the chair he broke wind loudly. He straightened up and faced Stephen, flushed with embarrassment. 'Excuse me,' he said. 'One too many onion bhajees in India.' He tried to wipe some dip from his forehead. 'Perhaps I should have that shower.'

Stephen nodded mutely and led him from the room. Under the table, Jorj was realising that maybe, just maybe, Rob James wasn't a robot.

A few metres above Jorj's head, the second half of the entertainment was beginning, a representation of Britain's finest hour. A hush fell as a single figure marched out into the arena, legs stiff and outstretched, as if his feet had offended his nose. He was short, with black, meticulously parted hair and a smudge on his top lip that wished it was a moustache. He wore a brown uniform and a red armband. He was Adolf Hitler, the man who had made a style of facial hair unwearable for the rest of time, along with other, more notorious crimes. He was confused, as well he might be. Being cloned from a strand of your own moustache over a century after you died is a bit difficult to adjust to, especially if you weren't very well adjusted to begin with. But crowds and public speaking held no fears for this man. He stood to attention, holding up his hand in salute. The crowd fell silent.

He cleared his throat, in German.

A huge shape flew through the air, catapulted from the side of the stadium. It was a bulldog, genetically modified to be over four metres tall, with red, white and blue fur. It looped high into the air, hanging there for a moment, whimpering slightly and representing British military might. Directly below, Hitler paused as he sensed he was no longer the centre of attention. The dog's nose dropped and it plummeted towards the ground. Hitler looked up in time to see a gaping canine maw centimetres from his face, as the falling British bulldog opened wide for one last meal. It swallowed the Führer whole before splattering itself over a wide area. The crowd went wild.

Ruck was the only one not to applaud. He was still reeling from his terrible realisation. He knew who had given the orders to Marcel. Orders about guns. He stood up. 'Excuse me a moment,' he muttered to Olivia as he squeezed past the other VIPs.

'He's coming now,' typed Olivia on her lifePod.

Ruck entered the underground tunnel and loitered in a small alcove. He dialled a number on his Pod, unaware of the watching cop a few metres away. The call was answered immediately.

'Yes?' The voice in his ears and the face on the screen belonged to Rob James.

'Stop that,' said Ruck. 'This is no time for games.'

Ruck's own face appeared on his wrist. 'Do you prefer this one?'

'No.'

'Don't blame you,' crowed the metallic voice.

'This is important,' Ruck hissed. 'What have you been playing at, young man?'

'Oh,' whined the voice. 'It was going to be a surprise.'

'It was a surprise, believe you me,' said Ruck grimly. 'Just give me the details.'

'I'm helping you, like you wanted,' said the voice proudly. 'You wanted to remind the world how dangerous stupidity is…'

'…Yes?'

'Something like your museum, that would prove once and for all that one idiot can cause a lot of damage?'

'Yes, yes, get on with it.'

'Well those people what you catched the other day…'

'Those people *that I caught*,' corrected Ruck.

'Those people think that Rob James is a robot, which is really stupid…'

'…Yes…'

'So,' concluded the voice smugly, 'I fixed it so they're gonna shoot him with an acid gun. Scar him for life, or kill him maybe. No one's gonna forget those idiots in a hurry.'

'What?!' Ruck's voice echoed around the tunnel and the watching cop jumped. 'How on earth did you think that was a good idea?' he cried.

'It is a good idea,' said the voice, sounding hurt. 'It does exactly what you wanted.'

'Oh yes, of course I want to shoot Rob James on Evolution Day,' wailed Ruck despairingly.

On the VIP platform, an appalled Olivia listened to Ruck's side of the conversation. She never dreamt Ruck could be planning something so despicable. She tapped at her lifePod, ordering all O'Connels staff to start an immediate search of the stadium.

Down in the tunnel, Ruck was feeling sick. 'This is unbelievable,' he said.

'I thought you'd be pleased,' protested the voice.

'Pleased?' moaned Ruck. 'You're an idiot.'

'Well screw you!' shouted the voice. 'This is the last time I try to help anyone. Screw everyone!'

'Just you wait till I get home.'

'No, just you wait. I'll show you, I'll show the world! So there!'

Ruck disconnected, took a few deep breaths and thought hard about the acid plan. It was inhuman, it was criminal, it would prove his point, there was no question about that. Olivia would never be able to bastardise his research if the plan succeeded. He thought a bit more, then made another call.

Marcel was trying to find the ladies dressing rooms when his lifePod rang. 'Monsieur,' he said.

'Marcel,' said Ruck, 'is everything going to plan?'

'But of course,' said Marcel. 'It must be an important plan, because I have never seen one like him. Softcom, they pay me to spread the lies about Rob James being a robot, but they have never gone so far like this.'

'No, I suppose not,' said Ruck. 'Could the plan be stopped?'

Marcel laughed. 'But the plan must be stopped, no? I think maybe you have the cops tipped up, they arrest the girl, big publicity for the robot lies. But this is not my department,' he continued in a more worried tone. 'You must stop it, Monsieur.'

Ruck stared at the wall for a moment, trying to see into the future. 'I don't think we need to worry about that,' he decided, hanging up.

In the lighting box, Abi tapped her foot impatiently. She had waited ten years to settle this debt, but the last few minutes were the worst. 'Where are you, Robot?' she muttered. 'Let's show everyone what you're made of.'

In the arena below, a hundred Adolf Hitlers were engaged in hand-to-hand combat with fifty Winston Churchills and fifty Margaret Thatchers. Strictly speaking the iron ladies were not historically accurate, but neither were the nunchuks that the Churchills were using.

Jorj was suffering from a guilty conscience. His conscience was feeling guilty because it wasn't doing enough to stop Jorj running away. He had seen with his own eyes that James wasn't a robot, yet he wasn't trying to prevent the man getting shot. Instead he was running around in a blind panic, attempting to save his own skin. His conscience tried another tack.

'Jorj,' it cooed, in a calming but slightly irritating internal voice, 'do you really think you're going to get away with this?'

Jorj stopped suddenly. It was working.

'Do you really think Softcom are going to stop looking for you after what you've done?'

Jorj rubbed his chin.

'The only way to get away with this is to stop it happening in the first place.'

Jorj nodded. His conscience was right; he had to go back to the lighting box. Unfortunately when it came to navigation, he was as much use as a plastic compass from a Christmas cracker.

Ruck returned to his seat beside Olivia. He was dazed, overwhelmed by the enormity of the decision he had just taken. 'Tell me,' he asked, looking for reassurance, 'what is it they say about the ends justifying the means?'

Olivia looked at him sharply. 'They say the ends don't justify the means,' she said.

'Do they?' asked Ruck. 'And do they ever say it the other way round, the ends *do* justify the means?'

'No.'

'Oh.' He scanned the roof of the stadium anxiously.

Olivia followed his line of sight and tapped a message to her troops. 'Search the roof.'

There was another huge roar from the crowd as Rob James appeared on the viewing platform. 'Rob,' shouted Olivia as he walked past.

'Not now, Olivia' said James. There was little love lost between their two corporations.

Olivia stayed where she was, not daring to risk getting caught by the assassin herself. She applied an extra layer of plastic to the side of her face closest to the podium.

Ruck nibbled a fingernail.

Jorj climbed a ladder and hoped it was the right one.

The last few Hitlers faced death by handbag.

Rob James looked through the notes for his speech.

Ruck chewed a finger.

Abi was thinking about her mother. Right now she would be in the park where her dad's ashes were scattered. 'I'm sorry I couldn't be there,' she muttered. 'I hope you understand.' She put her finger on the trigger.

Jorj climbed the ladder. A door opened below and light spilled into the shaft.

James got to his feet and approached the podium.

Ruck gnawed a knuckle.

Abi's finger tightened...

'Stop!' shouted Jorj, throwing himself into the lighting box.

Abi whirled round. 'What are you doing?' she cried. 'You traitor!'

'It's a mistake! He's not a robot!'

'Get lost, Jorj! This has nothing to do with you.'

Jorj had one hand on the rifle full of acid. 'Give me the gun,' he said.

'Wage slave!' shouted Abi, pulling back and kicking at him.

The crowd cheered once more as Rob James waved.

Jorj's muscles ached. This is a fine time to realise you're weaker than a girl, he thought.

Abi pulled again. One more yank should do it.

'Stop!' shouted K8 as she burst into the room.

Shocked, Abi let go of the rifle. Jorj pulled against thin air, flew across the room and landed in a heap.

K8 drew her O'Gun from its O'Holster.

Abi knew the game was up. But if she couldn't get Robot James, she could at least get some retribution elsewhere. She reached under her O'Connels jacket and drew another weapon.

Jorj struggled to his feet. Two O'Guns swung round to cover him.

240

'Drop the weapon!' shouted Abi. 'You're under arrest for attempted murder.'

Jorj's jaw dropped, as did the rifle. 'But...' he managed.

'No buts,' said Abi. 'You're in a lot of trouble.' I told you I'd never forgive you if you messed this up, she thought. Jorj slumped, defeated.

Harry ran up to the doorway and peered over his girlfriend's shoulder. 'Samantha Nice!' he exclaimed. 'I don't believe it! You're amazing.'

'For Christ's sake, Harry,' said K8. 'I am here, you know.'

Rob James finished his speech, boarded his rocket plane and headed for country number fifteen.

Ruck retreated to his laboratory, his plans, his mind and what was left of his hair in disarray. Olivia went with him. She had been informed of Jorj's capture and was hoping the Professor would confess before she arrested him too.

They entered a lift and descended into the subterranean warren. After the crowded filth of Wembley, Olivia was looking forward to the lab's sterile white corridors. She was totally unprepared when the elevator doors opened to reveal a dust storm; every surface was covered and motes hung in the air like lazy snow. 'What is going on?' she shrieked, backing into a corner of the lift.

'I don't know,' admitted Ruck grudgingly, 'but I'm going to find out. Do you have any spare nostril filters?' he asked, for once thankful for Olivia's allergies.

Olivia dropped the tiny objects into Ruck's palm, and then faced a terrible dilemma. Either she could look at the horrifying dust, or she could watch as Ruck shoved things up his nose. The particles made quite pleasing patterns as they moved through the air.

Ruck coated his skin with Olivia's liquid plastic, told her to wait in the lift and then strode out into the corridor. Olivia tried to follow him, and she vibrated for a few moments as her brain battled her phobias for control of her body. Her brain won through and she lurched out of the elevator.

Ruck looked over his shoulder. 'Are you, ah, sure you wouldn't rather wait there?' he asked hopefully.

'Mmm,' said Olivia through clenched teeth.

'Okay,' said Ruck as he followed the directions in his earpiece. 'We'll soon get to the bottom of this dust.' Olivia jerked along behind him, trying not to think about dust or bottoms.

They stopped outside a door that looked like all the others. 'I wasn't going to show you this,' Ruck said, looking guilty. 'It's not really finished, so maybe you'd like to wait out here?' Olivia glowered at Ruck and he hastily opened the door for her.

Inside was a desk, a computer and a great deal of dust. Ruck sat and faced the room's other door, which led away from the corridor. He cleared his throat.

'Oh, you're back,' boomed a deep metallic voice. 'Come to punish me have you?'

Ruck ignored Olivia's quizzical glances. 'Good evening,' he said quietly. 'We can talk about that later.'

'Alec, who is this?' asked Olivia. Ruck didn't answer.

'Are you ashamed of me or something?' asked the voice. 'I don't care actually. I don't need you anyway. I've decided what I'm going to do with my life.'

'Please introduce us,' demanded Olivia.

Ruck hung his head. 'Olivia, this is Darren,' he mumbled. 'Darren, this is…'

'I know who she is,' said Darren impatiently. 'Aren't you interested in what I'm going to do? It must be quite boring for you, after all it's only the rest of my life.' The last word made the speakers shake.

'Alright, Darren,' said Ruck, trying to assert his authority and forgetting that he had none. 'What do you want to do?'

'This,' said Darren.

The grey nanobot dust on the floor shifted and coalesced. The tiny machines formed themselves into a fist the size of a watermelon. It rose up, attached to more bots on the floor by a spindly arm. The fist whirled round at tremendous speed, crashing down and smashing furniture, computer screens and other equipment.

'I want to smash things,' said Darren. 'Smash smash smashy smash.'

'Stop!' said Ruck, rising to his feet. 'I demand that you stop!'

'Piss off.' Ruck and Olivia cowered in a corner while the destruction continued. The desk cracked and nanobots swarmed over the wreckage, seemingly disintegrating it, but actually turning it into more miniscule robots. So the fist grew larger, and smashed more and more until there was nothing but Ruck and Olivia left to destroy. The hand approached them, then very slowly extended its middle digit in a rock star's salute.

'Perhaps,' said Olivia imperiously, 'you would like to explain what's going on?'

'It's… complicated,' said Ruck.

'I'll make it easier,' said Darren. 'I'm coming out.' Before Ruck could protest, while Ruck was protesting and after Ruck had given up his protests, the fist was in action again, this time battering down one of the walls. It collapsed with a crash and nanobots oozed into the room beyond. Nothing could be seen through the haze of dust.

'Here I come!' said Darren, and he rushed over the rubble towards Ruck and Olivia. Olivia gasped.

Darren was, to put it bluntly, a brain in a jar. But this was not the cause of Olivia's surprise. Mankind has been putting brains in jars ever since they lost money by putting them in pies. Brains go into jars like footballers go into pop stars. Put a brain in a cardboard box, and the box will get soggy. Put it in a carrier bag and the handles will split or you'll leave it on the bus. But jars are just the job.

Although the jar was normal, the brain was not. As well as the traditional grey matter, the brain was augmented with various wires, LEDs and knobbly electronics bits. It appeared to be half brain, half computer, because that's exactly what it was. Olivia found this quite surprising, but not gaspworthy. The incongruous element was what the jar itself was sitting in, which was the driver's seat of a dune buggy.

'Vroom, vroom,' cried Darren, his voice emanating from speakers attached to the jar. The dune buggy was made of around three ¶illion nanobots, each controlled by the brain, together forming a fully functioning vehicle. It moved silently, so Darren had to provide the sound effects himself. He made the noise of a squeal of tyres and the buggy pulled a wheelie. As its front end rose, the car's form shifted and it momentarily resembled a rearing horse. Then it was down on four wheels again, speeding towards Ruck and Olivia.

'I'd run if I were you,' Darren suggested.

Ruck and Olivia agreed.

Marcel tried to leave Wembley shortly after Rob James's speech. In the arena they were trying to answer the age-old question, "How many Hitlers can you jump over in a double decker bus?" After several attempts the answer was still "none", but they were going to keep trying as long as there was a supply of unflattened Führers. Ignoring the cheers and occasional squelches, Marcel headed for the nearest way out.

He was within metres of an exit when a sign caught his eye: "Ladies Dressing Room". He sauntered in, confidently announcing that the afternoon was beautiful and so was he. There was a snarling sound and the door swung shut behind him, revealing another sign: "Caution – Thatchers."

Marcel was never seen again.

PART THREE

ABI, K8 and Harry handed Jorj to Softcom Special Investigations, who kneed, fisted and booted him down into the bowels of Wembley Stadium. His stolen lifePod was replaced with handcuffs, forearm cuffs, ankle cuffs, knee cuffs and thigh cuffs. He was well and truly cuffed, whichever way you looked at it. Having immobilised their prisoner, the agents turned off the lights and locked the door.

The cell's black emptiness suited Jorj's mood. He lay on the floor, cursing the day he had met Abi. Then, after a few moments' reflection, he assumed a more focused, positive attitude and just cursed Abi herself. When this began to pall, he found a crumb of comfort in the thought that he had reached rock bottom. Surely his life couldn't get any worse?

The lights came back on. Jorj groaned and struggled to lift his head from the floor. Ten men entered the room and formed a circle around him. Each man held a rifle and each rifle pointed at Jorj.

'Shut up!' Through the retina burn Jorj saw another man, standing slightly apart from the others. The cross around the man's neck indicated that he believed in god, despite the fact that he himself was clearly the result of a busy day in the divine workshop, the sort of day on which a pig might be mistakenly finished off as a wrinkled chimp, and then chucked in with the humans. He was in his late fifties, short, squat and ugly. He was wearing a cowboy hat, a sharply pressed suit, a shoelace tie and boots with spurs. To complete the look he was chewing a match, which was on fire. If the man was in charge, he looked less than convincing in the role. He had the gait of a small boy showing off for his parents, pleased with the attention but terrified that he may slip over. 'Shut up,' he said again, deeming the remark clever enough to warrant a second airing.

'I didn't–' started Jorj. Ten guns cocked. Jorj shut up.

The Pig Monkey flicked away his match, lit another and clamped it between his teeth. 'Strip,' he said. Another man unshackled Jorj, who reluctantly took off his clothes. 'Shut up,' drawled the Pig Monkey in an American accent. 'Put him in the tub.'

Jorj was dragged across the rough concrete floor and thrown into a vat of orange liquid. His captors struck him with the butts of their rifles, forcing him under the surface and pinning him down. As Jorj started to drown, his life flashed before his eyes. Under the circumstances he would have preferred something a bit more comforting, a cartoon or maybe a musical. He had seen his life before and hadn't liked it much the first time. He lost interest, then consciousness.

When Jorj awoke he was cuffed once more, but otherwise still naked. As he looked down at himself, he noticed that his skin was luminous orange. He stuck out his tongue and peered down his nose at it. Both were brightly dyed.

'You poking your tongue at me, boy?' Jorj looked up and saw the Pig Monkey leaning against a shotgun. The other men had disappeared. Jorj hastily reeled his tongue back in. 'You in a lot of trouble, boy. Tongues ain't gonna help you none. Point of fact, nothing's gonna help you.'

'You can't do this,' said Jorj, despite all the evidence to the contrary.

'You a terrorist. We can do whatever we want.'

'There's been a mistake. I'm not a terrorist.' Calm.

'I think you are.'

'You have to prove it.' Rational.

'I'll prove it at your trial.'

'Oh. Well we'll see. When is that?' Hopeful.

'Terrorists can be held indefinitely without trial.'

'But I'm not a terrorist.' Worried.

'You can prove that at your trial.'

'When is my trial?' Impatient.

'One, maybe two, hundred years.'

'That's ridiculous!' Horrified.

'You should have thought of that before you became a terrorist.'

'I'm not a terrorist.' Despairing.

'Now you see, this is getting us nowhere. If you ain't a terrorist, why are you sitting there with your dick in your hands all painted up like a freak? Well? I know you got a tongue, I seen it.'

Jorj didn't answer.

The man strutted towards him with the cocky swagger of a school bully. 'Now don't you be trying none of your terrorist tricks on me, boy. Anything happens to me, you'll be dead faster than you can say civil liberties. And if you're thinking of escaping, it ain't gonna work. You been eating too many carrots boy, 'cause you stick out like a sore dick.' He loomed over Jorj and sniggered. 'How is your dick, boy? Sore?'

Jorj shook his head and the man kicked him savagely in the groin.

'How about now?'

Jorj nodded and tried to stop crying. 'You got any hidden weapons boy?'

Jorj looked down at his naked form. 'No, sir,' he snivelled.

''Cause I can kill you if you got weapons. What should I do about that? Boy?'

'...You can have a look.'

'No, I don't think I'll do that. Maybe I should kill you now, just in case. You going to attack me boy?'

Jorj looked up at the man, terrified. 'No sir.'

''Cause I can kill you if you attack me. Matter of fact, I can kill you if I think you *might* attack me. Preeeee-emptive, they call that. I'll kill you, and it'll be self-defence. You thinking about attacking me? Boy?'

'...No, sir.'

'You thinking about looking at me in a funny way? 'Cause that's just asking for a killing.' Jorj's lip trembled and he dropped his head. 'Aw, don't cry, boy,' sneered the Pig Monkey. 'This is me being nice.'

Ruck burst out of Darren's lab and into the twisting, turning corridor. 'Come on,' he shouted at Olivia, who was already two metres ahead of him. He stabbed at his lifePod and a siren started to wail. Emergency lights bathed everything in a dim red glow.

'And how is that supposed to help?' demanded Olivia angrily.

'...Atmosphere?' suggested Ruck.

The dune buggy crashed through a wall behind them and skidded into the corridor. 'Yeah!' shouted Darren, as he sloshed about in his jar. 'I'm a speed demon! Whoooooooo!'

Panicking albino scientists ran into the corridor ahead of Olivia. She slowed and looked over her shoulder to see Ruck frowning with a finger in one ear. Darren had knocked out the guidance computer, and there were no whispered directions. Behind him, the car had grown limbs and was hitting out at the walls. 'Smashy smashy!' Darren yelled. 'Aaaargghh!'

Olivia came to a crossroads, the first of several thousand in the labyrinthine complex. 'Which way?' she yelled.

'...I... don't...' wheezed Ruck.

'Great!' shouted Olivia, whirling round.

'...know...' completed Ruck, catching up.

'So how do we get out?' asked Olivia urgently. She could see Darren's vehicle gaining on them, growing as the nanobots reproduced.

'Follow the scientists,' said Ruck, wondering if feeling sick and wanting a cigarette were signs of an impending heart attack.

'How do they know the way?' asked Olivia. Some nasty spikes were forming on the front of the buggy.

'They're mice,' said Ruck as he struggled forward, leaving Olivia behind. 'Part human, part mouse. Love being in labs, and very good at mazes.' Olivia ran on, quickly overtaking him.

'Oh! Yeah, I'm gonna smash you!' sang Darren as he sped after them. 'Oh! Yeah, I'm gonna bash you!' His terrible singing competed with a terrible rumble as the building began to collapse. The buggy was massive now, and several independent gobs of ooze streamed through the labs. These swallowed anything of interest: computers, experiments, the HumAnt farm, anything that wasn't running away screaming.

In one room a scientist was still working. He leant over Ken, the murderous We Care robot, tinkering with its insides. 'Any minute now,' said the scientist. 'Just got to finish—'

He didn't even finish his sentence. A sea of troublesome nanobots knocked the door in, sweeping the scientist off his feet. The minuscule machines swallowed their larger cousin Ken and rushed around its circuits, creating a new pathway here, making a new component there. Within seconds Ken had been reprogrammed again. It stood up, the head screen showing a pre-recorded customer care clip. 'Alright, sir,' smarmed an actress, 'let's start again from the beginning.' Ken walked off, letting fly with its fists. It threw the unfortunate scientist against the wall, breaking many bones in the process, including some rather important ones. 'Unfortunately that is not covered by your guarantee,' smiled another clip as Ken followed its new-found allies from the room.

Elsewhere, Darren's buggy was closing on Professor Ruck. A huge set of revolving blades erupted from the front of the vehicle, and Ruck could feel the breeze on the back of his neck.

'Faster!' yelled Olivia, who was still in front.

'Can't!'

Olivia ducked into an alcove and stopped. Ruck lumbered towards her, the blades centimetres away from his flapping Paisley lab coat. As he drew level, Olivia grimaced and threw herself at him. The knives just missed her feet as she and Ruck tumbled into the mouth of another corridor. The buggy sped past the junction, going too fast to turn.

Ruck was spread-eagled on the floor. He found himself nose to nose with Olivia, who lay sprawled on top of him. Just when you think your day can't get any worse, Ruck thought.

'Mmm,' moaned Olivia, her eyes shut and her hips gyrating.

'Olivia, ah, darling,' said Ruck. 'Perhaps this isn't the time for–'

'Get away, you moron,' growled Olivia through gritted teeth. 'I'm having a seizure.' Her whole body convulsed, revolted by the physical contact.

Ruck slid himself out from under her, then stood watching as Olivia's twitches slowly subsided. 'You saved my life,' he said finally.

'Don't remind me.'

'And… you touched me.'

Olivia's limbs flailed uncontrollably. 'I don't want to talk about it.'

'I'm…' Ruck smiled mischievously. 'Well, I'm touched.'

Olivia clutched her stomach and sat up. 'You're the only person who might know how to terminate this thing, that's all,' she said with ferocious cool. 'Now get moving.'

They listened for sounds of pursuit as they ran, but heard nothing. Neither did they find any pink-eyed scientists to follow. They didn't dare voice the thought that they were just taking turns at random.

After a few minutes, a wall of nanobots rose from the floor and blocked the way ahead. Ruck and Olivia turned and began to retrace their steps, but this route too was quickly sealed. Then the first wall started to move towards them.

'We're going to get crushed,' said Ruck.

'Keep your distance,' ordered Olivia. 'I don't want your blood in my hair.'

Ruck did as he was told. 'Any famous last words?' he asked.

'"Oh god please no" must be quite popular,' said Olivia grimly.

The wall was ten metres away, then five, then it stopped. They waited tensely for a few seconds, then breathed sighs of relief. Olivia sat reluctantly on the floor. 'I think,' she said, picking her words carefully, 'you should advise me what the hell is going on.'

Camden's eternal traffic jam circled slowly. Rob James's face was just visible between the flying cars, the huge screen still showing his Evolution Day progress. The image changed, and a young girl in an O'Connels uniform stared out. A caption flashed up, "Have you seen this person?" The picture froze on a close-up of the cop's face. It was Abi.

A hundred metres down, the same face was pouting sulkily. Abi paced the deserted tunnels like a caged animal, kicking at stones and swearing. 'Where are you?' she muttered. Conflicting emotions ran through her head: anger at Jorj for ruining her revenge, fear for Marcel who had missed their rendezvous, confusion and panic because she didn't know what to do, and the background loneliness that was always with her. Abi punched a wall as she let the anger take centre stage. 'Why, Jorj?' she said bitterly. 'Why?'

Later she was sitting on the floor with her head in her hands. She had let everyone down, Marcel, her father... Later still she was pacing again, staring upwards defiantly, her arms firmly crossed. So she was alone again, fine. She could look after herself, she'd had enough practice. First things first, she had to get rid of anything that might link her to the plot. She looked at her fake lifePod and nodded. It was time to rejoin the herd. She found her real Pod on the floor of the tunnel and put it on. The wolf had regained her sheep's clothing.

Abi decided to go up to the ticket hall, where her Pod would get a signal. Maybe Marcel had sent her a message. As she climbed the broken escalator, music news scrolled across her wrist. She was plugged in again. She picked up a pirate ear station, and her implanted speakers shook with one of her favourite tunes. A smile spread across her face, her head nodded and her feet carried her out into the street, towards home.

She only managed a few steps before she was stopped by the young arm of the law. A cop grabbed her shoulder and span her round, knocking her against a wall. 'That's her,' he said.

'Whatever,' sighed his spotty companion.

'Get off me,' shouted Abi, looking for an escape route. The two cops had her hemmed in against the wall. She would have to fight her way out.

'Abi Odiali, AKA Samantha Nice?' beamed the first cop.

'No,' said Abi, waiting for the right moment to strike.

'Yes,' contradicted the cop, laughing. He pointed at the huge screen that was once more showing her face.

Abi's heart sank. 'What have I done now ?'

'You're a hero,' chuckled the cop. 'You saved Rob James's life.'

'Oh,' Abi scowled. 'That.'

'You've got to come with us,' said the cop. 'We're taking you to Heathrow.'

'What if I don't want to?' Abi demanded.

'Whatever,' said the second youth.

'No,' corrected the first. 'You've got no choice. Every cop in London has been ordered to take you to the airport. But it's a good thing,' he smiled. 'You're going to Head Office. You're actually going to meet Rob James.'

'Really?' said Abi, with the faintest of smiles.

The Pig Monkey flicked a switch and Jorj's arms were nearly yanked from their sockets. The ceiling of the subterranean cell was a huge electro magnet, a fact that had previously escaped Jorj's attention. But as his iron handcuffs pulled him through the air, lifting his feet from the ground, the humming ceiling became more difficult to ignore. The cuffs attached themselves with a clank, and Jorj dangled painfully. To add to his discomfort, his pile of discarded clothes was directly in his line of sight, his hated work shoes sitting smugly on the top.

The Pig Monkey sniggered his approval. 'You ever been tortured before, boy?' he asked.

Jorj shook his head miserably.

'Oh, it's a whole heap of fun. I just know I'm gonna enjoy it.' The porcine primate moseyed over to a corner of the room and pressed a button. A section of the wall slid open to reveal an array of high tech whips, probes, blades and clamps. 'Daddy's home,' cooed the Pig Monkey, tenderly stroking the devices.

'I'll tell you anything, anything at all,' insisted Jorj.

'Woah, hold your horses, fella,' said his captor. 'If you're gonna spill the beans now, what's the point in me torturing you?'

'You don't have to torture me.'

The Pig Monkey scratched his head. 'Then why have I got these sweet babies?' he asked. 'These here are expensive gizmos. Wasn't much point in buying them if they ain't gonna get used.'

'Please…' mumbled Jorj. *This* was rock bottom, he realised. Things really couldn't get any worse now.

The Pig Monkey selected a bat, augmented with pointed electrical contacts. 'Did you miss me?' he whispered. He looked at Jorj. 'This here is very useful. Hostilities are initiated thusly…' He swung the bat through the air and blue sparks flew. 'Or it can be deployed inside the terrorist's ass.' The Pig Monkey smiled, and picked up another weapon. 'The itty bitty needles on this one attach themselves direct to the nerve endings. High impact pain on the nipple area, or inside the ass.'

Jorj winced as the man chose a third device.

'Come to poppa. Now just look at this one. Rotating blades, graters, spikes….' He fixed Jorj with an evil stare. 'Where do you think this one goes?'

'…My arse?' moaned Jorj reluctantly.

'"My arse",' mocked the Pig Monkey. 'I love the way you British scream that.'

'I wasn't screa… Oh. Oh I see.'

'You will be screaming, boy!' bellowed the man, advancing on Jorj. 'You're gonna wish your ass had never been born!' The blades whirled and buzzed. 'I am defending all that is good and pure in the world!' yelled the Pig Monkey, brandishing the weapon maniacally. 'Folks should be allowed to live free from terror and violence!' The graters scraped at the air a few centimetres from Jorj's skin.

The man paused, his attention caught by a movement on the floor. He turned to look at the pile of Jorj's clothing. It was wriggling.

Jorj's work shoes had picked up a few ¿illion nanobots several nights before, while fleeing Ruck's labs. Signals from Darren had caused the robots to reproduce, and Jorj's shoes and clothes had been completely consumed, leaving behind a bundle of voracious, microscopic machines. The Pig Monkey did not know this, which is why he made such a terrible mistake.

'Now what the hell fire tarnation is going on here?' he demanded, scowling at the ex-garments. The jelly inside his head excreted a thought, and he decided to fix the problem with violence. He kicked the ball of nanobots.

His leg disappeared up to the knee. The man screamed and pulled out a bloody stump teeming with hungry dust. His foot and shin had been devoured, turned instantly into more machines. He lost his balance and fell over backwards, bellowing with pain and rage. 'Gimme back my leg, you son of a bitch! I will not rest until I have avenged my innocent leg!' He used his slicer and scraper to smash at the tiny robots. That was his second mistake.

The impact threw splashes of bots onto his remaining foot. The bots made quick work of leg number two, ripping apart the flesh atom by atom. The man screamed again and started clubbing his own thighs. The tide of tiny devices flowed upwards, making *short* work of his sexual organs (insert your own joke here). 'Daddy!' sobbed the man. 'Help me da–' The rest became a sickening gurgle as his lungs were eaten away. The last thing the Pig Monkey saw was a pulpy red feeding frenzy moving towards his eyes, consuming his mouth, his nose, and then he could see no more. He could still feel, for a second or two, pain greater than a kick in the testicles multiplied by migraines to the power of childbirth. Then he was gone, leaving behind a soggy, seething mess.

Jorj hung above it all, horrified. He resolved never again to think that he had reached rock bottom, as this clearly just provoked the universe into proving him wrong.

A metre or so below him, the pool of hungry nanobots continued to expand.

Professor Ruck told a story about a boy, unlike other boys. Special. A boy raised, for reasons of necessity, apart from the rest of the world. For the world couldn't, or wouldn't, understand him. So the little boy, strange already, became stranger still. Who knew what was going on in the recesses of his mind? Who would reach out to him? It was a sad story, and as Ruck drew to a close he brushed away a tiny tear.

'Question,' said Olivia finally. 'Are you really saying you've crossed a brain with a computer and put it in a jar?'

'I tried a box but it got soggy.'

'Unbelievable,' said Olivia. 'And this was your model for a new improved human.' She thought for a moment. 'I guess no one has done this before?'

'No,' said Ruck proudly. 'He's totally original.'

'That's one word for it. So you're the subject matter expert. How old is he?'

'Six months. But he's a super computer, and he learns very quickly. And then there's his sessions on the growth spurter, so in real terms he's maybe fifteen.'

'So taking on board the nanotechnology, we're competing against an omnipotent teenage boy. May god help us all.'

'Now who's being far-fetched? But he's surprisingly mature. It is amazing how well he uses the nanotech. He's multitasking to an incredible extent, more than I'd ever thought possible...'

'Then perhaps going forwards he can smash us to pieces and write sappy poems at the same time. Okay, initial thoughts: our best practice is to lay off the computer and invest in the human angle. Try to grow some empathy or compassion. He can't be a total monster. Whose DNA did you use?'

'Mine. I suppose you could say he's my son.'

'We're bust.' Olivia shook her head. 'Why didn't you keep him on the growth spurter?' she groaned. 'Wait until he was in his thirties? He'd be more settled, fatalistic, boring?'

'You have to do it in small doses,' explained Ruck, 'and once he reached fifteen he refused to go on it again.'

'Well you should have forced him.'

Ruck was indignant. 'That's no way to raise a child. You have to reason with them, not bully them...'

Olivia raised her eyebrows.

'Look, it's not easy being a parent you know.'

'I think you've demonstrated that,' Olivia said. She walked to the far end of their cell, putting as much distance between Ruck and herself as possible.

Ruck appealed to her back. 'It wasn't supposed to turn out like this. I was doing it for the best.' There was no response. Ruck frowned. He couldn't afford to lose his powerful ally. 'Olivia, please, don't let this come between us.'

Olivia whirled round. 'Us?' she said scornfully. 'There is no "us". I only put "us" on the table so I could get up to speed with your dumb plans.'

'What?' screeched Ruck. 'My plans are far from dumb.'

Olivia gestured at the walls that imprisoned them. 'I don't think you're going to win the Nobel Prize. And trying to kill Rob James wasn't exactly smart.'

Ruck turned white. 'I, ah, don't know what you're talking about.'

The floor lurched beneath their feet and they both fell to the ground. The shaking continued, as if their cell was travelling somehow. Olivia looked quizzically at Ruck, who shrugged angrily.

'So,' said Olivia after a few minutes, 'aren't you even slightly upset that I'm not in love with you?'

'Hardly,' said Ruck cheerfully. 'I only agreed to go out with you so you would take my ideas to The Board.'

'What!…You were using me?'

'Yup.'

'How dare you!'

'You were using me.'

'Agreed! Did you really think I'd consider a joint venture with a man in a lime green tie?'

'At least I don't eat my dinner with a straw!'

'I never want to see you again as long as I live!'

'Suits me!'

They looked angrily at their five metre square prison, then turned their backs on each other. They fumed silently for several hours, until the rocking motion of the room sent them both to sleep.

The home of Softcom, and of Rob James, was known as Head Office. It was a sparkling rectangular block two hundred storeys high, which didn't so much scrape the sky as puncture it. According to Softcom, the building symbolised their ambition to reach ever higher; their detractors called it Rob James's one fingered salute to the world. But the most remarkable aspect of Head Office was not its height, but its location. Instead of being in an urban business district, competing for space with similarly lanky neighbours, the building was situated in lush green parkland somewhere in Upstate New York.

Abi stood nervously outside the main entrance. She looked up at the building, and saw every light blazing against the night sky. 'Come on then,' she muttered, 'I'll take you all on.' Clenching her fists, she walked through the gargantuan revolving doors.

The foyer was a cavernous space and Abi half expected to see clouds billowing overhead. The walls were lined with huge abstract paintings and vast motivational posters. To Abi's left was a picture of a chicken in flight, with the caption 'Losing is for losers.' A hectare of marble floor stretched before her, leading to dozens of lifts that constantly swallowed up and spat out passengers. People crisscrossed briskly in front of her, and a deafening hubbub filled the air. Abi's head swam.

'Abi Odiali?' A blonde man in his early twenties was smiling beside her.

'Yes,' admitted Abi.

'My name's Lee, I'm an intern here. I'll be looking after you until Mr James returns from his ED duties. I guess about now he'll be in...'

'Los Angeles,' supplied Abi automatically.

'Right,' grinned Lee. 'I suppose you want the tour?'

Abi wanted the tour like a fish wants to be shown the inside of a shark's mouth. But she felt helpless to resist as Lee led her through an endless series of dull, open plan offices. She sneered privately at the suited drones scurrying around her.

'This is the nightshift,' explained Lee. 'Each department has three shifts to ensure twenty-four hour productivity.'

'Oh,' said Abi.

'That's Matt Bozkurt,' Lee continued, proudly pointing out another busy bee. 'He's trebled transparency in the Australasian economy.'

'Oh.'

Head Office would have epitomised the boring corporate environment of Abi's nightmares, but for one thing: the money. Softcom had a lot more money to throw around, which didn't just mean that the desks were more expensive or that the water coolers were cooler. It meant there was a lot of money thrown around. Wherever Abi looked, there was cash. Buckets of coins held meeting room doors open. Stacks of notes propped up wonky desks. Messages were scrawled on hundred dollar bills. As Abi and Lee walked past, a woman opened a cupboard and was buried by an avalanche of fivers. The workers could hardly move for puddles of currency.

'Er,' said Abi. 'What's the story with...'

'The money?' asked Lee, sniffily. 'Everyone always asks about the money. I would have thought it was obvious,' he continued, wiping his nose on some passing pesos. 'After the Takeover we abolished physical cash, everyone knows that. But we decided to keep it all, just in case. So all the banks delivered their stocks here and,' he concluded, a little embarrassed, 'we've been too busy to work out where to put it.'

They continued the tour until Abi could hardly think. Although it was Monday night local time, it was Tuesday morning Abi time, and she was exhausted. She yawned pointedly several times before Lee finally got the message. 'I'll take you to your apartment,' he said.

Leaving the lobby, they took an electric buggy to the rear of Head Office. Abi was shocked to find a small town, which had previously been entirely hidden behind the massive skyscraper. 'Houses, shops, bars, everything we need,' said Lee. 'All the employees live here, it's more efficient.' Abi wrinkled her nose but said nothing.

They stopped outside a single storey building fronted with a large, luxurious garden. 'This is yours,' said Lee, as he transferred the electronic key onto Abi's lifePod. 'Mr James will send for you tomorrow. Just call the reception desk if you need anything.'

The luxury continued inside the apartment. The carpets were deep, the furnishings were soft, and the rooms were huge. Abi counted five bedrooms before she found the kitchen and quickly transferred her attention to the contents of the fridge. Realising that the fruit and cold meat platter might be her last meal, she tried to enjoy it.

Next she attempted to relax with a soak in the tub. The bathroom was as well stocked as the rest of the house. There was a vast array of bubble baths, unguents and lotions, and even the toilet paper came in a variety of denominations.

For hours Jorj hung suspended above the growing nanobot pool. To begin with he was terrified, but even Jorj couldn't sustain a state of abject fear indefinitely. Eventually he was merely annoyed that he would be killed by a monster that had evolved from his work shoes.

When the nanobots reached the walls they started to eat through the hidden panels, revealing instruments of torture, computers and other devices. These objects were not devoured as the Pig Monkey had been; instead they floated on top of the bot soup, turning on and off seemingly at random. When the tiny machines discovered a camera, they immediately began to swing its lens around the room. As Jorj came into shot the movement stopped, and the camera zoomed in.

'…Hello?' said Jorj warily. The lens nodded up and down. Jorj racked his brain. What topic was suitable for a conversation between a man and his work shoes? Jorj suspected that in the whole of human history, he was the first person ever to contemplate such a question, and he wasn't sure he was up to the challenge. 'How's it going?' he tried. 'Sorry I haven't polished you much recently. But I lost my job, and haven't actually needed work shoes as such.' The camera shook from side to side. 'Mind you,' continued Jorj, 'you seem to have moved on from the whole work shoe thing yourself. Er…'

The nanobot pool churned and frothed. Waves broke against the walls, dissolving secret doors and revealing yet more equipment. The robot dust surged over the appliances, and Jorj groaned. Why hadn't he just badmouthed trainers?

The nanobots found some speakers and the storm subsided. Darren's voice echoed around the cell. 'Jesus, that's better,' he said. 'Alright, dude, how's it hanging?' A delighted cackle issued from the speakers. 'Get it, cos you're, like, hanging? From the ceiling?'

'...Hello?' said Jorj again.

'Yeah, hello. My name's Darren, and I'm not a pair of shoes, by the way.'

'Okay. I'm Jorj.'

'Yeah, I know who you are. Nice paintjob, mate, very cool.'

Jorj looked at his bright orange skin. 'It makes me look like a terrorist,' he said nervously.

'Yeah, wicked,' said Darren. 'So, what kind of music do you like?'

'Er... what?' Jorj decided he was hallucinating. Partly because of the unbelievable things he had seen, but mainly because someone was trying to be nice to him. On recent evidence, that was just too far-fetched.

'I like extreme rock,' said Darren happily. 'Der ner ner ner ner, that sort of thing.'

'Are you a hallucination?' asked Jorj.

'No,' replied Darren. 'Why, are you on drugs? Hey, can you get me some, this is so coooooool.'

'I'm not on drugs,' said Jorj. He tried to flex his aching shoulders. 'I am in quite a lot of pain,' he said to himself. 'Maybe that's it.'

Darren's camera swept upwards, taking in the cuffs from which Jorj was dangling. 'Jesus, that looks totally bad actually. Don't worry, mate, I'll get you down.'

'No!' yelped Jorj, but it was too late. A geyser of bots erupted from the floor and plastered themselves against the ceiling. Jorj moaned as the voracious machines swarmed over his wrists, consuming the cuffs. Within seconds his bonds gave way, and he fell with a splash into the pool below. 'Get off! Don't eat me!' cried Jorj as he thrashed about, knee deep in dust.

'Chillax,' urged Darren. 'They won't bite, we're friends.'

'Oh,' said Jorj, feeling rather foolish. 'Thanks, er, friend.'

'Darren,' said Darren. 'So, what do you want to do? We could chill, hang out, kick back…'

'That sounds great,' said Jorj, slowly rubbing his chin. 'But someone's bound to come and check on me soon. I'm a sort of prisoner.'

'Cool!' exclaimed Darren. 'A jailbreak! Hold tight!'

Jorj looked around the ruined room for something to hold on to, as nanobot walls shot up around him. He, the speakers and the camera were encased in a transparent sphere. 'Wha–' started Jorj, as he plummeted downwards and everything turned black.

Several hours later, Olivia awoke to find that her cell had stopped moving. She stood quickly and wondered how to brush the dirt from her clothes without cross-contaminating her hand. She settled for shaking herself like a dog, adding fresh impetus to her shudders by glancing now and then at Ruck's sleeping form.

Her ablution solution completed, Olivia turned her attention to the walls, tapping them with a booted foot. 'Hello?' she called. 'Darren? Can somebody keep me in the loop?' There was no reply. Olivia checked her lifePod but there was no signal. She couldn't even find out the time, although she correctly estimated that it was early on Tuesday morning.

As he lay sprawled on the floor, Ruck incorrectly estimated that it was time Olivia apologised to him. He rolled over, turning his back on his erstwhile girlfriend.

'We've stopped moving,' said Olivia.

Ruck rolled back indignantly. 'I know that,' he said. 'Just how stupid do you think I am?'

Olivia resisted the urge to answer. 'Don't be counterproductive,' she said. 'Whatever our differences, we need to take a more proactive attitude, or we'll never achieve closure.'

'What are you talking about? And why bother asking me,' said Ruck, 'if all my ideas are so idiotic?'

'Because you're the smee,' Olivia said.

'The what?' Ruck erupted.

'The Subject Matter Expert,' said Olivia patiently. 'You know more about Darren than anyone else. We need to fully examine the situation, really drill down to a granular level.'

Ruck tried to ignore this incomprehensible request. 'There's one thing I don't understand,' he said slowly.

'Good,' encouraged Olivia, 'what?'

'If I'm so dumb, and you were only pretending to be interested in me...'

'Yes?' Olivia sighed.

'What about the other night at my house? When we, when we, ah..?'

'Did we?' asked Olivia sharply.

'I don't know.'

'I don't know either.' She stared at him, weighing up her options. 'Okay,' she said decisively, 'if it's going to increase your focus, I'll admit it. I gave you Prohypnall. I was going to inter-rogate you under hypnosis.' She tensed, waiting for Ruck's angry response.

Ruck laughed. 'You drugged me?' he chuckled.

'Yes,' said Olivia, frowning. 'Why are you laughing?'

'Because I drugged you. I was going to hypnotise you so you'd support me at The Board. I put Prohypnall in your drink.' Ruck tensed, knowing how little Olivia would appreciate him tampering with her water.

Olivia grinned. 'So I said you were feeling sleepy…'

'And I said you were feeling sleepy…'

'And we both fell asleep.'

'And we didn't have sex!'

'Brilliant!' exclaimed Olivia.

'Fantastic,' said Ruck, and they smiled warmly at each other for the first time.

Sometime after midday their cell began to move once more. Ruck and Olivia were pressed flat against the floor, and they struggled to breathe as the room shot upwards. The movement stopped as suddenly as it had begun. The nanobot walls blocking the ends of the corridor dissolved and flowed away, and cautiously Ruck and Olivia left their cell side by side.

They found themselves in a vast underground cavern, the size of St Paul's O'Connels in central London. The floor, walls and ceiling were made of a grimy black substance. Coal, thought Ruck, realising that they were in a mine. Two tunnels in the distance led to parts unknown, while a third shaft provided access to the surface, judging by the thin trickle of sunlight it deposited. Lava lamps and red ceiling lights provided additional illumina-tion, revealing some rather unusual decorations. Black was a common theme. There was a black banner with a skull and cross-bones on it, ragged strips of black material hung from the ceiling beside massive posters of rock stars dressed in black leather. A few pictures of naked orange terrorists and psychopaths provided light relief. There were cans of lager and bottles of whiskey strewn about the place, and screens hanging from the ceiling showed rock videos or horror films (it was hard to tell which). Crude graffiti was etched everywhere: The Dogs, Screw Everything and Up Yours Grandad. Scattered amongst the mess were computers and other bits of equipment pilfered from Ruck's labs. In the centre of it all was Darren, his dune buggy replaced by a stage, two metres high. Standing on the stage was a pedestal made of writhing nanobot snakes and naked women, on top of which was Darren's jar. 'Pretty cool, huh?' he said.

Ruck shook his head. 'I don't know how you can live like this,' he said.

'I knew you wouldn't understand,' Darren whined.

'I brought you up better than this.'

'I don't care what you think!' A drift of dust formed into a giant hand, which flexed its fingers menacingly.

Ruck turned to Olivia. 'I'm sorry,' he apologised. 'I don't know where he gets it from.'

Olivia rolled her eyes and turned to face the jar. 'I think your room is very nice, Darren,' she said in a lilting, patronising tone.

The huge hand came to rest on the floor. 'It's not a room. It's a lair.'

'And it's a very nice one.'

'It's not nice,' said Darren. 'It's cool and grimy and underground.'

'We can see that,' said Ruck sarcastically.

'Oh god, don't you know anything? Not "underground" as in under the ground, stupid, "underground" as in cool and grimy. You are so thick, Dad, you're really—'

'Hot and clean?'

The giant hand formed a fist.

'Why is your lair under the ground Darren?' asked Olivia quickly.

'Wouldn't you like to know?'

'I know,' said Ruck. 'It's a coal mine, isn't it? Darren needs carbon to make more nanobots. He can make them out of anything, but carbon lasts longest. And the coal in this mine is a huge supply.'

Darren simulated the sound of a slow handclap. 'You're not totally stupid, then.'

'I made you,' bristled Ruck.

'Shut up. Come and stand next to me. Leave your girlfriend there.'

'I'm not his girlfriend.'

'You shut up as well. Come and stand on the other side.'

Reluctantly they crossed the cavern and flanked Darren's stage. The ground trembled beneath their feet and two vast columns sprouted from the floor, carrying them up into the air. The pillars rose until they were fifteen metres high. More tiny machines formed transparent tubes around the tops of the columns, leaving the human occupants staring out like fish in bowls.

'There,' taunted Darren, 'see how you like living in a jar.'

'I don't like it,' said Ruck matter-of-factly.

'And neither do I,' said Darren. He thumped his massive fist, and the whole cavern shook. 'Just shut up,' he warned. 'I've got a friend coming round, and I don't want you embarrassing me.'

'What friend?' asked Ruck scornfully.

'I've got friends,' crowed Darren. 'You don't know everything about me. His name's Jorj, and he's on his way already actually, so there.'

'Can I ask you a question?' asked Olivia, who was quite enjoying being sealed in a jar.

'Do what you like,' said Darren.

'What are you going to do with all your little robots?'

'Oh, nothing much,' laughed Darren. 'Just...........' He overdid the dramatic pause. '................take over the world!' He tried out an evil laugh.

'I was afraid this might happen,' said Ruck, calling across to the other pillar.

'Why?' Olivia shouted back.

'That's my boy,' said Ruck with a shrug.

Olivia closed her eyes and furrowed her brow. 'When do you intend to action this proposal?' she asked.

'Very soon,' said Darren. 'I'll just make a quick phone call, then it's smashing time. Dad's girlfriend, you must have Rob James's number?'

Abi awoke at nine a.m. New York time and leapt out of bed. She roamed the apartment, shaking her head at the ostentatious luxury, before picking at a hearty breakfast. She felt energised, powerful, and she couldn't keep still. As she paced and fidgeted she knocked over a glass, which smashed on the floor. Abi made a big show of disposing of the fragments, glad of something to distract her thoughts. Next she turned her attention to the wardrobot, selecting the least businesslike garments she could find. She had just finished strategically ripping her jeans when Lee the intern arrived. He was not impressed by her appearance. 'You do know you're going to meet Rob James?' he asked.

'He's going to meet me,' corrected Abi, spreading her arms wide. 'And here I am.'

Rob James's office took up an entire wing at the base of the massive skyscraper. Lee led Abi through a multitude of metal, firearms and explosives detectors before they eventually reached a pair of lustrous wooden doors. Lee took a deep breath, raised a fist to knock, and Abi beat him to it, rat-a-tatting out a cheerful rhythm. 'Come in,' called a voice. Abi flung open the doors.

Rob James's office was big, that was the first thing Abi noticed. It was also the second and third things, that's how big it was. You could have fitted Abi's entire apartment into it several times. It was decorated in an old fashioned style; dark wooden book cases ran along one wall, an elaborate series of French windows with views of rolling fields made up another, there was plush, plum coloured carpet underfoot and an ornate ceiling overhead. The book cases were empty apart from three discs, which contained every book ever written: one disc for fiction, one for non- fiction and one for chick-lit novels with titles featuring the words shopping, shoes or chocolate. In the far corner was a desk that could quite happily have doubled as a five-aside football pitch, apart from the clusters of screens, in-trays, out-trays, family photos and the risk of falling off the edge.

A man emerged from behind the desk, advancing to greet his guest. 'Thank you Lee,' he called. Lee sagged, disappointed, and walked away. Sweating slightly, Abi approached Rob James.

He was shorter than she had expected, in his late forties, wearing an open-necked shirt tucked into beige trousers. His hair was dark and thick, the cause of constant transplant speculation. His features were large; a prominent nose and a wide mouth competed for room on his long face. He was not attractive, but he had learnt to do the best with what he had, helped by a charming smile. The small lack of symmetry in his face and the hint of unevenness in his teeth gave him a trustworthy air and made people relax in his presence. Abi was surprised; she hadn't been prepared for quite how lifelike the robot would look.

James was scrutinising Abi just as thoroughly. As they met in the middle of the room, he stuck out a hand in greeting. Abi took it cautiously, half expecting an electric shock or an unbreakable grip. James's hand exerted just the right amount of pressure, neither the feeble grip of a loser nor the macho squeeze of a man with something to prove. Abi's flesh crawled at her enemy's touch.

'Miss Odiali, I am very pleased to meet you,' James said. His accent was hard to place; American certainly, but not broad enough to tie down to any particular state or city.

'Yeah,' said Abi inarticulately.

James tried to smooth over his guest's discomfort. 'Shall we sit down?' he smiled, guiding her towards a pair of leather chairs beside a fireplace. One of the seats was already occupied by a stack of money, which James pushed onto the floor with a sheepish grin. As Abi carefully lowered herself into the chair, she couldn't help noticing that some of the cash had fallen in the fire, but James didn't seem to mind.

'You'll have to forgive me if I seem a little tired,' he said. 'Evolution Day only finished a few hours ago, and I've just got back from Samoa.'

'Right,' said Abi.

'I thought that's where samosas come from, but it seems I was wrong.'

'Oh.'

'It's a shame, I was looking forward to some sort of vegetable samosa based celebration.'

'I see.'

James smiled. 'I guess you're not in the mood for small talk.' He laughed inclusively, then stared into Abi's eyes. 'I'll come straight to the point Miss Odiali... or may I call you Abi?' he asked.

Abi shrugged.

'Abi, I would like to thank you, with the utmost sincerity, for saving my life in London.'

Abi looked at the floor. 'That's okay,' she mumbled.

James looked at her kindly. 'Abi, I'll be honest with you. That's not the only reason I brought you here today.'

Abi didn't dare look up in case the machine identified the hatred written on her face.

'Abi,' James continued, 'the Native Americans believed that when you save someone's life, your spirit becomes linked to theirs forever and you're essentially the same person.' James waited for Abi to fill the pause.

'Really?' she said, wishing the robot would get on with it.

'Probably,' James shrugged. 'They believed a whole load of crazy crap.' He paused again for a laugh or a smile, but none came. Instead an artificial female voice issued from hidden speakers. 'Sorry to disturb you, Mr James,' it purred, 'but there is an urgent call for you.'

'I'm busy,' snapped James. 'Take a message.'

'This call's priority level has been estimated at–'

'Thank you, computer,' said James firmly. He smiled apologetically. 'You just can't program the staff,' he said. 'The point I was trying to make is this: I want you to trust me, and I have to be able to trust you. Because I know what really happened in London.'

Abi's muscles tensed.

'I need to explain some–'

Abi sprang at him. Her knees struck James in the chest and his chair tipped over backwards. They tumbled to the floor. Doors opened at either end of the room and armed men burst in, shouting. James was winded, no match for Abi, who quickly held him in a headlock. She produced a shard of glass from her pocket and held it to James's throat. 'Don't come any closer!' she shouted.

'Do as she says,' wheezed James, and the approaching security guards stopped.

'Put your guns down!'

James nodded very, very carefully, and the men did as they were told.

Abi was panting, suddenly drenched in sweat. She tried to stop her knife hand shaking. 'This is it,' she said to herself.

James forced himself to breathe steadily. 'What?' he asked.

'I'm going to see your real face,' laughed Abi. 'Your circuits and wires.'

'Abi,' said James urgently, 'I know you believe I'm a robot, and I need to explain why you think that, before you do something we'll both regret.'

'I won't regret it,' said Abi dismissively.

'Just give me three minutes,' begged James.

Abi could feel the robot shaking. Now was hardly the time for second thoughts, but she was shocked at how warm and soft the machine felt. 'Go on,' she said.

James and the watching security guards relaxed ever so slightly.

'I know all the rumours about me being a robot,' said James, 'because I started those rumours.'

'I don't believe you,' said Abi, tightening her grip.

'I know you like conspiracy theories,' continued James quickly, 'so try this one for size. Ninety-five per cent of all conspiracy theories are made up by the government. I know that sounds like the biggest paranoid fantasy of them all, but it's true. I'm a robot. We faked the Mars landings. Okay Cola killed Santa. All made up by Softcom, or previous ruling bodies.'

Abi shook her head. 'Why would you do that?'

'To distract people from the five per cent of conspiracy theories that are actually true. So the suspicious people waste their time looking for the lizard men that rule the world instead of investigating more important stuff.' James sensed that he was getting through, and he slowed his sales pitch to a more natural tempo. 'And the fake theories discredit the real ones. If someone says Softcom is monitoring Shareholders' lifePods, the public just lumps him in with those who think TV screens can read people's minds. He's written off as a crank. It's very successful.'

Abi could feel a vein throbbing in James's neck. 'Prove it,' she demanded.

'I can,' said James, 'but I need to talk to my computer. Is that alright?'

'No tricks,' said Abi. 'I can cut this face off very quickly.'

'Understood,' said James. 'Computer,' he continued, 'this is Rob James. Activate voice control.'

The soothing female voice returned. 'Please state your password.'

James blushed. 'Password,' he muttered, shamefaced. The security guards whispered to each other and smiled.

'Accepted.'

'Computer, open the file on Softcom agent Marcel Patric.' A life-size hologram of Marcel appeared in the middle of the room, surrounded by various text and symbols. Abi gasped. 'Computer,' continued James, 'play Marcel Patric's safety disc.'

The hologram of Marcel started to speak. 'But I do not understand why you should want this, if I am to be operating under the duvet,' he said.

An irritated female voice could be heard from off camera. 'Undercover,' she corrected.

'Trust me,' said Marcel with a twinkle in his eye, 'I know where I will be operating.'

'Can we get on with this?' the unseen woman said tetchily. 'This could save your life someday. If O'Connels get hold of you and charge you with inciting…'

'Mademoiselle,' interrupted Marcel, 'I am very careful who gets hold of me. And I am exciting, not inciting.'

'Just read what's on the screen,' snapped the woman.

'Ah, very well.' The image of Marcel looked into the camera.

'I, Marcel Patric, am working for Softcom to spread rumours and conspiracy theories about Rob James. I work freelance on my own and also senior Softcom staff will contact me to hush up trouble.' A smile oozed across his face. 'I am the first choice for dealing with gullible young ladies.'

'That's not on the screen,' complained the woman.

'Just planting a useful rumour of my own,' said Marcel, waggling his eyebrows. 'All my actions are sponsored by Softcom,' he concluded. He blew a kiss towards the lens. 'That was for your own personal use,' he smarmed, facing off camera once more.

'Thanks,' the voice said, 'but if I want to throw up the thought of you will be enough. Next!'

The hologram froze. Abi continued to stare at it, horrified. 'You bastard,' she breathed.

'He was only doing his job,' said Rob James.

'I was talking to you,' said Abi.

'Oh. Well I'm only doing my job too,' James replied. 'I'm sorry that you got caught up in this, Abi, entrapment was never our intention. But now I need your help. Marcel Patric is missing, and I need to find out why he put you in this position. So if you'll let me go…'

'No,' said Abi quietly. 'Maybe you're not a robot,' she whispered. Across the room the security guards struggled to hear. 'That makes it worse. You killed thousands of people. You're selfish, greedy—'

'No, Abi,' said James, his heart racing. 'You're a Shareholder, I've always acted in your best interest.'

'Tell that to my father.'

'…I don't—'

'You killed him.'

A security guard reached slowly for the gun at his feet.

'Don't move,' snarled Abi, moving the shard of glass closer to James's throat.

'I've never met your father,' babbled James. 'You're holding me responsible for things I have no control over. I acted in good faith…'

'You killed my father,' said Abi, tears streaming down her face.

'I have children myself,' said James. 'Computer, show Bob and Josie.' Holographic images of two children hung in the air.

Abi shook her head. She drew her blade across James's throat, grazing the skin. Her eyes followed a tiny speck of blood as it trickled down the glass. As it reached her finger she dropped the weapon and released her hold on James's neck. She stepped to one side and watched as the guards snatched up their guns and shot her.

The nanobot bubble sped along a deserted, overgrown motorway, leaving a small trench in its wake as it literally ate up the road. Jorj stared out at the passing greenery. 'So we're outside the city,' he said numbly.

'Yeah, I've told you,' answered Darren.

'What if I want to go back in?' Jorj asked.

'You wanted to escape,' reminded Darren. 'Anyway, I'll look after you. We're mates, mate.'

'Yeah,' said Jorj, brightening a little. Although Darren hadn't explained exactly who he was, Jorj thought he had managed to fill in the blanks. Darren was a new kind of hacker, he decided. Instead of attacking Softcom in cyberspace, he was attacking them physically, using the nanobots to breach SSI strongholds. From their conversation Jorj had deduced that Darren was in his early teens, which made him a socially awkward whiz kid, a classic hacker type. Jorj sympathised with the child. He too spent much of his time immersed in technology, finding it easier to communicate through chat worlds and messageboards than in real life.

'Do you like computer games, Darren?' he asked.

'Love 'em,' Darren replied.

'Me too, mate,' smiled Jorj.

Through the miracle of multitasking, Darren was able to converse with Jorj and place a phone call to Rob James at the same time. It was a testament to Ruck's skills as a computer engineer that Darren was able to perform these operations simultaneously, without one affecting the other. Unfortunately, the actual content of the conversations was an indictment of Ruck's skills as a parent.

'Oi, Robbie James, where the hell are you?' Darren asked. 'Wh-y are we waiting,' he sang, this conversation being routed across the Atlantic and also through speakers in the brain's underground base. Many miles away, his friendly chat with Jorj was continuing unaffected. Meanwhile, his whiney 'Wh-y are we waiting?' echoed around the cave.

Ruck fidgeted nervously. 'Stop it, Darren, he might come through any minute.' This wasn't how the Professor had envisaged his creation's unveiling.

Darren increased the volume and changed styles, blending a rap with attempts to sing a guitar solo. 'Why are we waiting my homie? Der ner ner-ner ner ner! Yo! Yo! Ain't got no time to wait, bitch!'

Ruck groaned.

The screens hanging from the ceiling turned on, showing Rob James's face. He looked rather flustered, and had a fresh plaster on his Adam's apple. 'Good day,' he said.

'Hold on, I haven't finished,' snapped Darren. 'Der ner ner-ner ner ner, shit!'

Ruck held his head in his hands.

James maintained a poker face, waiting for a few seconds to ensure that Darren had stopped. 'I'm sorry I kept you,' he said finally. 'Are you receiving my image? I don't seem to have any pictures from you.'

Darren tutted. 'That's because I'm not sending any, you moron.'

Ruck's face crumbled dismally.

James turned his head and spoke to someone off camera, but his words could still be heard in the cave. 'Why am I taking this call?' he asked. The response was not picked up. '...Linked with Wembley?' James asked. '...So Parka and Odiali both visited this lab? Who is Ruck, anyway?'

Ruck's fists beat the floor of his bowl.

'The lab collapsed when? Why am I only hearing this now?' As he listened to the answer, James looked a little embarrassed. 'Yeah, I did get a message, I think I may have deleted it by mistake.' He turned back to the camera. 'I'm sorry about that. I don't think we've been introduced, my name is Rob James.'

'I know that,' said Darren sarcastically. 'Rob James, prepare to meet thy doom!' he continued, in what he thought was a dramatic, portentous voice.

Ruck clamped his hands over his ears, unable to take any more. On the other pillar, Olivia glanced at her lifePod and realised that it had picked up a signal from Darren's communications channel. She hastily composed a message.

'I am your destiny!' continued Darren. 'Your, oh, you know, what's it called? When bad things happen to you?'

'I see,' said James, unmoved. 'Sorry, I didn't catch the name?'

'Darren.'

'And what can I do for you today, Darren?'

'Naff all.'

James looked off camera again. 'Well, what—'

'Worry about yourself, not me.'

'Why should I be worried, Darren?'

Near the cavern entrance, a vast mound of nanobots started to move. They flowed upwards towards the surface, like water on a rewinding film. The two flying cameras that had previously belonged to the HumAnts ascended with the tiny machines, and Darren began to transmit the pictures. 'I'll show you why you should be worried,' he boomed.

And James was worried.

For a moment the screen showed nothing but blackness. Then a tiny speck of blue appeared, growing quickly as the camera shot out of the mineshaft. Sky filled the screen as the point of view rose higher, then it pitched forward vertiginously. A Non community lay spread out below. Two hundred years previously it had been a prosperous town, where life revolved around the mine as life on Earth revolves around the sun. When the mine closed the town began its inevitable slide towards the third world. Life Itself™ shares had not been advertised here.

The camera swooped low over the settlement. As with all Non communities, the population had fallen dramatically since the Takeover. The buildings skirting the town were derelict and crumbling, destroyed during the lawlessness that followed the separation of the haves from the have nots. The streets nearer the centre were still inhabited, the houses patched and repaired with materials salvaged from their fallen brethren.

In the town square, market day was coming to an end. Produce grown in the surrounding fields had been traded for livestock, knitted clothing or plastic status symbols fished from local land-fill sites. The camera picked out one man proudly wearing crisp packets on his hands.

Dominating the town square was the O'Connels building, its new, prefabricated walls looking out of place among the surrounding bricks and stone. O'Connels did not maintain law and order here; the Non's legal system was their own affair. O'Connels was there to fit basic, traceable lifePods and to sell food. Not satisfied with the huge gap between rich and poor, the corporations still sucked money from the Nons in return for O'Subsistence Burgers or, for those rich beyond the dreams of having rice, expired Okay Cola. The O'Connels building was staffed by Nons, who were paid in food.

Rob James watched as the camera flew through the streets, passing over groups of young, thin people. He grew impatient; he was one of the few Shareholders who knew what it was really like outside the cities; thus far the display had been a complete waste of time. The camera returned to the mine and hovered above the entrance, focusing on the shadows within.

At first James thought it was a trick of the light. The shadows seemed to be spilling out of the mine and into the afternoon sunshine. But as the flow intensified it became obvious that something was leaving the shaft, a stream at first, and then a torrent. It was like a black river, a liquid more glutinous than water, and capable of flowing uphill. A hollow dip beside the mine shaft was quickly filled and the resultant pool rose up, squashing itself into a ball. This was no liquid. This was nothing James had ever seen before. The ball rolled towards some ruined buildings and swallowed them whole. The sphere of nanobots left nothing in its wake, no evidence that the buildings had ever existed. Even the grass was stripped from the earth. The ball moved on, growing with every revolution, and fresh bots continued to flow from the mine. Everything in their path was instantly devoured, creating more tiny machines. Where once there was a shack, now there was an empty space. Where once there was a ruined crane, now there was nothing. Where once there was, now there wasn't.

The camera followed the ball as it smashed into the outskirts of the town, knocking down buildings like skittles. The sphere flattened and fattened as it consumed the wreckage. A giant hammer grew from the middle of the blob, its head the size of a tennis court. Screams could be heard from the town centre as the hammer smashed everything within its radius.

The picture cut back to the pit. A ~illion nanobots had formed an immense black cannon, pointing towards the town. The base of the barrel thickened, then the bulge shot upwards as the gun vomited a bullet bigger than a bus. As the projectile crashed down in the suburbs, the gun changed aim and fired again, and again. Soon the town was encircled by twenty independent blobs of bots, all smashing and swelling, and all moving towards the centre.

Now James saw terrified people stampeding towards the market square, as the nanobots herded the survivors together. Several men tried to escape down a side street, but their screams dissuaded others from following. Some went inside buildings, presumably because they lacked paper bags to put over their heads. The majority stood still or ran helplessly to and fro, not knowing what to do. There was a pause, filled with the sounds of grinding, crushing and dying, getting closer.

A black wave of nanobots crashed down the town's main street, brushing aside buildings as it went. It stopped just short of the crowded square, freezing into a wall. For a second there was a sigh of relief, then letters emerged, embossed on the wall's surface: "Your all going to die!!!!!"

People threw bricks and stones at the bots, which was like trying to stop a stampeding elephant with a barrage of mushy peas. The wall grew a dozen mouths that surged forward, swallowing their victims whole. Tentacles flailed out, grabbing people and pulling them inside the black mass. Balls of bots were fired, punching holes through arms, chests and heads. Within minutes, there was no one left.

Rob James watched it all in horrifying close-up. Just when he could take no more, the camera flew upwards, providing an aerial view of the town. A massive fist was punching buildings into dust. An enormous guitar was smashing earthwards again and again. A humanoid figure twenty metres tall was break dancing, with the emphasis on "break". Smaller clumps of bots pounced on the few remaining people. The town was completely destroyed, covered by the rising tide of tiny machines.

Jorj was enjoying himself for the first time in ages, chatting with his new friend Darren. They had a lot in common, and they bantered easily about technology and computer games. Darren was eager to please, excited by the prospect of friendship. This gave Jorj an unfamiliar buzz of superiority; for once he had met someone less experienced and more socially inept than himself. Deep down he knew that he was on the run, fleeing a grisly murder scene, but Jorj trusted his friend to look after him.

The bubble travelled through the open countryside, giving Jorj a sense of freedom he had never felt in the city. And it was interesting to see how the other 99.7 per cent lived. He had passed primitive villages, men riding horses and women washing clothes in a river. It was a far cry from the Handforths and the landfill site, and Jorj was pleased to see that not all Nons had it so bad. He skirted a heavily fortified farm, where crops were planted for

Shareholders, and minefields were sown for Nons. 'Where are we going?' Jorj asked at last.

'I'm taking you to my base,' said Darren. 'But I want to show you something first. We're nearly there.'

They crested a hilltop just as the nanobot flood engulfed the town below. Jorj's mouth gaped as he watched the hammers and guitars pulverising the buildings. 'Bang, crash,' chuckled Darren. He opened the roof of the bubble so Jorj could hear the screams.

'Are there… people down there?' Jorj asked weakly.

'Not for much longer.'

Jorj could see them now, tiny forms running for their lives and falling some way short of the target. Within seconds each person was nothing more than a little red smear. Jorj felt sick. He closed his eyes, but could still hear the sounds of destruction, terror and death.

'So,' asked Darren cheerfully, 'what's your favourite football team?'

(Jorj and Rob James weren't the only ones watching the destruction. Down in the depths of Darren's mine, away from the main chamber, the HumAnt farm nestled amongst other salvaged lab equipment. Darren had appropriated the insects' cameras to record his triumph, just as he had used them to discover the nanotechnology in the first place. In return the footage was being relayed into the colony, providing the HumAnts with their first television for two days. It had been worth the wait. The graphic, high tech slaughter was must-see-TV. The orgy of violence and suffering washed over the mutated insects, their Ruck and Olivia banners forgotten on the floor. They had a new hero now. How could they not worship Darren, who was as powerful as a god and who was bringing them the finest TV they had ever seen?)

Abi opened her eyes. Something was wrong. She sat up and rubbed her head groggily. What was the problem? She peered through the film fogging her eyes and realised that she was back in the guest apartment. That wasn't right. Something about... Oh yes. She was supposed to be dead.

She stood up shakily, her wobbly legs almost pitching her back onto the bed. She kicked the floor. It was insulting. She had been in Rob James's office, holding his life by a thread, and she hadn't deserved fatal force? Tranquiliser darts; did they think she was a little girl?

She stamped her way into the kitchen, looking for something to drink. As she opened cupboard after cupboard she realised with a wry smile that all the glasses had been removed. 'I'll kill you with my bare hands,' she muttered, before sticking her head under the tap.

There was a knock at the door. Abi ran to the lounge, her hair dripping. She crouched near the front door. 'Who's there?' she asked

'Rob James,' said a voice from outside.

'Want some more, do you?' taunted Abi.

'Can I come in?' James asked.

'Like I could stop you,' said Abi, backing away from the door.

Rob James entered, alone. He looked very tired. 'Do you mind if I sit down?' he said, waving at a chair.

'It's your planet,' said Abi, keeping her distance.

James flopped into the seat. 'I need your help Abi,' he said, looking her in the eye.

Abi laughed shortly and shook her head. 'I hate you, remember? That's what the broken glass was all about?'

James looked at her steadily. 'Why do you hate me, Abi?' he asked.

Abi gave another sarcastic laugh. 'It's got something to do with you taking over the world,' she said. 'Evil dictators don't do it for me.'

James sighed. 'You know it's not really possible for one man to rule the world,' he said. 'These days I'm a figurehead, that's all. I work on small projects that interest me,' he continued, slipping easily into a familiar patter. 'Recently I've been looking at education, trying to make a positive difference to young people.'

Abi rolled her eyes.

'Okay,' said James, raising his voice for the first time, 'do you know what I was supposed to be doing today?'

Abi looked at the ground. '...Oppressing something?'

'Testing a new range of pasta sauces,' said James. 'Not exactly the bombing of Dresden is it?'

Abi looked up defiantly. 'You killed my father,' she said.

James didn't flinch. 'Now we're getting somewhere,' he said. 'Do you want to sit down?'

Abi shook her head.

'Okay, but this might be difficult. Since you mentioned your father in my office, we've been doing some research, and we've found some footage.' He tapped at his lifePod and a nearby screen came to life. 'It's from a security camera, so the quality isn't—'

'Shut up.' Abi dropped to her knees and stared at the screen.

The image was grainy, low resolution. There was no sound. Abi saw the interior of a supermarket, well stocked with food but empty of people. There was a caption displaying the time and date. August

17th 2050, the day of the Takeover. The picture cut to show a different part of the shop, the front window visible behind a row of checkouts. A heaving group of people could be seen outside the store. The glass shattered as a metal bar smashed silently into the shop. Behind the gaping frame, holding the other end of the bar, was a man. He was in his thirties, dreadlocked with broad shoulders.

'That's him,' breathed Abi, tears streaming down her face.

The man dropped his makeshift weapon and climbed through the broken window, the cheap camera recording the movement as a series of silent tableaux. Abi's father ignored the tills and moved out of shot. Behind him, dozens of people entered the shop.

The footage cut to another part of the store, an aisle suddenly jammed with pushing, desperate people. Abi's father was briefly visible, then quickly lost in the crowd. The shelves were cleared within seconds. A bag was snatched and the crowd turned in on itself, fighting, grabbing and struggling. Abi's father appeared near the edge of one frame, a large man tugging at his coat pocket. In the next shot he had pulled away, with one foot on an empty shelf. The camera caught another image and this time he was climbing higher, his back to the crowd. Next he had almost reached the top, his head wedged over the uppermost shelf, but a hand was pulling him down. He clung onto the shelves, but they were tilting. The crowd below was moving away. And now the shelves were toppling over, and Abi's father was falling with them. James turned off the screen.

'His neck was broken,' said Abi quietly.

James nodded and opened his mouth to speak.

'No,' Abi said. She stood abruptly and left the room.

When Abi returned her eyes were dry and she wore an air of determined composure. 'Say what you've got to say,' she said, looming over James.

'Abi, I didn't kill your father,' he said calmly. 'It was an accident.'

'It was your fault,' shouted Abi, her composure lost already. 'Do you think he would have been there if you hadn't turned the power off? Do you think he always broke into supermarkets?'

'No, of course not.'

'I know you weren't there. It's still your fault.'

James paused for a moment. 'Who was your father stealing the food for?' he asked.

Abi looked at him in horror. 'No,' she said, recoiling. 'That's not fair.'

'Who was the food for?'

Abi turned her back on him and walked towards the door. 'Me,' she said. 'He was there because of me.'

'Abi, I–'

'But it's not my fault,' she snarled, whirling round to face him once more. 'Don't you dare say it's my fault,' she warned, her arm raised.

'It's not your fault,' soothed James. 'I would never say that, and you must never think it.' He paused again. 'Abi, did you ever wonder why I took over the world?'

She shrugged angrily.

'You're too young to remember, but the world wasn't exactly doing well before I came along. There was no cooperation, no centralised planning. No one was taking the long view because politicians had to be popular in the short term to get re-elected. There were wars, nations were fighting over resources, pushing and shoving, trying to get what they could for themselves.' His eyes flicked to the blank TV screen.

'Oh no,' sneered Abi. 'So the world was like that supermarket, and you made it all better? How stupid do you think I am?'

'I don't think you're stupid,' explained James calmly. 'I'm just telling you what happened. I had to provide for my family, just like your father did. Only my family was a bit bigger: every single Softcom shareholder. The way things were going, maybe the planet wouldn't have lasted much longer. I had a chance to safeguard my family's future, and I took it. I'm not going to apologise for that.'

'What about my family?' demanded Abi.

'What happened to your father was a tragic accident,' said James. 'But you're also part of a much bigger family. You're a Shareholder, and rejecting that isn't going to help anyone.'

Abi had lost control of the argument, and she could feel it pulling her in directions she didn't like or understand. 'Why are we even having this conversation?' she said at last.

'Because you're part of my family,' said James simply. 'And because I need your help.'

'How can I help *you*?'

'It's complicated,' said James. 'I can show you, but I don't think I should. It's very… disturbing.'

'I want to see it,' said Abi, obeying one of the basic rules of film advertising.

James activated the screen again, and Abi watched Darren's attack on the town. 'That's enough,' she said, as the first few victims were devoured.

'I did warn you,' said James, stopping the clip.

'I'm not joining your film club,' said Abi hollowly.

'Let me join a few dots,' said James. 'What you just saw are nanobots, billions of microscopic machines. They came from a lab run by a man called Professor Ruck. We know you visited there on Thursday night, along with the gunman Jorj Parka. A different group of nanobots helped Parka escape early this morning.'

'Jorj escaped?' interrupted Abi.

'Yes. I thought you'd be pleased about that.'

Abi suddenly realised she hadn't given Jorj a single thought. And he had been right about Rob James, right to stop her shooting the acid gun. She hadn't exactly repaid the favour. 'Of course I'm pleased he escaped,' she said guiltily. 'Is he okay now?'

'We don't know,' said James. 'He's no longer wearing a lifePod.'

Abi frowned, her bottom lip down turned. She thought about Jorj, the pleasure he had taken in throwing the rancid garbage around on their way back into London. As she thought about their time together outside the city, she suddenly realised why she had lost the argument with James. 'What about the people in that clip?' she challenged.

'The Nons?' replied James, puzzled.

'I've been outside. I've seen what it's like,' Abi said tartly. 'Who's looking after the Nons?'

James gestured impatiently. 'They aren't my responsibility,' he said.

'But you own the whole planet,' Abi cried. 'Whose responsibility are they?' She pointed at the TV. 'In that supermarket most people got some food. If you'd been there, you would have taken it all.'

'I would have taken it for you, and all the other Shareholders,' reminded James.

'What about the Nons?'

'You can't please all the people all the time.'

'They are people, then?' demanded Abi. 'You're not treating them like people.'

James paused, trying to reduce the tension. 'Do you know what the number one complaint is amongst children?' he asked finally. 'Actually, if they've seen enough commercials it will be "I want it", but that's not the one. "It's not fair". You sound like a child.'

'I do not,' said Abi defensively.

'I can't blame you, because it's not a nice lesson to learn. But I'm afraid life's not fair.'

'For god's sake. You could make it fairer. You own the world!'

'You can't blame me for human nature, Abi,' said James quietly. 'Can you name one time in the whole of history when resources were evenly distributed? One time when men were equal? You can't. Even when we were cavemen, the strongest man would get the nicest, juiciest bits of mammoth for himself and his family.'

'But you were in the ideal position,' said Abi angrily. 'You could have changed all that. How about some self-sacrifice instead of selfishness?'

James looked at her steadily, the suggestion of a smile on his lips. 'We can talk about this later,' he said. 'The situation with the nanobots is my top priority. Can we just agree that Darren is a bigger monster than I am and move on?'

'Who's Darren?' asked Abi, marking their truce with a pout.

'Darren is who's controlling the nanobots. He came from Ruck's lab too, so I'm hoping maybe you saw him.'

'I might have heard him,' Abi admitted grudgingly. 'What else do you know about him?'

'We've received a transmission from a hostage inside the mine. Apparently Darren has the personality of a fifteen year old boy.'

'A fifteen year old boy?' scoffed Abi. 'There's no way a boy could do all that.'

'Look at his base,' said James, and the screen showed the images that Olivia had attached to her message. Abi looked at the posters of rock bands, terrorists and naked women, the bottles, graffiti and general mess. Her nose wrinkled. She could almost smell it. 'You've got to stop him,' she said.

'How? Conventional missiles won't work, there's too many bots. Biological and chemical weapons will have no effect. Ground forces are obviously no use. A nuclear strike might do it, but at what cost? Plus we'd never be able to keep that quiet.' James stared at Abi. 'We need a way of getting close to Darren.'

Abi shook her head. It was obvious what they should do, but she wasn't about to start working for Rob James. Then she considered the dying Nons, and Jorj, who had last been seen with Darren's bots. She owed Jorj, if no one else. Plus she could still hear what she had just said, about selfishness and sacrifice. 'I've got an idea,' she announced, raising her head proudly.

'Really?' asked James, his expression the epitome of surprise.

'I know something that can crush a fifteen year old boy like that.' Abi clicked her fingers. 'And he can't resist it.'

'What?' smiled James.

'A nineteen year old girl.' Abi nodded smugly to herself.

'Oh,' said James mildly, 'that is a good idea.' He stood up. 'Come on, we've got a lot to do.'

As Abi followed him through the front door, she had a feeling she had been led into a trap.

Ruck watched the screens in Darren's base, showing the nanobots advancing across the countryside. It was awe-inspiring. Such power, and it had all come from his labs. If only it had fallen into the right hands, he thought, those hands of course being the ones currently protruding from a pair of beige and lavender cuffs.

Olivia was not watching the screens. Early on in the display she had seen a grubby Non crying with terror, and she could tell that things had only got less hygienic from there. 'Darren,' she said eventually, 'we need to talk.'

'Sorry, Grandma,' chuckled Darren, 'but you ain't my type.'

'I am chairperson of The Board,' continued Olivia frostily. 'I can offer you many things. You say you want world domination, and there are many territories unneeded by our Shareholders that could be made available to you. Controlling the Non population is a challenge we could face together–'

'Boring,' warbled Darren.

'We can sell you practically anything you can think of…' Olivia offered.

'Der, I don't have any money.'

Olivia smiled. 'We can lend you money, Darren.'

The snakes supporting Darren's jar writhed angrily. 'What part of "Stuff yourself" don't you understand?'

Olivia hesitated. 'You haven't told me to, er…' The tendons in Olivia's neck tightened as she forced out the unpleasantly bodily phrase. '…stuff myself.'

'Stuff yourself!' shouted Darren gleefully.

Jorj's transparent sphere tumbled down the mineshaft and quickly melted away. Jorj was left standing in the centre of the cavern, a few metres from the stage on which Darren's jar stood. He was still dazed with shock after seeing Darren's army in action.

'Jorjman!' bellowed the brain. 'Welcome to my lair, dude. Cool, innit?'

'Yes,' said Jorj obediently. He tried to take in his new surroundings, but his brain kept replaying the Non massacre.

'What's the best bit?' Darren asked.

'All of it,' said Jorj. 'It's all brilliant, you're brilliant.'

'Aw, thanks mate. The posters..?'

'Brilliant.'

'The laser lamps?'

'Very brilliant.' Jorj was trying not to notice the two people trapped at the top of the pillars. He covered his groin, suddenly aware of his nudity.

'Don't worry about the fossils,' said Darren. 'They won't bother us. Any more questions?'

Jorj noticed the brain bubbling in its liquid. 'Er, what's that?' he asked nervously.

Darren hesitated. 'That's me, Jorjman.'

'Of course it is,' gabbled Jorj. 'Brilliant, totally brilliant and cool and amazing.'

'Will…girls like me?' asked Darren quietly.

'Of course,' lied Jorj. 'You'll be a girl magnet, obviously not trying to imply that you're some sort of machine, I mean they'll love you, girls will absolutely fall at your…they will really like you.'

'Wicked,' boomed Darren, accompanying himself with a burst of guitar. 'That's what I always thought anyway. So what do you want to do? Play some games?'

'I will do whatever you want me to,' said Jorj emphatically. A console appeared in front of him and he let Darren beat him at computer games until he fell asleep.

The next morning, Abi stood uncertainly in the early sunlight. Her trip across the Atlantic had been bone-achingly fast, and she was still a little disorientated. The rocket plane had dropped her at a small Non community on the edge of Darren's ever expanding nanobot sea. The Nons had fled several hours previously, abandoning their primitive, crudely built homes. Abi was on the outskirts of the village, standing on the roof of a lopsided wooden shack. She shivered.

She was not dressed in her normal style. Her micro skirt was more garnish than garment, and her other clothes revealed so much flesh that they might have been wearing her rather than the other way round. Long leather boots and gaudy make up completed the look. Abi felt stupid, defenceless and more naked than she actually was, which was only just possible. She longed for her screen dress, with its camouflage of scrolling slogans. Instead she was surrounded by messages of a different kind, painted on a forest of signs and banners: "I Luv Darren!", "Darren Rocks!!!", "My other boyfriend is an omnipotent teenager" and "Brains in jars do it with a screw on top!". Abi hoped the display wasn't too subtle for Darren.

Mist hung in the air, robbing the sun of most of its light and heat. Abi peered out at the deserted village. Front doors hung open and rags drooped limply from washing lines. The Nons had not wasted any time in clearing out. The silence was creepy, but infinitely preferable to the sound that replaced it.

It was a quiet, sighing, hissing, grinding noise, like tiny, miserable snakes rubbing each other up the wrong way. Abi turned from the village and looked out into the fog. A dark stain was spreading towards her across the grass. The blob undulated and rippled as it insinuated its way forwards, quickly reaching an outlying shed. The nanobots surrounded the building and tore it down, destroying it from the ground up. Abi's legs trembled. 'I love you, Darren!' she yelled unconvincingly. 'Darren rules!' A camera flew over her head, paused for a moment in mid air, then came back for a second look. It swooped around the rooftop, exhaustively mapping every square centimetre of Abi's flesh. She smiled weakly and waved a placard. The nanobots surrounded the shack, shifting menacingly like a boxer flexing his muscles. 'How about it, Darren?' Abi mumbled. 'You and me?' She leant forward and jiggled her behind.

A huge wave erupted from the nanobot sea. The building was completely engulfed, swallowed up and sucked down.

The liquid in Darren's jar bubbled with excitement. 'Oh man, this is so cool,' he said. 'Finally, someone realises how much I rock.'

Ruck looked down from atop his pillar. 'Now, ah, son, don't rush into anything you're not, ah, comfortable with,' he said, looking decidedly uncomfortable himself.

'Eurgh, shut up,' whined Darren. 'I don't need advice from you. I'll leave the old people sex to you and your girlfriend.'

'I'm not his girlfriend,' said Olivia automatically, her eyes locked to a screen showing Abi on top of the shack.

Jorj was also staring at the screen, aghast. He shuffled backwards, trying to get away from the image of the girl. 'What's she doing here?' he moaned. She'd already cost him his job, pointed guns at him, got him kidnapped, volunteered him for suicide missions, arrested him... Jorj twitched nervously. This time he was going to lose a limb at least, he could feel it.

On the screen Abi's shack was swamped by nanobots and she disappeared. Jorj felt a tiny swell of relief, a selfish feeling that triggered a tidal wave of guilt. 'Don't kill her,' he suggested meekly. 'She doesn't deserve that.' Darren didn't respond. 'Is she dead?' Jorj asked quietly. '…Is she dead?'

'Is she dead?' asked Rob James.

All around him uniformed men and women tapped at keyboards and peered at readouts that hung in mid air. The command room's main screen showed nothing but seething nanobots, barely distinguishable from the snow of empty static. Moments earlier Abi had been clearly visible, before the tiny machines enveloped her.

James stared impotently at the screens. 'Where's Miriam Herczeg?' he snapped. 'Get me someone from Peace Dove. We need to go to Plan B.'

'The girl's alive,' called a female operator. 'I'm getting faint signals from her lifePod.'

'And the device?' James asked.

'Still functioning.'

'Good.'

'She's moving,' announced another technician. 'Tracking the location now.'

On the main screen a bulge appeared on the surface of the bot soup, marking Abi's location. It travelled swiftly away from the village, towards Darren's mine.

'Jorjman,' said Darren, 'get over here.' The snakes on his plinth writhed urgently.

Jorj approached the brain, one hand clamped over his groin. 'Hello?' he said, 'er, mate, buddy.'

'Did you see her?' Darren asked conspiratorially. 'The one with the tits?'

'Oh yes,' said Jorj leadenly. 'I saw her.'

'Yeah, well I saw her first,' snarled Darren. 'Keep your hands off.'

'That won't be a problem,' Jorj promised.

'I know she was with you when she came to my lab…'

'Whose lab?' enquired Ruck, peering down from his pillar.

'Shut up!' exploded Darren. 'This is a private conversation. Jesus, what do I have to do to get some privacy around here?'

'You could release us,' Olivia suggested.

'You shut up as well,' snapped Darren. 'Anyway,' he continued in a whisper, 'she's mine now.'

'Okay,' confirmed Jorj. 'I think you're probably perfect for each other.'

'Brilliant,' said Darren. '…So, Jorjman, mate…. what do I do?'

Oh, god no, thought Jorj. 'You do know about the, er, birds and the bees don't you?' he asked.

Darren thought for a moment. 'No.'

Jorj shifted from foot to foot. 'Oh. Well, er, men and women are different, physically, in this sort of area.' He waggled the hand that covered his groin. 'And when they love each other very much, or if they just want to, they, er, try to patch up their differences…'

'You mean shagging?'

'Yes.'

'I know all about shagging,' said Darren derisively. 'I'm not stupid. What have birds and bees got to do with it?'

'I don't know really.'

'Jee-zus. I just need to know how I can get to shag her.'

Jorj scratched his head with his free hand. This was hardly his area of expertise either. 'Well, you should stop calling her "The one with the tits" for a start. She's called Abi. Learn her name, girls like that.'

'Abi,' sighed Darren dreamily. 'Don't you think that's the most beautiful name you've ever heard?'

'Hmm,' evaded Jorj. 'And then I guess you need to make a good first impression.'

'This is pure gold, Jorjman,' said Darren gratefully. 'So what do you think I should do? I could kill someone. Hey, I could kill you!' A drift of nanobots slowly slithered towards Jorj's naked orange feet.

'No, I don't think she'd like that,' Jorj said quickly, privately admitting that, given Abi's past form, Darren had probably hit the nail on the head. 'I'm her friend, remember? In fact,' he continued hopefully, 'if anything bad happened to me, that would be a real turn off for her.'

'Are you sure?'

'Positive.' Jorj thought for a moment. 'Be nice to Abi,' he said carefully. 'Treat her well. Show her your sensitive side.'

Darren's liquid bubbled. 'I don't think I've got a sensitive side. I could pretend to have one, would that be alright?'

'That's fine,' said Jorj. 'That's what all men do.' He stared at Darren's jar. 'Now when you say "shag", there could be a few problems. You're not exactly equipped for...'

The brain thrashed about angrily. 'I'm not an idiot. I just need to get ready, that's all.' He paused for a moment as he consulted one of his cameras. 'Oh god, oh god she'll be here in a minute, everyone shut up, I've got so much to do!'

Nanobots from all over the cave flowed towards their dithering master. These machines were more colourful than the coal dust destroying the outside world. There were green bots made of grass, red bots made of bricks and blue bots made of blue bricks. Darren's plinth swelled visibly.

Jorj wondered if Abi knew what she was letting herself in for. 'Remember,' he said seriously, 'no means no. And so does get off. And stop it.'

Darren's jar was now completely hidden by a writhing blur of multicoloured bots. 'Don't cramp my style, Jorjman,' he said. 'Get out of here.'

Telling himself he had done all he could, Jorj wobbled to the edge of the circle of light, and disappeared down a gloomy tunnel.

Abi was still standing on the roof of the shack, her banners crumpled and creased. A hard nanobot shell arched a few centimetres above her head, completely encasing the building and blocking out the sunlight. She lurched in the darkness as the shack pitched and rolled on the nanobot sea. She fell heavily against the new carapace, and was very relieved when the tiny machines didn't try to eat her.

Her ears popped as she fell down the mineshaft into Darren's base. After a surprisingly gentle landing the nanobot shell disappeared. Dazzled by the sudden influx of light, Abi grabbed an "I love Darren" placard with which to defend herself. She leapt forward as the roof buckled and splintered beneath her, landing heavily on the cave floor. Behind her the shack was crushed and devoured.

'There goes my deposit,' Abi muttered. She looked around. She was standing in a huge underground cavern, lit by red and green lights hanging from the ceiling several hundred metres above her head. The uneven floor stretched beyond the pool of illumination, and the entrances to two passageways were just visible in the distance. Behind was the wide, gaping shaft that led to the surface.

In the centre of the cavern Abi saw vast screens, banks of control panels and tangles of wires. Two thin columns stood fifteen metres high, each topped with a clear cylinder. Abi couldn't be sure, but it looked as if each tube contained a person. Less mistakable was the figure at the centre of it all.

Like everything else in the cave, it was huge. Five metres tall, it stood with its legs apart and its hands on its hips. Its trousers were tight, especially around the crotch, which bulged alarmingly. Abi forced her eyes away from the groin and upwards over the figure's torso. Muscles rippled under a flimsy shirt. Its neck looked more like a thigh. The face had the rugged good looks of a commercial rock star.

The figure waved his arms triumphantly above his head, flexing his massive biceps. There was a deafening blast of guitar that almost knocked Abi over. A conveyer belt formed beneath her, carrying her forward until she was standing at the figure's feet. A leer of naked lust spread across the enormous face. 'I like you,' mumbled Darren.

Abi smiled weakly and half heartedly waggled her "I love Darren" placard.

Darren looked at the girl cowering before him and licked his lips. 'Do you…' he started, then stopped abruptly. Inside his head cavity the brain wriggled. Relays flashed and processors whirred as he tried to think of a charming, witty, irresistible conclusion to the unfinished sentence. '…come here often?' he asked finally, hating himself.

Abi stared up at him, her eyes wide with fear. She tried a girlish giggle. 'Oh, you,' she trilled unconvincingly. She let her placard drop to the floor.

Darren felt a sudden rush of confidence. He was doing it. He was talking to a girl. 'Make yourself comfortable,' he boomed, waving an arm expansively.

Abi looked around with distaste. Boys' bedrooms were always pretty minging, and this place was no exception. 'How?' she asked cautiously, mindful of the two people trapped in their transparent tubes.

'Take a seat,' said Darren gallantly. He was really getting the hang of this now. 'Your legs must be tired from being so sexy,' he oozed.

Abi forced another dutiful titter and looked around for the chair. Nanobots flowed forwards and resolved themselves into a seat. Abi eyed it nervously.

'It's alright,' said the brain, 'it won't bite.'

'It'd better not,' Abi muttered. As she eased herself into the chair, she could have sworn the cushion was giving her buttocks a squeeze. 'Hey!' she exclaimed.

'What?' asked Darren, smirking to himself. Abi slapped the arm of the chair and the tiny machines released their grip. 'Can I take your coat?' Darren asked.

'I'm not wearing a coat,' Abi pointed out.

'Then can I take any of your other clothes?' Darren persisted hopefully. 'Bra, pants..?'

Abi hid her disgust with another giggle.

'That was smooth,' said Darren, running his fingers through his hair. 'You should watch this, Dad, you might learn something.'

Ruck pointed at a screen showing the rampaging nanobot army. 'Actually, I'm watching–'

'Shut up, Dad.'

Olivia stared thoughtfully at Abi, and remained silent.

'So can I take your bra or pants?' asked Darren.

'Maybe later,' said Abi. 'So, I was wondering if you'd seen someone called Jorj?' she asked hopefully.

'Don't worry, babe, he won't disturb us,' replied Darren.

'But is he here?' pressed Abi. 'What have you two been up to?'

'I don't want to talk about work,' said Darren nonchalantly. His head grew a bowler hat, which he plucked off and sent spinning through the air. A nanobot hat stand sprang up, catching the bowler on one of its hooks. 'This is our time,' Darren smarmed. 'Let's not talk shop.'

'So what do you want to do?'

'Shag.'

'Oh,' said Abi. Things were not going well.

Jorj walked quickly along the tunnel, looking for somewhere to hide. He crouched behind a large boulder, but even he couldn't sleep in that position. He moved on, and eventually the tunnel opened up into a small chamber. Jorj peered cautiously inside.

The room was full of scientific equipment: microscopes, chemicals and computers that had been salvaged from Ruck's lab. The HumAnt farm was perched on an uneven ledge, but Jorj didn't notice it. He was too busy staring at Ken.

The reprogrammed customer care machine was stamping around the small space, wielding a circular saw. The blade buzzed as it sliced through the air, then screamed as Ken plunged it into a wall. Jorj clutched his neck anxiously, turned around and ran away.

(The HumAnts were also taking an interest in their new surroundings. The TV was still showing Darren's nanobot army, but the destruction had lost its fascination. Perhaps the insects had become desensitised to the violence; certainly Darren's rampages had become less inventive. The nanobots no longer formed themselves into towering spires or amusing arses, and they were expanding at a slower, more workmanlike pace. The HumAnts wandered about their farm, inspecting walls cracked by their journey underground, and looking at Ken. Only one insect remained in front of the TV, still proudly holding a Ruck banner. She fiddled with the remote control, and to her delight she found a camera that was pointing at her hero. As she put some of her feet up on the sofa, several other HumAnts came to join her.)

'So you're sure this will work, Miriam?' asked James.

A small, hard faced woman with prematurely grey hair stared out from one of the monitor screens. 'Nothing is a hundred per cent, Rob,' she said. 'Due to the downturn in defence spending post-Takeover–'

'We own the planet, Miriam,' snapped Rob, unable to resist the pull of an old argument. 'Who were we defending ourselves against?'

'You tell me, Rob,' she replied innocently.

'Just tell me if this is going to work,' ordered James.

'As soon as the device comes into contact with the liquid in the brain's jar, it's bye-bye Darren. At least.'

'What do you mean?'

'You told us to make sure,' smiled Miriam. 'It's amazing how much explosive material you can fit into a space that small.'

'It's a suicide mission,' stated James. 'Why wasn't I told?'

'You own the whole planet,' mimicked Miriam. 'People die all the time. Do you really want to be told about every death?'

'Maybe someone should be.'

'I'm not sure who'd apply for that job. Goths, I suppose.'

'This is serious, Miriam.'

'Isn't everything? You're a big picture man,' Miriam soothed. 'You have to leave the details to other people, or nothing gets done.'

James stared at the screen, his own reflected face merging with that of the woman. 'What did you tell Abi?' he asked.

'That the device would cause an extremely localised explosion.'

'We lied to her.'

'No, Rob,' Miriam corrected. 'Everything is localised from a certain perspective. On a global scale, twenty square kilometres isn't that big.'

'So,' said Darren, 'let's do sex.'

Abi pretended to be shocked. 'You're a fast mover,' she stalled.

'Ten thousand terahertz,' boasted Darren.

'We should get to know each other first, though,' continued Abi quickly. 'I want to... find out what makes you tick. I want to see the real you,' she said, following a script suggested by Softcom.

Darren was unconvinced. 'I prefer the shagging idea,' he said stubbornly.

'How about a game of strip poker?' Abi asked with a flash of inspiration. Darren looked at her blankly. 'It's a card game. Whoever loses has to take off some of their clothes.'

Darren seemed a lot more receptive to this suggestion. 'And then I get to poke her?' he asked.

Abi faked yet another giggle. 'And if you lose,' she said, 'you show me what's going on inside that wonderful body of yours.'

'I've got a quicker idea,' Darren gabbled. 'Let's draw cards and the lowest loses.'

Abi shrugged. 'Okay, fine. Where are the cards?'

'All under control,' Darren grinned. A large screen displayed a green baize surface and a pack of virtual cards. 'I'll go first,' said Darren. 'Are aces high or low?'

Abi shrugged again. 'High,' she said.

The cards on the screen fanned out. One danced from the pack and flipped over. 'The ace of spades, the ace of spades!' cried Darren. 'Dah na na-na-na na na nah! Dah na na-na-na na na nah! Your turn, Abi. Just say "stop".'

'Stop,' said Abi resignedly. A card somersaulted from the pack.

'The minus seven of hearts,' cackled Darren, 'what a shame.'

'Grow up,' ordered Abi, her mask momentarily slipping. 'That's stupid.'

'The cards never lie,' Darren said. 'Strip, strip, strip, strip.'

'Alright,' Abi grumbled, 'but I'm not playing that again.' She stuck out a leg and slowly, slowly peeled off her thigh length boot. Darren lost control of the nanobots in his face and his jaw hit the ground. 'I think we need another game,' said Abi, growing in confidence. She had found Darren's Achilles heel, although, as with most men, it wasn't in his foot.

'Eug,' said Darren, his chin still resting on the floor.

'What did you say?'

Darren shook himself and hoisted his jaw back up. 'Leg,' he mumbled.

'That's right,' patronised Abi. 'And we have to play something else if you're going to see any more,' she murmured, brazenly indicating her brassiere. Darren goggled at her, his eyes popping out for a closer look.

'I know,' said Abi. 'We'll each think of a number. If you guess mine, I'll take something off, and if I guess yours, you show me what you're made of. Okay?'

Darren grunted.

'I'll go first,' said Abi, standing up and sticking her chest out. 'What number am I thinking of?'

'…Two,' mumbled Darren, addressing her breasts.

Abi shook her head and various other parts. 'Now you think of a number. Got one?'

'Ug.'

Abi put her hands to her temples and breathed in deeply. 'Yes, yes, it's coming through. Is it a zero? Two zeroes? No… It's my tits.'

'How did you know?' asked Darren, amazed.

'Ah-ha!' cried Abi. 'You lose! Show me what you've got.'

Darren backed away. 'I don't want to,' he whined.

Abi almost pitied him. Although five metres tall, he was still just a little boy. She smiled reassuringly. 'It's alright Darren. I know you're not like other men. That's why I like you. But if I don't see the real you I'm not going to play again.'

Darren looked unconvinced.

'You know, I've got a lot more to show you,' Abi continued, before finding a reason to bend over. She wiggled awkwardly.

Darren's eyes were bulging again. 'Okay,' he grinned.

Abi deftly palmed the small device she had been carrying in her waistband. If the Softcom geeks were right, the egg shaped object would explode as soon as it came into contact with the liquid in Darren's jar. Abi took a deep breath and chewed her lip uncertainly. Could she actually kill him?

Darren knelt down in front of her. 'I'll only do this if I can have a go on your tits afterwards,' he said.

Abi clutched the gadget with a new resolve. 'Fine,' she said.

Darren brought his massive head level with her chest. As Abi looked down, the nanobots in Darren's skull rippled and moved. A hole appeared in the top, like a ball of clay on a potter's wheel opening out into a bowl. As the gap widened, Abi could see the jar inside, and the brain inside that, quivering slightly. She raised the device. Her arm muscles tensed.

'You're in a lot of trouble, Darren,' said a voice.

Darren reassembled his lid and stood up. Abi looked around for the source of the interruption, eventually finding Ruck in his transparent cage.

'Shut up, Dad,' said Darren. 'You're just jealous cos I'm gonna shag this great bird.'

Ruck bristled. 'That has nothing to do with it,' he said uncomfortably.

Darren put his hands on his head to ensure everything was back in place. 'Now then,' he grinned, 'I think somebody mentioned something about tits?'

'Oh well done,' said Olivia sarcastically, calling across to Ruck. Noticing Abi's sleight of hand, she had realised Ruck had scuppered some sort of plan.

'What have I done?' asked Ruck.

'You're a real low flier,' hissed Olivia.

'What are you talking about?' asked Darren. He looked from Olivia to Ruck to Abi, who was hiding something behind her back. 'What's that?' he asked.

'Nothing,' said Abi, trying to return the egg to her waistband. In her haste it slipped from her grasp and fell to the floor.

Darren blushed, red nanobots rushing to his cheeks. Not for the first time, he wished he knew more about female anatomy. 'Are you... ovulating?' he asked.

Abi could only manage an 'Er...'

Darren accessed a variety of websites concerning the human female reproductive system. After stopping for a second look at some of the pictures, he realised there was something suspicious about Abi laying eggs. Nanobots swarmed over the device and took it to their master. 'This is a weapon,' said Darren, shocked.

'Er...'

'Were you going to use this on me?'

'Er...' Abi panicked and started to run for the shaft that led to the surface. She had only taken a few steps when a whirlwind of nanobots rose up from the floor, imprisoning her behind rotating bars.

Darren paced up and down, then stopped as the full horror of the situation dawned on him. 'So,' he said incredulously, 'does this mean... you don't really want to sleep with me?'

Rob James sat in the control room, anxiously watching the screens. 'Will we definitely see the explosion?' he asked.

Miriam Herczeg smiled humourlessly. 'You may even feel it,' she said.

James looked at a clock. 'She should have done it by now,' he said. 'Something's–' His lifePod rang. 'Rob James,' he said, answering it. As he listened to the voice in his ear, he turned pale. '...How can I help you Darren?' he said. '...I see... Abi?... Darren, are you... Yes I did.' James stared at his wrist more closely. '…Yes I can… My…ass?… Darren? Hello?' James let his hand drop. He looked at the anxious operations team. 'Bad news,' he announced simply. 'Miriam, get the nukes ready.'

'Yeah I know I called you,' said Darren to Rob James. 'I'm just calling to say you're a loser basically… Sending a girl to do your dirty work, very brave I don't think.'

'He didn't send me,' interrupted Abi. She was still trapped in the shimmering nanobot cage. The solid bars span around her at tremendous speed, distorting Abi's view of the cave like hazy glass. 'I volunteered,' she said defiantly.

'You volunteered?' mocked Darren. 'For a suicide mission?'

'…What?'

Darren tossed the egg between his huge hands. 'There's enough explosives in here to blow up this whole base. Didn't they tell you?'

'You bastard!' yelled Abi.

'Did you hear that, Robbie?' enquired Darren, resuming his phone call. 'Sounds like you've made another enemy.' He whispered theatrically, 'Shall we teach him a lesson, Abi?'

Abi tried to think for a moment. 'Yes,' she said, without much conviction.

Near the entrance to the cavern, seven ♣illion nanobots began to move. A vast structure rose out of the dust. It looked like a bulbous cigar with a pointy tip, the tip itself topped with a thin antenna to make it even more pointy. The base had sleek, curvaceous fins and a great big cone for flames to shoot out of. It was the archetypal rocket; if someone was planning to build a missile, this was the design they would have in mind before they considered all the boring things like aerodynamics and power to weight ratios. Supported by a web-like gantry, it pointed up the mine shaft at a forty-five degree angle. A door was open in the rocket's side, presumably waiting for the intrepid crew or the nuclear devices. Darren manoeuvred a camera above the missile. 'Do you see that Rob?' he asked. 'That's gonna kick you right in the arse.' He disconnected, and leant over Abi's whirling cage. 'So, I guess it's just you and me against the world, baby,' he leered.

Abi sat on the floor, hugging her knees. Every decision she had ever made had been wrong. 'Leave me alone,' she said.

'Leave you alone?' mocked Darren. 'What, so you can try to escape?'

'You said I'd be cut to pieces,' said Abi in a monotone, indicating the spinning bars.

'Oh.' Darren looked sad. 'Cheer up,' he said awkwardly. 'We were having fun earlier, weren't we?'

Abi didn't reply.

'Another game of… what was it called? You taking your clothes off?'

'We've had enough games,' said Abi.

Darren rubbed his chin. 'If I let you out, how do I know I can trust you?'

Abi shrugged.

'Do you really hate Rob James?'

Abi laughed mirthlessly. 'Yes,' she said. 'That's one thing you can rely on.'

'Then I've got it,' said Darren triumphantly. Inside the cage a pedestal appeared, topped with a big red button. 'You can launch the missile,' he said. 'It's going to smash up Head Office. If you do that, I'll let you go.'

Abi looked balefully at the button beside her. Why couldn't the world just leave her alone for five minutes?

'You'll be evil like me,' encouraged Darren. 'You'll like it. You get to laugh like this.' Darren's maniacal laughter echoed around the chamber.

'I'll think about it,' said Abi. And she did.

'You're in a lot of trouble, Darren,' called Ruck again.

'Stop saying that,' said the giant, the stamping of his massive foot dislodging streams of coal dust from the ceiling. 'I caught her, didn't I? I am capable of running my own evil plans, you know.'

'I'm not talking about her,' said Ruck smugly.

'Well I'm going to catch Jorj as well. I'm doing it now, alright?'

'I'm not–'

'Will you stop interfering? This is my base, I can do what I want.'

Abi moved away from the button. Jorj was here. Maybe there was still hope.

Down in the depths of the mine, Ken the customer care robot received new orders. He carefully placed the circular saw next to the HumAnt farm and stomped from the room. The insects didn't notice. They were transfixed by the television screens again. Ruck had made the transition from star to has-been to ironic icon. The ants were enjoying his suffering, and were delighted when their camera picked out Olivia O'Connel atop the other pillar. The "will they won't they" intrigue started all over again and the HumAnts settled themselves on their sofas.

Jorj jogged down yet another tunnel, wheezing raggedly. He was spending most of his life running down corridors or tunnels these days, but he wasn't getting any better at it. He stopped for a moment to examine the walls around him. They were studded with objects from Ruck's lab, held in place by a coating of nanobots. There were bits of computers, jars of chemicals, anything that Darren had considered valuable. There was also a liberal sprinkling of useless debris: bricks, carpet tiles, white coats. Jorj pulled out one such garment and put it on gratefully. It was a little wrinkled in places, but at least it covered Jorj's little wrinkled places.

A few metres later Jorj found a drinks machine. He realised how thirsty he was, and typed in the code for a fizzy orange. The drink did not appear, and Jorj felt stupid. Of course the machine wouldn't work down here. He gave it a thump anyway.

'Ow,' said the machine in a quavering male voice.

'What?' said Jorj, recoiling in alarm.

'Nothing,' said the machine.

Jorj thought for a moment. 'Where's my fizzy orange?' he demanded.

'Sorry about that,' said the machine. 'You might have more luck if you try plain water, that's double zero.'

'Bil?' said Jorj.

'Jorj?' said Bil.

'Oh my god, Bil!' exclaimed Jorj. 'What have they done to you?' Jorj had seen lots of unbelievable things recently, but this was too much.

'I don't know,' said Bil, sounding scared. 'What have they done to me?'

'You mean you don't know? Oh god. You'd better prepare yourself for a shock, Bil.'

'What is it?'

'They've… they've turned you into a drinks machine. I'm so sorry.' Jorj clutched at the wall for support.

'Oh. Well, I don't think they have.'

'There's no point denying it. You have to be strong, Bil.'

'It's just that when the building collapsed, and all these weird things started appearing, I hid in a drinks machine. I've been in here for ages.' Bil stuck a hand through the cup dispenser and gave a little wave.

'Oh, I see. Sorry if I worried you.'

'That's alright. It's an easy mistake to make.' Bil didn't sound too sure.

Jorj looked up and down the tunnel and considered his options. 'Is there room for another one?' he asked.

'No,' said Bil firmly.

'We've got to get you out of there,' decided Jorj. 'You're not exactly convincing. We'll find somewhere better.'

'Okay,' said Bil. 'I should get out anyway. I can't feel my right arm.' A hatch in the side of the machine popped open and Jorj's ex-flatmate slowly squeezed himself out. His back was hunched and his limbs were twisted from their contortions inside the machine. His clothes were ripped and dirty, and where he wasn't black with oil he was white with dehydrated coffee creaming powder. He stared at the floor. 'To be honest,' he said, 'being headhunted hasn't turned out how I'd hoped.'

Jorj felt a pang of pity. 'I haven't had an easy time of it either.'

Bil twisted his neck, looked at Jorj and burst out laughing. 'What happened to you?' he spluttered. 'You look ridiculous.'

Jorj blushed beneath his orange dye. 'Steady on,' he said.

'Have the Norwegians been giving you a hard time?'

'They're about the only ones who haven't. Come on.'

They moved slowly down the tunnel, Bil limping and hobbling. 'Don't tell anyone,' he said, 'but I'm thinking of taking early retirement. The job's not what it used to be. Buildings falling on you, brains in jars chasing you with hammers, it's a young man's game.'

As they walked past an alcove two metal hands reached out and grabbed them by the scruffs of their necks. 'I'm just going to put you on hold, please bear with me,' said Ken, lifting them off the ground. Jorj and Bil kicked ineffectually at their unseen assailant. 'Please continue to hold. Your business is important to us.' Ken marched up the corridor, carrying his screaming captives and playing them something relaxing from the Four Seasons.

'Miriam, how long until the nukes are ready?' demanded James.

'At least ten minutes,' said the grey woman on the screen. 'If the maintenance budgets had been–'

'I get your point,' James interrupted. 'What if Darren launches his missile first?'

'We have no data on that,' said Miriam. 'A missile made of nano-bots? Our normal counter-measures are unlikely to be effective.'

'Then I suggest you hurry up,' James said. He turned to address a technician at his side. 'Start evacuating non-essential personnel from Head Office.'

'You're in a lot of trouble, Darren,' called Ruck for the third time.

Darren sighed. 'Jee-zus, will you stop saying that?'

(The HumAnts watched cheerfully. You could say this for the Professor, he never let you down. There he was, imprisoned at the top of a fifteen-metre column, at the mercy of Darren and his invincible army, and he still thought he knew best. His face filled the little TV screen as their camera zoomed in for a close up.)

'It's true,' said Ruck calmly.

Darren looked around at his base, at his muscular nanobot body and at his captives. 'It is so not true,' he whined. 'For your information, my robot has just caught Jorjman *and* someone else, so now the base is totally secure, actually.'

Abi groaned and shook her head.

'Look at the screens,' said Ruck patiently. 'Notice anything different?'

(The HumAnts waved their Professor Ruck banners happily. Their flying camera manoeuvred to face a screen showing Darren's miniscule soldiers.)

Olivia and Darren also looked at the screens, but Abi had other things on her mind. If Jorj was unable to rescue her, she would have to play the sex card more effectively. She fiddled with her bra, hoping that it might separate her from the others and lift her out of trouble.

The nanobots on the screen were pursuing a group of Nons on horseback. The machines had formed rolling spheres as before, but this time something was different. The Nons were easily outrunning the bots, and when the people changed direction the machines were slow to adjust their course. At the rear of the group a young girl was having difficulties. As Darren and his captives watched, the child fell from her mount. A nanobot sphere bulged and oozed over her, swallowing the girl completely. Olivia tensed, ready to look away at the first sign of gore. But then the child stood up, brushed off the bots and climbed back onto her horse, her skin only slightly grazed.

'It's a classic mistake,' proclaimed Ruck, as if delivering a lecture. 'You've over-expanded in every direction. You've stretched yourself too thin. You must have over a ¬illion bots by now. Even you can't process data that quickly. Controlling all the units out there, building your missile, doing whatever else you're doing down here, it's too much for you. You've become slow and vulnerable. I'm right, aren't I?'

All eyes turned to Darren. 'Yes,' he mumbled.

(The HumAnts went crazy, stamping their tiny feet and throwing celebratory streamers at the screen. They always supported the little guy, for obvious reasons.)

Olivia was impressed. 'You're right,' she said slowly. 'I guess by the law of averages it had to happen eventually.'

Abi fluttered her eyelashes at Darren. 'You can, er, expand in my direction,' she said, attempting a sexy pose. 'Just get rid of these bars…'

Ruck clapped his hands triumphantly. 'It's a familiar pattern,' he said. 'It's like the rise and fall of the Roman empire.'

'I'll give you a bit of rise and fall,' said Abi with a smile. She was getting the hang of it.

Ruck ignored the interruption. 'There's no way you can attack Head Office. You'll be lucky to hold on to what you've got.'

'You can hold on to what I've go–'

'Will you be quiet? I'm trying to make a serious point.'

'I'm just trying to get out of here, Coco,' spat Abi.

'You're right,' said Darren, and they all looked at him once more. 'I'm at full capacity. But it's no biggie. I've got it sorted.' He laughed. 'You are going to be soooo pissed when I tell you. Ha!'

The pause lengthened. 'What?' asked Ruck.

'Wouldn't you like to know?' gloated Darren.

'Yes,' they chorused.

'Alright,' said Darren with a grin. 'What it is, basically, is that one of you is gonna donate your brain and I'm gonna upload my personality onto it, and that's gonna go to Head Office.' There was a shocked silence. 'So like, I'll just cut the top of your head off, take out the brain, then I'll put these chips and stuff into it, your personality will be wiped and there'll be two of me. Double the capacity, it's gonna be awesome!'

Abi broke the silence first. 'Which one of us?' she asked.

'Don't worry, it won't be you,' said Darren. 'Brains aren't exactly your best feature.' He turned to Ruck and Olivia. 'I mean, look at her tits. No, Dad, it's gonna be you or your girlfriend.'

'I am not his girlfriend,' breathed Olivia.

'Any volunteers?' asked Darren.

(The HumAnts were amazed. Forget Darren's army, this was the finest television they had ever seen. It had comedy, tragedy, human interest, plot twists and cliffhangers. The only thing missing was a way for them to influence the result. Tiny digits pressed red buttons on their remote control, but to no avail. They chattered excitedly, antennae waving, discussing the relative merits of Ruck and Olivia, who should escape and who should die. Everything else was forgotten as their tiny brains were caught in an ecstasy of gossip, scandal and voyeurism.)

Ruck looked to the opposite pillar. 'This is awkward,' he said. Olivia glared back at him.

Darren faked a yawn. 'I haven't got all day, you know,' he said. 'If no one's going to volunteer, Dad can decide.'

'What?' asked Ruck and Olivia, both equally horrified.

'Give me a name,' said Darren with a smile. 'Who's it gonna be for the old...' He whistled and the top of his head flipped open. A hand rummaged inside his skull while he crossed his eyes and stuck his tongue out.

(The HumAnts shushed each other and stared at the screen.)

Everyone looked expectantly at Ruck.

Some calming Vivaldi wafted into the room, quickly followed by Ken, Jorj and Bil. Jorj was protesting desperately. 'Remember the good old days? When you beat me up on that travelator?'

'I can refer you to my supervisor,' said Ken, 'but he's only going to say the same as me.'

'Ken,' boomed Darren as they drew near. 'Nice to see you.'

Abi smiled sadly at Jorj and gave him a little wave. Jorj groaned, gave up his struggles and hung limply from the robot's outstretched arm.

'Welcome to the handset helpline,' said Ken. 'My name is Ken, how can I help?'

'I notice you've easily caught and restrained those intruders,' gloated Darren.

'I'm sorry, sir, that's just our company policy,' said Ken.

'Don't apologise. Put them down.'

'Please listen carefully to the following options. If you are complaining about a noisy neighbour, say "yes" now.'

'Ken–'

'I did not recognise your choice. If you have noticed an unusual smell, say "yes" now.'

Darren turned to Abi and gave her a sickly smile. 'I kept him independent because I thought it might be good to have someone else to talk to. Even I can't be right about everything.' He looked at the robot again. 'Put them down,' he yelled.

'If you are calling to complain about our automated menu system, please hang up in disgust now.'

'For god's sake,' said Darren. He hacked into Ken's operating system, and the robot slumped lifelessly. Bil and Jorj dropped from its drooping fingers. Darren frowned at them. 'Jorjman, did you know Abi was planning to kill us all?' he asked.

'Doesn't surprise me,' said Jorj, rubbing his neck.

'It wasn't my fault,' said Abi.

'That makes a change,' snapped Jorj, who could see no advantage in biting his tongue. 'You've not exactly been a force for good in my life recently.'

'We should talk about this later,' suggested Abi, exasperation creeping into her voice. 'We're in the same boat if you hadn't noticed.'

'Oh good,' said Jorj. 'I'm sure you'll manage to capsize it or throw me overboard.'

'This isn't helping.'

'Why didn't you warn me about her?' interrupted Darren, hurt. 'I thought we were friends.'

'You did offer to kill me just to impress her,' reminded Jorj, unable to turn off the sarcasm. 'That wasn't very friendly.'

'Oh, this friendship is over,' said Darren. 'Abi, love, don't move.' The spinning bars slowed, stopped and disappeared. 'Jorj the Traitor, old man, go and stand next to her,' said Darren.

Jorj complied, supporting Bil who was still half crippled from his time inside the drinks machine. A stream of nanobots whirled up from the floor and encased them all in another cyclonic cage.

Abi looked at the orange man penitently. 'Look, I know things haven't worked out,' she started.

'Don't bother,' said Jorj, backing away. 'Unless you've got a plan that will actually help me, I don't want to know. And just to clarify, getting me fired, or ejected, or arrested is not my idea of help.'

Abi pouted moodily. 'None of that was meant to happen. I was trying to do the right thing.'

'Well you're not very good at it,' replied Jorj irritably. 'If you must do something, why not try doing the wrong thing? You'll probably end up rescuing us all or finding some buried treasure or something.'

Abi treated Jorj to a thousand watt glare. He took a few more steps backwards and brushed against the rotating bars. The tiny robots cut through the back of his lab coat, and it fell to the floor in two halves. Jorj let out an involuntary sob. 'Why? Frame me, torture me, kill me, but why do I have to be naked?' He collapsed and shook his head. 'Someone up there must really hate me.'

Darren looked down at him. 'Er, that would be me,' he said. 'Now if you two can shut up for a minute, we're in the middle of something quite important.' He turned to Ruck again. 'Well? Have you decided who's for the chop?'

(Many of the HumAnts had been holding their breath since the last time Ruck had been asked. They quickly ex- and inhaled so they could hold it again. One of them fainted.)

Olivia opened her mouth to speak.

'Uh uh uh,' admonished Darren. 'No conferring.'

Ruck coughed nervously and looked around him.

'I'm going to have to hurry you,' said Darren.

'Get on with it,' shouted Abi.

'Me,' mumbled Ruck. 'Take me.'

Olivia stared, dumbfounded. 'That… that was really stupid,' she said finally.

'Thanks a lot,' snapped Ruck.

'I mean, thank you. Thank you. I didn't forecast that. The scenario allowed you to save yourself, but you didn't. You rejected the sensible, logical–'

'Alright, don't rub it in.' The column on which Ruck was standing slowly sank towards the ground.

A sudden thought hit Olivia. 'Do you have a plan?' she hissed down at him.

Ruck snorted. 'No,' he said sadly.

(Down in the depths of the mine the HumAnts stood and gave their hero a silent ovation. Tiny eyes glistened with even smaller tears as they watched Ruck's slow descent.)

Even Darren seemed to feel the momentousness of the occasion. He avoided eye contact with Ruck. 'Wow,' he intoned. 'I guess there comes a time in every man's life when he kills his own father…'

'No there doesn't,' snapped Ruck irritably. 'Don't be an idiot.'

'Oh, that does it,' growled Darren. 'Ken!'

The robot jerked back to life.

'Take him down. You know what to do.'

Ken marched swiftly over, seized the uncomplaining Ruck, and dragged him into the darkness.

Olivia shrieked. 'Alec! Alec! I'm sorry. Thank you! I… I… I don't know what to say.'

Ruck's irritated shrug suggested he had more important things on his mind.

Darren felt the disapproving stares of his prisoners. 'Don't look at me like that,' he said. 'I'm an evil mastermind, yeah? I do evil things.'

'Rob?' said Miriam, appearing on a screen. 'We've run some simulations of the nanobot missile scenario.'

'And?'

'Not good. The guidance system will be unlike anything we're prepared for, and probably unjammable. It will be fast enough to outmanoeuvre our anti-missile missiles.'

'Any good news?' asked James.

'The nukes will be ready in six minutes,' smiled Miriam.

James laughed mirthlessly. 'That's the best you can do?' He shook his head. 'Today was going to be such an easy day. I was going to test pasta sauces.'

'It's all linked Rob,' said Miriam. 'If Darren wins there won't be any more pasta.'

James shrugged. 'So you can't make a carbonara without launching nukes?'

Miriam nodded encouragingly. 'Five minutes thirty seconds,' she said.

Jorj was sitting on the floor, hiding his nakedness. Abi was trying to attract his attention. She picked up a lump of coal and threw it at him, hoping that a gentle tap might make him turn round. It struck him painfully behind the ear. 'Ow!' he cried, standing up. 'Haven't you done enough damage?' he asked, gesturing angrily.

'Cover yourself up, Jorj,' said Abi, averting her eyes.

Jorj placed a hand in front of his nether regions, suddenly feeling very small. 'Don't leave me in here with her,' he appealed to Darren. 'I thought we were friends.'

'Sorry, Jorj,' said Darren. 'You're just one of them.'

'One of who?' asked Jorj indignantly. 'I've never joined in with anything in my life.'

'One of them humans.'

'You're fifty per cent human, Darren,' called Olivia from her lonely jar. 'Doesn't that mean anything?'

'Nope.'

'Listen to your human side,' Olivia pleaded. 'There must be good in there somewhere.'

'Oh yeah, cos humans are so much better than computers and robots, aren't they?' said Darren. 'You lot are so big headed, but you're rubbish. Can you work out the square root of thirty seven million in your head? I can, but maths is boring so I don't want to. Can you plug yourself into a computer and set the course of that missile just by thinking about it?'

Darren's forefinger sprouted several mechanical appendages which he plugged into a nearby terminal. 'No. You couldn't even remember the pass code. Four four one three six nine two eight one zero five seven nine two zero eight six three nine one seven five one eight three five four nine six zero eight two four zero six three seven zero zero six two seven three one nine two four eight zero seven six nine two eight eight six...'

'I've got a plan,' hissed Abi.

'Oh no,' Jorj said, wishing he had two hands free so he could stick his fingers in his ears.

'You'll be perfectly safe,' promised Abi. 'Just distract him.' Jorj pretended not to hear.

'...three seven five zero one two four one eight six five one one zero three five one nine two eight four zero nine zero two nine six two zero one eight one one seven zero five five four two nine seven three six eight,' Darren finished. 'Did you get that? Come on, it's only a hundred digits long. No? You're rubbish. Can you do this?' His face turned into two fingers that flicked V signs at his captives. 'No. I think you'll find that computers are better than people and I am better than you.' He rotated the finger that was plugged into the computer. Over by the entrance the giant missile realigned itself. 'There. I'm coming to get you, Mr James.'

Bil had been watching proceedings with interest and had reached a decision. He straightened a torn and stained item that had once been a tie. 'Good morning, sir,' he said humbly. 'I was wondering if, when you have a moment, I could request a transfer to another department? I feel my skills are more suited to accounts or purchase ledger rather than...' He looked around, taking in the cave, Darren and his fellow prisoners. '...Whatever this is. Marketing, or what have you.'

Darren's enormous eyes blinked. 'I dunno what you're talking about.'

'I—'

'And I don't care. Shut up.' Darren looked at his wrist, which had sprouted a watch. He made a popping noise with his lips. 'Not long now till Dad's brain is ready for the missile,' he said to Abi. 'Then you can press that button.'

'Yes, that button,' said Abi meaningfully, staring at Jorj.

'Anyone fancy going for a drink after?' Darren asked.

'Oh yes,' said Bil.

'Not you, mate. Abi? We could get really pissed.'

'We could do something now if you're bored,' said Abi innocently. 'A little distraction. Jorj, any ideas?'

'Er, no not really,' said Jorj, avoiding her gaze.

'Strip poker?' suggested Darren.

'I think Jorj, has already lost that one,' said Abi. 'But why don't you two boys have a game of something? You like computer games, don't you Jorj? Don't you?' she repeated firmly.

'…Yes,' Jorj admitted, looking up reluctantly.

'Thanks,' mouthed Abi. 'You'll be okay, I promise.'

'Okay, Jorjman, I'll beat you again,' said Darren. 'To the death!'

'What?' asked Abi, horrified.

'…That sounds about right,' mumbled Jorj. 'Thanks, Abi, thanks a lot.'

Abi's face creased with useless sympathy.

The cage grew a computer, a pair of net goggles and two gloves. 'My choice of game,' said Darren. 'Only one rule, if you lose, you die.'

'And if *you* lose?' asked Abi. 'He might lose, mightn't he, Jorj?' she asked, trying to encourage her ally.

'I never lose,' boasted Darren.

'Maybe I can teach you how,' said Jorj pathetically. 'It's one of the only things I'm good at.' He picked up the gloves and stared mournfully at Abi. 'Mind you, recently I have had some help.'

Ruck thumped Ken as the robot dragged him down a tunnel. 'Let me go, damn you. Damn thing,' shouted the Professor.

'If you continue to use that sort of language I will terminate the call,' said Ken.

'Just stop it, you bastard!'

'I'm hanging up now, sir.'

Ruck started to choke as his throat was lifted into the air. 'Aargh… Put me down, please, please.'

'Good manners cost nothing, sir,' said the robot, lowering his arm.

Ruck's legs trailed out behind him, scraping painfully along the floor. 'I want to complain,' he said.

'All complaints must be made in writing,' said Ken.

'There's been a mistake, it's really very simple–'
'All complaints must be made in writing.'
They continued towards the circular saw.

Jorj put on his goggles and almost crashed into a brick wall. He was in a blue car, an old fashioned, ground-locked, dirty car, travelling at high speed. His gloved hands flexed and he gripped the virtual wheel, twisting it sharply to the left and narrowly avoiding the obstacle. 'No fair!' he yelled. 'I wasn't ready. Sorry,' he added, as a startled pedestrian flew over the bonnet.

Darren shot past in a red open topped sports car, his virtual form matching his nanobot body. 'Try the road, Jorjman,' he laughed, as his hair billowed in the breeze.

In the real world, Darren was standing stock still, all his spare processing power routed into the game. Abi, Bil and Olivia were watching a three-dimensional projection of the contest. The red car maintained its lead, as Jorj fought to control his vehicle. His appearance was less flattering than Darren's; the blue car was being driven by a stickman with a round head, spindly arms and a face comprised of two dots and a bendy line. 'Come on,' he shouted. In the real world Jorj stood in the cage, lurching from side to side, lashing out at nothing. In the game the stickman punched the steering wheel in frustration.

Darren's car approached a bridge that crossed a river. It was rising to allow the passage of a tall ship and Jorj watched as Darren hit the ramp at speed. 'Where'd he go?' he asked, just before his own car hit the bridge. Warning sirens sounded and the ship's foghorn blared as he shot up the ramp and launched over the river. 'Can I swim in this game?' the stickman shouted desperately.

The blue car flew, then fell through the air. It hit the road on the other side of the river. In the cave nanobots beneath Jorj's feet jolted his body painfully.

Jorj's stick hands sounded a triumphant fanfare on the horn, before he realised that something was wrong. He had landed in empty, derelict dockland and there was no sign of Darren's car. 'Where is he?' Jorj asked again. The answer came from above. A red propeller-powered biplane swooped down a few hundred metres ahead of the blue car, heading straight for it, guns blazing. Clumps of dirt flew into the air on either side as the bullets just missed the vehicle. Jorj swerved desperately, keeping his round head as low as possible. The plane came nearer and nearer, until Jorj could see Darren grinning in the cockpit. There was a ping of bullet on bonnet as the plane zoomed overhead, then turned around for the next attack.

Jorj pressed all the buttons on the dashboard, looking for the one that changed the car into a plane. Nothing. He took his hands off the wheel and tried combinations of gestures, hoping that the plane could be spawned by a special move. Up, down, up, down, point, left, right, left, right, fist. Nothing.

'He's cheating,' Abi yelled. Jorj heard her voice above the engine roar from his implanted speakers. 'He's making up the rules as he goes along.'

Jorj swore bitterly. Buildings had sprung up on either side of the car, forcing him down a narrow canyon. Darren's plane overtook the vehicle, then came back fast and low, on a collision course.

'Come on Jorj, you can do it!' yelled Abi.

'I don't understand what's going on,' shouted Bil.

The car and the plane sped towards each other, the bonnet heading straight for the plane's nose. At the last minute Jorj flung his vehicle to one side, scraping up sparks against the wall. The car just missed the plane's fuselage and smashed through its wing. The plane swung round and flew into the wall, exploding in an orange fireball.

'Yes!' cheered Abi. 'Come on!'

Jorj slammed on the brakes and tumbled from his vehicle. 'I've won!' he called triumphantly.

'Not yet you haven't,' grumbled Darren. The virtual scene shifted and Jorj found himself in a graveyard, surrounded by zombies.

'Three minutes, Rob,' said Miriam.

'I've never been to England,' said Rob James. 'Apart from an hour on E-Day, and that doesn't count.'

'Probably best not to now,' said Miriam. 'For thirty years or so.'

James sighed.

'I hear Australia's better anyhow,' continued Miriam brightly. 'Like England 2.0, and they've fixed the rain.'

'Hmm,' said James. 'I heard the Australians put beetroot in their hamburgers.'

Miriam grimaced. 'That's plain wrong. We've got some nukes left if you want to teach them a lesson.'

The undead nearest to Jorj looked up and unignored him, rubbing their stomachs unsatiatedly. 'Brains,' they moaned unsilently, before shaking unfriendly fists in his direction.

'Help!' shouted Jorj. 'What do I do?'

'Which one are you?' asked Bil.

Abi was watching the spinning bars. She looked up at the projection of the game. 'There's a flamethrower by your feet,' she called.

'Thanks!' shouted Jorj, grabbing the weapon. He moved through the crowd, making unappetising undead toast as he went. Darren was waiting for him on the other side of the graveyard. Jorj raised the flamethrower, his finger on the trigger. A fire extinguisher appeared in Darren's hands, and a smug grin arrived on his face. Flame met foam and steam filled the air, obscuring Jorj from Darren's view.

'Where are you?' Darren whined.

'He's behind you,' Abi lied.

Darren turned round, but Jorj wasn't there. Instead the stickman was lying on the ground, still hidden by the steam. He grabbed Darren's ankles and pulled him over. Jorj stood up, lifting his disorientated opponent and throwing him to the approaching zombies.

'You're good at this,' laughed Abi. The stickman smiled.

The scene changed again, and Jorj found himself beside a busy road. 'After this car!' shouted Abi, and he advanced one lane. 'Not yet!' Abi warned.

Jorj quickly crossed the road and reached the river on the other side. He jumped onto a log and was about to leap on a turtle's back when Darren changed the rules again. Every time Jorj got the upper hand Darren would switch games. They shot space invaders, arranged multicoloured blocks and collected coins, Jorj almost winning every time.

Each change required more of Darren's processing power, and Abi watched happily as the rotating bars of their prison slowed down. Not long now. Above her head the scene changed again, and now the projection showed an ornate chessboard floating between Darren and the stickman. 'Your move,' Darren said.

Jorj stared blankly at the board. 'I didn't think chess was your style,' he said, stalling for time.

Darren shrugged and indicated the board impatiently.

'Are you sure you wouldn't prefer Guess Who?' asked Jorj. He studied the chessmen intently. 'Does your piece have a horse's face?' he asked.

'Can't you even play chess?' taunted his opponent.

'I can play, I'm just surprised that you can,' said Jorj defiantly. 'This one, to this square here.'

Darren looked at the board and pulled out a shotgun.

'Look out!' yelled Bil.

Jorj was already diving to one side, and Darren's shot just missed him. 'I need a gun!' he shouted, but no one could help him. Darren was standing over him, the barrel of the shotgun brushing his unhappy face. 'You lose,' he said, his trigger finger tightening.

'Hey, big boy.' Abi's voice floated across cyberspace. 'Wanna come and see me? Or should that be the other way round?' She had worked on her chat up lines while waiting for the spinning bars to slow enough to let her through.

Darren paused the game and returned his attention to the real world. He looked at his prisoners and realised Abi was missing. 'Where are you?' he yelled.

'I'm inside your giant missile,' Abi cooed seductively. 'Now that really is the wrong way round.'

Darren looked at the rocket. The hatch in the side was open. 'Get out right now,' he said.

'I'm naked,' Abi sang.

'Stay there.' Darren leapt from his plinth and rushed towards the missile, shedding nanobots from his body as he ran. As he climbed the gantry his gargantuan form had shrunk to a more normal size, enabling him to squeeze through the hatch. Bil watched in bewilderment as Darren disappeared inside the rocket. A howl of disappointment echoed around the chamber. 'You're not naked,' Darren moaned.

Abi pushed past him and leapt onto the gantry, kicking the hatch shut behind her. 'Jorj!' she shouted.

Darren's voice could still be heard from speakers outside the rocket. 'It's not fair,' he said, banging on the door. 'I only wanted to see some boobs.'

'Jorj!' repeated Abi as she swung down to the ground. 'Press the button!'

Jorj had removed his gloves and goggles and was looking around in confusion. 'Press the button!' barked Olivia. Jorj noticed the pedestal beside him and did as he was told.

The missile's engine fired, shaking the cave and knocking everyone off their feet. Olivia climbed from the jar on top of her shaking pillar and moved quickly towards the ground. The rocket shook itself free from the gantry and took off, flying up the tunnel, out of sight and out of the mine.

Inside the missile, Darren flew into a rage. His shouts still boomed from speakers in the cave. 'Oh, that does it! You are going to get such a smashing!' Nanobot hammers began to form at the edges of the cavern.

Abi ran towards the others, fleeing the massive hammers that were pulverising everything in their path.

'Not so funny now, is it?' asked Darren, from inside the speeding missile. The hammers were only a few metres away. 'Who's laughing now? I am. Me.' Darren's speech became punctuated with static, the signal weakening as he travelled further and further away. The movement of the hammers became slower and less coordinated, their instructions becoming garbled as Darren sped across the Atlantic. 'You've made a real mistake this ti…' The taunting faded completely as Darren flew out of range. The hammers came to a halt, then crumbled into dust. Olivia jumped the last couple of metres to the ground as her pillar dissolved.

Abi, Jorj and Bil whooped and cheered in celebration. They jumped up and down and hugged each other, Jorj taking care to keep one hand just below waist height. 'You did it,' he said.

'We did it,' corrected Abi.

'I still don't know what's going on,' said Bil.

They congratulated each other noisily, and it was some time before Olivia's voice could be heard.

'You do realise what you've done?' she said, walking towards them.

'Well, der,' said Abi. 'We've escaped.'

'Well, der,' mocked Olivia. 'And you've despatched Darren to Head Office.'

'So?' said Abi, smiling dangerously.

'Fifteen seconds until the nukes can launch,' announced Miriam Herczeg. 'Ten, nine, eight–'

'He's fired first,' yelled a technician, pointing at a radar screen. A green dot was shooting away from the mine.

'Six, five, four–'

'Wait,' ordered James. 'What's onboard the missile?' he asked.

'It's broadcasting,' said a technician. 'On speakers now.'

Darren's laugh filled the control room. 'I'm coming to get you, Robbie,' he sang.

'Abort the strike on the mine,' said James. 'Concentrate on bringing down that missile.'

Miriam hid her disappointment. 'Firing laser satellites,' she reported. 'No hit. Just passes straight through it.'

James dragged a hand across his brow. 'Jam on all frequencies.'

'No change.'

Rob James closed his eyes.

'I don't care if he's going to Head Office,' said Abi stubbornly. 'Rob James was going to kill us all, remember?'

'Revenge has no place on our agenda,' insisted Olivia. 'If Darren takes over Head Office, he's not going to stop at killing Rob James. He'll bring down the whole of Life Itself™. Civilisation will collapse.'

'Good,' said Abi. 'Things need to be shaken up a bit.'

'Darren's a monster,' pointed out Bil.

'So's Rob James,' said Abi. Bil was shocked. He didn't believe in badmouthing top management.

Jorj was in front of a computer screen. 'There's nothing we can do anyway,' he said. 'I've tried to access the missile's guidance systems, but we need that hundred digit pass code.'

'Oh dear,' smiled Abi.

'Is anyone's Eye Camera working?' asked Olivia. 'Maybe we recorded the code?' They all checked and shook their heads. Olivia crumpled. She was born for business class; she knew she wouldn't last long in economy. 'I hope you're happy,' she said.

'Mankind will survive,' Abi preached. 'But only if we learn to help our neighbours, act collectively–'

'We're done for,' said Jorj gloomily.

'No,' Abi urged. 'We can respect other points of view…'

'I know the code,' said Bil.

'…listen to each other, think about the less fortunate, the little man…'

Bil hobbled over and tugged at her sleeve. 'I know the code,' he repeated.

'Shh a minute Bil,' said Abi.

'People aren't like that,' said Olivia. 'They can't be trusted to act in the best interests of the planet.'

'I know the code.'

'You're living in a dream world, Abi,' said Jorj. 'Wake up and… what was that Bil?'

'I know the code.'

'How?'

'I remembered it.'

'But it's a hundred digits long,' said Olivia.

'It was easy.'

'Don't tell us,' warned Abi.

Bil looked at her and shook his head. 'Sorry, miss,' he said, inflating his chest. 'But I'm a company man.'

'Go on then,' said Jorj, fingers poised above the keyboard.

Abi pushed him away and stood in front of the computer. 'No,' she said. 'I'm not going to let you.'

'Anti-missile missiles launched.'

'Well?' demanded James.

'No good,' said Miriam. 'Darren's too fast. We can't stop him.'

'This is crazy,' said Jorj. 'Darren could wipe out mankind.'

Abi resolutely blocked the computer. She could hear her destiny again, telling her what to do. Everything she had endured had been for a reason, to teach her this lesson. 'Maybe that's a good thing,' she said. 'What's so good about people anyway? They're greedy, selfish, stupid...'

'That's not true,' said Jorj.

'Isn't it?' asked Abi. Rob James's words came unbidden to her lips. 'You name me one time when humans shared things equally. Even cavemen killed each other for the best bits of mammoth.'

Jorj stared at her. Something had gone very wrong with her programming. If she had been a robot, he might have known how to fix her. 'What have cavemen got to do with anything?' he asked gently.

'Forget them,' snapped Abi, annoyed with herself for using her enemy's argument. 'I mean, look around you. What have we got here and now that's worth saving? Bil, you're just a happy little worker. You'll do whatever the companies want.'

'That's almost right,' smiled Bil, pleased with the compliment. 'But I do more than they want. Under-promise, over-deliver.'

'Exactly,' said Abi. 'Jorj, you don't believe in anything, except a quiet life and to hell with everyone else.'

Jorj struggled to find a defence against this attack.

'And you...' Abi pointed at Olivia O'Connel. 'Who are you, anyway?'

Olivia blinked guiltily. 'Me? I'm... no one.'

'What's your name?'

'Jane?' lied Olivia. 'Jane O'... Schwartz?'

'And what do you do?'

'Nothing really, nothing.'

'There,' said Abi triumphantly. 'The human race. Not worth all the fuss.' She leant against the computer, dizzy with power.

'You forgot someone,' said Jorj quietly.

Abi folded her arms. 'What?'

'What about you?' Jorj asked. 'You always try to do the right thing, you said so yourself. You're not selfish or any of those things.'

'And a lot of good it's done me,' said Abi.

'It has,' insisted Jorj, improvising desperately. 'It's made you worth saving.'

'Shut up,' said Abi unconvincingly.

'No,' said Jorj. 'This isn't you. You're an optimist. The glass is half full.'

'Ooh, I could do with a drink.'

'Shut up, Bil. Come on Abi, you believe in… stuff. A better way of doing, er, things. For people. Um.'

'…Do I?'

'Yes,' said Jorj, amazed that his incoherent ramblings were working. He edged towards the computer. 'You've got to always remember that.' Their eyes met. Abi was trembling, confused. Jorj smiled. 'And you've got to realise,' he said, 'that genocide rarely makes things better.'

Abi laughed, and let Jorj push her out of the way. He snatched up the keyboard. 'Come on then, Bil,' he said. 'I don't know how you've remembered this code, but you'd better be right.'

'Okay,' said Bil, 'it's black tea two sugars, forty-four, white fresh grind coffee with one sugar, thirteen, orange squash, sixty-nine, instant coffee extra cream, twenty-eight…' Jorj could hardly type, he was laughing so hard.

Abi stood apart from the others, overwhelmed, tears leaking from her eyes. Olivia approached her gingerly. 'There there,' she muttered, patting the girl delicately on the shoulder. It took Abi a few moments to shrug her off.

'Instant coffee with cream and one sugar, twenty-nine, chicken soup extra noodles, seventy-three and weak lemon squash, sixty-eight.' Bil took a deep breath and smiled.

'I'm in,' said Jorj. 'Where do we want to send him? France?' he suggested hopefully.

'I think space would be better,' advised Olivia.

'Okay,' said Jorj, fingers already tapping at the keyboard, 'straight up.' Bil and Olivia watched anxiously. 'That's it,' he said, a few seconds later. 'He's just left the atmosphere.'

Jorj and Bil whooped and cheered in celebration. Abi soon joined in, gratefully taking her place in the group. They gave each other high fives, Jorj taking care to keep one hand down low. They congratulated each other loudly, until Olivia's voice cut through the noise. 'Your celebrations are premature,' she said.

'What is it now?' demanded Jorj.

'Alec... Professor Ruck is currently having his brain cut out.' An unwelcome tear hung in the corner of Olivia's eye before making a run for it down her cheek. 'You may have eliminated Darren,' she said, furiously brushing away the interloper, 'but any minute now his identical twin will be launched.'

'You're a real killjoy, you know that?' said Jorj.

'Maybe we can stop it,' said Abi eagerly, leading the charge across the cave. They stopped just short of the tunnel's threshold and shook their heads.

It was no use. The tunnel was full of dust and lab equipment. Deprived of Darren's instructions, the nanobots supporting the entrance had crumbled back into individual particles, blocking it completely. Ruck was doomed, and so were they.

The HumAnts couldn't believe their luck when Ken dragged a screaming Professor Ruck into their cave. They would have a ringside seat for the finale. Banners were waved and a chorus of tiny cheers rose up as Ruck was pulled past the farm. Ant faces pressed against the glass, songs were sung and several more insects fainted. The atmosphere was amazing. Bets were placed on the method of Ruck's escape. Ken crushed in a rock fall was the favourite, although there were good odds on Ruck talking his way out.

Ruck also couldn't believe his luck, although his perspective was somewhat different. Ken threw him onto a table, knocking the breath from his body. He tried to wriggle free but Ken pinned him down and strapped his legs to the bench. 'I won't keep you long, sir,' said the robot, securing Ruck's left arm. As the machine walked round to fix Ruck's other limb, it noticed something was wrong. The table, like most other things in the room, had been damaged on the journey from London. The last strap was missing.

The HumAnts noticed it too. Hurried bets were placed on Ruck simply untying himself and running away. It had seemed like a dull option before, but now it looked quite likely.

Ken stamped around the room in an artificial rage, smashing everything in its path. Ruck saw his chance and started picking at the straps with his free hand.

The HumAnts gripped each other's pincers.

Ken returned to the table and broke Ruck's free arm with a single blow. Ruck howled in pain and lay still, resigned to his fate.

The HumAnts also howled. It couldn't end like this, not after all they'd been through. It had to have a happy ending.

Ken stomped towards the ant farm and the circular saw. As the robot reached over to pick up its weapon, the HumAnts swarmed out of a hole in their tank. They advanced onto the saw, and then onto Ken's fingers. More than a hundred insects ran all over Ken's body as the robot marched back to the table, holding the saw above Ruck's head. The HumAnts found cracks in Ken's casing and dashed inside, infiltrating the mechanisms. They clambered over transistors, capacitors and diodes. Antennae waggled urgently as the insects surged deeper and deeper into the heart of the robot. Ken's finger rested on the saw's power switch. The ants marched onwards; many were electrocuted and fell by the wayside. Still they forced their way through the cramped interior of the robot, the darkness lit by sparks that marked the departure of another HumAnt to the great couch in the sky. Smoke started to pour from Ken's casing as the short circuits continued. The robot spasmed, dropping the saw to the ground. The ants reached the robot's power supply. Without a second thought, the tiny creature who was Ruck's biggest fan bit through the connecting leads and burnt to a crisp. The robot slumped and its lights went out.

Carefully and painfully, Ruck began to undo the straps with his broken arm. 'Thank you, my children,' he said, blinking away a tear. 'You died for my sins.'

The staff at Head Office began celebrating as soon as the missile blasted into space. Unscheduled breaks were the order of the day, and joyful colleagues hugged each other before awkwardly detaching themselves.

A handful of personnel remained in the command room, monitoring footage of the mine. It was several hours before a group of people slowly pulled themselves out of the mineshaft. There were five of them, two women and three men, all tired, dirty and happy. The youngest woman stuck two fingers up at the sky, knowing that James would be watching.

But Rob wasn't there. Gratefully letting the big picture slip out of focus, he'd turned his attention closer to home. He was sitting at a table in a small kitchen, away from the hubbub of Head Office. His wife spooned some pasta into a couple of bowls and sat opposite him. 'Busy morning?' she asked.

Rob shook his head. 'Work stays at work,' he admonished wearily. He lifted some pasta to his mouth. It was smothered in a rich sauce, topped with chunks of real lobster.

'I think this might be the best one yet,' opined his wife.

'It's good,' said Rob, smacking his lips. He smiled happily at his wife. 'You know,' he said, 'to save something this good… Maybe a small nuclear strike wouldn't have been so unreasonable.'

By the time Darren regained control of the guidance systems, the nanobot missile had already left the atmosphere. Reinstating the original course would have taken seconds, but fortunately his teenage attention span didn't last that long. He had a new idea.

In space no one can hear you sing guitar solos, but anyone with a radio tuned to the correct frequency would have heard the ship's strange message to the cosmos: 'Der ner ner-ner ner ner, yeah! I'm a Space Pirate, baby! Gonna find me an alien sex queen! Der ner ner-ner ner ner…'

A few days later...

Ruck was in his office, his arm in a sling, slowly packing up his stupidity exhibition. He was moving on. A swift enquiry into the Darren affair had relieved him of his funding and what was left of his laboratory. It could have been so much worse.

He hadn't spoken to Olivia since they were rescued from Darren's mine. She had testified at the enquiry, and Ruck had expected her to reveal his complicity in the plan to shoot Rob James, or his part in Darren's early misdemeanours. To his amazement, Olivia had barely mentioned him. The enquiry decided to punish Ruck for creating Darren in the first place, but not for aiding and abetting him. The Professor still couldn't believe it. He could only assume that gratitude had clouded Olivia's judgement. His stupid act of kindness, volunteering to become Darren's clone, had been balanced with another act, equally stupid and equally kind.

Ruck would have plenty of time to mull over this equation. He had been given a teaching post at a Softcom University, although it had been made abundantly clear that he was expected to learn from the students rather than the other way round.

Brijit opened the office door without knocking. 'There's a package arrived for you, Professor,' she said.

'Put it on my desk,' Ruck ordered. He looked up. 'What on earth are you wearing?' he asked incredulously.

Brijit simpered. 'It's the latest thing,' she said, swishing her carrier bag skirt. 'It's a Karen Handforth original. I got it from that new boutique, Bert's Barrow, everyone's talking about it.' Her styrofoam shoes creaked as she walked over to the desk, and the unspooled cassette tapes swathing her arms rustled as she put down the parcel.

Ruck smiled to himself. 'I always said you had *rubbish* taste,' he said, almost pleasantly.

'Oh, Professor, I'm going to miss you,' cried Brijit, approaching him with open arms. 'Deep down you're just a big pussy cat, aren't you?'

'No!' squawked Ruck, backing away in alarm. 'No I'm not!'

Brijit shook her head knowingly and closed the door behind her.

Ruck mopped his brow and turned his attention to the package. It was a flat square shape, about fifty centimetres on each side, wrapped in brown paper. Turning it over, Ruck saw a message written on the back. 'With many thanks, an essential addition to your museum of stupidity, O.O'C.'

Only able to use one hand, Ruck tore through the wrapper with difficulty. He looked at the gift and his own face stared back at him. It was a mirror.

Abi wandered happily across the wasteland outside the city walls. She spotted a group of Nons dragging sacks of produce towards the tourist enclave, and aimed her lifePod at them.

There had been no public recognition for the efforts of Abi, Jorj and Bil, for which she was extremely grateful. A televised medal ceremony, or even a single photograph of her shaking hands with Rob James would have been the cruellest punishment she could imagine.

Instead there had been a private gathering at Head Office. Rob James had said a few words of thanks, and they had each been awarded several hundred shares in Life Itself™. Then James showed them a huge list of careers and asked them all to choose a job for life, the highest reward a corporation could offer. Jorj and Bil had chosen happily, but Abi had refused. She had a better idea.

So while Abi was walking the dead earth outside the city, her mother was starting her new permanent position, her temping days finally over. If Abi needed money she could always return to data muling. For the present she was happy living frugally, contributing as little as possible to the system.

Abi had redistributed most of the Life Itself™ shares that Rob James had given her. Her first priority had been to find Shiny and his family. Mr Handforth had been less than pleased to see her, calling her a snooty bloody Shareholder, a perspective that shifted when she transferred some stock to his lifePod. She had put the Handforths in touch with Bert, and by all accounts they were already thriving within the city walls.

Now, a few day later, Abi roamed the Non zone, handing out her remaining shares at random. She was disguised in rags to avoid attention, but had allowed herself one personal touch. An animated badge on her chest showed Rob James, his shirt and tie disappearing to reveal bare skin, which quickly turned bright orange.

Abi pressed a button on her Pod and transferred some shares to the distant Nons. A few moments later they realised their change in fortune, and started to run towards the city gates. They couldn't wait to get inside, to start buying burgers, trainers and software.

Jorj ran along the travelator, cursing. He was late for work, and on his first day as well. He could have taken a flying car for nothing, but he kept forgetting about his new shares and the increased privileges to which he was now entitled.

It had taken a long time to apply the make up that covered his orange dye, and he had been further delayed by a phone call from Bil. The old man had been anxious to talk about his new job, managing the canteen of a beverage factory. When Bil had started to explain the numbering system on the drinks machine for a second time, Jorj had politely hung up on him.

When Jorj finally arrived at work, his punctuality wasn't mentioned. Everyone was very friendly, and the first few hours were spent on a tour. By the time all the introductions were over, Jorj was itching to get on with the job.

'So that's everyone,' concluded his guide. 'I hope you'll enjoy yourself here at the Institute of Sleep Research.'

'I'm sure I will,' said Jorj, happily sticking electrodes to his temples. 'Is that my bed there?' It was. Jorj climbed in and pulled the covers over himself. 'Right,' he said, 'let's get to work.' He closed his eyes, smiled and fell asleep.

The surviving HumAnts had returned to their glass colony. A Softcom Special Investigations team had found them in Darren's mine, and had taken them to a lab for further study. The insects had not paid much attention, being far too busy erecting a statue to their fallen comrades. An air of mourning permeated the farm, and not just for the ants that had perished inside Ken the robot. The screens that had hypnotised the tiny creatures for so long were also dead. Unable to live vicariously through Ruck and Olivia, the ants believed they had lost something special, something big. They felt hollow and empty.

But after a while the insects left the couch behind. They began fixing the colony, or playing football, or making patterns out of leaves, or talking to each other. They began to feel that they might have gained something, and lost nothing. Their previous obsessions started to look a bit weird. That's when one of the HumAnts decided to record the story of Ruck, as a lesson for future generations. He wrote a book.

And what happened to this book, this story of ants and scientists, of monsters and televisions? Well, it's certainly not the book you're holding now. Honestly, can you read ant language? And just look at the size of it. A book written by an ant would be much smaller than this one.

Thanks to all at Picnic Publishing and to Lesley Thorne and Leah Middleton at Aitken Alexander, without whom this novel would have been twice as long and half as good. Thanks too to everyone who read the early drafts and who helped me cut out the bad bits (e.g. clumsy phrases likes 'thanks too to'): Matt Avery, Simon Allen, Matt Collins, Matthew Pountney, Gilleon Moulds, Amy Coughlin, Lee Clarke, Alec Christie, Alex Newman, Chris Coleman, Ian Buchan, Andy Cassels and Anthony MacMurray (eventually). Thanks to Ian Bass for the wonderful illustrations. I'll always be grateful to Barry Evans, beacause he didn't force me to sign to Barry's Booklegs. Special thanks to my parents and to John Schwartz, without whom you would not be reading this (or the rest of the book, which hopefully was a bit more entertaining).

www.picnic-publishing.co.uk